The Collected Supernatural and Weird Fiction of Charles Dickens Volume 1

The Collected Supernatural and Weird Fiction of Charles Dickens Volume 1

Contains two novellas 'A Christmas Carol'
and 'A House to let' and nineteen
short stories to chill the blood

Charles Dickens

LEONAUR

The Collected
Supernatural and Weird
Fiction of Charles Dickens
Volume 1
Contains two novellas 'A Christmas Carol'
and 'A House to let' and nineteen
short stories to chill the blood
by Charles Dickens

FIRST EDITION

Leonaur is an imprint
of Oakpast Ltd

Copyright in this form © 2009 Oakpast Ltd

ISBN: 978-1-84677-846-9 (hardcover)
ISBN: 978-1-84677-845-2 (softcover)

http://www.leonaur.com

Publisher's Notes

Contents

A Christmas Carol

CHAPTER 1

MARLEY'S GHOST

Marley was dead: to begin with. There is no doubt whatever about that. The register of his burial was signed by the clergyman, the clerk, the undertaker, and the chief mourner. Scrooge signed it. And Scrooge's name was good upon 'Change, for anything he chose to put his hand to. Old Marley was as dead as a door-nail.

Mind! I don't mean to say that I know, of my own knowledge, what there is particularly dead about a door-nail. I might have been inclined, myself, to regard a coffin-nail as the deadest piece of ironmongery in the trade. But the wisdom of our ancestors is in the simile; and my unhallowed hands shall not disturb it, or the Country's done for. You will therefore permit me to repeat, emphatically, that Marley was as dead as a door-nail.

Scrooge knew he was dead? Of course he did. How could it be otherwise? Scrooge and he were partners for I don't know how many years. Scrooge was his sole executor, his sole administrator, his sole assign, his sole residuary legatee, his sole friend, and sole mourner. And even Scrooge was not so dreadfully cut up by the sad event, but that he was an excellent man of business on the very day of the funeral, and solemnised it with an undoubted bargain.

The mention of Marley's funeral brings me back to the point I started from. There is no doubt that Marley was dead. This must be distinctly understood, or nothing wonderful can come of the story I am going to relate. If we were not perfectly convinced that Hamlet's Father died before the play began, there would be nothing more remarkable in his taking a stroll at night, in an easterly wind, upon his own ramparts, than there would be in any other middle-aged gentleman rashly turning out after dark in a breezy spot—say Saint Paul's Churchyard for instance-literally to astonish his son's weak mind.

Scrooge never painted out Old Marley's name. There it stood, years afterwards, above the ware-house door: Scrooge and Marley. The firm was known as Scrooge and Marley. Sometimes people new to the business called Scrooge 'Scrooge', and sometimes 'Marley', but he answered to both names. It was all the same to him.

Oh! But he was a tight-fisted hand at the grindstone, Scrooge! a squeezing, wrenching, grasping, scraping, clutching, covetous old sinner! Hard and sharp as flint, from which no steel had ever struck out generous fire; secret, and self-contained, and solitary as an oyster. The cold within him froze his old features, nipped his pointed nose, shrivelled his cheek, stiffened his gait; made his eyes red, his thin lips blue; and spoke out shrewdly in his grating voice. A frosty rime was on his head, and on his eyebrows, and his wiry chin. He carried his own low temperature always about with him; he iced his office in the dog-days; and didn't thaw it one degree at Christmas.

External heat and cold had little influence on Scrooge. No warmth could warm, no wintry weather chill him. No wind that blew was bitterer than he, no falling snow was more intent upon its purpose, no pelting rain less open to entreaty. Foul weather didn't know where to have him. The heaviest rain, and snow, and hail, and sleet, could boast of the advantage over him in only one respect. They often came down handsomely, and Scrooge never did.

Nobody ever stopped him in the street to say, with gladsome looks, "My dear Scrooge, how are you. When will you come to see me." No beggars implored him to bestow a trifle, no children asked him what it was o'clock, no man or woman ever once in all his life inquired the way to such and such a place, of Scrooge. Even the blindmen's dogs appeared to know him; and when they saw him coming on, would tug their owners into doorways and up courts; and then would wag their tails as though they said, "No eye at all is better than an evil eye, dark master!"

But what did Scrooge care! It was the very thing he liked. To edge his way along the crowded paths of life, warning all human sympathy to keep its distance, was what the knowing ones call nuts to Scrooge.

Once upon a time—of all the good days in the year, on Christmas Eve—old Scrooge sat busy in his counting-house. It was cold, bleak, biting weather: foggy withal: and he could hear the people in the court outside, go wheezing up and down, beating their hands upon their breasts, and stamping their feet upon the pavement stones to warm them. The city clocks had only just gone three, but it was quite dark already: it had not been light all day: and candles were flaring in the windows of the neighbouring offices, like ruddy smears upon the palpable brown air. The fog came pouring in at every chink and keyhole, and was so dense without, that although the court was of the narrowest, the houses opposite were mere phantoms. To see the dingy cloud come drooping down, obscuring everything, one might have thought that Nature lived hard by, and was brewing on a large scale.

The door of Scrooge's counting-house was open that he might keep his eye upon his clerk, who in a dismal little cell beyond, a sort of tank, was copying letters. Scrooge had a very small fire, but the clerk's fire was so very much smaller that it looked like one coal. But he couldn't replenish it, for Scrooge kept the coal-box in his own room; and so surely as the clerk came in with the shovel, the master predicted that it would be necessary for them to part. Wherefore the clerk put on his white comforter, and tried to warm himself at the candle; in which effort, not being a man of a strong imagination, he failed.

"A merry Christmas, uncle! God save you!" cried a cheerful

voice. It was the voice of Scrooge's nephew, who came upon him so quickly that this was the first intimation he had of his approach.

"Bah!" said Scrooge, "Humbug!"

He had so heated himself with rapid walking in the fog and frost, this nephew of Scrooge's, that he was all in a glow; his face was ruddy and handsome; his eyes sparkled, and his breath smoked again.

"Christmas a humbug, uncle!" said Scrooge's nephew. "You don't mean that, I am sure."

"I do," said Scrooge. "Merry Christmas! What right have you to be merry? what reason have you to be merry? You're poor enough."

"Come, then," returned the nephew gaily. "What right have you to be dismal? what reason have you to be morose? You're rich enough."

Scrooge having no better answer ready on the spur of the moment, said, "Bah!" again; and followed it up with "Humbug."

"Don't be cross, uncle," said the nephew.

"What else can I be," returned the uncle, "when I live in such a world of fools as this Merry Christmas! Out upon merry Christmas. What's Christmas time to you but a time for paying bills without money; a time for finding yourself a year older, but not an hour richer; a time for balancing your books and having every item in 'em through a round dozen of months presented dead against you? If I could work my will," said Scrooge indignantly, "every idiot who goes about with "Merry Christmas" on his lips, should be boiled with his own pudding, and buried with a stake of holly through his heart. He should!"

"Uncle!" pleaded the nephew.

"Nephew!" returned the uncle, sternly, "keep Christmas in your own way, and let me keep it in mine."

"Keep it!" repeated Scrooge's nephew. "But you don't keep it."

"Let me leave it alone, then," said Scrooge. "Much good may it do you! Much good it has ever done you!"

"There are many things from which I might have derived good, by which I have not profited, I dare say," returned the nephew: "Christmas among the rest. But I am sure I have always thought of Christmas time, when it has come round—apart from the veneration due to its sacred name and origin, if anything belonging to it can be apart from that—as a good time: a kind, forgiving, charitable, pleasant time: the only time I know of, in the long calendar of the year, when men and women seem by one consent to open their shut-up hearts freely, and to think of people below them as if they really were fellow-passengers to the grave, and not another race of creatures bound on other journeys. And therefore, uncle, though it has never put a scrap of gold or silver in my pocket, I believe that it has done me good, and will do me good; and I say, God bless it!"

The clerk in the tank involuntarily applauded. Becoming immediately sensible of the impropriety, he poked the fire, and extinguished the last frail spark forever.

"Let me hear another sound from you," said Scrooge, " and you'll keep your Christmas by losing your situation. You're quite a powerful speaker, sir," he added, turning to his nephew. "I wonder you don't go into Parliament."

"Don't be angry, uncle. Come! Dine with us tomorrow."

Scrooge said that he would see him—yes, indeed he did. He went the whole length of the expression, and said that he would see him in that extremity first.

"But why?" cried Scrooge's nephew. "Why?"

"Why did you get married?" said Scrooge.

"Because I fell in love."

"Because you fell in love!" growled Scrooge, as if that were the only one thing in the world more ridiculous than a merry Christmas. "Good afternoon!"

"Nay, uncle, but you never came to see me before that happened. Why give it as a reason for not coming now?"

"Good afternoon," said Scrooge.

"I want nothing from you; I ask nothing of you; why cannot we be friends?"

"Good afternoon," said Scrooge.

"I am sorry, with all my heart, to find you so resolute. We have never had any quarrel, to which I have been a party. But I have made the trial in homage to Christmas, and I'll keep my Christmas humour to the last. So A Merry Christmas, uncle!"

"Good afternoon!" said Scrooge.

"And A Happy New Year!"

"Good afternoon!" said Scrooge.

His nephew left the room without an angry word, notwithstanding. He stopped at the outer door to bestow the greeting of the season on the clerk, who, cold as he was, was warmer than Scrooge; for he returned them cordially.

"There's another fellow," muttered Scrooge; who overheard him: "my clerk, with fifteen shillings a week, and a wife and family, talking about a merry Christmas. I'll retire to Bedlam."

This lunatic, in letting Scrooge's nephew out, had let two other people in. They were portly gentlemen, pleasant to behold, and now stood, with their hats off, in Scrooge's office. They had books and papers in their hands, and bowed to him.

"Scrooge and Marley's, I believe," said one of the gentlemen, referring to his list. "Have I the pleasure of addressing Mr Scrooge, or Mr Marley?"

"Mr Marley has been dead these seven years," Scrooge replied. "He died seven years ago, this very night."

"We have no doubt his liberality is well represented by his surviving partner," said the gentleman, presenting his credentials.

It certainly was; for they had been two kindred spirits. At the ominous word "liberality", Scrooge frowned, and shook his head, and handed the credentials back.

"At this festive season of the year, Mr Scrooge," said the gentleman, taking up a pen, "it is more than usually desirable that we should make some slight provision for the Poor and destitute, who suffer greatly at the present time. Many thousands are in want of common necessaries; hundreds of thousands are in want of common comforts, sir."

"Are there no prisons?" asked Scrooge.

"Plenty of prisons," said the gentleman, laying down the pen again.

"And the Union workhouses?" demanded Scrooge. "Are they still in operation?"

"They are. Still," returned the gentleman, " I wish I could say they were not."

"The Treadmill and the Poor Law are in full vigour, then?" said Scrooge.

"Both very busy, sir."

"Oh! I was afraid, from what you said at first, that something had occurred to stop them in their useful course," said Scrooge. "I'm very glad to hear it."

"Under the impression that they scarcely furnish Christian cheer of mind or body to the multitude," returned the gentleman, "a few of us are endeavouring to raise a fund to buy the Poor some meat and drink, and means of warmth. We choose this time, because it is a time, of all others, when Want is keenly felt, and Abundance rejoices. What shall I put you down for?"

"Nothing!" Scrooge replied.

"You wish to be anonymous?"

"I wish to be left alone," said Scrooge. "Since you ask me what I wish, gentlemen, that is my answer. I don't make merry myself at Christmas and I can't afford to make idle people merry. I help to support the establishments I have mentioned: they cost enough: and those who are badly off must go there."

"Many can't go there; and many would rather die."

"If they would rather die," said Scrooge, "they had better do it, and decrease the surplus population. Besides—excuse me—I don't know that."

"But you might know it," observed the gentleman.

"It's not my business," Scrooge returned. "It's enough for a man to understand his own business, and not to interfere with other people's. Mine occupies me constantly. Good afternoon, gentlemen!"

Seeing clearly that it would be useless to pursue their point, the gentlemen withdrew. Scrooge resumed his labours with an improved opinion of himself, and in a more facetious temper than was usual with him.

Meanwhile the fog and darkness thickened so, that people ran about with flaring links, proffering their services to go before horses in carriages, and conduct them on their way. The ancient tower of a church, whose gruff old bell was always peeping slily down at Scrooge out of a gothic window in the wall, became invisible, and struck the hours and quarters in the clouds, with tremulous vibrations afterwards as if its teeth were chattering in its frozen head up there. The cold became intense. In the main street, at the corner of the court, some labourers were repairing the gas-pipes, and had lighted a great fire in a brazier, round which a party of ragged men and boys were gathered: warming their hands and winking their eyes before the blaze in rapture. The water-plug being left in solitude, its overflowings sullenly congealed, and turned to misanthropic ice. The brightness of the shops where holly sprigs and berries crackled in the lamp-heat of the windows, made pale faces ruddy as they passed. Poulterers' and grocers' trades became a splendid joke: a glorious pageant, with which it was next to impossible to believe that such dull principles as bargain and sale had anything to do. The Lord Mayor, in the stronghold of the might Mansion House, gave orders to his fifty cooks and butlers to keep Christmas as a Lord Mayor's household should; and even the little tailor, whom he had fined five shillings on the previous Monday for being drunk and bloodthirsty in the streets, stirred up tomorrow's pudding in his garret, while his lean wife and the baby sallied out to buy the beef.

Foggier yet, and colder! Piercing, searching, biting cold. If the good Saint Dunstan had but nipped the Evil Spirit's nose with a touch of such weather as that, instead of using his familiar weapons, then indeed he would have roared to lusty purpose. The owner of one scant young nose, gnawed and mumbled by the hungry cold as bones are gnawed by dogs, stooped down at Scrooge's keyhole to regale him with a Christmas carol: but at the first sound of—

God bless you, merry gentleman!
May nothing you dismay!

Scrooge seized the ruler with such energy of action that the singer fled in terror, leaving the keyhole to the fog and even more congenial frost.

At length the hour of shutting up the counting-house arrived. With an ill-will Scrooge dismounted from his stool, and tacitly admitted the fact to the expectant clerk in the Tank, who instantly snuffed his candle out, and put on his hat.

"You'll want all day tomorrow, I suppose?" said Scrooge.

"If quite convenient, Sir."

"It's not convenient," said Scrooge, "and it's not fair. If I was to stop half-a-crown for it, you'd think yourself ill-used, I'll be bound?"

The clerk smiled faintly.

"And yet," said Scrooge, "you don't think me ill-used, when I pay a day's wages for no work."

The clerk observed that it was only once a year.

"A poor excuse for picking a man's pocket every twenty-fifth of December!" said Scrooge, buttoning his great-coat to the chin. "But I suppose you must have the whole day. Be here all the earlier next morning!"

The clerk promised that he would; and Scrooge walked out with a growl. The office was closed in a twinkling, and the clerk, with the long ends of his white comforter dangling below his waist (for he boasted no great-coat), went down a slide on Cornhill, at the end of a lane of boys, twenty times, in honour of its being Christmas Eve, and then ran home to Camden Town as hard as he could pelt, to play at blindman's buff.

Scrooge took his melancholy dinner in his usual melancholy tavern; and having read all the newspapers, and beguiled the rest of the evening with his banker's-book, went home to bed. He lived in chambers which had once belonged to his deceased partner. They were a gloomy suite of rooms, in a lowering pile of building up a yard, where it had so little business to be, that one could scarcely help fancying it must have run there when it was a young house, playing at hide-and-seek with other houses, and have forgotten the way out again. It was old enough now, and dreary enough, for nobody lived in it but Scrooge, the other rooms being all let out as offices. The yard was so dark that even Scrooge, who knew its every stone, was fain to grope with his hands. The fog and frost so hung about the black old gateway of the house, that it seemed as if the Genius of the Weather sat in mournful meditation on the threshold.

Now, it is a fact, that there was nothing at all particular about the knocker on the door, except that it was very large. It is also a fact, that Scrooge had seen it, night and morning, during his whole residence in that place; also that Scrooge had as little of what is called fancy about him as any man in the City of London, even including—which is a bold word—the corporation, aldermen, and livery. Let it also be borne in mind that Scrooge had not bestowed one thought on Marley, since his last mention of his seven-year's dead partner that afternoon. And then let any man explain to me, if he can, how it happened that Scrooge, having his key in the lock of the door, saw in the knocker, without its undergoing any intermediate process of change: not a knocker, but Marley's face.

Marley's face. It was not in impenetrable shadow as the other objects in the yard were, but had a dismal light about it, like a bad lobster in a dark cellar. It was not angry or ferocious, but looked at Scrooge as Marley used to look: with ghostly spectacles turned up upon its ghostly forehead. The hair was curiously stirred, as if by breath or hot-air; and, though the eyes were wide open, they were perfectly motionless. That, and its livid colour, made it horrible; but its horror seemed to be in spite of the face and beyond its control, rather than a part of its own expression.

As Scrooge looked fixedly at this phenomenon, it was a knocker again.

To say that he was not startled, or that his blood was not conscious of a terrible sensation to which it had been a stranger from infancy, would be untrue. But he put his hand upon the key he had relinquished, turned it sturdily, walked in, and lighted his candle.

He did pause, with a moment's irresolution, before he shut the door; and he did look cautiously behind it first, as if he half expected to be terrified with the sight of Marley's pigtail sticking out into the hall. But there was nothing on the back of the door, except the screws and nuts that held the knocker on, so he said "Pooh, pooh!" and closed it with a bang.

The sound resounded through the house like thunder. Every room above, and every cask in the wine-merchant's cellars below, appeared to have a separate peal of echoes of its own. Scrooge was not a man to be frightened by echoes. He fastened the door, and walked across the hall, and up the stairs, slowly too: trimming his candle as he went.

You may talk vaguely about driving a coach-and-six up a good old flight of stairs, or through a bad young Act of Parliament; but I mean to say you might have got a hearse up that staircase, and taken it broadwise, with the splinter-bar towards the wall and the door towards the balustrades: and done it easy. There was plenty of width for that, and room to spare; which is perhaps the reason why Scrooge thought he saw a locomotive hearse going on before him in the gloom. Half-a-dozen gas-lamps out of the street wouldn't have lighted the entry too well, so you may suppose that it was pretty dark with Scrooge's dip.

Up Scrooge went, not caring a button for that: darkness is cheap, and Scrooge liked it. But before he shut his heavy door, he walked through his rooms to see that all was right. He had just enough recollection of the face to desire to do that.

Sitting-room, bed-room, lumber-room. All as they should be. Nobody under the table, nobody under the sofa; a small fire in the grate; spoon and basin ready; and the little saucepan of gruel (Scrooge has a cold in his head) upon the hob. Nobody under the bed; nobody in the closet; nobody in his dressing-gown, which was hanging up in a suspicious attitude against the wall. Lumber-room as usual. Old fire-guard, old shoes, two fish-baskets, washing-stand on three legs, and a poker.

Quite satisfied, he closed his door, and locked himself in; double-locked himself in, which was not his custom. Thus secured against surprise, he took off his cravat; put on his dressing-gown and slippers, and his night-cap; and sat down before the fire to take his gruel.

It was a very low fire indeed; nothing on such a bitter night. He was obliged to sit close to it, and brood over it, before he could extract the least sensation of warmth from such a handful of fuel. The fireplace was an old one, built by some Dutch merchant long ago, and paved all round with quaint Dutch tiles, designed to illustrate the Scriptures. There were Cains and Abels, Pharaoh's daughters, Queens of Sheba, Angelic messengers descending through the air on clouds like feather-beds, Abrahams, Belshazzars, Apostles putting off to sea in butter-boats, hundreds of figures to attract his thoughts; and yet that face of Marley, seven years dead, came like the ancient Prophet's rod, and swallowed up the whole. If each smooth tile had been a blank at first, with power to shape some picture on its surface from the disjointed fragments of his thoughts, there would have been a copy of old Marley's head on every one.

"Humbug!" said Scrooge; and walked across the room.

After several turns, he sat down again. As he threw his head back in the chair, his glance happened to rest upon a bell, a disused bell, that hung in the room, and communicated for some purpose now forgotten with a chamber in the highest story of the building. It was with great astonishment, and with a strange, inexplicable dread, that as he looked, he saw this bell begin to swing. It swung so softly in the outset that it scarcely made a sound; but soon it rang out loudly, and so did every bell in the house.

This might have lasted half a minute, or a minute, but it seemed an hour. The bells ceased as they had begun, together. They were succeeded by a clanking noise, deep down below; as if some person were dragging a heavy chain over the casks in the wine-merchant's cellar. Scrooge then remembered to have heard that ghosts in haunted houses were described as dragging chains.

The cellar-door flew open with a booming sound, and then he heard the noise much louder, on the floors below; then coming up the stairs; then coming straight towards his door.

"It's humbug still!" said Scrooge. "I won't believe it."

His colour changed though, when, without a pause, it came on through the heavy door, and passed into the room before his eyes. Upon its coming in, the dying flame leaped up, as though it cried, "I know him! Marley's Ghost!" and fell again.

The same face: the very same. Marley in his pigtail, usual waistcoat, tights, and boots; the tassels on the latter bristling, like his pigtail, and his coat-skirts, and the hair upon his head. The chain he drew was clasped about his middle. It was long, and wound about him like a tail; and it was made (for Scrooge observed it closely) of cash-boxes, keys, padlocks, ledgers, deeds, and heavy purses wrought in steel. His body was transparent; so that Scrooge, observing him, and looking through his waistcoat, could see the two buttons on his coat behind.

Scrooge had often heard it said that Marley had no bowels, but he had never believed it until now.

No, nor did he believe it even now. Though he looked the phantom through and through, and saw it standing before him; though he felt the chilling influence of its death-cold eyes; and marked the very texture of the folded kerchief bound about its head and chin, which wrapper he had not observed before; he was still incredulous, and fought against his senses.

"How now!" said Scrooge, caustic and cold as ever. "What do you want with me?"

"Much!"—Marley's voice, no doubt about it.

"Who are you?"

"Ask me who I was."

"Who were you then." said Scrooge, raising his voice. "You're particular, for a shade." He was going to say "to a shade," but substituted this, as more appropriate.

"In life I was your partner, Jacob Marley."

"Can you—can you sit down?" asked Scrooge, looking doubtfully at him.

"I can."

"Do it, then."

Scrooge asked the question, because he didn't know whether a ghost so transparent might find himself in a condition to take a chair; and felt that in the event of its being impossible, it might involve the necessity of an embarrassing explanation. But the ghost sat down on the opposite side of the fireplace, as if he were quite used to it.

"You don't believe in me," observed the Ghost.

"I don't," said Scrooge.

"What evidence would you have of my reality beyond that of your senses?"

"I don't know," said Scrooge.

"Why do you doubt your senses?"

"Because," said Scrooge, "a little thing affects them. A slight disorder of the stomach makes them cheats. You may be an undigested bit of beef, a blot of mustard, a crumb of cheese, a fragment of an underdone potato. There's more of gravy than of grave about you, whatever you are!"

Scrooge was not much in the habit of cracking jokes, nor did he feel, in his heart, by any means waggish then. The truth is, that he tried to be smart, as a means of distracting his own attention, and keeping down his terror; for the spectre's voice disturbed the very marrow in his bones.

To sit, staring at those fixed, glazed eyes, in silence for a moment, would play, Scrooge felt, the very deuce with him. There was something very awful, too, in the spectre's being provided with an infernal atmosphere of its own. Scrooge could not feel it himself, but this was clearly the case; for though the Ghost sat perfectly motionless, its hair, and skirts, and tassels, were still agitated as by the hot vapour from an oven.

"You see this toothpick?" said Scrooge, returning quickly to the charge, for the reason just assigned; and wishing, though it were only for a second, to divert the vision's stony gaze from himself.

"I do," replied the Ghost.

"You are not looking at it," said Scrooge.

"But I see it," said the Ghost, "notwithstanding."

"Well!" returned Scrooge, "I have but to swallow this, and be for the rest of my days persecuted by a legion of goblins, all of my own creation. Humbug, I tell you; humbug!"

At this the spirit raised a frightful cry, and shook its chain with such a dismal and appalling noise, that Scrooge held on tight to his chair, to save himself from falling in a swoon. But how much greater was his horror, when the phantom taking off the bandage round its head, as if it were too warm to wear indoors, its lower jaw dropped down upon its breast!

Scrooge fell upon his knees, and clasped his hands before his face.

"Mercy!" he said. "Dreadful apparition, why do you trouble me?"

"Man of the worldly mind!" replied the Ghost, "do you believe in me or not?"

"I do," said Scrooge. "I must. But why do spirits walk the earth, and why do they come to me?"

"It is required of every man," the Ghost returned, "that the spirit within him should walk abroad among his fellow-men, and travel far and wide; and if that spirit goes not forth in life, it is condemned to do so after death. It is doomed to wander through the world—oh, woe is me!—and witness what it cannot share, but might have shared on earth, and turned to happiness!"

Again the spectre raised a cry, and shook its chain, and wrung its shadowy hands.

"You are fettered," said Scrooge, trembling. "Tell me why?"

"I wear the chain I forged in life," replied the Ghost. "I made it link by link, and yard by yard; I girded it on of my own free will, and of my own free will I wore it. Is its pattern strange to you?"

Scrooge trembled more and more.

"Or would you know," pursued the Ghost, "the weight and length of the strong coil you bear yourself? It was full as heavy and as long as this, seven Christmas Eves ago. You have laboured on it, since. It is a ponderous chain!"

Scrooge glanced about him on the floor, in the expectation of finding himself surrounded by some fifty or sixty fathoms of iron cable: but he could see nothing.

"Jacob," he said, imploringly. "Old Jacob Marley, tell me more. Speak comfort to me, Jacob."

"I have none to give," the Ghost replied. "It comes from other regions, Ebenezer Scrooge, and is conveyed by other ministers, to other kinds of men. Nor can I tell you what I would. A very little more, is all permitted to me. I cannot rest, I cannot stay, I cannot linger anywhere. My spirit never walked beyond our counting-house—mark me!—in life my spirit never roved beyond the narrow limits of our money-changing hole; and weary journeys lie before me!"

It was a habit with Scrooge, whenever he became thoughtful, to put his hands in his breeches pockets. Pondering on what the Ghost had said, he did so now, but without lifting up his eyes, or getting off his knees.

"You must have been very slow about it, Jacob," Scrooge observed, in a business-like manner, though with humility and deference.

"Slow!" the Ghost repeated.

"Seven years dead," mused Scrooge. "And travelling all the time?"

"The whole time," said the Ghost. "No rest, no peace. Incessant torture of remorse."

"You travel fast?" said Scrooge.

"On the wings of the wind," replied the Ghost.

"You might have got over a great quantity of ground in seven years," said Scrooge.

The Ghost, on hearing this, set up another cry, and clanked its chain so hideously in the dead silence of the night, that the Ward would have been justified in indicting it for a nuisance.

"Oh! captive, bound, and double-ironed," cried the phantom, "not to know, that ages of incessant labour by immortal creatures, for this earth must pass into eternity before the good of which it is susceptible is all developed. Not to know that any Christian spirit working kindly in its little sphere, whatever it may be, will find its mortal life too short for its vast means of usefulness. Not to know that no space of regret can make amends for one life's opportunities misused! Yet such was I! Oh! such was I!"

"But you were always a good man of business, Jacob," faltered Scrooge, who now began to apply this to himself.

"Business!" cried the Ghost, wringing its hands again. "Mankind was my business. The common welfare was my business; charity, mercy, forbearance, and benevolence, were, all, my business. The dealings of my trade were but a drop of water in the comprehensive ocean of my business!"

It held up its chain at arm's length, as if that were the cause of all its unavailing grief, and flung it heavily upon the ground again.

"At this time of the rolling year," the spectre said, "I suffer most. Why did I walk through crowds of fellow-beings with my eyes turned down, and never raise them to that blessed Star which led the Wise Men to a poor abode? Were there no poor homes to which its light would have conducted me!"

Scrooge was very much dismayed to hear the spectre going on at this rate, and began to quake exceedingly.

"Hear me!" cried the Ghost. "My time is nearly gone."

"I will," said Scrooge. "But don't be hard upon me! Don't be flowery, Jacob! Pray!"

"How it is that I appear before you in a shape that you can see, I may not tell. I have sat invisible beside you many and many a day."

It was not an agreeable idea. Scrooge shivered, and wiped the perspiration from his brow.

"That is no light part of my penance," pursued the Ghost. "I am here tonight to warn you, that you have yet a chance and hope of escaping my fate. A chance and hope of my procuring,

Ebenezer."

"You were always a good friend to me," said Scrooge. "Thank'ee!"

"You will be haunted," resumed the Ghost, "by Three Spirits."

Scrooge's countenance fell almost as low as the Ghost's had done.

"Is that the chance and hope you mentioned, Jacob?" he demanded, in a faltering voice.

"It is."

"I—I think I'd rather not," said Scrooge.

"Without their visits," said the Ghost, "you cannot hope to shun the path I tread. Expect the first tomorrow, when the bell tolls One."

"Couldn't I take 'em all at once, and have it over, Jacob?" hinted Scrooge.

"Expect the second on the next night at the same hour. The third upon the next night when the last stroke of Twelve has ceased to vibrate. Look to see me no more; and look that, for your own sake, you remember what has passed between us."

When it had said these words, the spectre took its wrapper from the table, and bound it round its head, as before. Scrooge knew this, by the smart sound its teeth made, when the jaws were brought together by the bandage. He ventured to raise his eyes again, and found his supernatural visitor confronting him in an erect attitude, with its chain wound over and about its arm.

The apparition walked backward from him; and at every step it took, the window raised itself a little, so that when the spectre reached it, it was wide open.

It beckoned Scrooge to approach, which he did. When they were within two paces of each other, Marley's Ghost held up its hand, warning him to come no nearer. Scrooge stopped.

Not so much in obedience, as in surprise and fear: for on the raising of the hand, he became sensible of confused noises in the air; incoherent sounds of lamentation and regret; wailings inexpressibly sorrowful and self-accusatory. The spectre, after listening for a moment, joined in the mournful dirge; and floated out upon the bleak, dark night.

Scrooge followed to the window: desperate in his curiosity. He looked out.

The air was filled with phantoms, wandering hither and thither in restless haste, and moaning as they went. Every one of them wore chains like Marley's Ghost; some few (they might be guilty governments) were linked together; none were free. Many had been personally known to Scrooge in their lives. He had been quite familiar with one old ghost, in a white waistcoat, with a monstrous iron safe attached to its ankle, who cried piteously at being unable to assist a wretched woman with an infant, whom it saw below, upon a door-step. The misery with them all was, clearly, that they sought to interfere, for good, in human matters, and had lost the power for ever.

Whether these creatures faded into mist, or mist enshrouded them, he could not tell. But they and their spirit voices faded together; and the night became as it had been when he walked home.

Scrooge closed the window, and examined the door by which the Ghost had entered. It was double-locked, as he had locked it with his own hands, and the bolts were undisturbed. He tried to say "Humbug!" but stopped at the first syllable. And being, from the emotion he had undergone, or the fatigues of the day, or his glimpse of the Invisible World, or the dull conversation of the Ghost, or the lateness of the hour, much in need of repose; went straight to bed, without undressing, and fell asleep upon the instant.

CHAPTER 2
THE FIRST OF THE THREE SPIRITS

When Scrooge awoke, it was so dark, that looking out of bed, he could scarcely distinguish the transparent window from the opaque walls of his chamber. He was endeavouring to pierce the darkness with his ferret eyes, when the chimes of a neighbouring church struck the four quarters. So he listened for the hour.

To his great astonishment the heavy bell went on from six to seven, and from seven to eight, and regularly up to twelve; then stopped. Twelve! It was past two when he went to bed. The clock was wrong. An icicle must have got into the works. Twelve!

He touched the spring of his repeater, to correct this most preposterous clock. Its rapid little pulse beat twelve: and stopped.

"Why, it isn't possible," said Scrooge, "that I can have slept through a whole day and far into another night. It isn't possible that anything has happened to the sun, and this is twelve at noon!"

The idea being an alarming one, he scrambled out of bed, and groped his way to the window. He was obliged to rub the frost off with the sleeve of his dressing-gown before he could see anything; and could see very little then. All he could make out was, that it was still very foggy and extremely cold, and that there was no noise of people running to and fro, and making a great stir, as there unquestionably would have been if night had beaten off bright day, and taken possession of the world. This was a great relief, because "three days after sight of this First of Exchange pay to Mr. Ebenezer Scrooge or his order," and so forth, would have become a mere United States' security if there were no days to count by.

Scrooge went to be again, and thought, and 1 thought, and thought it over and over, and could make nothing of it. The more he thought, the more perplexed he was; and the more he endeavoured not to think, the more he thought Marley's Ghost bothered him exceedingly. Every time he resolved within himself, after mature inquiry, that it was all a dream, his mind flew back, like a strong spring released, to its first position, and presented the same problem to be worked all through, "Was it a dream or not?"

Scrooge lay in this state until the chime had gone three quarters more, when he remembered, on a sudden, that the Ghost had warned him of a visitation when the bell tolled one. He resolved to lie awake until the hour was past; and, considering that he could no more go to sleep than go to Heaven, this was perhaps the wisest resolution in his power.

The quarter was so long, that he was more than once con-vinced he must have sunk into a doze unconsciously, and missed the clock. At length it broke upon his listening ear.

"Ding, dong!"

"A quarter past," said Scrooge, counting.

"Ding, dong!"

"Half past!" said Scrooge.

"Ding, dong!"

"A quarter to it," said Scrooge.

"Ding, dong!"

"The hour itself," said Scrooge, triumphantly, "and nothing else!"

He spoke before the hour bell sounded, which it now did with a deep, dull, hollow, melancholy ONE. Light flashed up in the room upon the instant, and the curtains of his bed were drawn.

The curtains of his bed were drawn aside, I tell you, by a hand. Not the curtains at his feet, nor the curtains at his back, but those to which his face was addressed. The curtains of his bed were drawn aside; and Scrooge, starting up into a half-re-cumbent attitude, found himself face to face with the unearthly visitor who drew them: as close to it as I am now to you, and I am standing in the spirit at your elbow.

It was a strange figure—like a child: yet not so like a child as like an old man, viewed through some supernatural medium, which gave him the appearance of having receded from the view, and being diminished to a child's proportions. Its hair, which hung about its neck and down its back, was white as if with age; and yet the face had not a wrinkle in it, and the tenderest bloom was on the skin. The arms were very long and muscular; the hands the same, as if its hold were of uncommon strength. Its legs and feet, most delicately formed, were, like those upper members, bare. It wore a tunic of the purest white and round its waist was bound a lustrous belt, the sheen of which was beautiful. It held a branch of fresh green holly in its hand; and, in singular contradiction of that wintry emblem, had its dress trimmed with summer flowers. But the strangest thing about it was, that from the crown of its head there sprung a bright clear jet of light, by which all this was visible; and which was doubtless the occasion of its using, in its duller moments, a great extinguisher for a cap, which it now held under its arm.

Even this, though, when Scrooge looked at it with increasing steadiness, was not its strangest quality. For as its belt sparkled and glittered now in one part and now in another, and what was light one instant, at another time was dark, so the figure itself fluctuated in its distinctness: being now a thing with one arm, now with one leg, now with twenty legs, now a pair of legs without a head, now a head without a body: of which dissolving parts, no outline would be visible in the dense gloom wherein they melted away. And in the very wonder of this, it would be itself again; distinct and clear as ever.

"Are you the Spirit, sir, whose coming was foretold to me?" asked Scrooge.

"I am!"

The voice was soft and gentle. Singularly low, as if instead of being so close beside him, it were at a distance.

"Who, and what are you?" Scrooge demanded.

"I am the Ghost of Christmas Past."

"Long past?" inquired Scrooge: observant of its dwarfish stature.

"No. Your past."

Perhaps, Scrooge could not have told anybody why, if anybody could have asked him; but he had a special desire to see the Spirit in his cap; and begged him to be covered.

"What!" exclaimed the Ghost, "would you so soon put out, with worldly hands, the light I give? Is it not enough that you are one of those whose passions made this cap, and force me through whole trains of years to wear it low upon my brow!"

Scrooge reverently disclaimed all intention to offend or any knowledge of having wilfully bonneted the Spirit at any period of his life. He then made bold to inquire what business brought him there.

"Your welfare!" said the Ghost.

Scrooge expressed himself much obliged, but could not help thinking that a night of unbroken rest would have been more conducive to that end. The Spirit must have heard him thinking, for it said immediately:

"Your reclamation, then. Take heed!"

It put out its strong hand as it spoke, and clasped him gently by the arm.

"Rise! and walk with me!"

It would have been in vain for Scrooge to plead that the weather and the hour were not adapted to pedestrian purposes; that bed was warm, and the thermometer a long way below freezing; that he was clad but lightly in his slippers, dressing-gown, and nightcap; and that he had a cold upon him at that time. The grasp, though gentle as a woman's hand, was not to be resisted. He rose: but finding that the Spirit made towards the window, clasped his robe in supplication.

"I am mortal," Scrooge remonstrated, "and liable to fall."

"Bear but a touch of my hand there," said the Spirit, laying it upon his heart, "and you shall be upheld in more than this!"

As the words were spoken, they passed through the wall, and stood upon an open country road, with fields on either hand. The city had entirely vanished. Not a vestige of it was to be seen. The darkness and the mist had vanished with it, for it was a clear, cold, winter day, with snow upon the ground. "Good Heaven!" said Scrooge, clasping his hands together, as he looked about him. "I was bred in this place. I was a boy here!"

The Spirit gazed upon him mildly. Its gentle touch, though it had been light and instantaneous, appeared still present to the old man's sense of feeling. He was conscious of a thousand odours floating in the air, each one connected with a thousand thoughts, and hopes, and joys, and cares long, long, forgotten.

"Your lip is trembling," said the Ghost. "And what is that upon your cheek?"

Scrooge muttered, with an unusual catching in his voice, that it was a pimple; and begged the Ghost to lead him where he would.

"You recollect the way?" inquired the Spirit.

"Remember it!" cried Scrooge with fervour; "I could walk it blindfold."

"Strange to have forgotten it for so many years!" observed the Ghost. "Let us go on."

They walked along the road; Scrooge recognising every gate, and post, and tree; until a little market-town appeared in the distance, with its bridge, its church, and winding river. Some shaggy ponies now were seen trotting towards them with boys upon their backs, who called to other boys in country gigs and carts, driven by farmers. All these boys were in great spirits, and shouted to each other, until the broad fields were so full of merry music, that the crisp air laughed to hear it.

"These are but shadows of the things that have been," said the Ghost. "They have no consciousness of us."

The jocund travellers came on; and as they came, Scrooge knew and named them every one. Why was he rejoiced beyond all bounds to see them! Why did his cold eye glisten, and his heart leap up as they went past! Why was he filled with gladness when he heard them give each other Merry Christmas, as they parted at cross-roads and bye-ways, for their several homes! What was merry Christmas to Scrooge? Out upon merry Christmas! What good had it ever done to him?

"The school is not quite deserted," said the Ghost. "A solitary child, neglected by his friends, is left there still."

Scrooge said he knew it. And he sobbed.

They left the high-road, by a well-remembered lane, and soon approached a mansion of dull red brick, with a little weathercock-surmounted cupola, on the roof, and a bell hanging in it. It was a large house, but one of broken fortunes; for the spacious offices were little used, their walls were damp and mossy, their windows broken, and their gates decayed. Fowls clucked and strutted in the stables; and the coach-houses and sheds were over-run with grass. Nor was it more retentive of its ancient state, within; for entering the dreary hall, and glancing through the open doors of many rooms, they found them poorly furnished, cold, and vast. There was an earthy savour in the air, a chilly bareness in the place, which associated itself somehow with too much getting up by candle-light, and not too much to eat.

They went, the Ghost and Scrooge, across the hall, to a door at the back of the house. It opened before them, and disclosed a long, bare, melancholy room, made barer still by lines of plain deal forms and desks. At one of these a lonely boy was reading near a feeble fire; and Scrooge sat down upon a form, and wept to see his poor forgotten self as he used to be.

Not a latent echo in the house, not a squeak and scuffle from the mice behind the panelling, not a drip from the half-thawed water-spout in the dull yard behind, not a sigh among the leafless boughs of one despondent poplar, not the idle swinging of an empty store-house door, no, not a clicking in the fire, but fell upon the heart of Scrooge with a softening influence, and gave a freer passage to his tears.

The Spirit touched him on the arm, and pointed to his younger self, intent upon his reading. Suddenly a man, in foreign garments: wonderfully real and distinct to look at: stood outside the window, with an axe stuck in his belt, and leading an ass laden with wood by the bridle.

"Why, it's Ali Baba! " Scrooge exclaimed in ecstasy. "It's dear old honest Ali Baba! Yes, yes, I know! One Christmas time, when yonder solitary child was left here all alone, he did come, for the first time, just like that. Poor boy! And Valentine," said Scrooge, "and his wild brother, Orson; there they go! And what's his name, who was put down in his drawers, asleep, at the Gate of Damascus; don't you see him! And the Sultan's Groom turned upside-down by the Genii; there he is upon his head! Serve him right. I'm glad of it. What business had he to be married to the Princess!"

To hear Scrooge expending all the earnestness of his nature on such subjects, in a most extraordinary voice between laughing and crying; and to see his heightened and excited face; would have been a surprise to his business friends in the city, indeed.

"There's the Parrot!" cried Scrooge. "Green body and yellow tail, with a thing like a lettuce growing out of the top of his head; there he is! Poor Robin Crusoe, he called him, when he came home again after sailing round the island. "Poor Robin Crusoe, where have you been, Robin Crusoe?" The man thought he was dreaming, but he wasn't. It was the Parrot, you know. There goes Friday, running for his life to the little creek! Halloa! Hoop! Halloo!"

Then, with a rapidity of transition very foreign to his usual character, he said, in pity for his former self, "Poor boy!" and cried again.

"I wish," Scrooge muttered, putting his hand in his pocket, and looking about him, after drying his eyes with his cuff: "but it's too late now."

"What is the matter?" asked the Spirit.

"Nothing," said Scrooge. "Nothing. There was a boy singing a Christmas Carol at my door last night. I should like to have given him something: that's all."

The Ghost smiled thoughtfully, and waved its hand: saying as it did so, "Let us see another Christmas!"

Scrooge's former self grew larger at the words, and the room became a little darker and more dirty. The panels shrunk, the windows cracked; fragments of plaster fell out of the ceiling, and the naked laths were shown instead; but how all this was brought about, Scrooge knew no more than you do. He only knew that it was quite correct; that everything had happened so; that there he was, alone again, when all the other boys had gone home for the jolly holidays.

He was not reading now, but walking up and down despairingly. Scrooge looked at the Ghost, and with a mournful shaking of his head, glanced anxiously towards the door.

It opened; and a little girl, much younger than the boy, came darting in, and putting her arms about his neck, and often kissing him, addressed him as her "Dear, dear brother."

"I have come to bring you home, dear brother!" said the

child, clapping her tiny hands, and bending down to laugh. "To bring you home, home, home!"

"Home, little Fan?" returned the boy.

"Yes!" said the child, brimful of glee. "Home, for good and all. Home, forever and ever. Father is so much kinder than he used to be, that home's like Heaven! He spoke so gently to me one dear night when I was going to bed, that I was not afraid to ask him once more if you might come home; and he said Yes, you should; and sent me in a coach to bring you. And you're to be a man!" said the child, opening her eyes, "and are never to come back here; but first, we're to be together all the Christmas long, and have the merriest time in all the world."

"You are quite a woman, little Fan!" exclaimed the boy.

She clapped her hands and laughed, and tried to touch his head; but being too little, laughed again, and stood on tiptoe to embrace him. Then she began to drag him, in her childish eagerness, towards the door; and he, nothing loath to go, accompanied her.

A terrible voice in the hall cried."Bring down Master Scrooge's box, there! " and in the hall appeared the schoolmaster himself, who glared on Master Scrooge with a ferocious condescension, and threw him into a dreadful state of mind by shaking hands with him. He then conveyed him and his sister into the veriest old well of a shivering best-parlour that ever was seen, where the maps upon the wall, and the celestial and terrestrial globes in the windows, were waxy with cold. Here he produced a decanter of curiously light wine, and a block of curiously heavy cake, and administered instalments of those dainties to the young people: at the same time, sending out a meagre servant to offer a glass of something to the postboy, who answered that he thanked the gentleman, but if it was the same tap as he had tasted before, he had rather not. Master Scrooge's trunk being by this time tied on to the top of the chaise, the children bade the schoolmaster good-bye right willingly; and getting into it, drove gaily down the garden-sweep: the quick wheels dashing the hoar-frost and snow from off the dark leaves of the evergreens like spray.

"Always a delicate creature, whom a breath might have withered," said the Ghost. "But she had a large heart!"

"So she had," cried Scrooge. "You're right, I will not gainsay it, Spirit. God forbid!"

"She died a woman," said the Ghost, "and had, as I think, children."

"One child," Scrooge returned.

"True," said the Ghost. "Your nephew!"

Scrooge seemed uneasy in his mind; and answered briefly, "Yes."

Although they had but that moment left the school behind them, they were now in the busy thoroughfares of a city, where shadowy passengers passed and repassed; where shadowy carts and coaches battle for the way, and all the strife and tumult of a real city were. It was made plain enough, by the dressing of the shops, that here too it was Christmas time again; but it was evening, and the streets were lighted up.

The Ghost stopped at a certain warehouse door, and asked Scrooge if he knew it.

"Know it!" said Scrooge. "Was I apprenticed here!"

They went in. At sight of an old gentleman in a Welch wig, sitting behind such a high desk, that if he had been two inches taller he must have knocked his head against the ceiling, Scrooge cried in great excitement:

"Why, it's old Fezziwig! Bless his heart; it's Fezziwig alive again!"

Old Fezziwig laid down his pen, and looked up at the clock, which pointed to the hour of seven. He rubbed his hands; adjusted his capacious waistcoat; laughed all over himself, from his shows to his organ of benevolence; and called out in a comfortable, oily, rich, fat, jovial voice:

"Yo ho, there! Ebenezer! Dick!"

Scrooge's former self, now grown a young man, came briskly in, accompanied by his fellow-'prentice.

"Dick Wilkins, to be sure!" said Scrooge to the Ghost. "Bless me, yes. There he is. He was very much attached to me, was

Dick. Poor Dick! Dear, dear!"

"Yo ho, my boys!" said Fezziwig. "No more work tonight. Christmas Eve, Dick. Christmas, Ebenezer! Let's have the shutters up," cried old Fezziwig, with a sharp clap of his hands, "before a man can say, Jack Robinson!"

You wouldn't believe how those two fellows went at it! They charged into the street with the shutters—one, two, three—had 'em up in their places—four, five, six—barred 'em and pinned 'em—seven, eight, nine—and came back before you could have got to twelve, panting like race-horses.

"Hilli-ho!" cried old Fezziwig, skipping down from the high desk, with wonderful agility. "Clear away, my lads, and let's have lots of room here! Hilli-ho, Dick! Chirrup, Ebenezer!"

Clear away! There was nothing they wouldn't have cleared away, or couldn't have cleared away, with old Fezziwig looking on. It was done in a minute. Every movable was packed off, as if it were dismissed from public life for evermore; the floor was swept and watered, the lamps were trimmed, fuel was heaped upon the fire; and the warehouse was as snug, and warm, and dry, and bright a ball-room, as you would desire to see upon a winter's night.

In came a fiddler with a music-book, and went up to the lofty desk, and made an orchestra of it, and tuned like fifty stomach-aches. In came Mrs. Fezziwig, one vast substantial smile. In came the three Miss Fezziwigs, beaming and lovable. In came the six young followers whose hearts they broke. In came all the young men and women employed in the business. In came the housemaid, with her cousin, the baker. In came the cook, with her brother's particular friend, the milkman. In came the boy from over the way, who was suspected of not having board enough from his master; trying to hide himself behind the girl from next door but one, who was proved to have had her ears pulled by her Mistress.

In they all came, one after another; some shyly, some boldly, some gracefully, some awkwardly, some pushing, some pulling; in they all came, anyhow and everyhow. Away they all went, twenty couple at once; hands half round and back again the other way; down the middle and up again; round and round in various stages of affectionate grouping; old top couple always turning up in the wrong place; new top couple starting off again, as soon as they got there; all top couples at last, and not a bottom one to help them. When this result was brought about, old Fezziwig, clapping his hands to stop the dance, cried out, "Well done!" and the fiddler plunged his hot face into a pot of porter, especially provided for that purpose. But scorning rest, upon his reappearance, he instantly began again, though there were no dancers yet, as if the other fiddler had been carried home, exhausted, on a shutter, and he were a bran-new man resolved to beat him out of sight, or perish.

There were more dances, and there were forfeits, and more dances, and there was cake, and there was negus, and there was a great piece of Cold Roast, and there was a great piece of Cold Boiled, and there were mince-pies, and plenty of beer. But the great effect of the evening came after the Roast and Boiled, when the fiddler (an artful dog, mind! The sort of man who knew his business better than you or I could have told it him!) struck up "Sir Roger de Coverley." Then old Fezziwig stood out to dance with Mrs. Fezziwig. Top couple, too; with a good stiff piece of work cut out for them; three or four and twenty pair of partners; people who were not to be trifled with; people who would dance, and had no notion of walking.

But if they had been twice as many: ah, four times: old Fezziwig would have been a match for them, and so would Mrs. Fezziwig. As to her, she was worthy to be his partner in every sense of the term. If that's not high praise, tell me higher, and I'll use it. A positive light appeared to issue from Fezziwig's calves. They shone in every part of the dance like moons. You couldn't have predicted, at any given time, what would become of 'em next. And when old Fezziwig and Mrs. Fezziwig had gone all through the dance; advance and retire, hold hands with your partner, bow and curtsey; corkscrew; thread-the-needle, and back again to your place; Fezziwig cut—cut so deftly, that he appeared to wink with his legs, and came upon his feet again without a stagger.

When the clock struck eleven, this domestic ball broke up. Mr and Mrs Fezziwig took their stations, one on either side of the door, and shaking hands with every person individually as he or she went out, wished him or her a Merry Christmas. When everybody had retired but the two 'prentices, they did the same to them; and thus the cheerful voices died away, and the lads were left to their beds; which were under a counter in the back-shop.

During the whole of this time, Scrooge had acted like a man out of his wits. His heart and soul were in the scene, and with his former self. He corroborated everything, remembered everything, enjoyed everything, and underwent the strangest agitation. It was not until now, when the bright faces of his former self and Dick were turned from them, that he remembered the Ghost, and became conscious that it was looking full upon him, while the light upon its head burnt very clear.

"A small matter," said the Ghost, "to make these silly folks so full of gratitude."

"Small!" echoed Scrooge.

The Spirit signed to him to listen to the two apprentices, who were pouring out their hearts in praise of Fezziwig: and when he had done so, said,

"Why! Is it not? He has spent but a few pounds of your mortal money: three or four perhaps. Is that so much that he deserves this praise?"

"It isn't that," said Scrooge, heated by the remark, and speaking unconsciously like his former, not his latter, self. "It isn't that, Spirit. He has the power to render us happy or unhappy; to make our service light or burdensome; a pleasure or a toil. Say that his power lies in words and looks; in things so slight and insignificant that it is impossible to add and count 'em up: what then? The happiness he gives, is quite as great as if it cost a fortune."

He felt the Spirit's glance, and stopped.

"What is the matter?" asked the Ghost.

"Nothing particular," said Scrooge.

"Something, I think?" the Ghost insisted.

"No," said Scrooge, "No. I should like to be able to say a word or two to my clerk just now! That's all."

His former self turned down the lamps as he gave utterance to the wish; and Scrooge and the Ghost again stood side by side in the open air.

"My time grows short," observed the Spirit. "Quick!"

This was not addressed to Scrooge, or to any one whom he could see, but it produced an immediate effect. For again Scrooge saw himself. He was older now; a man in the prime of life. His face had not the harsh and rigid lines of later years; but it had begun to wear the signs of care and avarice. There was an eager, greedy, restless motion in the eye, which showed the passion that had taken root, and where the shadow of the growing tree would fall.

He was not alone, but sat by the side of a fair young girl in a mourning-dress: in whose eyes there were tears, which sparkled in the light that shone out of the Ghost of Christmas Past.

"It matters little," she said, softly. "To you, very little. Another idol has displaced me; and if it can cheer and comfort you in time to come, as I would have tried to do, I have no just cause to grieve."

"What Idol has displaced you?" he rejoined.

"A golden one."

"This is the even-handed dealing of the world!" he said. "There is nothing on which it is so hard as poverty; and there is nothing it professes to condemn with such severity as the pursuit of wealth!"

"You fear the world too much," she answered, gently. "All your other hopes have merged into the hope of being beyond the chance of its sordid reproach. I have seen your nobler aspirations fall off one by one, until the master-passion, Gain, engrosses you. Have I not?"

"What then?" he retorted. "Even if I have grown so much

wiser, what then? I am not changed towards you."

She shook her head.

"Am I?"

"Our contract is an old one. It was made when we were both poor and content to be so, until, in good season, we could improve our worldly fortune by our patient industry. You are changed. When it was made, you were another man."

"I was a boy," he said impatiently.

"Your own feeling tells you that you were not what you are," she returned. "I am. That which promised happiness when we were one in heart, is fraught with misery now that we are two. How often and how keenly I have thought of this, I will not say. It is enough that I have thought of it, and can release you."

"Have I ever sought release?"

"In words. No. Never."

"In what, then?"

"In a changed nature; in an altered spirit; in another atmosphere of life; another Hope as its great end. In everything that made my love of any worth or value in your sight. If this had never been between us," said the girl, looking mildly, but with steadiness, upon him; "tell me, would you seek me out and try to win me now? Ah, no!"

He seemed to yield to the justice of this supposition, in spite of himself. But he said with a struggle, "You think not."

"I would gladly think otherwise if I could," she answered, "Heaven knows! When I have learned a Truth like this, I know how strong and irresistible it must be. But if you were free today, tomorrow, yesterday, can even I believe that you would choose a dowerless girl—you who, in your very confidence with her, weigh everything by Gain: or, choosing her, if for a moment you were false enough to your one guiding principle to do so, do I not know that your repentance and regret would surely follow? I do; and I release you. With a full heart, for the love of him you once were."

He was about to speak; but with her head turned from him, she resumed.

"You may—the memory of what is past half makes me hope you will—have pain in this. A very, very brief time, and you will dismiss the recollection of it, gladly, as an unprofitable dream, from which it happened well that you awoke. May you be happy in the life you have chosen!"

She left him, and they parted.

"Spirit!" said Scrooge, "show me no more! Conduct me home. Why do you delight to torture me?"

"One shadow more!" exclaimed the Ghost.

"No more!" cried Scrooge. "No more. I don't wish to see it. Show me no more!"

But the relentless Ghost pinioned him in both his arms, and forced him to observe what happened next.

They were in another scene and place; a room, not very large or handsome, but full of comfort. Near to the winter fire sat a beautiful young girl, so like that last that Scrooge believed it was the same, until he saw her, now a comely matron, sitting opposite her daughter. The noise in this room was perfectly tumultuous, for there were more children there, than Scrooge in his agitated state of mind could count; and, unlike the celebrated herd in the poem, they were not forty children conducting themselves like one, but every child was conducting itself like forty. The consequences were uproarious beyond belief; but no one seemed to care; on the contrary, the mother and daughter laughed heartily, and enjoyed it very much; and the latter, soon beginning to mingle in the sports, got pillaged by the young brigands most ruthlessly.

What would I not have given to one of them! Though I never could have been so rude, no, no! I wouldn't for the wealth of all the world have crushed that braided hair, and torn it down; and for the precious little shoe, I wouldn't have plucked it off, God bless my soul! to save my life. As to measuring her waist in sport, as they did, bold young brood, I couldn't have done it; I should have expected my arm to have grown round it for a punishment, and never come straight again. And yet I should have dearly liked, I own, to have touched her lips; to have questioned her, that she might have opened them; to have looked upon the lashes of her downcast eyes, and never raised a blush; to have let loose waves of hair, an inch of which would be a keepsake beyond price: in short, I should have liked, I do confess, to have had the lightest licence of a child, and yet to have been man enough to know its value.

But now a knocking at the door was heard, and such a rush immediately ensued that she with laughing face and plundered dress was borne towards it the centre of a flushed and boisterous group, just in time to greet the father, who came home attended by a man laden with Christmas toys and presents. Then the shouting and the struggling, and the onslaught that was made on the defenceless porter! The scaling him, with chairs for ladders, to dive into his pockets, despoil him of brown-paper parcels, hold on tight by his cravat, hug him round the neck, pommel his back, and kick his legs in irrepressible affection! The shouts of wonder and delight with which the development of every package was received!

The terrible announcement that the baby had been taken in the act of putting a doll's frying-pan into his mouth, and was more than suspected of having swallowed a fictitious turkey, glued on a wooden platter! The immense relief of finding this a false alarm! The joy, and gratitude, and ecstasy! They are all indescribable alike. It is enough that by degrees the children and their emotions got out of the parlour, and by one stair at a time, up to the top of the house; where they went to bed, and so subsided.

And now Scrooge looked on more attentively than ever, when the master of the house, having his daughter leaning fondly on him, sat down with her and her mother at his own fireside; and when he thought that such another creature, quite as graceful and as full of promise, might have called him father, and been a spring-time in the haggard winter of his life, his sight grew very dim indeed.

"Belle," said the husband, turning to his wife with a smile, "I saw an old friend of yours this afternoon."

"Who was it?"

"Guess!"

"How can I? Tut, don't I know." she added in the same breath, laughing as he laughed. "Mr Scrooge."

"Mr Scrooge it was. I passed his office window; and as it was not shut up, and he had a candle inside, I could scarcely help seeing him. His partner lies upon the point of death, I hear; and there he sat alone. Quite alone in the world, I do believe."

"Spirit!" said Scrooge in a broken voice, "remove me from this place."

"I told you these were shadows of the things that have been," said the Ghost. "That they are what they are, do not blame me!"

"Remove me!" Scrooge exclaimed, "I cannot bear it!"

He turned upon the Ghost, and seeing that it looked upon him with a face, in which in some strange way there were fragments of all the faces it had shown him, wrestled with it.

"Leave me! Take me back. Haunt me no longer!"

In the struggle, if that can be called a struggle in which the Ghost with no visible resistance on its own part was undisturbed by any effort of its adversary, Scrooge observed that its light was burning high and bright; and dimly connecting that with its influence over him, he seized the extinguisher-cap, and by a sudden action pressed it down upon its head.

The Spirit dropped beneath it, so that the extinguisher covered its whole form; but though Scrooge pressed it down with all his force, he could not hide the light, which streamed from under it, in an unbroken flood upon the ground.

He was conscious of being exhausted, and overcome by an irresistible drowsiness; and, further, of being in his own bedroom. He gave the cap a parting squeeze, in which his hand relaxed; and had barely time to reel to bed, before he sank into a heavy sleep.

CHAPTER 3
THE SECOND OF THE THREE SPIRITS

Awakening in the middle of a prodigiously tough snore, and sitting up in bed to get his thoughts together, Scrooge had no occasion to be told that the bell was again upon the stroke of One. He felt that he was restored to consciousness in the right nick of time, for the especial purpose of holding a conference with the second messenger despatched to him through Jacob Marley's intervention. But, finding that he turned uncomfortably cold when he began to wonder which of his curtains this new spectre would draw back, he put them every one aside with his own hands; and lying down again, established a sharp look-out all round the bed. For he wished to challenge the Spirit on the moment of its appearance, and did not wish to be taken by surprise, and made nervous.

Gentlemen of the free-and-easy sort, who plume themselves on being acquainted with a move or two, and being usually equal to the time-of-day, express the wide range of their capacity for adventure by observing that they are good for anything from pitch-and-toss to manslaughter; between which opposite extremes, no doubt, there lies a tolerably wide and comprehensive range of subjects. Without venturing for Scrooge quite as hardily as this, I don't mind calling on you to believe that he was ready for a good broad field of strange appearances, and that nothing between a baby and rhinoceros would have astonished him very much.

Now, being prepared for almost anything, he was not by any means prepared for nothing; and, consequently, when the Bell struck One, and no shape appeared, he was taken with a violent fit of trembling. Five minutes, ten minutes, a quarter of an hour went by, yet nothing came. All this time, he lay upon his bed, the very core and centre of a blaze of ruddy light, which streamed upon it when the clock proclaimed the hour; and which, being only light, was more alarming than a dozen ghosts, as he was powerless to make out what it meant, or would be at; and was sometimes apprehensive that he might be at that very moment an interesting case of spontaneous combustion, without having the consolation of knowing it.

At last, however, he began to think—as you or I would have thought at first; for it is always the person not in the predicament who knows what ought to have been done in it, and would unquestionably have done it too—at last, I say, he began to think that the source and secret of this ghostly light might be in the adjoining room, from whence, on further tracing it, it seemed to shine. This idea taking full possession of his mind, he got up softly and shuffled in his slippers to the door.

The moment Scrooge's hand was on the lock, a strange voice called him by his name, and bade him enter. He obeyed.

It was his own room. There was no doubt about that. But it had undergone a surprising transformation. The walls and ceiling were so hung with living green, that it looked a perfect grove; from every part of which, bright gleaming berries glistened. The crisp leaves of holly, mistletoe, and ivy reflected back the light, as if so many little mirrors had been scattered there; and such a mighty blaze went roaring up the chimney, as that dull petrification of a hearth had never known in Scrooge's time, or Marley's, or for many and many a winter season gone.

Heaped up on the floor, to form a kind of throne, were turkeys, geese, game, poultry, brawn, great joints of meat, sucking-pigs, long wreaths of sausages, mince-pies, plum-puddings, barrels of oysters, red-hot chesnuts, cherry-cheeked apples, juicy oranges, luscious pears, immense twelfth-cakes, and seething bowls of punch, that made the chamber dim with their delicious steam. In easy state upon this couch, there sat a jolly Giant, glorious to see: who bore a glowing torch, in shape not unlike Plenty's horn, and held it up, high up, to shed its light on Scrooge, as he came peeping round the door.

"Come in!" exclaimed the Ghost. "Come in and know me better, man!"

Scrooge entered timidly, and hung his head before this Spirit. He was not the dogged Scrooge he had been; and though the Spirit's eyes were clear and kind, he did not like to meet them.

"I am the Ghost of Christmas Present," said the Spirit. "Look upon me!"

Scrooge reverently did so. It was clothed in one simple green robe, or mantle, bordered with white fur. This garment hung so loosely on the figure, that its capacious breast was bare, as if disdaining to be warded or concealed by any artifice. Its feet, observable beneath the ample folds of the garment, were also bare; and on its head it wore no other covering than a holly wreath, set here and there with shining icicles. Its dark brown curls were long and free: free as its genial face, its sparkling eye, its open hand, its cheery voice, its unconstrained demeanour, and its joyful air. Girded round its middle was an antique scabbard; but no sword was in it, and the ancient sheath was eaten up with rust.

"You have never seen the like of me before!" exclaimed the Spirit.

"Never," Scrooge made answer to it.

"Have never walked forth with the younger members of my family; meaning (for I am very young) my elder brothers born in these later years?" pursued the Phantom.

"I don't think I have," said Scrooge. "I am afraid I have not. Have you had many brothers, Spirit?"

"More than eighteen hundred," said the Ghost.

"A tremendous family to provide for!" muttered Scrooge.

The Ghost of Christmas Present rose.

"Spirit," said Scrooge submissively, "conduct me where you will. I went forth last night on compulsion, and I learnt a lesson which is working now. Tonight, if you have aught to teach me, let me profit by it."

"Touch my robe!"

Scrooge did as he was told, and held it fast.

Holly, mistletoe, red berries, ivy, turkeys, geese, game, poultry, brawn, meat, pigs, sausages, oysters, pies, puddings, fruit, and punch, all vanished instantly. So did the room, the fire, the ruddy glow, the hour of night, and they stood in the city streets on Christmas morning, where (for the weather was severe) the people made a rough, but brisk and not unpleasant kind of music, in scraping the snow from the pavement in front of their dwellings, and from the tops of their houses: whence it was mad delight to the boys to see it come plumping down into the road below, and splitting into artificial little snow-storms.

The house fronts looked black enough, and the windows blacker, contrasting with the smooth white sheet of snow upon the roofs, and with the dirtier snow upon the ground; which last deposit had been ploughed up in deep furrows by the heavy wheels of carts and wagons; furrows that crossed and recrossed each other hundreds of times where the great streets branched off; and made intricate channels, hard to trace in the thick yellow mud and icy water.

The sky was gloomy, and the shortest streets were choked up with a dingy mist, half thawed, half frozen, whose heavier particles descended in shower of sooty atoms, as if all the chimneys in Great Britain had, by one consent, caught fire, and were blazing away to their dear hearts' content. There was nothing very cheerful in the climate or the town, and yet was there an air of cheerfulness abroad that the clearest summer air and brightest summer sun might have endeavoured to diffuse in vain.

For the people who were shovelling away on the housetops were jovial and full of glee; calling out to one another from the parapets, and now and then exchanging a facetious snowball—better-natured missile far than many a wordy jest—laughing heartily if it went right and not less heartily if it went wrong. The poulterers' shops were still half open, and the fruiterers' were radiant in their glory. There were great, round, pot-bellied baskets of chestnuts, shaped like the waistcoats of jolly old gentlemen, lolling at the doors, and tumbling out into the street in their apoplectic opulence.

There were ruddy, brown-faced, broad-girthed Spanish Onions, shining in the fatness of their growth like Spanish Friars, and winking from their shelves in wanton slyness at the girls as they went by, and glanced demurely at the hung-up mistletoe. There were pears and apples, clustered high in blooming pyramids; there were bunches of grapes, made, in the shopkeepers' benevolence to dangle from conspicuous hooks, that people's mouths might water gratis as they passed; there were piles of filberts, mossy and brown, recalling, in their fragrance, ancient walks among the woods, and pleasant shufflings ankle deep through withered leaves; there were Norfolk Biffins, squab and swarthy, setting off the yellow of the oranges and lemons, and, in the great compactness of their juicy persons, urgently entreating and beseeching to be carried home in paper bags and eaten after dinner. The very gold and silver fish, set forth among these choice fruits in a bowl, though members of a dull and stagnant-blooded race, appeared to know that there was something going on; and, to a fish, went gasping round and round their little world in slow and passionless excitement.

The Grocers'! oh the Grocers'! nearly closed, with perhaps two shutters down, or one; but through those gaps such glimpses! It was not alone that the scales descending on the counter made a merry sound, or that the twine and roller parted company so briskly, or that the canisters were rattled up and down like juggling tricks, or even that the blended scents of tea and coffee were so grateful to the nose, or even that the raisins were so plentiful and rare, the almonds so extremely white, the sticks of cinnamon so long and straight, the other spices so delicious, the candied fruits so caked and spotted with molten sugar as to make the coldest lookers-on feel faint and subsequently bilious.

Nor was it that the figs were moist and pulpy, or that the French plums blushed in modest tartness from their highly-decorated boxes, or that everything was good to eat and in its Christmas dress; but the customers were all so hurried and so eager in the hopeful promise of the day, that they tumbled up against each other at the door, crashing their wicker baskets wildly, and left their purchases upon the counter, and came running back to fetch them, and committed hundreds of the like mistakes, in the best humour possible; while the Grocer and his people were so frank and fresh that the polished hearts with which they fastened their aprons behind might have been their own, worn outside for general inspection, and for Christmas daws to peck at if they chose.

But soon the steeples called good people all, to church and chapel, and away they came, flocking through the streets in their best clothes, and with their gayest faces. And at the same time there emerged from scores of bye-streets, lanes, and nameless turnings, innumerable people, carrying their dinners to the baker' shops. The sight of these poor revellers appeared to interest the Spirit very much, for he stood with Scrooge beside him in a baker's doorway, and taking off the covers as their bearers passed, sprinkled incense on their dinners from his torch. And it was a very uncommon kind of torch, for once or twice when there were angry words between some dinner-carriers who had jostled each other, he shed a few drops of water on them from it, and their good humour was restored directly. For they said, it was a shame to quarrel upon Christmas Day. And so it was! God love it, so it was!

In time the bells ceased, and the bakers' were shut up; and yet there was a genial shadowing forth of all these dinners and the progress of their cooking, in the thawed blotch of wet above each baker's oven; where the pavement smoked as if its stones were cooking too.

"Is there a peculiar flavour in what you sprinkle from your torch?" asked Scrooge.

"There is. My own."

"Would it apply to any kind of dinner on this day?" asked Scrooge.

"To any kindly given. To a poor one most."

"Why to a poor one most?" asked Scrooge.

"Because it needs it most."

"Spirit," said Scrooge, after a moment's thought, "I wonder you, of all the beings in the many worlds about us, should desire to cramp these people's opportunities of innocent enjoyment."

"I!" cried the Spirit.

"You would deprive them of their means of dining every seventh day, often the only day on which they can be said to dine at all," said Scrooge. "Wouldn't you?"

"I!" cried the Spirit.

"You seek to close these places on the Seventh Day?" said Scrooge. "And it comes to the same thing."

"I seek!" exclaimed the Spirit.

"Forgive me if I am wrong. It has been done in your name, or at least in that of your family," said Scrooge.

"There are some upon this earth of yours," returned the Spirit, "who lay claim to know us, and who do their deeds of passion, pride, ill-will, hatred, envy, bigotry, and selfishness in our name, who are as strange to us and all out kith and kin, as if they had never lived. Remember that, and charge their doings on themselves, not us."

Scrooge promised that he would; and they went on, invisible, as they had been before, into the suburbs of the town. It was a remarkable quality of the Ghost (which Scrooge had observed at the baker's), that notwithstanding his gigantic size, he could accommodate himself to any place with ease; and that he stood beneath a low roof quite as gracefully and like a supernatural creature, as it was possible he could have done in any lofty hall.

And perhaps it was the pleasure the good Spirit had in show-ing off this power of his, or else it was his own kind, generous, hearty nature, and his sympathy with all poor men, that led him straight to Scrooge's clerk's; for there he went, and took Scrooge with him, holding to his robe; and on the threshold of the door the Spirit smiled, and stopped to bless Bob Cratchit's dwelling with the sprinkling of his torch. Think of that! Bob had but fif-teen bob a-week himself; he pocketed on Saturdays but fifteen copies of his Christian name; and yet the Ghost of Christmas Present blessed his four-roomed house!

Then up rose Mrs Cratchit, Cratchit's wife, dressed out but poorly in a twice-turned gown, but brave in ribbons, which are cheap and make a goodly show for sixpence; and she laid the cloth, assisted by Belinda Cratchit, second of her daughters, also brave in ribbons; while Master Peter Cratchit plunged a fork into the saucepan of potatoes, and getting the corners of his monstrous shirt collar (Bob's private property, conferred upon his son and heir in honour of the day) into his mouth, rejoiced to find himself so gallantly attired, and yearned to show his linen in the fashionable Parks. And now two smaller Cratchits, boy and girl, came tearing in, screaming that outside the baker's they had smelt the goose, and known it for their own; and basking in luxurious thoughts of sage-and-onion, these young Cratchits danced about the table, and exalted Master Peter Cratchit to the skies, while he (not proud, although his collars nearly choked him) blew the fire, until the slow potatoes bubbling up, knocked loudly at the saucepan-lid to be let out and peeled.

"What has ever got your precious father then." said Mrs Cratchit. "And your brother, Tiny Tim! And Martha warn't as late last Christmas Day by half-an-hour!"

"Here's Martha, mother!" said a girl, appearing as she spoke.

"Here's Martha, mother!" cried the two young Cratchits. "Hurrah! There's such a goose, Martha!"

"Why, bless your heart alive, my dear, how late you are!" said Mrs Cratchit, kissing her a dozen times, and taking off her shawl and bonnet for her with officious zeal.

"We'd a deal of work to finish up last night," replied the girl, "and had to clear away this morning, mother!"

"Well! Never mind so long as you are come," said Mrs Cratchit. "Sit ye down before the fire, my dear, and have a warm, Lord bless ye!"

"No, no! There's father coming," cried the two young Cratchits, who were everywhere at once. "Hide, Martha, hide!"

So Martha hid herself, and in came little Bob, the father, with at least three feet of comforter exclusive of the fringe, hanging down before him; and his threadbare clothes darned up and brushed, to look seasonable; and Tiny Tim upon his shoulder. Alas for Tiny Tim, he bore a little crutch, and had his limbs supported by an iron frame!

"Why, where's our Martha?" cried Bob Cratchit, looking round.

"Not coming," said Mrs Cratchit.

"Not coming!" said Bob, with a sudden declension in his

high spirits; for he had been Tim's blood horse all the way from church, and had come home rampant. "Not coming upon Christmas Day!"

Martha didn't like to see him disappointed, if it were only in joke; so she came out prematurely from behind the closet door, and ran into his arms, while the two young Cratchits hustled Tiny Tim, and bore him off into the wash-house, that he might hear the pudding singing in the copper.

"And how did little Tim behave?" asked Mrs Cratchit, when she had rallied Bob on his credulity and Bob had hugged his daughter to his heart's content.

"As good as gold," said Bob, "and better. Somehow he gets thoughtful, sitting by himself so much, and thinks the strangest things you ever heard. He told me, coming home, that he hoped the people saw him in the church, because he was a cripple, and it might be pleasant to them to remember upon Christmas Day, who made lame beggars walk, and blind men see."

Bob's voice was tremulous when he told them this, and trembled more when he said that Tiny Tim was growing strong and hearty.

His active little crutch was heard upon the floor, and back came Tiny Tim before another word was spoken, escorted by his brother and sister to his stool before the fire; and while Bob, turning up his cuffs—as if, poor fellow, they were capable of being made more shabby—compounded some hot mixture in a jug with gin and lemons, and stirred it round and round and put it on the hob to simmer; Master Peter, and the two ubiquitous young Cratchits went to fetch the goose, with which they soon returned in high procession.

Such a bustle ensued that you might have thought a goose the rarest of all birds; a feathered phenomenon, to which a black swan was a matter of course; and in truth it was something very like it in that house. Mrs Cratchit made the gravy (ready beforehand in a little saucepan) hissing hot; Master Peter mashed the potatoes with incredible vigour; Miss Belinda sweetened up the apple-sauce; Martha dusted the hot plates; Bob took Tiny Tim beside him in a tiny corner at the table; the two young Cratchits set chairs for everybody, not forgetting themselves, and mounting guard upon their posts, crammed spoons into their mouths, lest they should shriek for goose before their turn came to be helped.

At last the dishes were set on, and grace was said. It was succeeded by a breathless pause, as Mrs Cratchit, looking slowly all along the carving-knife, prepared to plunge it in the breast; but when she did, and when the long expected gush of stuffing issued forth, one murmur of delight arose all round the board, and even Tiny Tim, excited by the two young Cratchits, beat on the table with the handle of his knife, and feebly cried Hurrah!

There never was such a goose. Bob said he didn't believe there ever was such a goose cooked. Its tenderness and flavour, size and cheapness, were the themes of universal admiration. Eked out by apple-sauce and mashed potatoes, it was a sufficient dinner for the whole family; indeed, as Mrs Cratchit said with great delight (surveying one small atom of a bone upon the dish), they hadn't ate it all at last! Yet everyone had had enough, and the youngest Cratchits in particular, were steeped in sage and onion to the eyebrows! But now, the plates being changed by Miss Belinda, Mrs Cratchit left the room alone—too nervous to bear witnesses—to take the pudding up, and bring it in.

Suppose it should not be done enough! Suppose it should break in turning out! Suppose somebody should have got over the wall of the back-yard, and stolen it, while they were merry with the goose: a supposition at which the two young Cratchits became livid! All sorts of horrors were supposed.

Hallo! A great deal of steam! The pudding was out of the copper. A smell like a washing-day! That was the cloth. A smell like an eating-house and a pastrycook's next door to each other, with a laundress's next door to that! That was the pudding. In half a minute Mrs Cratchit entered: flushed, but smiling proudly: with the pudding, like a speckled cannon-ball, so hard and firm, blazing in half of half-a-quartern of ignited brandy, and bedight with Christmas holly stuck into the top.

Oh, a wonderful pudding! Bob Cratchit said, and calmly too, that he regarded it as the greatest success achieved by Mrs Cratchit since their marriage. Mrs Cratchit said that now the weight was off her mind, she would confess she had had her doubts about the quantity of flour. Everybody had something to say about it, but nobody said or thought it was at all a small pudding for a large family. It would have been flat heresy to do so. Any Cratchit would have blushed to hint at such a thing.

At last the dinner was all done, the cloth was cleared, the hearth swept, and the fire made up. The compound in the jug being tasted, and considered perfect, apples and oranges were put upon the table, and a shovel-full of chesnuts on the fire. Then all the Cratchit family drew round the hearth, in what Bob Cratchit called a circle, meaning half a one; and at Bob Cratchit's elbow stood the family display of glass; two tumblers, and a custard-cup without a handle.

These held the hot stuff from the jug, however, as well as golden goblets would have done; and Bob served it out with beaming looks, while the chesnuts on the fire sputtered and cracked noisily. Then Bob proposed:

"A Merry Christmas to us all, my dears. God bless us!"

Which all the family re-echoed.

"God bless us every one!" said Tiny Tim, the last of all.

He sat very close to his father's side upon his little stool. Bob held his withered little hand in his, as if he loved the child, and wished to keep him by his side, and dreaded that he might be taken from him.

"Spirit," said Scrooge, with an interest he had never felt before, "tell me if Tiny Tim will live."

"I see a vacant seat," replied the Ghost, "in the poor chimney-corner, and a crutch without an owner, carefully preserved. If these shadows remain unaltered by the Future, the child will die."

"No, no," said Scrooge. "Oh, no, kind Spirit! say he will be spared."

"If these shadows remain unaltered by the Future, none other of my race," returned the Ghost, "will find him here. What then? If he be like to die, he had better do it, and decrease the surplus population."

Scrooge hung his head to hear his own words quoted by the Spirit, and was overcome with penitence and grief.

"Man," said the Ghost, "if man you be in heart, not adamant, forbear that wicked cant until you have discovered What the surplus is, and Where it is. Will you decide what men shall live, what men shall die? It may be, that in the sight of Heaven, you are more worthless and less fit to live than millions like this poor man's child. Oh God! to hear the Insect on the leaf pronouncing on the too much life among his hungry brothers in the dust!"

Scrooge bent before the Ghost's rebuke, and trembling cast his eyes upon the ground. But he raised them speedily, on hearing his own name.

"Mr Scrooge!" said Bob; "I'll give you Mr Scrooge, the Founder of the Feast!"

"The Founder of the Feast indeed!" cried Mrs Cratchit, reddening. "I wish I had him here. I'd give him a piece of my mind to feast upon, and I hope he'd have a good appetite for it."

"My dear," said Bob, "the children; Christmas Day."

"It should be Christmas Day, I am sure," said she, "on which one drinks the health of such an odious, stingy, hard, unfeeling man as Mr Scrooge. You know he is, Robert! Nobody knows it better than you do, poor fellow!"

"My dear," was Bob's mild answer, "Christmas Day."

"I'll drink his health for your sake and the Day's," said Mrs Cratchit, "not for his. Long life to him. A merry Christmas and a happy new year! He'll be very merry and very happy, I have no doubt!"

The children drank the toast after her. It was the first of their proceedings which had no heartiness. Tiny Tim drank it last of all, but he didn't care twopence for it. Scrooge was the Ogre of the family. The mention of his name cast a dark shadow on the party, which was not dispelled for full five minutes.

After it had passed away, they were ten times merrier than

before, from the mere relief of Scrooge the Baleful being done with. Bob Cratchit told them how he had a situation in his eye for Master Peter, which would bring in, if obtained, full five-and-sixpence weekly. The two young Cratchits laughed tremendously at the idea of Peter's being a man of business; and Peter himself looked thoughtfully at the fire from between his collars, as if he were deliberating what particular investments he should favour when he came into the receipt of that bewildering income.

Martha, who was a poor apprentice at a milliner's, then told them what kind of work she had to do, and how many hours she worked at a stretch, and how she meant to lie a-bed tomorrow morning for a good long rest; tomorrow being a holiday she passed at home. Also how she had seen a countess and a lord some days before, and how the lord "was much about as tall as Peter;" at which Peter pulled up his collars so high that you couldn't have seen his head if you had been there. All this time the chesnuts and the jug went round and round; and bye and bye they had a song, about a lost child travelling in the snow, from Tiny Tim; who had a plaintive little voice, and sang it very well indeed.

There was nothing of high mark in this. They were not a handsome family; they were not well dressed; their shoes were far from being water-proof; their clothes were scanty; and Peter might have known, and very likely did, the inside of a pawnbroker's. But, they were happy, grateful, pleased with one another, and contented with the time; and when they faded, and looked happier yet in the bright sprinklings of the Spirit's torch at parting, Scrooge had his eye upon them, and especially on Tiny Tim, until the last.

By this time it was getting dark, and snowing pretty heavily; and as Scrooge and the Spirit went along the streets, the brightness of the roaring fires in kitchens, parlours, and all sorts of rooms, was wonderful. Here, the flickering of the blaze showed preparations for a cosy dinner, with hot plates baking through and through before the fire, and deep red curtains, ready to be drawn to shut out cold and darkness. There all the children of the house were running out into the snow to meet their married sisters, brothers, cousins, uncles, aunts, and be the first to greet them. Here, again, were shadows on the window-blind of guests assembling; and there a group of handsome girls, all hooded and fur-booted, and all chattering at once, tripped lightly off to some near neighbour's house; where, woe upon the single man who saw them enter—artful witches, well they knew it—in a glow!

But, if you had judged from the numbers of people on their way to friendly gatherings, you might have thought that no one was at home to give them welcome when they got there, instead of every house expecting company, and piling up its fires half-chimney high. Blessings on it, how the Ghost exulted! How it bared its breadth of breast, and opened its capacious palm, and floated on, outpouring, with a generous hand, its bright and harmless mirth on everything within its reach! The very lamp-lighter, who ran on before, dotting the dusky street with specks of light, and who was dressed to spend the evening somewhere, laughed out loudly as the Spirit passed: though little kenned the lamplighter that he had any company but Christmas!

And now, without a word of warning from the Ghost, they stood upon a bleak and desert moor, where monstrous masses of rude stone were cast about, as though it were the burial-place of giants; and water spread itself wheresoever it listed; or would have done so, but for the frost that held it prisoner; and nothing grew but moss and furze, and coarse, rank grass. Down in the west the setting sun had left a streak of fiery red, which glared upon the desolation for an instant, like a sullen eye, and frowning lower, lower, lower yet, was lost in the thick gloom of darkest night.

"What place is this?" asked Scrooge.

"A place where Miners live, who labour in the bowels of the earth," returned the Spirit. "But they know me. See!"

A light shone from the window of a hut, and swiftly they advanced towards it. Passing through the wall of mud and stone, they found a cheerful company assembled round a glowing fire. An old, old man and woman, with their children and their children's children, and another generation beyond that, all decked out gaily in their holiday attire. The old man, in a voice that seldom rose above the howling of the wind upon the barren waste, was singing them a Christmas song: it had been a very old song when he was a boy; and from time to time they all joined in the chorus. So surely as they raised their voices, the old man got quite blithe and loud; and so surely as they stopped, his vigour sank again.

The Spirit did not tarry here, but bade Scrooge hold his robe, and passing on above the moor, sped whither? Not to sea? To sea. To Scrooge's horror, looking back, he saw the last of the land, a frightful range of rocks, behind them; and his ears were deafened by the thundering of water, as it rolled, and roared, and raged among the dreadful caverns it had worn, and fiercely tried to undermine the earth.

Built upon a dismal reef of sunken rocks, some league or so from shore, on which the waters chafed and dashed, the wild year through, there stood a solitary lighthouse. Great heaps of sea-weed clung to its base, and storm-birds—born of the wind one might suppose, as sea-weed of the water—rose and fell about it, like the waves they skimmed.

But even here, two men who watched the light had made a fire, that through the loophole in the thick stone wall shed out a ray of brightness on the awful sea. Joining their horny hands over the rough table at which they sat, they wished each other Merry Christmas in their can of grog; and one of them: the elder, too, with his face all damaged and scarred with hard weather, as the figure-head of an old ship might be: struck up a sturdy song that was like a Gale in itself.

Again the Ghost sped on, above the black and heaving sea—on, on—until, being far away, as he told Scrooge, from any shore, they lighted on a ship. They stood beside the helmsman at the wheel, the look-out in the bow, the officers who had the watch; dark, ghostly figures in their several stations; but every man among them hummed a Christmas tune, or had a Christmas thought, or spoke below his breath to his companion of some bygone Christmas Day, with homeward hopes belonging to it. And every man on board, waking or sleeping, good or bad, had had a kinder word for another on that day than on any day in the year; and had shared to some extent in its festivities; and had remembered those he cared for at a distance, and had known that they delighted to remember him.

It was a great surprise to Scrooge, while listening to the moaning of the wind, and thinking what a solemn thing it was to move on through the lonely darkness over an unknown abyss, whose depths were secrets as profound as Death: it was a great surprise to Scrooge, while thus engaged, to hear a hearty laugh. It was a much greater surprise to Scrooge to recognise it as his own nephew's and to find himself in a bright, dry, gleaming room, with the Spirit standing smiling by his side, and looking at that same nephew with approving affability!

"Ha, ha!" laughed Scrooge's nephew. "Ha, ha, ha!"

If you should happen, by any unlikely chance, to know a man more blest in a laugh than Scrooge's nephew, all I can say is, I should like to know him too. Introduce him to me, and I'll cultivate his acquaintance.

It is a fair, even-handed, noble adjustment of things, that while there is infection in disease and sorrow, there is nothing in the world so irresistibly contagious as laughter and good-humour. When Scrooge's nephew laughed in this way: holding his sides, rolling his head, and twisting his face into the most extravagant contortions: Scrooge's niece, by marriage, laughed as heartily as he. And their assembled friends being not a bit behindhand, roared out lustily.

"Ha, ha! Ha, ha, ha, ha!"

"He said that Christmas was a humbug, as I live!" cried Scrooge's nephew. "He believed it too!"

"More shame for him, Fred!" said Scrooge's niece, indignantly. Bless those women; they never do anything by halves. They are always in earnest.

She was very pretty: exceedingly pretty. With a dimpled, surprised-looking, capital face; a ripe little mouth, that seemed made to be kissed—as no doubt it was; all kinds of good little dots about her chin, that melted into one another when she laughed; and the sunniest pair of eyes you ever saw in any little creature's head. Altogether she was what you would have called provoking, you know; but satisfactory, too. Oh, perfectly satisfactory!

"He's a comical old fellow," said Scrooge's nephew, "that's the truth: and not so pleasant as he might be. However, his offences carry their own punishment, and I have nothing to say against him."

"I'm sure he is very rich, Fred," hinted Scrooge's niece. "At least you always tell me so."

"What of that, my dear!" said Scrooge's nephew. "His wealth is of no use to him. He don't do any good with it. He don't make himself comfortable with it. He hasn't the satisfaction of thinking—ha, ha, ha!—that he is ever going to benefit Us with it."

"I have no patience with him," observed Scrooge's niece. Scrooge's niece's sisters, and all the other ladies, expressed the same opinion.

"Oh, I have!" said Scrooge's nephew. "I am sorry for him; I couldn't be angry with him if I tried. Who suffers by his ill whims? Himself, always. Here, he takes it into his head to dislike us, and he won't come and dine with us. What's the consequence? He don't lose much of a dinner."

"Indeed, I think he loses a very good dinner," interrupted Scrooge's niece. Everybody else said the same, and they must be allowed to have been competent judges, because they had just had dinner; and, with the dessert upon the table, were clustered round the fire, by lamplight.

"Well! I'm very glad to hear it," said Scrooge's nephew, "because I haven't great faith in these young housekeepers. What do you say, Topper?"

Topper had clearly got his eye upon one of Scrooge's niece's sisters, for he answered that a bachelor was a wretched outcast, who had no right to express an opinion on the subject. Whereat Scrooge's niece's sister—the plump one with the lace tucker: not the one with the roses—blushed.

"Do go on, Fred," said Scrooge's niece, clapping her hands. "He never finishes what he begins to say. He is such a ridiculous fellow!"

Scrooge's nephew revelled in another laugh, and as it was impossible to keep the infection off; though the plump sister tried hard to do it with aromatic vinegar; his example was unanimously followed.

"I was only going to say," said Scrooge's nephew, "that the consequence of his taking a dislike to us, and not making merry with us, is, as I think, that he loses some pleasant moments, which could do him no harm. I am sure he loses pleasanter companions than he can find in his own thoughts, either in his mouldy old office, or his dusty chambers. I mean to give him the same chance every year, whether he likes it or not, for I pity him. He may rail at Christmas till he dies, but he can't help thinking better of it—I defy him—if he finds me going there, in good temper, year after year, and saying Uncle Scrooge, how are you? If it only puts him in the vein to leave his poor clerk fifty pounds, that's something; and I think I shook him yesterday."

It was their turn to laugh now at the notion of his shaking Scrooge. But being thoroughly good-natured, and not much caring what they laughed at, so that they laughed at any rate, he encouraged them in their merriment, and passed the bottle joyously.

After tea, they had some music. For they were a musical family, and knew what they were about, when they sung a Glee or Catch, I can assure you: especially Topper, who could growl away in the bass like a good one, and never swell the large veins in his forehead, or get red in the face over it. Scrooge's niece played well upon the harp; and played among other tunes a simple little air (a mere nothing: you might learn to whistle it in two minutes), which had been familiar to the child who fetched

Scrooge from the boarding-school, as he had been reminded by the Ghost of Christmas Past. When this strain of music sounded, all the things that Ghost had shown him, came upon his mind; he softened more and more; and thought that if he could have listened to it often, years ago, he might have cultivated the kindnesses of life for his own happiness with his own hands, without resorting to the sexton's spade that buried Jacob Marley.

But they didn't devote the whole evening to music. After a while they played at forfeits; for it is good to be children sometimes, and never better than at Christmas, when its mighty Founder was a child himself. Stop! There was first a game at blind-man's buff. Of course there was. And I no more believe Topper was really blind than I believe he had eyes in his boots. My opinion is, that it was a done thing between him and Scrooge's nephew; and that the Ghost of Christmas Present knew it. The way he went after that plump sister in the lace tucker, was an outrage on the credulity of human nature. Knocking down the fire-irons, tumbling over the chairs, bumping against the piano, smothering himself among the curtains, wherever she went, there went he. He always knew where the plump sister was. He wouldn't catch anybody else. If you had fallen up against him (as some of them did), on purpose, he would have made a feint of endeavouring to seize you, which would have been an affront to your understanding, and would instantly have sidled off in the direction of the plump sister.

She often cried out that it wasn't fair; and it really was not. But when at last, he caught her; when, in spite of all her silken rustlings, and her rapid flutterings past him, he got her into a corner whence there was no escape; then his conduct was the most execrable. For his pretending not to know her; his pretending that it was necessary to touch her head-dress, and further to assure himself of her identity by pressing a certain ring upon her finger, and a certain chain about her neck; was vile, monstrous. No doubt she told him her opinion of it, when, another blind-man being in office, they were so very confidential together, behind the curtains.

Scrooge's niece was not one of the blind-man's buff party, but was made comfortable with a large chair and a footstool, in a snug corner, where the Ghost and Scrooge were close behind her. But she joined in the forfeits, and loved her love to admiration with all the letters of the alphabet. Likewise at the game of How, When, and Where, she was very great, and to the secret joy of Scrooge's nephew, beat her sisters hollow: though they were sharp girls too, as Topper could have told you.

There might have been twenty people there, young and old, but they all played, and so did Scrooge; for, wholly forgetting in the interest he had in what was going on, that his voice made no sound in their ears, he sometimes came out with his guess quite loud, and vey often guessed quite right, too; for the sharpest needle, best Whitechapel, warranted not to cut in the eye, was not sharper than Scrooge; blunt as he took it in his head to be.

The Ghost was greatly pleased to find him in this mood, and looked upon him with such favour, that he begged like a boy to be allowed to stay until the guests departed. But this the Spirit said could not be done.

"Here is a new game," said Scrooge. "One half hour, Spirit, only one!"

It was a Game called Yes and No, where Scrooge's nephew had to think of something, and the rest must find out what; he only answering to their questions yes or no, as the case was. The brisk fire of questioning to which he was exposed, elicited from him that he was thinking of an animal, a live animal, rather a disagreeable animal, a savage animal, an animal that growled and grunted sometimes, and talked sometimes, and lived in London, and walked about the streets, and wasn't made a show of, and wasn't led by anybody, and didn't live in a menagerie, and was never killed in a market, and was not a horse, or an ass, or a cow, or a bull, or a tiger, or a dog, or a pig, or a cat, or a bear. At every fresh question that was put to him, this nephew burst into a fresh roar of laughter; and was so inexpressibly tickled, that he was obliged to get up off the sofa and stamp. At last the plump sister, falling into a similar state, cried out:

"I have found it out! I know what it is, Fred! I know what it is!"

"What is it?" cried Fred.

"It's your Uncle Scro-o-o-o-oge!"

Which it certainly was. Admiration was the universal sentiment, though some objected that the reply to "Is it a bear?" ought to have been "Yes;" inasmuch as an answer in the negative was sufficient to have diverted their thoughts from Mr Scrooge, supposing they had ever had any tendency that way.

"He has given us plenty of merriment, I am sure," said Fred, "and it would be ungrateful not to drink his health. Here is a glass of mulled wine ready to our hand at the moment; and I say, "Uncle Scrooge!"

"Well! Uncle Scrooge." they cried.

"A Merry Christmas and a Happy New Year to the old man, whatever he is!" said Scrooge's nephew. "He wouldn't take it from me, but may he have it, nevertheless. Uncle Scrooge!"

Uncle Scrooge had imperceptibly become so gay and light of heart, that he would have pledged the unconscious company in return, and thanked them in an inaudible speech, if the Ghost had given him time. But the whole scene passed off in the breath of the last word spoken by his nephew; and he and the Spirit were again upon their travels.

Much they saw, and far they went, and many homes they visited, but always with a happy end. The Spirit stood beside sick beds, and they were cheerful; on foreign lands, and they were close at home; by struggling men, and they were patient in their greater hope; by poverty, and it was rich. In almshouse, hospital, and jail, in misery's every refuge, where vain man in his little brief authority had not made fast the door and barred the Spirit out, he left his blessing, and taught Scrooge his precepts.

It was a long night, if it were only a night; but Scrooge had his doubts of this, because the Christmas Holidays appeared to be condensed into the space of time they passed together. It was strange, too, that while Scrooge remained unaltered in his outward form, the Ghost grew older, clearly older. Scrooge had observed this change, but never spoke of it, until they left a children's Twelfth Night party, when, looking at the Spirit as they stood together in an open place, he noticed that its hair was grey.

"Are spirits' lives so short?" asked Scrooge.

"My life upon this globe, is very brief," replied the Ghost. "It ends tonight."

"Tonight!" cried Scrooge.

"Tonight at midnight. Hark! The time is drawing near."

The chimes were ringing the three quarters past eleven at that moment.

"Forgive me if I am not justified in what I ask," said Scrooge, looking intently at the Spirit's robe, "but I see something strange, and not belonging to yourself, protruding from your skirts. Is it a foot or a claw!"

"It might be a claw, for the flesh there is upon it," was the Spirit's sorrowful reply. "Look here."

From the foldings of its robe, it brought two children; wretched, abject, frightful, hideous, miserable. They knelt down at its feet, and clung upon the outside of its garment.

"Oh, Man! look here. Look, look, down here!" exclaimed the Ghost.

They were a boy and girl. Yellow, meagre, ragged, scowling, wolfish; but prostrate, too, in their humility. Where graceful youth should have filled their features out, and touched them with its freshest tints, a stale and shrivelled hand, like that of age, had pinched, and twisted them, and pulled them into shreds. Where angels might have sat enthroned, devils lurked, and glared out menacing. No change, no degradation, no perversion of humanity, in any grade, through all the mysteries of wonderful creation, has monsters half so horrible and dread.

Scrooge started back, appalled. Having them shown to him in this way, he tried to say they were fine children, but the words choked themselves, rather than be parties to a lie of such enormous magnitude.

"Spirit! are they yours?" Scrooge could say no more.

"They are Man's," said the Spirit, looking down upon them. "And they cling to me, appealing from their fathers. This boy is Ignorance. This girl is Want. Beware them both, and all of their degree, but most of all beware this boy, for on his brow I see that written which is Doom, unless the writing be erased. Deny it!" cried the Spirit, stretching out its hand towards the city. "Slander those who tell it ye! Admit it for your factious purposes, and make it worse! And bide the end!"

"Have they no refuge or resource?" cried Scrooge.

"Are there no prisons?" said the Spirit, turning on him for the last time with his own words. "Are there no workhouses?"

The bell struck twelve.

Scrooge looked about him for the Ghost, and saw it not. As the last stroke ceased to vibrate, he remembered the prediction of old Jacob Marley, and lifting up his eyes, beheld a solemn Phantom, draped and hooded, coming, like a mist along the ground, towards him.

Chapter 4
The Last of the Spirits

The Phantom slowly, gravely, silently approached. When it came, Scrooge bent down upon his knee; for in the very air through which this Spirit moved it seemed to scatter gloom and mystery.

It was shrouded in a deep black garment, which concealed its head, its face, its form, and left nothing of it visible save one outstretched hand. But for this it would have been difficult to detach its figure from the night, and separate it from the darkness by which it was surrounded.

He felt that it was tall and stately when it came beside him, and that its mysterious presence filled him with a solemn dread. He knew no more, for the Spirit neither spoke nor moved.

"I am in the presence of the Ghost of Christmas Yet To Come?" said Scrooge.

The Spirit answered not, but pointed onward with its hand.

"You are about to show me shadows of the things that have

not happened, but will happen in the time before us," Scrooge pursued. "Is that so, Spirit?"

The upper portion of the garment was contracted for an instant in its folds, as if the Spirit had inclined its head. That was the only answer he received.

Although well used to ghostly company by this time, Scrooge feared the silent shape so much that his legs trembled beneath him, and he found that he could hardly stand when he prepared to follow it. The Spirit paused a moment, as observing his condition, and giving him time to recover.

But Scrooge was all the worse for this. It thrilled him with a vague uncertain horror, to know that behind the dusky shroud, there were ghostly eyes intently fixed upon him, while he, though he stretched his own to the utmost, could see nothing but a spectral hand and one great heap of black.

"Ghost of the Future!" he exclaimed, "I fear you more than any spectre I have seen. But as I know your purpose is to do me good, and as I hope to live to be another man from what I was, I am prepared to bear you company, and do it with a thankful heart. Will you not speak to me?"

It gave him no reply. The hand was pointed straight before them.

"Lead on!" said Scrooge. "Lead on! The night is waning fast, and it is precious time to me, I know. Lead on, Spirit!"

The Phantom moved away as it had come towards him. Scrooge followed in the shadow of its dress, which bore him up, he thought, and carried him along.

They scarcely seemed to enter the city; for the city rather seemed to spring up about them, and encompass them of its own act. But there they were, in the heart of it; on Change, amongst the merchants; who hurried up and down, and chinked the money in their pockets, and conversed in groups, and looked at their watches, and trifled thoughtfully with their great gold seals; and so forth, as Scrooge had seen them often.

The Spirit stopped beside one little knot of business men. Observing that the hand was pointed to them, Scrooge advanced to listen to their talk.

"No," said a great fat man with a monstrous chin, "I don't know much about it, either way. I only know he's dead."

"When did he die?" inquired another.

"Last night, I believe."

"Why, what was the matter with him?" asked a third, taking a vast quantity of snuff out of a very large snuff-box. "I thought he'd never die."

"God knows," said the first, with a yawn.

"What has he done with his money?" asked a red-faced gentleman with a pendulous excrescence on the end of his nose, that shook like the gills of a turkey-cock.

"I haven't heard," said the man with the large chin, yawning again. "Left it to his Company, perhaps. He hasn't left it to me. That's all I know."

This pleasantry was received with a general laugh.

"It's likely to be a very cheap funeral," said the same speaker; "for upon my life I don't know of anybody to go to it. Suppose we make up a party and volunteer?"

"I don't mind going if a lunch is provided," observed the gentleman with the excrescence on his nose. "But I must be fed, if I make one."

Another laugh.

"Well, I am the most disinterested among you, after all," said the first speaker, "for I never wear black gloves, and I never eat lunch. But I'll offer to go, if anybody else will. When I come to think of it, I'm not at all sure that I wasn't his most particular friend; for we used to stop and speak whenever we met. Bye, bye!"

Speakers and listeners strolled away, and mixed with other groups. Scrooge knew the men, and looked towards the Spirit for an explanation.

The Phantom glided on into a street. Its finger pointed to two persons meeting. Scrooge listened again, thinking that the explanation might lie here.

He knew these men, also, perfectly. They were men of business: very wealthy, and of great importance. He had made a point always of standing well in their esteem: in a business point of view, that is; strictly in a business point of view.

"How are you?" said one.

"How are you?" returned the other.

"Well!" said the first. "Old Scratch has got his own at last, hey?"

"So I am told," returned the second. "Cold, isn't it?"

"Seasonable for Christmas time. You're not a skater, I suppose?"

"No. No. Something else to think of. Good morning!"

Not another word. That was their meeting, their conversation, and their parting.

Scrooge was at first inclined to be surprised that the Spirit should attach importance to conversations apparently so trivial; but feeling assured that they must have some hidden purpose, he set himself to consider what it was likely to be. They could scarcely be supposed to have any bearing on the death of Jacob, his old partner, for that was Past, and this Ghost's province was the Future. Nor could he think of any one immediately connected with himself, to whom he could apply them. But nothing doubting that to whomsoever they applied they had some latent moral for his own improvement, he resolved to treasure up every word he heard, and everything he saw; and especially to observe the shadow of himself when it appeared. For he had an expectation that the conduct of his future self would give him the clue he missed, and would render the solution of these riddles easy.

He looked about in that very place for his own image; but another man stood in his accustomed corner, and though the clock pointed to his usual time of day for being there, he saw no likeness of himself among the multitudes that poured in through the Porch. It gave him little surprise, however; for he had been revolving in his mind a change of life, and thought and hoped he saw his new-born resolutions carried out in this.

Quiet and dark, beside him stood the Phantom, with its outstretched hand. When he roused himself from his thoughtful quest, he fancied from the turn of the hand, and its situation in reference to himself, that the Unseen Eyes were looking at him keenly. It made him shudder, and feel very cold.

They left the busy scene, and went into an obscure part of the town, where Scrooge had never penetrated before, although he recognised its situation, and its bad repute. The ways were foul and narrow; the shops and houses wretched; the people half-naked, drunken, slipshod, ugly. Alleys and archways, like so many cesspools, disgorged their offences of smell, and dirt, and life, upon the straggling streets; and the whole quarter reeked with crime, with filth, and misery.

Far in this den of infamous resort, there was a low-browed, beetling shop, below a pent-house roof, where iron, old rags, bottles, bones, and greasy offal, were bought. Upon the floor within, were piled up heaps of rusty keys, nails, chains, hinges, files, scales, weights, and refuse iron of all kinds. Secrets that few would like to scrutinise were bred and hidden in mountains of unseemly rags, masses of corrupted fat, and sepulchres of bones. Sitting in among the wares he dealt in, by a charcoal stove, made of old bricks, was a grey-haired rascal, nearly seventy years of age; who had screened himself from the cold air without, by a frousy curtaining of miscellaneous tatters, hung upon a line; and smoked his pipe in all the luxury of calm retirement.

Scrooge and the Phantom came into the presence of this man, just as a woman with a heavy bundle slunk into the shop. But she had scarcely entered, when another woman, similarly laden, came in too; and she was closely followed by a man in faded black, who was no less startled by the sight of them, than they had been upon the recognition of each other. After a short period of blank astonishment, in which the old man with the pipe had joined them, they all three burst into a laugh.

"Let the charwoman alone to be the first!" cried she who had entered first. "Let the laundress alone to be the second; and let the undertaker's man alone to be the third. Look here, old Joe, here's a chance! If we haven't all three met here without meaning it!"

"You couldn't have met in a better place," said old Joe, removing his pipe from his mouth. "Come into the parlour. You were made free of it long ago, you know; and the other two an't strangers. Stop till I shut the door of the shop. Ah! How it skreeks! There an't such a rusty bit of metal in the place as its own hinges, I believe; and I'm sure there's no such old bones here, as mine. Ha, ha! We're all suitable to our calling, we're well matched. Come into the parlour. Come into the parlour."

The parlour was the space behind the screen of rags. The old man raked the fire together with an old stair-rod, and having trimmed his smoky lamp (for it was night), with the stem of his pipe, put it in his mouth again.

While he did this, the woman who had already spoken threw her bundle on the floor, and sat down in a flaunting manner on a stool; crossing her elbows on her knees, and looking with a bold defiance at the other two.

"What odds then! What odds, Mrs Dilber?" said the woman. "Every person has a right to take care of themselves. He always did!"

"That's true, indeed!" said the laundress. "No man more so."

"Why then, don't stand staring as if you was afraid, woman; who's the wiser? We're not going to pick holes in each other's coats, I suppose?"

"No, indeed!" said Mrs Dilber and the man together. "We should hope not."

"Very well, then!" cried the woman. "That's enough. Who's the worse for the loss of a few things like these? Not a dead man, I suppose."

"No, indeed!" said Mrs Dilber, laughing.

"If he wanted to keep 'em after he was dead, a wicked old screw," pursued the woman, "why wasn't he natural in his lifetime? If he had been, he'd have had somebody to look after him when he was struck with Death, instead of lying gasping out his last there, alone by himself."

"It's the truest word that ever was spoke," said Mrs Dilber.

"It's a judgment on him."

"I wish it was a little heavier judgment," replied the woman; "and it should have been, you may depend upon it, if I could have laid my hands on anything else. Open that bundle, old Joe, and let me know the value of it. Speak out plain. I'm not afraid to be the first, nor afraid for them to see it. We know pretty well that we were helping ourselves, before we met here, I believe. It's no sin. Open the bundle, Joe."

But the gallantry of her friends would not allow of this; and the man in faded black, mounting the breach first, produced his plunder. It was not extensive. A seal or two, a pencil-case, a pair of sleeve-buttons, and a brooch of no great value, were all. They were severally examined and appraised by old Joe, who chalked the sums he was disposed to give for each, upon the wall, and added them up into a total when he found there was nothing more to come.

"That's your account," said Joe, "and I wouldn't give another sixpence, if I was to be boiled for not doing it. Who's next?"

Mrs Dilber was next. Sheets and towels, a little wearing apparel, two old-fashioned silver teaspoons, a pair of sugar-tongs, and a few boots. Her account was stated on the wall in the same manner.

"I always give too much to ladies. It's a weakness of mine, and that's the way I ruin myself," said old Joe. "That's your account. If you asked me for another penny, and made it an open question, I'd repent of being so liberal and knock off half-a-crown."

"And now undo my bundle, Joe," said the first woman.

Joe went down on his knees for the greater convenience of opening it, and having unfastened a great many knots, dragged out a large and heavy roll of some dark stuff.

"What do you call this." said Joe. "Bed-curtains!"

"Ah!" returned the woman, laughing and leaning forward on her crossed arms. "Bed-curtains!"

"You don't mean to say you took them down, rings and all, with him lying there?" said Joe.

"Yes I do," replied the woman. "Why not?"

"You were born to make your fortune," said Joe, "and you'll certainly do it."

"I certainly shan't hold my hand, when I can get anything in it by reaching it out, for the sake of such a man as He was, I promise you, Joe," returned the woman coolly. "don't drop that oil upon the blankets, now."

"His blankets?" asked Joe.

"Whose else's do you think?" replied the woman. "He isn't likely to take cold without 'em, I dare say."

"I hope he didn't die of anything catching? Eh?" said old Joe, stopping in his work, and looking up.

"Don't you be afraid of that," returned the woman. "I an't so fond of his company that I'd loiter about him for such things, if he did. Ah! you may look through that shirt till your eyes ache; but you won't find a hole in it, nor a threadbare place. It's the best he had, and a fine one too. They'd have wasted it, if it hadn't been for me."

"What do you call wasting of it?" asked old Joe.

"Putting it on him to be buried in, to be sure," replied the woman with a laugh. "Somebody was fool enough to do it, but I took it off again. If calico an't good enough for such a purpose, it isn't good enough for anything. It's quite as becoming to the body. He can't look uglier than he did in that one."

Scrooge listened to this dialogue in horror. As they sat grouped about their spoil, in the scanty light afforded by the old man's lamp, he viewed them with a detestation and disgust, which could hardly have been greater, though they had been obscene demons, marketing the corpse itself.

"Ha, ha!" laughed the same woman, when old Joe, producing a flannel bag with money in it, told out their several gains upon the ground. "This is the end of it, you see! He frightened every one away from him when he was alive, to profit us when he was dead! Ha, ha, ha!"

"Spirit!" said Scrooge, shuddering from head to foot. "I see, I see. The case of this unhappy man might be my own. My life tends that way, now. Merciful Heaven, what is this!"

He recoiled in terror, for the scene had changed, and now he almost touched a bed: a bare, uncurtained bed: on which, beneath a ragged sheet, there lay a something covered up, which, though it was dumb, announced itself in awful language.

The room was very dark, too dark to be observed with any accuracy, though Scrooge glanced round it in obedience to a secret impulse, anxious to know what kind of room it was. A pale light, rising in the outer air, fell straight upon the bed; and on it, plundered and bereft, unwatched, unwept, uncared for, was the body of this man.

Scrooge glanced towards the Phantom. Its steady hand was pointed to the head. The cover was so carelessly adjusted that the slightest raising of it, the motion of a finger upon Scrooge's part, would have disclosed the face. He thought of it, felt how easy it would be to do, and longed to do it; but had no more power to withdraw the veil than to dismiss the spectre at his side.

Oh cold, cold, rigid, dreadful Death, set up thine altar here, and dress it with such terrors as thou hast at thy command: for this is thy dominion! But of the loved, revered, and honoured head, thou canst not turn one hair to thy dread purposes, or make one feature odious. It is not that the hand is heavy and will fall down when released; it is not that the heart and pulse are still; but that the hand was open, generous, and true; the heart brave, warm, and tender; and the pulse a man's. Strike, Shadow, strike! And see his good deeds springing from the wound, to sow the world with life immortal.

No voice pronounced these words in Scrooge's ears, and yet he heard them when he looked upon the bed. He thought, if this man could be raised up now, what would be his foremost thoughts? Avarice, hard-dealing, griping cares? They have brought him to a rich end, truly!

He lay, in the dark empty house, with not a man, a woman, or a child, to say that he was kind to me in this or that, and for the memory of one kind word I will be kind to him. A cat was tearing at the door, and there was a sound of gnawing rats beneath the hearth-stone. What they wanted in the room of death, and why they were so restless and disturbed, Scrooge did not dare to think.

"Spirit!" he said, "this is a fearful place. In leaving it, I shall not leave its lesson, trust me. Let us go!"

Still the Ghost pointed with an unmoved finger to the head.

"I understand you," Scrooge returned, "and I would do it, if I could. But I have not the power, Spirit. I have not the power."

Again it seemed to look upon him.

"If there is any person in the town, who feels emotion caused by this man's death," said Scrooge quite agonised, "show that person to me, Spirit, I beseech you!"

The Phantom spread its dark robe before him for a moment, like a wing; and withdrawing it, revealed a room by daylight, where a mother and her children were.

She was expecting some one, and with anxious eagerness; for she walked up and down the room; started at every sound; looked out from the window; glanced at the clock; tried, but in vain, to work with her needle; and could hardly bear the voices of the children in their play.

At length the long-expected knock was heard. She hurried to the door, and met her husband; a man whose face was care-worn and depressed, though he was young. There was a remarkable expression in it now; a kind of serious delight of which he felt ashamed, and which he struggled to repress.

He sat down to the dinner that had been boarding for him by the fire; and when she asked him faintly what news (which was not until after a long silence), he appeared embarrassed how to answer.

"Is it good." she said, "or bad?"—to help him.

"Bad," he answered.

"We are quite ruined?"

"No. There is hope yet, Caroline."

"If he relents," she said, amazed, "there is. Nothing is past hope, if such a miracle has happened."

"He is past relenting," said her husband. "He is dead."

She was a mild and patient creature if her face spoke truth;

but she was thankful in her soul to hear it, and she said so, with clasped hands. She prayed forgiveness the next moment, and was sorry; but the first was the emotion of her heart.

"What the half-drunken woman whom I told you of last night, said to me, when I tried to see him and obtain a week's delay; and what I thought was a mere excuse to avoid me; turns out to have been quite true. He was not only very ill, but dying, then."

"To whom will our debt be transferred?"

"I don't know. But before that time we shall be ready with the money; and even though we were not, it would be a bad fortune indeed to find so merciless a creditor in his successor. We may sleep tonight with light hearts, Caroline!"

Yes. Soften it as they would, their hearts were lighter. The children's faces, hushed and clustered round to hear what they so little understood, were brighter; and it was a happier house for this man's death! The only emotion that the Ghost could show him, caused by the event, was one of pleasure.

"Let me see some tenderness connected with a death," said Scrooge; "or that dark chamber, Spirit, which we left just now, will be forever present to me."

The Ghost conducted him through several streets familiar to his feet; and as they went along, Scrooge looked here and there to find himself, but nowhere was he to be seen. They entered poor Bob Cratchit's house; the dwelling he had visited before; and found the mother and the children seated round the fire.

Quiet. Very quiet. The noisy little Cratchits were as still as statues in one corner, and sat looking up at Peter, who had a book before him. The mother and her daughters were engaged in sewing. But surely they were very quiet!

And he took a child, and set him in the midst of them.

Where had Scrooge heard those words? He had not dreamed them. The boy must have read them out, as he and the Spirit crossed the threshold. Why did he not go on?

The mother laid her work upon the table, and put her hand

up to her face.

"The colour hurts my eyes," she said.

The colour? Ah, poor Tiny Tim!

"They're better now again," said Cratchit's wife. "It makes them weak by candle-light; and I wouldn't show weak eyes to your father when he comes home, for the world. It must be near his time."

"Past it rather," Peter answered, shutting up his book. "But I think he has walked a little slower than he used, these few last evenings, mother."

They were very quiet again. At last she said, and in a steady, cheerful voice, that only faltered once:

"I have known him walk with—I have known him walk with Tiny Tim upon his shoulder, very fast indeed."

"And so have I," cried Peter. "Often."

"And so have I!" exclaimed another. So had all.

"But he was very light to carry," she resumed, intent upon her work, "and his father loved him so, that it was no trouble: no trouble. And there is your father at the door!"

She hurried out to meet him; and little Bob in his comforter—he had need of it, poor fellow—came in. His tea was ready for him on the hob, and they all tried who should help him to it most. Then the two young Cratchits got upon his knees and laid, each child a little cheek, against his face, as if they said, "Don't mind it, father. Don't be grieved!"

Bob was very cheerful with them, and spoke pleasantly to all the family. He looked at the work upon the table, and praised the industry and speed of Mrs Cratchit and the girls. They would be done long before Sunday, he said.

"Sunday! You went today, then, Robert?" said his wife.

"Yes, my dear," returned Bob. "I wish you could have gone. It would have done you good to see how green a place it is. But you'll see it often. I promised him that I would walk there on a Sunday. My little, little child!" cried Bob. "My little child!"

He broke down all at once. He couldn't help it. If he could have helped it, he and his child would have been farther apart perhaps than they were.

He left the room, and went up-stairs into the room above, which was lighted cheerfully, and hung with Christmas. There was a chair set close beside the child, and there were signs of someone having been there, lately. Poor Bob sat down in it, and when he had thought a little and composed himself, he kissed the little face. He was reconciled to what had happened, and went down again quite happy.

They drew about the fire, and talked; the girls and mother working still. Bob told them of the extraordinary kindness of Mr Scrooge's nephew, whom he had scarcely seen but once, and who, meeting him in the street that day, and seeing that he looked a little—"just a little down you know," said Bob, inquired what had happened to distress him. "On which," said Bob, "for he is the pleasantest-spoken gentleman you ever heard, I told him. "I am heartily sorry for it, Mr Cratchit," he said, "and heartily sorry for your good wife." By the bye, how he ever knew that, I don't know."

"Knew what, my dear?"

"Why, that you were a good wife," replied Bob.

"Everybody knows that." said Peter.

"Very well observed, my boy." cried Bob. "I hope they do. "Heartily sorry," he said, "for your good wife. If I can be of service to you in any way," he said, giving me his card, "that's where I live. Pray come to me." Now, it wasn't," cried Bob, "for the sake of anything he might be able to do for us, so much as for his kind way, that this was quite delightful. It really seemed as if he had known our Tiny Tim, and felt with us."

"I'm sure he's a good soul!" said Mrs Cratchit.

"You would be surer of it, my dear," returned Bob, "if you saw and spoke to him. I shouldn't be at all surprised, mark what I say, if he got Peter a better situation."

"Only hear that, Peter," said Mrs Cratchit.

"And then," cried one of the girls, "Peter will be keeping company with someone, and setting up for himself."

"Get along with you!" retorted Peter, grinning.

"It's just as likely as not," said Bob, "one of these days; though there's plenty of time for that, my dear. But however and whenever we part from one another, I am sure we shall none of us forget poor Tiny Tim—shall we—or this first parting that there was among us?"

"Never, father!" cried they all.

"And I know," said Bob, "I know, my dears, that when we recollect how patient and how mild he was; although he was a little, little child; we shall not quarrel easily among ourselves, and forget poor Tiny Tim in doing it."

"No, never, father!" they all cried again.

"I am very happy," said little Bob, "I am very happy!"

Mrs Cratchit kissed him, his daughters kissed him, the two young Cratchits kissed him, and Peter and himself shook hands. Spirit of Tiny Tim, thy childish essence was from God!

"Spectre," said Scrooge, "something informs me that our parting moment is at hand. I know it, but I know not how. Tell me what man that was whom we saw lying dead?"

The Ghost of Christmas Yet To Come conveyed him, as before—though at a different time, he thought: indeed, there seemed no order in these latter visions, save that they were in the Future—into the resorts of business men, but showed him not himself. Indeed, the Spirit did not stay for anything, but went straight on, as to the end just now desired, until besought by Scrooge to tarry for a moment.

"This court," said Scrooge, "through which we hurry now, is where my place of occupation is, and has been for a length of time. I see the house. Let me behold what I shall be, in days to come."

The Spirit stopped; the hand was pointed elsewhere.

"The house is yonder," Scrooge exclaimed. "Why do you point away?"

The inexorable finger underwent no change.

Scrooge hastened to the window of his office, and looked in. It was an office still, but not his. The furniture was not the same, and the figure in the chair was not himself. The Phantom pointed as before.

He joined it once again, and wondering why and whither he had gone, accompanied it until they reached an iron gate. He paused to look round before entering.

A churchyard. Here, then, the wretched man whose name he had now to learn, lay underneath the ground. It was a worthy place. Walled in by houses; overrun by grass and weeds, the growth of vegetation's death, not life; choked up with too much burying; fat with repleted appetite. A worthy place!

The Spirit stood among the graves, and pointed down to One. He advanced towards it trembling. The Phantom was exactly as it had been, but he dreaded that he saw new meaning in its solemn shape.

"Before I draw nearer to that stone to which you point," said Scrooge, "answer me one question. Are these the shadows of the things that Will be, or are they shadows of things that May be, only?"

Still the Ghost pointed downward to the grave by which it stood.

"Men's courses will foreshadow certain ends, to which, if persevered in, they must lead," said Scrooge. "But if the courses be departed from, the ends will change. Say it is thus with what you show me!"

The Spirit was immovable as ever.

Scrooge crept towards it, trembling as he went; and following the finger, read upon the stone of the neglected grave his own name, Ebenezer Scrooge.

"Am I that man who lay upon the bed?" he cried, upon his knees.

The finger pointed from the grave to him, and back again.

"No, Spirit! Oh no, no!"

The finger still was there.

"Spirit!" he cried, tight clutching at its robe, "hear me! I am not the man I was. I will not be the man I must have been but for this intercourse. Why show me this, if I am past all hope?"

For the first time the hand appeared to shake.

"Good Spirit," he pursued, as down upon the ground he fell before it: "Your nature intercedes for me, and pities me. Assure me that I yet may change these shadows you have shown me, by an altered life!"

The kind hand trembled.

"I will honour Christmas in my heart, and try to keep it all the year. I will live in the Past, the Present, and the Future. The Spirits of all Three shall strive within me. I will not shut out the lessons that they teach. Oh, tell me I may sponge away the writing on this stone!"

In his agony, he caught the spectral hand. It sought to free itself, but he was strong in his entreaty, and detained it. The Spirit, stronger yet, repulsed him.

Holding up his hands in a last prayer to have his fate reversed, he saw an alteration in the Phantom's hood and dress. It shrunk, collapsed, and dwindled down into a bedpost.

Chapter 5
The End of it

Yes! and the bedpost was his own. The bed was his own, the room was his own. Best and happiest of all, the time before him was his own, to make amends in!

"I will live in the Past, the Present, and the Future!" Scrooge repeated, as he scrambled out of bed. "The Spirits of all Three shall strive within me. Oh Jacob Marley! Heaven, and the Christmas Time be praised for this! I say it on my knees, old Jacob; on my knees!"

He was so fluttered and so glowing with his good intentions, that his broken voice would scarcely answer to his call. He had been sobbing violently in his conflict with the Spirit, and his face was wet with tears.

"They are not torn down," cried Scrooge, folding one of his bed-curtains in his arms, "they are not torn down, rings and all. They are here: I am here: the shadows of the things that would have been, may be dispelled. They will be. I know they will!"

His hands were busy with his garments all this time: turning them inside out, putting them on upside down, tearing them, mislaying them, making them parties to every kind of extravagance.

"I don't know what to do!" cried Scrooge, laughing and crying in the same breath; and making a perfect *Laocoön* of himself with his stockings. "I am as light as a feather, I am as happy as an angel, I am as merry as a school-boy. I am as giddy as a drunken man. A merry Christmas to every-body! A happy New Year to all the world! Hallo here! Whoop! Hallo!"

He had frisked into the sitting-room, and was now standing there: perfectly winded.

"There's the saucepan that the gruel was in!" cried Scrooge, starting off again, and going round the fireplace. "There's the door, by which the Ghost of Jacob Marley entered! There's the corner where the Ghost of Christmas Present, sat! There's the window where I saw the wandering Spirits! It's all right, it's all true, it all happened. Ha ha ha!"

Really, for a man who had been out of practice for so many years, it was a splendid laugh, a most illustrious laugh. The father of a long, long line of brilliant laughs!

"I don't know what day of the month it is!" said Scrooge. "I don't know how long I've been among the Spirits. I don't know anything. I'm quite a baby. Never mind. I don't care. I'd rather be a baby. Hallo! Whoop! Hallo here!"

He was checked in his transports by the churches ringing out the lustiest peals he had ever heard. Clash, clang, hammer, ding, dong, bell. Bell, dong, ding, hammer, clang, clash! Oh, glorious, glorious!

Running to the window, he opened it, and put out his head. No fog, no mist, clear, bright, jovial stirring, cold, cold, piping for the blood to dance to; Golden sunlight; Heavenly sky; sweet fresh air; merry bells. Oh, glorious. Glorious!

"What's today?" cried Scrooge, calling downward to a boy in Sunday clothes, who perhaps had loitered in to look about him.

"Eh?" returned the boy, with all his might of wonder.

"What's today, my fine fellow?" said Scrooge.

"Today?" replied the boy. "Why, Christmas Day."

"It's Christmas Day!" said Scrooge to himself. "I haven't missed it. The Spirits have done it all in one night. They can do anything they like. Of course they can. Of course they can. Hallo, my fine fellow!"

"Hallo!" returned the boy

"Do you know the Poulterer's, in the next street but one, at the corner?" Scrooge inquired.

"I should hope I did," replied the lad.

"An intelligent boy!" said Scrooge. "A remarkable boy! Do you know whether they've sold the prize Turkey that was hanging up there? Not the little prize Turkey; the big one?"

"What, the one as big as me?" returned the boy.

"What a delightful boy!" said Scrooge. "It's a pleasure to talk to him. Yes, my buck!"

"It's hanging there now," replied the boy.

"Is it?" said Scrooge. "Go and buy it."

"Walk-er!" exclaimed the boy.

"No, no," said Scrooge, "I am in earnest. Go and buy it, and tell 'em to bring it here, that I may give them the direction where to take it. Come back with the man, and I'll give you a shilling. Come back with him in less than five minutes, and I'll give you half-a-crown!"

"I'll send it to Bob Cratchit's!" whispered Scrooge, rubbing his hands, and splitting with a laugh. "He sha'n't know who sends it. It's twice the size of Tiny Tim. Joe Miller never made such a joke as sending it to Bob's will be!"

The hand in which he wrote the address was not a steady one, but write it he did, somehow, and went down stairs to open the street door, ready for the coming of the poulterer's man. As he stood there, waiting his arrival, the knocker caught his eye.

"I shall love it, as long as I live!" cried Scrooge, patting it with his hand. "I scarcely ever looked at it before. What an honest expression it has in its face! It's a wonderful knocker!—Here's the Turkey. Hallo! Whoop! How are you! Merry Christmas!"

It was a Turkey! He never could have stood upon his legs, that bird. He would have snapped 'em short off in a minute, like sticks of sealing-wax.

"Why, it's impossible to carry that to Camden Town," said Scrooge. "You must have a cab."

The chuckle with which he said this, and the chuckle with which he paid for the Turkey, and the chuckle with which he paid for the cab, and the chuckle with which he recompensed the boy, were only to be exceeded by the chuckle with which he sat down breathless in his chair again, and chuckled till he cried.

Shaving was not an easy task, for his hand continued to shake very much; and shaving requires attention, even when you don't dance while you are at it. But if he had cut the end of his nose off, he would have put a piece of sticking-plaster over it, and been quite satisfied.

He dressed himself all in his best, and at last got out into the streets. The people were by this time pouring forth, as he had seen them with the Ghost of Christmas Present; and walking with his hands behind him, Scrooge regarded every one with a delighted smile. He looked so irresistibly pleasant, in a word, that three or four good-humoured fellows said, "Good morning, sir! A merry Christmas to you!" And Scrooge said often afterwards, that of all the blithe sounds he had ever heard, those were the blithest in his ears.

He had not gone far, when coming on towards him he beheld the portly gentleman, who had walked into his counting-house the day before, and said, "Scrooge and Marley's, I believe?" It sent a pang across his heart to think how this old gentleman would look upon him when they met; but he knew what path lay straight before him, and he took it.

"My dear sir," said Scrooge, quickening his pace, and taking the old gentleman by both his hands. "How do you do? I hope you succeeded yesterday. It was very kind of you. A merry Christmas to you, sir!"

"Mr Scrooge?"

"Yes," said Scrooge. "That is my name, and I fear it may not be pleasant to you. Allow me to ask your pardon. And will you have the goodness —" here Scrooge whispered in his ear.

"Lord bless me!" cried the gentleman, as if his breath were gone. "My dear Mr Scrooge, are you serious?"

"If you please," said Scrooge. "Not a farthing less. A great many back-payments are included in it, I assure you. Will you do me that favour?"

"My dear sir," said the other, shaking hands with him. "I don't know what to say to such munifi——;"

"Don't say anything, please," retorted Scrooge. "Come and see me. Will you come and see me?"

"I will!" cried the old gentleman. And it was clear he meant to do it.

"Thank 'ee," said Scrooge. "I am much obliged to you. I thank you fifty times. Bless you!"

He went to church, and walked about the streets, and watched the people hurrying to and fro, and patted children on the head, and questioned beggars, and looked down into the kitchens of houses, and up to the windows: and found that everything could yield him pleasure. He had never dreamed that any walk—that anything—could give him so much happiness. In the afternoon he turned his steps towards his nephew's house.

He passed the door a dozen times, before he had the courage to go up and knock. But he made a dash, and did it:

"Is your master at home, my dear?" said Scrooge to the girl. Nice girl! Very.

"Yes, sir."

"Where is he, my love?" said Scrooge.

"He's in the dining-room, sir, along with mistress. I'll show you upstairs, if you please."

"Thank 'ee. He knows me," said Scrooge, with his hand already on the dining-room lock. "I'll go in here, my dear."

He turned it gently, and sidled his face in, round the door. They were looking at the table (which was spread out in great array); for these young housekeepers are always nervous on such points, and like to see that everything is right.

"Fred!" said Scrooge.

Dear heart alive, how his niece by marriage started! Scrooge had forgotten, for the moment, about her sitting in the corner with the footstool, or he wouldn't have done it, on any account.

"Why bless my soul!" cried Fred, "who's that?"

"It's I. Your uncle Scrooge. I have come to dinner. Will you let me in, Fred?"

Let him in! It is a mercy he didn't shake his arm off. He was at home in five minutes. Nothing could be heartier. His niece looked just the same. So did Topper when he came. So did the plump sister when she came. So did every one when they came. Wonderful party, wonderful games, wonderful unanimity, wonder-ful happiness!

But he was early at the office next morning. Oh, he was early there. If he could only be there first, and catch Bob Cratchit coming late! That was the thing he had set his heart upon.

And he did it; yes he did! The clock struck nine. No Bob. A quarter past. No Bob. He was full eighteen minutes and a half, behind his time. Scrooge sat with his door wide open, that he might see him come into the Tank.

His hat was off, before he opened the door; his comforter too. He was on his stool in a jiffy; driving away with his pen, as if he were trying to overtake nine o'clock.

"Hallo!" growled Scrooge, in his accustomed voice, as near as he could feign it. "What do you mean by coming here at this time of day."

"I am very sorry, sir," said Bob. "I am behind my time."

"You are?" repeated Scrooge. "Yes. I think you are. Step this way, if you please."

"It's only once a year, sir," pleaded Bob, appearing from the Tank. "It shall not be repeated. I was making rather merry yesterday, sir."

"Now, I'll tell you what, my friend," said Scrooge, "I am not going to stand this sort of thing any longer. And therefore," he continued, leaping from his stool, and giving Bob such a dig in the waistcoat that he staggered back into the Tank again: "and therefore I am about to raise your salary!"

Bob trembled, and got a little nearer to the ruler. He had a momentary idea of knocking Scrooge down with it; holding him, and calling to the people in the court for help and a strait-waistcoat.

"A merry Christmas, Bob!" said Scrooge, with an earnestness that could not be mistaken, as he clapped him on the back. "A merrier Christmas, Bob, my good fellow, than I have given you for many a year! I'll raise your salary, and endeavour to assist your struggling family, and we will discuss your affairs this very afternoon, over a Christmas bowl of smoking bishop, Bob! Make up the fires, and buy another coal-scuttle before you dot another i, Bob Cratchit."

Scrooge was better than his word. He did it all, and infinitely more; and to Tiny Tim, who did not die, he was a second father. He became as good a friend, as good a master, and as good a man, as the good old city knew, or any other good old city, town, or borough, in the good old world. Some people laughed to see the alteration in him, but he let them laugh, and little heeded them; for he was wise enough to know that nothing ever happened on this globe, for good, at which some people did not have their fill of laughter in the outset; and knowing that such as these would be blind anyway, he thought it quite as well that they should wrinkle up their eyes in grins, as have the malady in less attractive forms. His own heart laughed: and that was quite enough for him.

He had no further intercourse with Spirits, but lived upon the Total Abstinence Principle, ever afterwards; and it was always said of him, that he knew how to keep Christmas well, if any man alive possessed the knowledge. May that be truly said of us, and all of us! And so, as Tiny Tim observed, God Bless Us, Every One!

A Child's Dream of a Star

There was once a child, and he strolled about a good deal, and thought of a number of things. He had a sister, who was a child too, and his constant companion. These two used to wonder all day long. They wondered at the beauty of the flowers; they wondered at the height and blueness of the sky; they wondered at the depth of the bright water; they wondered at the goodness and the power of GOD who made the lovely world.

They used to say to one another, sometimes, Supposing all the children upon earth were to die, would the flowers, and the water, and the sky be sorry? They believed they would be sorry. For, said they, the buds are the children of the flowers, and the little playful streams that gambol down the hillsides are the children of the water; and the smallest bright specks playing at hide and seek in the sky all night, must surely be the children of the stars; and they would all be grieved to see their playmates, the children of men, no more.

There was one clear shining star that used to come out in the sky before the rest, near the church spire, above the graves. It was larger and more beautiful, they thought, than all the others, and every night they watched for it, standing hand in hand at a window. Whoever saw it first cried out, 'I see the star!' And often they cried out both together, knowing so well when it would rise, and where. So they grew to be such friends with it, that, before lying down in their beds, they always looked out once again, to bid it goodnight; and when they were turning round to sleep, they used to say, 'God bless the star!'

But while she was still very young, oh, very, very young, the sister drooped, and came to be so weak that she could no longer stand in the window at night; and then the child looked sadly out by himself, and when he saw the star, turned round and said to the patient pale face on the bed, 'I see the star!' and then a smile would come upon the face, and a little weak voice used to say, 'God bless my brother and the star!'

And so the time came all too soon! when the child looked out alone, and when there was no face on the bed; and when there was a little grave among the graves, not there before; and when the star made long rays down towards him, as he saw it through his tears.

Now, these rays were so bright, and they seemed to make such a shining way from earth to Heaven, that when the child went to his solitary bed, he dreamed about the star; and dreamed that, lying where he was, he saw a train of people taken up that sparkling road by angels. And the star, opening, showed him a great world of light, where many more such angels waited to receive them.

All these angels, who were waiting, turned their beaming eyes upon the people who were carried up into the star; and some came out from the long rows in which they stood, and fell upon the people's necks, and kissed them tenderly, and went away with them down avenues of light, and were so happy in their company, that lying in his bed he wept for joy.

But, there were many angels who did not go with them, and among them one he knew. The patient face that once had lain upon the bed was glorified and radiant, but his heart found out his sister among all the host.

His sister's angel lingered near the entrance of the star, and said to the leader among those who had brought the people thither:

'Is my brother come?'

And he said 'No.'

She was turning hopefully away, when the child stretched out his arms, and cried, 'O, sister, I am here! Take me!' and then she turned her beaming eyes upon him, and it was night; and the star was shining into the room, making long rays down towards him as he saw it through his tears.

From that hour forth, the child looked out upon the star as on the home he was to go to, when his time should come; and he thought that he did not belong to the earth alone, but to the star too, because of his sister's angel gone before.

There was a baby born to be a brother to the child; and while he was so little that he never yet had spoken word, he stretched his tiny form out on his bed, and died.

Again the child dreamed of the open star, and of the company of angels, and the train of people, and the rows of angels with their beaming eyes all turned upon those people's faces.

Said his sister's angel to the leader:

'Is my brother come?'

And he said, 'Not that one, but another.'

As the child beheld his brother's angel in her arms, he cried, 'O, sister, I am here! Take me!' And she turned and smiled upon him, and the star was shining.

He grew to be a young man, and was busy at his books when an old servant came to him and said:

'Thy mother is no more. I bring her blessing on her darling son!'

Again at night he saw the star, and all that former company. Said his sister's angel to the leader.

'Is my brother come?'

And he said, 'Thy mother!'

A mighty cry of joy went forth through all the star, because the mother was reunited to her two children. And he stretched out his arms and cried, 'O, mother, sister, and brother, I am here! Take me!' And they answered him, 'Not yet,' and the star was shining.

He grew to be a man, whose hair was turning grey, and he was sitting in his chair by the fireside, heavy with grief, and with his face bedewed with tears, when the star opened once again.

Said his sister's angel to the leader: 'Is my brother come?'

And he said, 'Nay, but his maiden daughter.'

And the man who had been the child saw his daughter, newly lost to him, a celestial creature among those three, and he said, 'My daughter's head is on my sister's bosom, and her arm is around my mother's neck, and at her feet there is the baby of old time, and I can bear the parting from her, GOD be praised!'

And the star was shining.

Thus the child came to be an old man, and his once smooth face was wrinkled, and his steps were slow and feeble, and his back was bent. And one night as he lay upon his bed, his children standing round, he cried, as he had cried so long ago:

'I see the star!'

They whispered one another, 'He is dying.'

And he said, 'I am. My age is falling from me like a garment, and I move towards the star as a child. And O, my Father, now I thank thee that it has so often opened, to receive those dear ones who await me!'

And the star was shining; and it shines upon his grave.

The Mother's Eyes

My old companion tells me it is midnight. The fire glows brightly, crackling with a sharp and cheerful sound as if it loved to burn. The merry cricket on the hearth (my constant visitor), this ruddy blaze, my clock, and I, seem to share the world among us, and to be the only things awake. The wind, high and boisterous but now, has died away and hoarsely mutters in its sleep. I love all times and seasons each in its turn, and am apt perhaps to think the present one the best, but past or coming I always love this peaceful time of night, when long buried thoughts favoured by the gloom and silence steal from their graves and haunt the scenes of faded happiness and hope.

The popular faith in ghosts has a remarkable affinity with the whole current of our thoughts at such an hour as this, and seems to be their necessary and natural consequence. For who can wonder that man should feel a vague belief in tales of disembodied spirits wandering through those places which they once dearly affected, when he himself, scarcely less separated from his old world than they, is forever lingering upon past emotions and bygone times, and hovering, the ghost of his former self, about the places and people that warmed his heart of old?

It is thus that at this quiet hour I haunt the house where I was born, the rooms I used to tread, the scenes of my infancy, my boyhood and my youth; it is thus that I prowl around my buried treasure (though not of gold or silver) and mourn my loss; it is thus that I revisit the ashes of extinguished fires, and take my silent stand at old bedsides. If my spirit should ever glide back to this chamber when my body is mingled with *the* dust, it will but follow the course it often look in the old man's lifetime and add but one more change to the subjects of its contemplation.

In all my idle speculations I am greatly assisted by various legends connected with my venerable house, which are current in the neighbourhood, and are so numerous that there is scarce a cupboard or corner that has not some dismal story of its own. When I first entertained thoughts of becoming its tenant I was assured mat it was haunted from roof to cellar, and I believe the bad opinion in which my neighbours once held me had its rise in my not being torn to pieces or at least distracted with terror on the night I took possession: in either of which cases I should doubtless have arrived by a short cut at the very summit of popularity.

But traditions and rumours all taken into account, who so abets me in every fancy and chimes with my every thought, as my dear deaf friend; and how often have I cause to bless the day that brought us two together! Of all days in the year I rejoice to think that it should have been Christmas Day, with which from childhood we associate something, friendly, hearty, and sincere.

I had walked out to cheer myself with the happiness of others, and in the little tokens of festivity and rejoicing of which the streets and houses present so many upon that day, had lost some hours. Now I stopped to look at a merry party hurrying through the snow on foot to their place of meeting, and now turned back to see a whole coachful of children safely deposited at the welcome house. At one time, I admired how carefully the working-man carried the baby in its gaudy hat and feathers, and how his wife, trudging patiently on behind, forgot even her care of her gay clothes, in exchanging greetings with the child as it crowed and laughed over the famer's shoulder; at another, I pleased myself with some passing scene of gallantry or courtship, and was glad to believe that for a season half the world of poverty was gay.

As the day closed in, I still rambled through the streets, feeling a companionship in the bright fires that cast their warm reflection on the windows as I passed, and losing all sense of my own loneliness in imagining the sociality and kind-fellowship that everywhere prevailed. At length I happened to stop before a Tavern and, encountering a Bill of Fare in the window, it all at once brought it into my head to wonder what kind of people dined alone in Taverns upon Christmas Day.

Solitary men are accustomed, I suppose, unconsciously to look upon solitude as their own peculiar property. I had sat alone in my room on many, many, anniversaries of this great holiday, and had never regarded it but as one of universal assemblage and rejoicing. I had excepted, and with an aching heart, a crowd of prisoners and beggars, but *these* were not the men for whom the Tavern doors were open. Had they any customers, or was it a mere form? A form no doubt.

Trying to feel quite sure of this I walked away, but before I had gone many paces, I stopped and looked back. There was a provoking air of business in the lamp above the door, which I could not overcome. I began to be afraid there might be many customers—young men perhaps struggling with the world, ut-ter strangers in this great place, whose friends lived at a long distance off, and whose means were too slender to enable them to make the journey. The supposition gave rise to so many dis-tressing little pictures that in preference to carrying them home with me, I determined to encounter the realities. So I turned, and walked in.

I was at once glad and sorry to find that there was only one person in the dining-room; glad to know that there were not more, and sorry to think that he should be there by himself. He did not look so old as I, but like me he was advanced in life, and his hair was nearly white. Though I made more noise in enter-ing and seating myself than was quite necessary, with the view of attracting his attention and saluting him in the good old form of that time of year, he did not raise his head but sat with it resting on his hand, musing over his half-finished meal.

I called for something which would give me an excuse for remaining in the room (I had dined early as my housekeeper was engaged at night to partake of some friend's good cheer) and sat where I could observe without intruding on him. After a time he looked up. He was aware that somebody had entered, but could see very little of me as I sat in the shade and he in the light. He was sad and thoughtful, and I forbore to trouble him by speaking.

Let me believe that it was something better than curiosity which riveted my attention and impelled me strongly towards this gentleman. I never saw so patient and kind a face. He should have been surrounded by friends, and yet here he sat dejected and alone when all men had their friends about them. As often as he roused himself from his reverie he would fall into it again, and it was plain that whatever were the subject of his thoughts they were of a melancholy kind, and would not be controlled.

He was not used to solitude. I was sure of that, for I know by myself that if he had been, his manner would have been different and he would have taken some slight interest in the arrival of another. I could not fail to mark that he had no appetite—that he tried to eat in vain—that time after time the plate was pushed away, and he relapsed into his former posture.

His mind was wandering among old Christmas Days, I thought. Many of them sprung up together, not with a long gap between each but in unbroken succession like days of the week. It was a great change to find himself for the first time (I quite settled that it *was* the first) in an empty silent room with no soul to care for. I could not help following him in imagination through crowds of pleasant faces, and then coming back to that dull place with its bough of mistletoe sickening in the gas, and sprigs of holly parched up already by a Simoom of roast and boiled. The very waiter had gone home, and his representative, a poor, lean hungry man, was keeping Christmas in his jacket.

I grew still more interested in my friend. His dinner done, a decanter of wine was placed before him. It remained untouched for a long time, but at length with a quivering hand he filled a glass and raised it to his lips. Some tender wish to which he had been accustomed to give utterance on that day, or some beloved name that he had been used to pledge, trembled upon them at the moment. He put it down very hastily—took it up once more—again put it down—pressed his hand upon his face—yes—and tears stole down his cheeks, I am certain.

Without pausing to consider whether I did right or wrong, I stepped across the room, and sitting down beside him laid my hand gently on his arm.

"My friend," I said, "forgive me if I beseech you to take comfort and consolation from the lips of an old man. I will not preach to you what I have not practised, indeed. Whatever be your grief, be of a good heart—be of a good heart, pray!"

"I see that you speak earnestly," he replied, "and kindly I am very sure, but—"

I nodded my head to show that I understood what he would I say, for I had already gathered from a certain fixed expression in his face and from the attention with which he watched me while I spoke, that his sense of hearing was destroyed, "There should be a freemasonry between us," said I, pointing from himself to me to explain my meaning—"if not in our grey hairs, at least in our misfortunes. You see that I am but I a poor cripple."

I have never felt so happy under my affliction since the trying moment of my first becoming conscious of it, as when he took my hand in his with a smile that has lighted my path in life from that day, and we sat down side by side.

This was the beginning of my friendship with the deaf gentleman, and when was ever the slight and easy service of a kind word in season, repaid by such attachment and devotion as he has shown to me!

He produced a little set of tablets and a pencil to facilitate our conversation, on that our first acquaintance, and I well remember how awkward and constrained I was in writing down my share of the dialogue, and how easily he guessed my meaning before I had written half of what I had to say. He told me in a faltering voice that he had not been accustomed to be alone on that day—that it had always been a little festival with him—and seeing that I glanced at his dress in the expectation that he wore mourning, he added hastily that it was not that; if it had been, he thought he could have borne it better. From that time to the present we have never touched upon this theme.

Upon every return of the same day we have been together, and although we make it our annual custom to drink to each hand in hand after dinner, and to recall with affectionate garrulity every circumstance of our first meeting, we always avoid this one as if by mutual consent.

Meantime we have gone on strengthening in our friendship and regard and forming an attachment which, I trust and believe, will only be interrupted by death, to be renewed in another existence. I scarcely know how we communicate as we do, but he has long since ceased to be deaf to me. He is frequently the companion of my walks, and even in crowded streets replies to my slightest look or gesture as though he could read my thoughts. From the vast number of objects which pass in rapid succession before our eyes, we frequently select the same for some particular notice or remark, and when one of these little coincidences occurs I cannot describe the pleasure that animates my friend, or the beaming countenance he will preserve for half an hour afterwards at least.

He is a great thinker from living so much within himself, and having a lively imagination has a facility of conceiving and enlarging upon odd ideas which renders him invaluable to our little body, and greatly astonishes our two friends. His powers in this respect are much assisted by a large pipe which he assures us once belonged to a German Student. Be this as it may, it has undoubtedly a very ancient and mysterious appearance, and is of such capacity that it takes three hours and a half to smoke it out. I have reason to believe that my barber, who is the chief authority of a knot of gossips who congregate every evening at a small tobacconist's hard by, has related anecdotes of this pipe and the grim figures that are carved upon its bowl at which all the smokers in the neighbourhood have stood aghast, and I know that my housekeeper, while she holds it in high veneration, has a superstitious feeling connected with it which would render her exceedingly unwilling to be left alone in its company after dark.

Whatever sorrow my deaf friend has known, and whatever grief may linger in some secret corner of his heart, he is now a cheerful, placid, happy creature. Misfortune can never have fallen upon such a man but for some good purpose, and when I see its traces in his gentle nature and his earnest feeling, I am the less disposed to murmur at such trials as I may have undergone myself.

With regard to the pipe, I have a theory of my own; I cannot help thinking that it is in some manner connected with the event that brought us together, for I remember that it was a long time before he even talked about it; that when he did, he grew reserved and melancholy; and that it was a long time yet before he brought it forth. I have no curiosity, however, upon this subject, for I know mat it promotes his tranquillity and comfort, and I need no other inducement to regard it with my utmost favour.

Such is the deaf gentleman. I can call up his figure now, clad in sober grey, and seated in the chimney corner. As he puffs out the smoke from his favourite pipe he casts a look on me brimful of cordiality and friendship, and says all manner of kind and genial things in a cheerful smile; then he raises his eyes to my clock which is just about to strike, and glancing from it to me and back again, seems to divide his heart between us. For myself, it is not too much to say that I would gladly part with one of my poor limbs, could he but hear the old clock's voice.

This is my friend and this is the story he told me.

THE CLOCK CASE
A Confession found in a prison in the time of Charles the Second.

I held a lieutenant's commission in his Majesty's army, and served abroad in the campaigns of 1677 and 1678. The treaty of Nimeguen being concluded, I returned home, and retiring from the service, withdrew to a small estate lying a few miles east of London, which I had recently acquired in right of my wife.

This is the last night I have to live, and I will set down the naked truth without disguise. I was never a brave man, and had always been from my childhood of a secret, sullen, distrustful nature. I speak of myself as if I had passed from the world; for while I write this, my grave is digging, and my name is written in the black-book of death.

Soon after my return to England, my only brother was seized with mortal illness. This circumstance gave me slight or no pain; for since we had been men, we had associated but very little together. He was open-hearted and generous, handsomer than I, more accomplished, and generally beloved. Those who sought my acquaintance abroad or at home, because they were friends of his, seldom attached themselves to me long, and would usually say, in our first conversation, that they were surprised to find two brothers so unlike in their manners and appearance. It was my habit to lead them on to this avowal; for I knew what comparisons they must draw between us; and having a rankling envy in my heart, I sought to justify it to myself.

We had married two sisters. This additional tie between us, as it may appear to some, only estranged us the more. His wife knew me well. I never struggled with any secret jealousy or gall when she was present but that woman knew it as well as I did. I never raised my eyes at such times but I found hers fixed upon me; I never bent them on the ground or looked another way but I felt that she overlooked me always. It was an inexpressible relief to me when we quarrelled, and a greater relief still when I heard abroad that she was dead. It seems to me now as if some strange and terrible foreshadowing of what has happened since must have hung over us then. I was afraid of her; she haunted me; her fixed and steady look comes back upon me now, like the memory of a dark dream, and makes my blood run cold.

She died shortly after giving birth to a child—a boy. When my brother knew that all hope of his own recovery was past, he called my wife to his bedside, and confided this orphan, a child of four years old, to her protection. He bequeathed to him all the property he had, and willed that, in case of his child's death, it should pass to my wife, as the only acknowledgment he could make her for her care and love. He exchanged a few brotherly words with me, deploring our long separation; and being exhausted, fell into a slumber, from which he never awoke.

We had no children; and as there had been a strong affection between the sisters, and my wife had almost supplied the place of a mother to this boy, she loved him as if he had been her own. The child was ardently attached to her; but he was his mother's image in face and spirit, and always mistrusted me.

I can scarcely fix the date when the feeling first came upon me; but I soon began to be uneasy when this child was by. I never roused myself from some moody train of thought but I marked him looking at me; not with mere childish wonder, but with something of the purpose and meaning that I had so often noted in his mother. It was no effort of my fancy, founded on close resemblance of feature and expression. I never could look the boy down. He feared me, but seemed by some instinct to despise me while he did so; and even when he drew back beneath my gaze—as he would when we were alone, to get nearer to the door—he would keep his bright eyes upon me still.

Perhaps I hide the truth from myself, but I do not think that, when this began, I meditated to do him any wrong. I may have thought how serviceable his inheritance would be to us, and may have wished him dead; but I believe I had no thought of compassing his death. Neither did the idea come upon me at once, but by very slow degrees, presenting itself at first in dim shapes at a very great distance, as men may think of an earthquake or the last day; then drawing nearer and nearer, and losing something of its horror and improbability; then coming to be part and parcel—nay nearly the whole sum and substance—of my daily thoughts, and resolving itself into a question of means and safety; not of doing or abstaining from the deed.

While this was going on within me, I never could bear that the child should see me looking at him, and yet I was under a fascination which made it a kind of business with me to contemplate his slight and fragile figure and think how easily it might be done. Sometimes I would steal upstairs and watch him as he slept; but usually I hovered in the garden near the window of the room in which he learnt his little tasks; and there, as he sat upon a low seat beside my wife, I would peer at him for hours together from behind a tree; starting, like the guilty wretch I was, at every rustling of a leaf, and still gliding back to look and start again.

Hard by our cottage, but quite out of sight, and (if there were any wind astir) of hearing too, was a deep sheet of water. I spent days in shaping with my pocket-knife a rough model of a boat, which I finished at last and dropped in the child's way. Then I withdrew to a secret place, which he must pass if he stole away alone to swim this bauble, and lurked there for his coming. He came neither that day nor the next, though I waited from noon till nightfall. I was sure that I had him in my net, for I had heard him prattling of the toy, and knew that in his infant pleasure he kept it by his side in bed. I felt no weariness or fatigue, but waited patiently, and on the third day he passed me, running joyously along, with his silken hair streaming in the wind, and he singing—God have mercy upon me!—singing a merry ballad,—who could hardly lisp the words.

I stole down after him, creeping under certain shrubs which grow in that place, and none but devils know with what terror I, a strong, full-grown man, tracked the footsteps of that baby as he approached the water's brink. I was close upon him, had sunk upon my knee and raised my hand to thrust him in, when he saw my shadow in the stream and turned him round.

His mother's ghost was looking from his eyes. The sun burst forth from behind a cloud; it shone in the bright sky, the glistening earth, the clear water, the sparkling drops of rain upon the leaves. There were eyes in everything. The whole great universe of light was there to see the murder done. I know not what he said; he came of bold and manly blood, and, child as he was, he did not crouch or fawn upon me. I heard him cry that he would try to love me,—not that he did,—and then I saw him running back towards the house. The next I saw was my own sword naked in my hand, and he lying at my feet stark dead,—dabbled here and there with blood, but otherwise no different from what I had seen him in his sleep—in the same attitude too, with his cheek resting upon his little hand.

I took him in my arms and laid him—very gently now that he was dead—in a thicket. My wife was from home that day, and would not return until the next. Our bedroom window, the only sleeping-room on that side of the house, was but a few feet from the ground, and I resolved to descend from it at night and bury him in the garden. I had no thought that I had failed in my design, no thought that the water would be dragged and nothing found, that the money must now lie waste, since I must encourage the idea that the child was lost or stolen. All my thoughts were bound up and knotted together in the one absorbing necessity of hiding what I had done.

How I felt when they came to tell me that the child was missing, when I ordered scouts in all directions, when I gasped and trembled at every one's approach, no tongue can tell or mind of man conceive. I buried him that night. When I parted the boughs and looked into the dark thicket, there was a glow-worm shining like the visible spirit of God upon the murdered child. I glanced down into his grave when I had placed him there, and still it gleamed upon his breast; an eye of fire looking up to Heaven in supplication to the stars that watched me at my work.

I had to meet my wife, and break the news, and give her hope that the child would soon be found. All this I did,—with some appearance, I suppose, of being sincere, for I was the object of no suspicion. This done, I sat at the bedroom window all day long, and watched the spot where the dreadful secret lay.

It was in a piece of ground which had been dug up to be newly turfed, and which I had chosen on that account, as the traces of my spade were less likely to attract attention. The men who laid down the grass must have thought me mad. I called to them continually to expedite their work, ran out and worked beside them, trod down the earth with my feet, and hurried them with frantic eagerness. They had finished their task before night, and then I thought myself comparatively safe.

I slept,—not as men do who awake refreshed and cheerful, but I did sleep, passing from vague and shadowy dreams of being hunted down, to visions of the plot of grass, through which now a hand, and now a foot, and now the head itself was starting out. At this point I always woke and stole to the window, to make sure that it was not really so. That done, I crept to bed again; and thus I spent the night in fits and starts, getting up and lying down full twenty times, and dreaming the same dream over and over again,—which was far worse than lying awake, for every dream had a whole night's suffering of its own. Once I thought the child was alive, and that I had never tried to kill him. To wake from that dream was the most dreadful agony of all.

The next day I sat at the window again, never once taking my eyes from the place, which, although it was covered by the grass, was as plain to me—its shape, its size, its depth, its jagged sides, and all—as if it had been open to the light of day. When a servant walked across it, I felt as if he must sink in; when he had passed, I looked to see that his feet had not worn the edges. If a bird lighted there, I was in terror lest by some tremendous interposition it should be instrumental in the discovery; if a breath of air sighed across it, to me it whispered murder. There was not a sight or a sound—how ordinary, mean, or unimportant soever—but was fraught with fear. And in this state of ceaseless watching I spent three days.

On the fourth there came to the gate one who had served with me abroad, accompanied by a brother officer of his whom I had never seen. I felt that I could not bear to be out of sight of the place. It was a summer evening, and I bade my people take a table and a flask of wine into the garden. Then I sat down *with my chair upon the grave*, and being assured that nobody could disturb it now without my knowledge, tried to drink and talk.

They hoped that my wife was well,—that she was not obliged to keep her chamber,—that they had not frightened her away. What could I do but tell them with a faltering tongue about the child? The officer whom I did not know was a down-looking man, and kept his eyes upon the ground while I was speaking. Even that terrified me. I could not divest myself of the idea that he saw something there which caused him to suspect the truth. I asked him hurriedly if he supposed that—and stopped. 'That the child has been murdered?' said he, looking mildly at me: 'O no! what could a man gain by murdering a poor child?' I could have told him what a man gained by such a deed, no one better: but I held my peace and shivered as with an ague.

Mistaking my emotion, they were endeavouring to cheer me with the hope that the boy would certainly be found,- great cheer that was for me!—when we heard a low deep howl, and presently there sprung over the wall two great dogs, who, bounding into the garden, repeated the baying sound we had heard before.

'Bloodhounds!' cried my visitors.

What need to tell me that! I had never seen one of that kind in all my life, but I knew what they were and for what purpose they had come. I grasped the elbows of my chair, and neither spoke nor moved.

'They are of the genuine breed,' said the man whom I had known abroad, 'and being out for exercise have no doubt escaped from their keeper.'

Both he and his friend turned to look at the dogs, who with their noses to the ground moved restlessly about, running to and fro, and up and down, and across, and round in circles, careering about like wild things, and all this time taking no notice of us, but ever and again repeating the yell we had heard already, then dropping their noses to the ground again and tracking earnestly here and there. They now began to snuff the earth more eagerly than they had done yet, and although they were still very restless, no longer beat about in such wide circuits, but kept near to one spot, and constantly diminished the distance between themselves and me.

At last they came up close to the great chair on which I sat, and raising their frightful howl once more, tried to tear away the wooden rails that kept them from the ground beneath. I saw how I looked, in the faces of the two who were with me.

'They scent some prey,' said they, both together.

'They scent no prey!' cried I.

'In Heaven's name, move!' said the one I knew, very earnestly, 'or you will be torn to pieces.'

'Let them tear me from limb to limb, I'll never leave this place!' cried I. 'Are dogs to hurry men to shameful deaths? Hew them down, cut them in pieces.'

'There is some foul mystery here!' said the officer whom I did not know, drawing his sword. 'In King Charles's name, assist me to secure this man.'

They both set upon me and forced me away, though I fought and bit and caught at them like a madman. After a struggle, they got me quietly between them; and then, my God! I saw the angry dogs tearing at the earth and throwing it up into the air like water.

What more have I to tell? That I fell upon my knees, and with chattering teeth confessed the truth, and prayed to be forgiven. That I have since denied, and now confess to it again. That I have been tried for the crime, found guilty, and sentenced. That I have not the courage to anticipate my doom, or to bear up manfully against it. That I have no compassion, no consolation, no hope, no friend. That my wife has happily lost for the time those faculties which would enable her to know my misery or hers. That I am alone in this stone dungeon with my evil spirit, and that I die tomorrow.

A House to Let

I had been living at Tunbridge Wells and nowhere else, going on for ten years, when my medical man—very clever in his
profession, and the prettiest player I ever saw in my life of a hand
at Long Whist, which was a noble and a princely game before
Short was heard of—said to me, one day, as he sat feeling my
pulse on the actual sofa which my poor dear sister Jane worked
before her spine came on, and laid her on a board for fifteen
months at a stretch—the most upright woman that ever lived-
said to me, "What we want, ma'am, is a fillip."

"Good gracious, goodness gracious, Doctor Towers!" says I,
quite startled at the man, for he was so christened himself:"don't
talk as if you were alluding to people's names; but say what you
mean."

"I mean, my dear ma'am, that we want a little change of air
and scene."

"Bless the man!" said I; "does he mean we or me!"

"I mean you, ma'am."

"Then Lard forgive you, Doctor Towers," I said; "why don't
you get into a habit of expressing yourself in a straightforward
manner, like a loyal subject of our gracious Queen Victoria, and
a member of the Church of England?"

Towers laughed, as he generally does when he has fidgeted
me into any of my impatient ways—one of my states, as I call
them—and then he began,—"Tone, ma'am, Tone, is all you re-

quire!"

He appealed to Trottle, who just then came in with the coal-scuttle, looking, in his nice black suit, like an amiable man putting on coals from motives of benevolence.

Trottle (whom I always call my right hand) has been in my service two-and-thirty years. He entered my service, far away from England. He is the best of creatures, and the most respectable of men; but, opinionated.

"What you want, ma'am," says Trottle, making up the fire in his quiet and skilful way, "is Tone."

"Lard forgive you both!" says I, bursting out a-laughing; "I see you are in a conspiracy against me, so I suppose you must do what you like with me, and take me to London for a change."

For some weeks Towers had hinted at London, and consequently I was prepared for him. When we had got to this point, we got on so expeditiously, that Trottle was packed off to London next day but one, to find some sort of place for me to lay my troublesome old head in.

Trottle came back to me at the Wells after two days' absence, with accounts of a charming place that could be taken for six months certain, with liberty to renew on the same terms for another six, and which really did afford every accommodation that I wanted. "Could you really find no fault at all in the rooms, Trottle?" I asked him.

"Not a single one, ma'am. They are exactly suitable to you. There is not a fault in them. There is but one fault outside of them."

"And what's that?"

"They are opposite a House to Let."

"O!" I said, considering of it. "But is that such a very great objection?"

"I think it my duty to mention it, ma'am. It is a dull object to look at. Otherwise, I was so greatly pleased with the lodging that I should have closed with the terms at once, as I had your authority to do."

Trottle thinking so highly of the place, in my interest, I wished not to disappoint him. Consequently I said:

"The empty House may let, perhaps."

"O, dear no, ma'am," said Trottle, shaking his head with decision; "it won't let. It never does let, ma'am."

"Mercy me! Why not?"

"Nobody knows, ma'am. All I have to mention is, ma'am, that the House won't let!"

"How long has this unfortunate House been to let, in the name of Fortune?" said I.

"Ever so long," said Trottle. "Years."

"Is it in ruins?"

"It's a good deal out of repair, ma'am, but it's not in ruins."

The long and the short of this business was, that next day I had a pair of post-horses put to my chariot—for, I never travel by railway: not that I have anything to say against railways, except that they came in when I was too old to take to them; and that they made ducks and drakes of a few turnpike-bonds I had—and so I went up myself, with Trottle in the rumble, to look at the inside of this same lodging, and at the outside of this same House.

As I say, I went and saw for myself. The lodging was perfect. That, I was sure it would be; because Trottle is the best judge of comfort I know. The empty house was an eyesore; and that I was sure it would be too, for the same reason. However, setting the one thing against the other, the good against the bad, the lodging very soon got the victory over the House. My lawyer, Mr. Squares, of Crown Office Row; Temple, drew up an agreement; which his young man jabbered over so dreadfully when he read it to me, that I didn't understand one word of it except my own name; and hardly that, and I signed it, and the other party signed it, and, in three weeks' time, I moved my old bones, bag and baggage, up to London.

For the first month or so, I arranged to leave Trottle at the Wells. I made this arrangement, not only because there was a good deal to take care of in the way of my school-children and pensioners, and also of a new stove in the hall to air the house in my absence, which appeared to me calculated to blow up and burst; but, like-wise because I suspect Trottle (though the steadiest of men, and a widower between sixty and seventy) to be what I call rather a Phi-landerer. I mean, that when any friend comes down to see me and brings a maid, Trottle is always remarkably ready to show that maid the Wells of an evening; and that I have more than once noticed the shadow of his arm, outside the room door nearly opposite my chair, encircling that maid's waist on the landing, like a table-cloth brush.

Therefore, I thought it just as well, before any London Phi-landering took place, that I should have a little time to look round me, and to see what girls were in and about the place. So, nobody stayed with me in my new lodging at first after Trottle had established me there safe and sound, but Peggy Flobbins, my maid; a most affectionate and attached woman, who never was an object of Philandering since I have known her, and is not likely to begin to become so after nine-and-twenty years next March.

It was the fifth of November when I first breakfasted in my new rooms. The Guys were going about in the brown fog, like magnified monsters of insects in table-beer, and there was a Guy resting on the door-steps of the House to Let. I put on my glasses, partly to see how the boys were pleased with what I sent them out by Peggy, and partly to make sure that she didn't approach too near the ridiculous object, which of course was full of sky-rockets, and might go off into bangs at any moment. In this way it happened that the first time I ever looked at the House to Let, after I became its opposite neighbour, I had my glasses on. And this might not have happened once in fifty times, for my sight is uncommonly good for my time of life; and I wear glasses as little as I can, for fear of spoiling it.

I knew already that it was a ten-roomed house, very dirty, and much dilapidated; that the area-rails were rusty and peeling away, and that two or three of them were wanting, or half-want-ing; that there were broken panes of glass in the windows, and blotches of mud on other panes, which the boys had thrown at them; that there was quite a collection of stones in the area, also proceeding from those Young Mischiefs; that there were games chalked on the pavement before the house, and likenesses of ghosts chalked on the street-door; that the windows were all darkened by rotting old blinds, or shutters, or both; that the bills "To Let," had curled up, as if the damp air of the place had given them cramps; or had dropped down into corners, as if they were no more. I had seen all this on my first visit, and I had remarked to Trottle, that the lower part of the black board about terms was split away; that the rest had become illegible, and that the very stone of the door-steps was broken across. Notwithstanding, I sat at my breakfast table on that Please to Remember the fifth of November morning, staring at the House through my glasses, as if I had never looked at it before.

All at once—in the first-floor window on my right—down in a low corner, at a hole in a blind or a shutter—I found that I was looking at a secret Eye. The reflection of my fire may have touched it and made it shine; but, I saw it shine and vanish.

The eye might have seen me, or it might not have seen me, sitting there in the glow of my fire—you can take which probability you prefer, without offence—but something struck through my frame, as if the sparkle of this eye had been electric, and had flashed straight at me. It had such an effect upon me, that I could not remain by myself, and I rang for Flobbins, and invented some little jobs for her, to keep her in the room. After my breakfast was cleared away, I sat in the same place with my glasses on, moving my head, now so, and now so, trying whether, with the shining of my fire and the flaws in the window-glass, I could reproduce any sparkle seeming to be up there, that was like the sparkle of an eye. But no; I could make nothing like it. I could make ripples and crooked lines in the front of the House to Let, and I could even twist one window up and loop it into another; but, I could make no eye, nor anything like an eye. So I convinced myself that I really had seen an eye.

Well, to be sure I could not get rid of the impression of this eye, and it troubled me and troubled me, until it was almost a torment. I don't think I was previously inclined to concern my head much about the opposite House; but, after this eye, my head was full of the house; and I thought of little else than the house, and I watched the house, and I talked about the house, and I dreamed of the house. In all this, I fully believe now, there was a good Providence. But, you will judge for yourself about that, bye-and-bye.

My landlord was a butler, who had married a cook, and set up housekeeping. They had not kept house longer than a couple of years, and they knew no more about the House to Let than I did. Neither could I find out anything concerning it among the trades-people or otherwise; further than what Trottle had told me at first. It had been empty, some said six years, some said eight, some said ten. It never did let, they all agreed, and it never would let.

I soon felt convinced that I should work myself into one of my states about the House; and I soon did. I lived for a whole month
in a flurry, that was always getting worse. Towers's prescriptions, which I had brought to London with me, were of no more use than nothing. In the cold winter sunlight, in the thick winter fog, in the black winter rain, in the white winter snow, the House was equally on my mind. I have heard, as everybody else has, of a spirit's haunting a house; but I have had my own personal experience of a house's haunting a spirit; for that House haunted mine.

In all that month's time, I never saw anyone go into the House nor come out of the House. I supposed that such a thing must take place sometimes, in the dead of the night, or the glimmer of the morning; but, I never saw it done. I got no relief from having my curtains drawn when it came on dark, and shutting out the House. The Eye then began to shine in my fire.

I am a single old woman. I should say at once, without being at all afraid of the name, I am an old maid; only that I am older than the phrase would express. The time was when I had my love-trouble, but, it is long and long ago. He was killed at sea

(Dear Heaven rest his blessed head!) when I was twenty-five. I have all my life, since ever I can remember, been deeply fond of children. I have always felt such a love for them, that I have had my sorrowful and sinful times when I have fancied something must have gone wrong in my life—something must have been turned aside from its original intention I mean—or I should have been the proud and happy mother of many children, and a fond old grandmother this day. I have soon known better in the cheerfulness and contentment that God has blessed me with and given me abundant reason for; and yet I have had to dry my eyes even then, when I have thought of my dear, brave, hopeful, handsome, bright-eyed Charley, and the trust meant to cheer me with. Charley was my youngest brother, and he went to India. He married there, and sent his gentle little wife home to me to be confined, and she was to go back to him, and the baby was to be left with me, and I was to bring it up. It never belonged to this life.

It took its silent place among the other incidents in my story that might have been, but never were. I had hardly time to whisper to her "Dead my own!" or she to answer, "Ashes to ashes, dust to dust! O lay it on my breast and comfort Charley!" when she had gone to seek her baby at Our Saviour's feet. I went to Charley, and I told him there was nothing left but me, poor me; and I lived with Charley, out there, several years. He was a man of fifty, when he fell asleep in my arms. His face had changed to be almost old and a little stern; but, it softened, and softened when I laid it down that I might cry and pray beside it; and, when I looked at it for the last time, it was my dear, untroubled, handsome, youthful Charley of long ago.—I was going on to tell that the loneliness of the House to Let brought back all these recollections, and that they had quite pierced my heart one evening, when Flobbins, opening the door, and looking very much as if she wanted to laugh but thought better of it, said: "Mr. Jabez Jarber, ma'am!"

Upon which Mr. Jarber ambled in, in his usual absurd way, saying:"Sophonisba!"

Which I am obliged to confess is my name. A pretty one and proper one enough when it was given to me: but, a good many years out of date now, and always sounding particularly high-flown and comical from his lips. So I said, sharply:

"Though it is Sophonisba, Jarber, you are not obliged to mention it, that *I* see."

In reply to this observation, the ridiculous man put the tips of my five right-hand fingers to his lips, and said again, with an aggravating accent on the third syllable:

"Sophon*is*ba!"

I don't burn lamps, because I can't abide the smell of oil, and wax candles belonged to my day. I hope the convenient situation of one of my tall old candlesticks on the table at my elbow will be my excuse for saying, that if he did that again, I would chop his toes with it. (I am sorry to add that when I told him so, I knew his toes to be tender.) But, really, at my time of life and at Jarber's, it is too much of a good thing. There is an orchestra still standing in the open air at the Wells, before which, in the presence of a throng of fine company, I have walked a minuet with Jarber. But, there is a house still standing, in which I have worn a pinafore, and had a tooth drawn by fastening a thread to the tooth and the door-handle, and toddling away from the door.

And how should I look now, at my years, in a pinafore, or having a door for my dentist? Besides, Jarber always was more or less an absurd man. He was sweetly dressed, and beautifully perfumed, and many girls of my day would have given their ears for him; though I am bound to add that he never cared a fig for them, or their advances either, and that he was very constant to me. For, he not only proposed to me before my love-happiness ended in sorrow, but afterwards too: not once, nor yet twice: nor will we say how many times. However many they were, or however few they were, the last time he paid me that compliment was immediately after he had presented me with a digestive dinner-pill stuck on the point of a pin.

And I said on that occasion, laughing heartily, "Now, Jarber, if you don't know that two people whose united ages would make about a hundred and fifty, have got to be old, I do; and I beg to swallow this nonsense in the form of this pill" (which I took on the spot), "and I request to, hear no more of it."

After that, he conducted himself pretty well. He was always a little squeezed man, was Jarber, in little sprigged waistcoats; and he had always little legs and a little smile, and a little voice, and little round-about ways. As long as I can remember him he was always going little errands for people, and carrying little gossip.

At this present time when he called me "Sophonisba!" he had a little old-fashioned lodging in that new neighbourhood of mine. I had not seen him for two or three years, but I had heard that he still went out with a little perspective-glass and stood on door-steps in Saint James's Street, to see the nobility go to Court; and went in his little cloak and galoshes outside Willis's rooms to see them go to Almack's; and caught the frightfullest colds, and got himself trodden upon by coachmen and linkmen, until he went home to his landlady a mass of bruises, and had to be nursed for a month.

Jarber took off his little fur-collared cloak, and sat down opposite me, with his little cane and hat in his hand.

"Let us have no more Sophonisbaing, if YOU please, Jarber," I said. "Call me Sarah. How do you do? I hope you are pretty well."

"Thank you. And you?" said Jarber.

"I am as well as an old woman can expect to be."

Jarber was beginning:

"Say, not old, Sophon—" but I looked at the candlestick, and he left off; pretending not to have said anything.

"I am infirm, of course," I said, "and so are you. Let us both be thankful it's no worse."

"Is it possible that you look worried?" said Jarber.

"It is very possible. I have no doubt it is the fact."

"And what has worried my Soph—, soft-hearted friend," said Jarber.

"Something not easy, I suppose, to comprehend. I am worried to death by a House to Let, over the way."

Jarber went with his little tiptoe step to the window-curtains, peeped out, and looked round at me.

"Yes," said I, in answer: "that house."

After peeping out again, Jarber came back to his chair with a tender air, and asked: "How does it worry you, S—arah?"

"It is a mystery to me," said I. "Of course every house IS a mystery, more or less; but, something that I don't care to mention" (for truly the Eye was so slight a thing to mention that I was more than half ashamed of it), "has made that House so mysterious to me, and has so fixed it in my mind, that I have had no peace for a month. I foresee that I shall have no peace, either, until Trottle comes to me, next Monday."

I might have mentioned before, that there is a long-standing jealousy between Trottle and Jarber; and that there is never any love lost between those two.

"TROTTLE," petulantly repeated Jarber, with a little flourish of his cane; "how is TROTTLE to restore the lost peace of Sarah?"

"He will exert himself to find out something about the House. I have fallen into that state about it, that I really must discover by some means or other, good or bad, fair or foul, how and why it is that that House remains To Let."

"And why Trottle? Why not," putting his little hat to his heart; "why not, Jarber?"

"To tell you the truth, I have never thought of Jarber in the matter. And now I do think of Jarber, through your having the kindness to suggest him—for which I am really and truly obliged to you—I don't think he could do it."

"Sarah!"

"I think it would be too much for you, Jarber."

"Sarah!"

"There would be coming and going, and fetching and carrying, Jarber, and you might catch cold."

"Sarah! What can be done by Trottle, can be done by me. I am on terms of acquaintance with every person of responsibility in this parish. I am intimate at the Circulating Library. I converse daily with the Assessed Taxes. I lodge with the Water Rate. I know the Medical Man. I lounge habitually at the House Agent's. I dine with the Churchwardens. I move to the Guardians. Trottle! A person in the sphere of a domestic, and totally unknown to society!"

"Don't be warm, Jarber. In mentioning Trottle, I have naturally relied on my Right-Hand, who would take any trouble to gratify even a whim of his old mistress's. But, if you can find out anything to help to unravel the mystery of this House to Let, I shall be fully as much obliged to you as if there was never a Trottle in the land."

Jarber rose and put on his little cloak. A couple of fierce brass lions held it tight round his little throat; but a couple of the mildest hares might have done that, I am sure. "Sarah," he said, "I go. Expect me on Monday evening, the Sixth, when perhaps you will give me a cup of tea;—may I ask for no Green? *Adieu!*"

This was on a Thursday, the second of December. When I reflected that Trottle would come back on Monday, too, I had My misgivings as to the difficulty of keeping the two powers from open warfare, and indeed I was more uneasy than I quite like to confess. However, the empty House swallowed up that thought next morning, as it swallowed up most other thoughts now, and the House quite preyed upon me all that day, and all the Saturday.

It was a very wet Sunday: raining and blowing from morning to night. When the bells rang for afternoon church, they seemed to ring in the commotion of the puddles as well as in the wind, and they sounded very loud and dismal indeed, and the street looked very dismal indeed, and the House looked dismallest of all.

I was reading my prayers near the light, and my fire was growing in the darkening window-glass, when, looking up, as I prayed for the fatherless children and widows and all who were desolate and oppressed,—I saw the Eye again. It passed in a moment, as it had done before; but, this time, I was inwardly more convinced that I had seen it.

Well to be sure, I HAD a night that night! Whenever I closed my own eyes, it was to see eyes. Next morning, at an unreasonably, and I should have said (but for that railroad) an impossibly early hour, comes Trottle. As soon as he had told me all about the Wells, I told him all about the House. He listened with as great interest and attention as I could possibly wish, until I came to Jabez Jarber, when he cooled in an instant, and became opinionated.

"Now, Trottle," I said, pretending not to notice, "when Mr. Jarber comes back this evening, we must all lay our heads together."

"I should hardly think that would be wanted, ma'am; Mr. Jarber's head is surely equal to anything."

Being determined not to notice, I said again, that we must all lay our heads together.

"Whatever you order, ma'am, shall be obeyed. Still, it cannot be doubted, I should think, that Mr. Jarber's head is equal, if not superior, to any pressure that can be brought to bear upon it."

This was provoking; and his way, when he came in and out all through the day, of pretending not to see the House to Let, was more provoking still. However, being quite resolved not to notice, I gave no sign whatever that I did notice. But, when evening came, and he showed in Jarber, and, when Jarber wouldn't be helped off with his cloak, and poked his cane into cane chairbacks and china ornaments and his own eye, in trying to unclasp his brazen lions of himself (which he couldn't do, after all), I could have shaken them both.

As it was, I only shook the teapot, and made the tea. Jarber had brought from under his cloak, a roll of paper, with which he had triumphantly pointed over the way, like the Ghost of Hamlet's Father appearing to the late Mr. Kemble, and which he had laid on the table.

"A discovery?" said I, pointing to it, when he was seated, and had got his teacup.—"Don't go, Trottle."

"The first of a series of discoveries," answered Jarber. "Account of a former tenant, compiled from the Water Rate, and

Medical Man."

"Don't go, Trottle," I repeated. For, I saw him making imperceptibly to the door.

"Begging your pardon, ma'am, I might be in Mr. Jarber's way?"

Jarber looked that he decidedly thought he might be. I relieved myself with a good angry croak, and said—always determined not to notice:

"Have the goodness to sit down, if you please, Trottle. I wish you to hear this."

Trottle bowed in the stiffest manner, and took the remotest chair he could find. Even that, he moved close to the draught from the keyhole of the door.

"Firstly," Jarber began, after sipping his tea, "would my Sophon—"

"Begin again, Jarber," said I.

"Would you be much surprised, if this House to Let should turn out to be the property of a relation of your own?"

"I should indeed be very much surprised."

"Then it belongs to your first cousin (I learn, by the way, that he is ill at this time) George Forley."

"Then that is a bad beginning. I cannot deny that George Forley stands in the relation of first cousin to me; but I hold no communication with him. George Forley has been a hard, bitter, stony father to a child now dead. George Forley was most implacable and unrelenting to one of his two daughters who made a poor marriage. George Forley brought all the weight of his band to bear as heavily against that crushed thing, as he brought it to bear lightly, favouringly, and advantageously upon her sister, who made a rich marriage. I hope that, with the measure George Forley meted, it may not be measured out to him again. I will give George Forley no worse wish."

I was strong upon the subject, and I could not keep the tears out of my eyes; for, that young girl's was a cruel story, and I had dropped many a tear over it before.

"The house being George Forley's," said I, "is almost enough to account for there being a Fate upon it, if Fate there is. Is there anything about George Forley in those sheets of paper?"

"Not a word."

"I am glad to hear it. Please to read on. Trottle, why don't you come nearer? Why do you sit mortifying yourself in those arctic regions? Come nearer."

"Thank you, ma'am; I am quite near enough to Mr. Jarber."

Jarber rounded his chair, to get his back full to my opinionated friend and servant, and, beginning to read, tossed the words at him over his (Jabez Jarber's) own ear and shoulder.

He read what follows:

CHAPTER 2
THE MANCHESTER MARRIAGE

Mr. and Mrs. Openshaw came from Manchester to London and took the House To Let. He had been, what is called in Lancashire, a Salesman for a large manufacturing firm, who were extending their business, and opening a warehouse in London; where Mr. Openshaw was now to superintend the business. He rather enjoyed the change of residence; having a kind of curiosity about London, which he had never yet been able to gratify in his brief visits to the metropolis. At the same time he had an odd, shrewd, contempt for the inhabitants; whom he had always pictured to himself as fine, lazy people; caring nothing but for fashion and aristocracy, and lounging away their days in Bond Street, and such places; ruining good English, and ready in their turn to despise him as a provincial.

The hours that the men of business kept in the city scandalised him too; accustomed as he was to the early dinners of Manchester folk, and the consequently far longer evenings. Still, he was pleased to go to London; though he would not for the world have confessed it, even to himself, and always spoke of the step to his friends as one demanded of him by the interests of his employers, and sweetened to him by a considerable increase of salary. His salary indeed was so liberal that he might have been justified in taking a much larger House than this one, had he not thought himself bound to set an example to Londoners of how little a Manchester man of business cared for show. Inside, however, he furnished the House with an unusual degree of comfort, and, in the winter time, he insisted on keeping up as large fires as the grates would allow, in every room where the temperature was in the least chilly.

Moreover, his northern sense of hospitality was such, that, if he were at home, he could hardly suffer a visitor to leave the house without forcing meat and drink upon him. Every servant in the house was well warmed, well fed, and kindly treated; for their master scorned all petty saving in aught that conduced to comfort; while he amused himself by following out all his accustomed habits and individual ways in defiance of what any of his new neighbours might think.

His wife was a pretty, gentle woman, of suitable age and character. He was forty-two, she thirty-five. He was loud and decided; she soft and yielding. They had two children or rather, I should say, she had two; for the elder, a girl of eleven, was Mrs. Openshaw's child by Frank Wilson her first husband. The younger was a little boy, Edwin, who could just prattle, and to whom his father delighted to speak in the broadest and most unintelligible Lancashire dialect, in order to keep up what he called the true Saxon accent.

Mrs. Openshaw's Christian-name was Alice, and her first husband had been her own cousin. She was the orphan niece of a sea-captain in Liverpool: a quiet, grave little creature, of great personal attraction when she was fifteen or sixteen, with regular features and a blooming complexion. But she was very shy, and believed herself to be very stupid and awkward; and was frequently scolded by her aunt, her own uncle's second wife. So when her cousin, Frank Wilson, came home from a long absence at sea, and first was kind and protective to her; secondly, attentive and thirdly, desperately in love with her, she hardly knew how to be grateful enough to him.

It is true she would have preferred his remaining in the first or second stages of behaviour; for his violent love puzzled and frightened her. Her uncle neither helped nor hindered the love affair though it was going on under his own eyes. Frank's stepmother had such a variable temper, that there was no knowing whether what she liked one day she would like the next, or not. At length she went to such extremes of crossness, that Alice was only too glad to shut her eyes and rush blindly at the chance of escape from domestic tyranny offered her by a marriage with her cousin; and, liking him better than anyone in the world except her uncle (who was at this time at sea) she went off one morning and was married to him; her only bridesmaid being the housemaid at her aunt's.

The consequence was, that Frank and his wife went into lodgings, and Mrs. Wilson refused to see them, and turned away Norah, the warm-hearted housemaid; whom they accordingly took into their service. When Captain Wilson returned from his voyage, he was very cordial with the young couple, and spent many an evening at their lodgings; smoking his pipe, and sipping his grog; but he told them that, for quietness' sake, he could not ask them to his own house; for his wife was bitter against them. They were not very unhappy about this.

The seed of future unhappiness lay rather in Frank's vehement, passionate disposition; which led him to resent his wife's shyness and want of demonstration as failures in conjugal duty. He was already tormenting himself, and her too, in a slighter degree, by apprehensions and imaginations of what might befall her during his approaching absence at sea. At last he went to his father and urged him to insist upon Alice's being once more received under his roof; the more especially as there was now a prospect of her confinement while her husband was away on his voyage.

Captain Wilson was, as he himself expressed it, "breaking up," and unwilling to undergo the excitement of a scene; yet he felt that what his son said was true. So he went to his wife. And before Frank went to sea, he had the comfort of seeing his wife installed in her old little garret in his father's house. To have placed her in the one best spare room was a step beyond

Mrs. Wilson's powers of submission or generosity. The worst part about it, however, was that the faithful Norah had to be dismissed. Her place as housemaid had been filled up; and, even had it not, she had forfeited Mrs. Wilson's good opinion forever. She comforted her young master and mistress by pleasant prophecies of the time when they would have a household of their own; of which, in whatever service she might be in the meantime, she should be sure to form part.

Almost the last action Frank Wilson did, before setting sail, was going with Alice to see Norah once more at her mother's house. And then he went away. Alice's father-in-law grew more and more feeble as winter advanced. She was of great use to her step-mother in nursing and amusing him; and, although there was anxiety enough in the household, there was perhaps more of peace than there had been for years; for Mrs. Wilson had not a bad heart, and was softened by the visible approach of death to one whom she loved, and touched by the lonely condition of the young creature, expecting her first confinement in her husband's absence. To this relenting mood Norah owed the permission to come and nurse Alice when her baby was born, and to remain to attend on Captain Wilson.

Before one letter had been received from Frank (who had sailed for the East Indies and China), his father died. Alice was always glad to remember that he had held her baby in his arms, and kissed and blessed it before his death. After that, and the consequent examination into the state of his affairs, it was found that he had left far less property than people had been led by his style of living to imagine; and, what money there was, was all settled upon his wife, and at her disposal after her death. This did not signify much to Alice, as Frank was now first mate of his ship, and, in another voyage or two, would be captain. Meanwhile he had left her some hundreds (all his savings) in the bank.

It became time for Alice to hear from her husband. One letter from the Cape she had already received. The next was to announce his arrival in India. As week after week passed over, and no intelligence of the ship's arrival reached the office of the

owners, and the Captain's wife was in the same state of ignorant suspense as Alice herself, her fears grew most oppressive. At
length the day came when, in reply to her inquiry at the Ship-
ping Office, they told her that the owners had given up Hope of
ever hearing more of the Betsy-Jane, and had sent in their claim
upon the underwriters. Now that he was gone forever, she first
felt a yearning, longing love for the kind cousin, the dear friend,
the sympathising protector, whom she should never see again,-
first felt a passionate desire to show him his child, whom she
had hitherto rather craved to have all to herself—her own sole
possession. Her grief was, however, noiseless, and quiet—rather
to the scandal of Mrs. Wilson; who bewailed her stepson as if
he and she had always lived together in perfect harmony, and
who evidently thought it her duty to burst into fresh tears at
every strange face she saw; dwelling on his poor young widow's
desolate state, and the helplessness of the fatherless child, with an
unction, as if she liked the excitement of the sorrowful story.

So passed away the first days of Alice's widowhood. Bye-and-
bye things subsided into their natural and tranquil course. But,
as if this young creature was always to be in some heavy trouble,
her ewe-lamb began to be ailing, pining and sickly. The child's
mysterious illness turned out to be some affection of the spine
likely to affect health; but not to shorten life—at least so the doctors said. But the long dreary suffering of one whom a mother
loves as Alice loved her only child, is hard to look forward to.
Only Norah guessed what Alice suffered; no one but God knew.
And so it fell out, that when Mrs. Wilson, the elder, came to
her one day in violent distress, occasioned by a very material
diminution in the value the property that her husband had left
her—a diminution which made her income barely enough to
support herself, much less Alice—the latter could hardly understand how anything which did not touch health or life could
cause such grief; and she received the intelligence with irritating
composure.

But when, that afternoon, the little sick child was brought
in, and the grandmother—who after all loved it well—began a

fresh moan over her losses to its unconscious ears—saying how she had planned to consult this or that doctor, and to give it this or that comfort or luxury in after yearn but that now all chance of this had passed away—Alice's heart was touched, and she drew near to Mrs. Wilson with unwonted caresses, and, in a spirit not unlike to that of, Ruth, entreated, that come what would, they might remain together.

After much discussion in succeeding days, it was arranged that Mrs. Wilson should take a house in Manchester, furnishing it partly with what furniture she had, and providing the rest with Alice's remaining two hundred pounds. Mrs. Wilson was herself a Manchester woman, and naturally longed to return to her native town. Some connections of her own at that time required lodgings, for which they were willing to pay pretty handsomely. Alice undertook the active superintendence and superior work of the household. Norah, willing faithful Norah, offered to cook, scour, do anything in short, so that, she might but remain with them. The plan succeeded. For some years their first lodgers remained with them, and all went smoothly,—with the one sad exception of the little girl's increasing deformity. How that mother loved that child, is not for words to tell!

Then came a break of misfortune. Their lodgers left, and no one succeeded to them. After some months they had to remove to a smaller house; and Alice's tender conscience was torn by the idea that she ought not to be a burden to her mother-in-law, but ought to go out and seek her own maintenance. And leave her child! The thought came like the sweeping boom of a funeral bell over her heart.

Bye-and-bye, Mr. Openshaw came to lodge with them. He had started in life as the errand-boy and sweeper-out of a warehouse; had struggled up through all the grades of employment in the place, fighting his way through the hard striving Manchester life with strong pushing energy of character. Every spare moment of time had been sternly given up to self-teaching. He was a capital accountant, a good French and German scholar, a keen, far-seeing tradesman; understanding markets, and the bearing of events, both near and distant, on trade: and yet, with such vivid attention to present details, that I do not think he ever saw a group of flowers in the fields without thinking whether their colours would, or would not, form harmonious contrasts in the coming spring muslins and prints. He went to debating societies, and threw himself with all his heart and soul into politics; esteeming, it must be owned, every man a fool or a knave who differed from him, and overthrowing his opponents rather by the loud strength of his language than the calm strength if his logic. There was something of the Yankee in all this. Indeed his theory ran parallel to the famous Yankee motto—*England flogs creation, and Manchester flogs England.*

Such a man, as may be fancied, had had no time for falling in love, or any such nonsense. At the age when most young men go through their courting and matrimony, he had not the means of keeping a wife, and was far too practical to think of having one. And now that he was in easy circumstances, a rising man, he considered women almost as incumbrances to the world, with whom a man had better have as little to do as possible. His first impression of Alice was indistinct, and he did not care enough about her to make it distinct. "A pretty yea-nay kind of woman," would have been his description of her, if he had been pushed into a corner.

He was rather afraid, in the beginning, that her quiet ways arose from a listlessness and laziness of character which would have been exceedingly discordant to his active energetic nature. But, when he found out the punctuality with which his wishes were attended to, and her work was done; when he was called in the morning at the very stroke of the clock, his shaving-water scalding hot, his fire bright, his coffee made exactly as his peculiar fancy dictated, (for he was a man who had his theory about everything, based upon what he knew of science, and often perfectly original)—then he began to think: not that Alice had any peculiar merit; but that he had got into remarkably good lodgings: his restlessness wore away, and he began to consider himself as almost settled for life in them.

Mr. Openshaw had been too busy, all his life, to be introspective. He did not know that he had any tenderness in his nature; and if he had become conscious of its abstract existence, he would have considered it as a manifestation of disease in some part of his nature. But he was decoyed into pity unawares; and pity led on to tenderness. That little helpless child—always carried about by one of the three busy women of the house, or else patiently threading coloured beads in the chair from which, by no effort of its own, could it ever move; the great grave blue eyes, full of serious, not uncheerful, expression, giving to the small delicate face a look beyond its years; the soft plaintive voice dropping out but few words, so unlike the continual prattle of a child—caught Mr. Openshaw's attention in spite of himself.

One day—he half scorned himself for doing so—he cut short his dinner-hour to go in search of some toy which should take the place of those eternal beads. I forget what he bought; but, when he gave the present (which he took care to do in a short abrupt manner, and when no one was by to see him) he was almost thrilled by the flash of delight that came over that child's face, and could not help all through that afternoon going over and over again the picture left on his memory, by the bright effect of unexpected joy on the little girl's face.

When he returned home, he found his slippers placed by his sitting-room fire; and even more careful attention paid to his fancies than was habitual in those model lodgings. When Alice had taken the last of his tea-things away—she had been silent as usual till then—she stood for an instant with the door in her hand. Mr. Openshaw looked as if he were deep in his book, though in fact he did not see a line; but was heartily wishing the woman would be gone, and not make any palaver of gratitude. But she only said:

"I am very much obliged to you, sir. Thank you very much," and was gone, even before he could send her away with a "There, my good woman, that's enough!"

For some time longer he took no apparent notice of the child. He even hardened his heart into disregarding her sudden flush of colour, and little timid smile of recognition, when he saw her by chance. But, after all, this could not last forever; and, having a second time given way to tenderness, there was no relapse. The insidious enemy having thus entered his heart, in the guise of compassion to the child, soon assumed the more dangerous form of interest in the mother. He was aware of this change of feeling, despised himself for it, struggled with it nay, internally yielded to it and cherished it, long before he suffered the slightest expression of it, by word, action, or look, to escape him.

He watched Alice's docile obedient ways to her stepmother; the love which she had inspired in the rough Norah (roughened by the wear and tear of sorrow and years); but above all, he saw the wild, deep, passionate affection existing between her and her child. They spoke little to anyone else, or when any one else was by; but, when alone together, they talked, and murmured, and cooed, and chattered so continually, that Mr. Openshaw first wondered what they could find to say to each other, and next became irritated because they were always so grave and silent with him.

All this time, he was perpetually devising small new pleasures for the child. His thoughts ran, in a pertinacious way, upon the desolate life before her; and often he came back from his day's work loaded with the very thing Alice had been longing for, but had not been able to procure. One time it was a little chair for drawing the little sufferer along the streets, and many an evening that ensuing summer Mr. Openshaw drew her along himself, regardless of the remarks of his acquaintances. One day in autumn he put down his newspaper, as Alice came in with the breakfast, and said, in as indifferent a voice as he could assume: "Mrs. Frank, is there any reason why we two should not put up our horses together?"

Alice stood still in perplexed wonder. What did he mean? He had resumed the reading of his newspaper, as if he did not expect any answer; so she found silence her safest course, and went on quietly arranging his breakfast without another word passing between them. Just as he was leaving the house, to go to the warehouse as usual, he turned back and put his head into the bright, neat, tidy kitchen, where all the women breakfasted in the morning:

"You'll think of what I said, Mrs. Frank" (this was her name with the lodgers), "and let me have your opinion upon it to-night." Alice was thankful that her mother and Norah were too busy talking together to attend much to this speech. She determined not to think about it at all through the day; and, of course, the effort not to think made her think all the more. At night she sent up Norah with his tea. But Mr. Openshaw almost knocked Norah down as she was going out at the door, by pushing past her and calling out "Mrs. Frank!" in an impatient voice, at the top of the stairs.

Alice went up, rather than seem to have affixed too much meaning to his words.

"Well, Mrs. Frank," he said, "what answer? Don't make it too long; for I have lots of office-work to get through tonight."

"I hardly know what you meant, sir," said truthful Alice.

"Well! I should have thought you might have guessed. You're not new at this sort of work, and I am. However, I'll make it plain this time. Will you have me to be thy wedded husband, and serve me, and love me, and honour me, and all that sort of thing? Because if you will, I will do as much by you, and be a father to your child—and that's more than is put in the prayer-book. Now, I'm a man of my word; and what I say, I feel; and what I promise, I'll do. Now, for your answer!"

Alice was silent. He began to make the tea, as if her reply was a matter of perfect indifference to him; but, as soon as that was done, he became impatient.

"Well?" said he.

"How long, sir, may I have to think over it?"

"Three minutes!" (looking at his watch). "You've had two already—that makes five. Be a sensible woman, say Yes, and sit down to tea with me, and we'll talk it over together; for, after tea, I shall be busy; say No" (he hesitated a moment to try and keep his voice in the same tone), "and I shan't say another word about it, but pay up a year's rent for my rooms tomorrow, and be off. Time's up! Yes or no?"

"If you please, sir,—you have been so good to little Ailsie—"

"There, sit down comfortably by me on the sofa, and let us have our tea together. I am glad to find you are as good and sensible as I took for."

And this was Alice Wilson's second wooing.

Mr. Openshaw's will was too strong, and his circumstances too good, for him not to carry all before him. He settled Mrs. Wilson in a comfortable house of her own, and made her quite independent of lodgers. The little that Alice said with regard to future plans was in Norah's behalf.

"No," said Mr. Openshaw. "Norah shall take care of the old lady as long as she lives; and, after that, she shall either come and live with us, or, if she likes it better, she shall have a provision for life—for your sake, missus. No one who has been good to you or the child shall go unrewarded. But even the little one will be better for some fresh stuff about her. Get her a bright, sensible girl as a nurse: one who won't go rubbing her with calf's-foot jelly as Norah does; wasting good stuff outside that ought to go in, but will follow doctors' directions; which, as you must see pretty clearly by this time, Norah won't; because they give the poor little wench pain.

"Now, I'm not above being nesh for other folks myself. I can stand a good blow, and never change colour; but, set me in the operating-room in the infirmary, and I turn as sick as a girl. Yet, if need were, I would hold the little wench on my knees while she screeched with pain, if it were to do her poor back good. Nay, nay, wench! keep your white looks for the time when it comes—I don't say it ever will. But this I know, Norah will spare the child and cheat the doctor if she can. Now, I say, give the bairn a year or two's chance, and then, when the pack of doctors have done their best—and, maybe, the old lady has gone—we'll have Norah back, or do better for her."

The pack of doctors could do no good to little Ailsie. She was beyond their power. But her father (for so he insisted on being called, and also on Alice's no longer retaining the appellation of Mama, but becoming henceforward Mother), by his healthy cheerfulness of manner, his clear decision of purpose, his odd turns and quirks of humour, added to his real strong love for the helpless little girl, infused a new element of brightness and confidence into her life; and, though her back remained the same, her general health was strengthened, and Alice—never going beyond a smile herself—had the pleasure of seeing her child taught to laugh.

As for Alice's own life, it was happier than it had ever been. Mr. Openshaw required no demonstration, no expressions of affection from her. Indeed, these would rather have disgusted him. Alice could love deeply, but could not talk about it. The perpetual requirement of loving words, looks, and caresses, and misconstruing their absence into absence of love, had been the great trial of her former married life. Now, all went on clear and straight, under the guidance of her husband's strong sense, warm heart, and powerful will. Year by year their worldly prosperity increased.

At Mrs. Wilson's death, Norah came back to them, as nurse to the newly-born little Edwin; into which post she was not installed without a pretty strong oration on the part of the proud and happy father; who declared that if he found out that Norah ever tried to screen the boy by a falsehood, or to make him nesh either in body or mind, she should go that very day. Norah and Mr. Openshaw were not on the most thoroughly cordial terms; neither of them fully recognising or appreciating the other's best qualities.

This was the previous history of the Lancashire family who had now removed to London, and had come to occupy the House.

They had been there about a year, when Mr. Openshaw suddenly informed his wife that he had determined to heal long-standing feuds, and had asked his uncle and aunt Chadwick to come and pay them a visit and see London. Mrs. Openshaw had never seen this uncle and aunt of her husband's. Years before she had married him, there had been a quarrel. All she knew was, that Mr. Chadwick was a small manufacturer in a country town in South Lancashire. She was extremely pleased that the breach was to be healed, and began making preparations to render their visit pleasant.

They arrived at last. Going to see London was such an event to them, that Mrs. Chadwick had made all new linen fresh for the occasion—from night-caps downwards; and, as for gowns, ribbons, and collars, she might have been going into the wilds of Canada where never a shop is, so large was her stock. A fortnight before the day of her departure for London, she had formally called to take leave of all her acquaintance; saying she should need all the intermediate time for packing up. It was like a second wedding in her imagination; and, to complete the resemblance which an entirely new wardrobe made between the two events, her husband brought her back from Manchester, on the last market-day before they set off, a gorgeous pearl and amethyst brooch, saying, "Lunnon should see that Lancashire folks knew a handsome thing when they saw it."

For some time after Mr. and Mrs. Chadwick arrived at the Openshaws', there was no opportunity for wearing this brooch; but at length they obtained an order to see Buckingham Palace, and the spirit of loyalty demanded that Mrs. Chadwick should wear her best clothes in visiting the abode of her sovereign. On her return, she hastily changed her dress; for Mr. Openshaw had planned that they should go to Richmond, drink tea and return by moonlight. Accordingly, about five o'clock, Mr. and Mrs. Openshaw and Mr. and Mrs. Chadwick set off.

The housemaid and cook sate below, Norah hardly knew where. She was always engrossed in the nursery, in tending her two children, and in sitting by the restless, excitable Ailsie till she fell asleep. Bye-and-bye, the housemaid Bessy tapped gently at the door. Norah went to her, and they spoke in whispers.

"Nurse! there's someone downstairs wants you."

"Wants me! Who is it?"

"A gentleman—"

"A gentleman? Nonsense!"

"Well! a man, then, and he asks for you, and he rung at the front door bell, and has walked into the dining-room."

"You should never have let him," exclaimed Norah, "master and missus out—"

"I did not want him to come in; but when he heard you lived here, he walked past me, and sat down on the first chair, and said, 'Tell her to come and speak to me.' There is no gas lighted in the room, and supper is all set out."

"He'll be off with the spoons!" exclaimed Norah, putting the housemaid's fear into words, and preparing to leave the room, first, however, giving a look to Ailsie, sleeping soundly and calmly.

Downstairs she went, uneasy fears stirring in her bosom. Before she entered the dining-room she provided herself with a candle, and, with it in her hand, she went in, looking round her in the darkness for her visitor.

He was standing up, holding by the table. Norah and he looked at each other; gradual recognition coming into their eyes. "Norah?" at length he asked.

"Who are you?" asked Norah, with the sharp tones of alarm and incredulity. "I don't know you:" trying, by futile words of disbelief, to do away with the terrible fact before her.

"Am I so changed?" he said, pathetically. "I daresay I am. But, Norah, tell me!" he breathed hard, "where is my wife? Is she—is she alive?"

He came nearer to Norah, and would have taken her hand; but she backed away from him; looking at him all the time with staring eyes, as if he were some horrible object. Yet he was a handsome, bronzed, good-looking fellow, with beard and moustache, giving him a foreign-looking aspect; but his eyes! there was no mistaking those eager, beautiful eyes—the very same that Norah had watched not half-an-hour ago, till sleep stole softly over them.

"Tell me, Norah—I can bear it—I have feared it so often. Is she dead?" Norah still kept silence. "She is dead!" He hung on Norah's words and looks, as if for confirmation or contradiction.

"What shall I do?" groaned Norah. "O, sir! why did you come? How did you find me out? where have you been? We thought you dead, we did, indeed!" She poured out words and questions to gain time, as if time would help her.

"Norah! answer me this question, straight, by yes or no—Is my wife dead?"

"No, she is not!" said Norah, slowly and heavily.

"O what a relief! Did she receive my letters? But perhaps you don't know. Why did you leave her? Where is she? O Norah, tell me all quickly!"

"Mr. Frank!" said Norah at last, almost driven to bay by her terror lest her mistress should return at any moment, and find him there—unable to consider what was best to be done or said—rushing at something decisive, because she could not endure her present state: "Mr. Frank! we never heard a line from you, and the shipowners said you had gone down, you and everyone else. We thought you were dead, if ever man was, and poor Miss Alice and her little sick, helpless child! O, sir, you must guess it," cried the poor creature at last, bursting out into a passionate fit of crying, "for indeed I cannot tell it. But it was no one's fault. God help us all this night!"

Norah had sate down. She trembled too much to stand. He took her hands in his. He squeezed them hard, as if by physical pressure, the truth could be wrung out.

"Norah!" This time his tone was calm, stagnant as despair. "She has married again!"

Norah shook her head sadly. The grasp slowly relaxed. The man had fainted.

There was brandy in the room. Norah forced some drops into Mr. Frank's mouth, chafed his hands, and—when mere animal life returned, before the mind poured in its flood of memories and thoughts—she lifted him up, and rested his head against her

132

knees. Then she put a few crumbs of bread taken from the sup-per-table, soaked in brandy into his mouth. Suddenly he sprang to his feet.

"Where is she? Tell me this instant." He looked so wild, so mad, so desperate, that Norah felt herself to be in bodily danger; but her time of dread had gone by. She had been afraid to tell him the truth, and then she had been a coward. Now, her wits were sharpened by the sense of his desperate state. He must leave the house. She would pity him afterwards; but now she must rather command and upbraid; for he must leave the house before her mistress came home. That one necessity stood clear before her.

"She is not here; that is enough for you to know. Nor can I say exactly where she is" (which was true to the letter if not to the spirit). "Go away, and tell me where to find you tomorrow, and I will tell you all. My master and mistress may come back at any minute, and then what would become of me with a strange man in the house?"

Such an argument was too petty to touch his excited mind.

"I don't care for your master and mistress. If your master is a man, he must feel for me poor shipwrecked sailor that I am—kept for years a prisoner amongst savages, always, always, always thinking of my wife and my home—dreaming of her by night, talking to her, though she could not hear, by day. I loved her more than all heaven and earth put together. Tell me where she is, this instant, you wretched woman, who salved over her wick-edness to her, as you do to me."

The clock struck ten. Desperate positions require desperate measures.

"If you will leave the house now, I will come to you tomor-row and tell you all. What is more, you shall see your child now. She lies sleeping upstairs. O, sir, you have a child, you do not know that as yet—a little weakly girl—with just a heart and soul beyond her years. We have reared her up with such care: We watched her, for we thought for many a year she might die any day, and we tended her, and no hard thing has come near

133

her, and no rough word has ever been said to her. And now you, come and will take her life into your hand, and will crush it. Strangers to her have been kind to her; but her own father—Mr. Frank, I am her nurse, and I love her, and I tend her, and I would do anything for her that I could. Her mother's heart beats as hers beats; and, if she suffers a pain, her mother trembles all over.

"If she is happy, it is her mother that smiles and is glad. If she is growing stronger, her mother is healthy: if she dwindles, her mother languishes. If she dies—well, I don't know: it is not every one can lie down and die when they wish it. Come upstairs, Mr. Frank, and see your child. Seeing her will do good to your poor heart. Then go away, in God's name, just this one night— tomorrow, if need be, you can do anything—kill us all if you will, or show yourself—a great grand man, whom God will bless forever and ever. Come, Mr. Frank, the look of a sleeping child is sure to give peace."

She led him upstairs; at first almost helping his steps, till they came near the nursery door. She had almost forgotten the existence of little Edwin. It struck upon her with affright as the shaded light fell upon the other cot; but she skilfully threw that corner of the room into darkness, and let the light fall on the sleeping Ailsie. The child had thrown down the coverings, and her deformity, as she lay with her back to them, was plainly visible through her slight night-gown. Her little face, deprived of the lustre of her eyes, looked wan and pinched, and had a pathetic expression in it, even as she slept.

The poor father looked and looked with hungry, wistful eyes, into which the big tears came swelling up slowly, and dropped heavily down, as he stood trembling and shaking all over. Norah was angry with herself for growing impatient of the length of time that long lingering gaze lasted. She thought that she waited for full half-an-hour before Frank stirred. And then—instead of going away—he sank down on his knees by the bedside, and buried his face in the clothes. Little Ailsie stirred uneasily. Norah pulled him up in terror. She could afford no more time even for prayer in her extremity of fear; for surely the next moment would bring her mistress home. She took him forcibly by the arm; but, as he was going, his eye lighted on the other bed: he stopped. Intelligence came back into his face. His hands clenched.

"His child?" he asked.

"Her child," replied Norah. "God watches over him," said she instinctively; for Frank's looks excited her fears, and she needed to remind herself of the Protector of the helpless.

"God has not watched over me," he said, in despair; his thoughts apparently recoiling on his own desolate, deserted state. But Norah had no time for pity. Tomorrow she would be as compassionate as her heart prompted. At length she guided him downstairs and shut the outer door and bolted it—as if by bolts to keep out facts.

Then she went back into the dining-room and effaced all traces of his presence as far as she could. She went upstairs to the nursery and sate there, her head on her hand, thinking what was to come of all this misery. It seemed to her very long before they did return; yet it was hardly eleven o'clock. She so heard the loud, hearty Lancashire voices on the stairs; and, for the first time, she understood the contrast of the desolation of the poor man who had so lately gone forth in lonely despair.

It almost put her out of patience to see Mrs. Openshaw come in, calmly smiling, handsomely dressed, happy, easy, to inquire after her children.

"Did Ailsie go to sleep comfortably?" she whispered to Norah.

"Yes."

Her mother bent over her, looking at her slumbers with the soft eyes of love. How little she dreamed who had looked on her last! Then she went to Edwin, with perhaps less wistful anxiety in her countenance, but more of pride. She took off her things, to go down to supper. Norah saw her no more that night.

Beside the door into the passage, the sleeping-nursery opened out of Mr. and Mrs. Openshaw's room, in order that they might have the children more immediately under their own eyes. Early the next summer morning Mrs. Openshaw was awakened by Ailsie's startled call of "Mother! mother!" She sprang up, put on her dressing-gown, and went to her child. Ailsie was only half awake, and in a not uncommon state of terror.

"Who was he, mother? Tell me!"

"Who, my darling? No one is here. You have been dreaming love. Waken up quite. See, it is broad daylight."

"Yes," said Ailsie, looking round her; then clinging to her mother, said, "but a man was here in the night, mother."

"Nonsense, little goose. No man has ever come near you!"

"Yes, he did. He stood there. Just by Norah. A man with hair and a beard. And he knelt down and said his prayers. Norah knows he was here, mother" (half angrily, as Mrs. Openshaw shook her head in smiling incredulity).

"Well! we will ask Norah when she comes," said Mrs. Openshaw, soothingly. "But we won't talk any more about him now. It is not five o'clock; it is too early for you to get up. Shall I fetch you a book and read to you?"

"Don't leave me, mother," said the child, clinging to her. So Mrs. Openshaw sate on the bedside talking to Ailsie, and telling her of what they had done at Richmond the evening before, until the little girl's eyes slowly closed and she once more fell asleep.

"What was the matter?" asked Mr. Openshaw, as his wife returned to bed. "Ailsie wakened up in a fright, with some story of a man having been in the room to say his prayers,—a dream, I suppose." And no more was said at the time.

Mrs. Openshaw had almost forgotten the whole affair when she got up about seven o'clock. But, bye-and-bye, she heard a sharp altercation going on in the nursery. Norah speaking angrily to Ailsie, a most unusual thing. Both Mr. and Mrs. Openshaw listened in astonishment.

"Hold your tongue, Ailsie I let me hear none of your dreams; never let me hear you tell that story again!" Ailsie began to cry.

Mr. Openshaw opened the door of communication before his wife could say a word.

"Norah, come here!"

The nurse stood at the door, defiant. She perceived she had been heard, but she was desperate.

"Don't let me hear you speak in that manner to Ailsie again," he said sternly, and shut the door.

Norah was infinitely relieved; for she had dreaded some questioning; and a little blame for sharp speaking was what she could well bear, if cross-examination was let alone.

Downstairs they went, Mr. Openshaw carrying Ailsie; the sturdy Edwin coming step by step, right foot foremost, always holding his mother's hand. Each child was placed in a chair by the breakfast-table, and then Mr. and Mrs. Openshaw stood together at the window, awaiting their visitors' appearance and making plans for the day. There was a pause. Suddenly Mr. Openshaw turned to Ailsie, and said:

"What a little goosy somebody is with her dreams, waking up poor, tired mother in the middle of the night with a story of a man being in the room."

"Father! I'm sure I saw him," said Ailsie, half crying. "I don't want to make Norah angry; but I was not asleep, for all she says I was. I had been asleep,—and I awakened up quite wide awake though I was so frightened. I kept my eyes nearly shut, and I saw the man quite plain. A great brown man with a beard. He said his prayers. And then he looked at Edwin. And then Norah took him by the arm and led him away, after they had whispered a bit together."

"Now, my little woman must be reasonable," said Mr. Openshaw, who was always patient with Ailsie. "There was no man in the house last night at all. No man comes into the house as you know, if you think; much less goes up into the nursery. But sometimes we dream something has happened, and the dream is so like reality, that you are not the first person, little woman, who has stood out that the thing has really happened."

"But, indeed it was not a dream!" said Ailsie, beginning to cry.

Just then Mr. and Mrs. Chadwick came down, looking grave

and discomposed. All during breakfast time they were silent and uncomfortable. As soon as the breakfast things were taken away, and the children had been carried upstairs, Mr. Chadwick began in an evidently preconcerted manner to inquire if his nephew was certain that all his servants were honest; for, that Mrs. Chadwick had that morning missed a very valuable brooch, which she had worn the day before. She remembered taking it off when she came home from Buckingham Palace. Mr. Openshaw's face contracted into hard lines: grew like what it was before he had known his wife and her child. He rang the bell even before his uncle had done speaking. It was answered by the housemaid.

"Mary, was any one here last night while we were away?"

"A man, sir, came to speak to Norah."

"To speak to Norah! Who was he? How long did he stay?"

"I'm sure I can't tell, sir. He came—perhaps about nine. I went up to tell Norah in the nursery, and she came down to speak to him. She let him out, sir. She will know who he was, and how long he stayed."

She waited a moment to be asked any more questions, but she was not, so she went away.

A minute afterwards Openshaw made as though he were going out of the room; but his wife laid her hand on his arm:

"Do not speak to her before the children," she said, in her low, quiet voice. "I will go up and question her."

"No! I must speak to her. You must know," said he, turning to his uncle and aunt, "my missus has an old servant, as faithful as ever woman was, I do believe, as far as love goes,—but, at the same time, who does not always speak truth, as even the missus must allow. Now, my notion is, that this Norah of ours has been come over by some good-for-nothing chap (for she's at the time o' life when they say women pray for husbands—'any, good Lord, any,') and has let him into our house, and the chap has made off with your brooch, and m'appen many another thing beside. It's only saying that Norah is soft-hearted, and does not stick at a white lie—that's all, missus."

It was curious to notice how his tone, his eyes, his whole face changed as he spoke to his wife; but he was the resolute man through all. She knew better than to oppose him; so she went upstairs, and told Norah her master wanted to speak to her, and that she would take care of the children in the meanwhile.

Norah rose to go without a word. Her thoughts were these:

"If they tear me to pieces they shall never know through me. He may come,—and then just Lord have mercy upon us all: for some of us are dead folk to a certainty. But he shall do it; not me."

You may fancy, now, her look of determination as she faced her master alone in the dining-room; Mr. and Mrs. Chadwick having left the affair in their nephew's hands, seeing that he took it up with such vehemence.

"Norah! Who was that man that came to my house last night?"

"Man, sir!" As if infinitely; surprised but it was only to gain time.

"Yes; the man whom Mary let in; whom she went upstairs to the nursery to tell you about; whom you came down to speak to; the same chap, I make no doubt, whom you took into the nursery to have your talk out with; whom Ailsie saw, and afterwards dreamed about; thinking, poor wench! she saw him say his prayers, when nothing, I'll be bound, was farther from his thoughts; who took Mrs. Chadwick's brooch, value ten pounds. Now, Norah! Don't go off! I am as sure as that my name's Thomas Openshaw, that you knew nothing of this robbery.

"But I do think you've been imposed on, and that's the truth. Some good-for-nothing chap has been making up to you, and you've been just like all other women, and have turned a soft place in your heart to him; and he came last night a-lovyering, and you had him up in the nursery, and he made use of his opportunities, and made off with a few things on his way down! Come, now, Norah: it's no blame to you, only you must not be such a fool again. Tell us," he continued, "what name he gave you, Norah? I'll be bound it was not the right one; but it will be a clue for the police."

Norah drew herself up. "You may ask that question, and taunt me with my being single, and with my credulity, as you will, Master Openshaw. You'll get no answer from me. As for the brooch, and the story of theft and burglary; if any friend ever came to see me (which I defy you to prove, and deny), he'd be just as much above doing such a thing as you yourself, Mr. Openshaw, and more so, too; for I'm not at all sure as everything you have is rightly come by, or would be yours long, if every man had his own." She meant, of course, his wife; but he understood her to refer to his property in goods and chattels.

"Now, my good woman," said he, "I'll just tell you truly, I never trusted you out and out; but my wife liked you, and I thought you had many a good point about you. If you once begin to sauce me, I'll have the police to you, and get out the truth in a court of justice, if you'll not tell it me quietly and civilly here. Now the best thing you can do is quietly to tell me who the fellow is. Look here! a man comes to my house; asks for you; you take him upstairs, a valuable brooch is missing next day; we know that you, and Mary, and cook, are honest; but you refuse to tell us who the man is. Indeed you've told one lie already about him, saying no one was here last night. Now I just put it to you, what do you think a policeman would say to this, or a magistrate? A magistrate would soon make you tell the truth, my good woman."

"There's never the creature born that should get it out of me," said Norah. "Not unless I choose to tell."

"I've a great mind to see," said Mr. Openshaw, growing angry at the defiance. Then, checking himself, he thought before he spoke again:

"Norah, for your missus's sake I don't want to go to extremities. Be a sensible woman, if you can. It's no great disgrace, after all, to have been taken in. I ask you once more—as a friend—who was this man whom you let into my house last night?"

No answer. He repeated the question in an impatient tone. Still no answer. Norah's lips were set in determination not to speak.

"Then there is but one thing to be done. I shall send for a policeman."

"You will not," said Norah, starting forwards. "You shall not, sir! No policeman shall touch me. I know nothing of the brooch, but I know this: ever since I was four-and-twenty I have thought more of your wife than of myself: ever since I saw her, a poor motherless girl put upon in her uncle's house, I have thought more of serving her than of serving myself! I have cared for her and her child, as nobody ever cared for me. I don't cast blame on you, sir, but I say it's ill giving up one's life to any one; for, at the end, they will turn round upon you, and forsake you. Why does not my missus come herself to suspect me? Maybe she is gone for the police? But I don't stay here, either for police, or magistrate, or master. You're an unlucky lot. I believe there's a curse on you. I'll leave you this very day. Yes! I leave that poor Ailsie, too. I will! No good will ever come to you!"

Mr. Openshaw was utterly astonished at this speech; most of which was completely unintelligible to him, as may easily be supposed. Before he could make up his mind what to say, or what to do, Norah had left the room. I do not think he had ever really intended to send for the police to this old servant of his wife's; for he had never for a moment doubted her perfect honesty. But he had intended to compel her to tell him who the man was, and in this he was baffled. He was, consequently, much irritated. He returned to his uncle and aunt in a state of great annoyance and perplexity, and told them he could get nothing out of the woman; that some man had been in the house the night before; but that she refused to tell who he was. At this moment his wife came in, greatly agitated, and asked what had happened to Norah; for that she had put on her things in passionate haste, and had left the house.

"This looks suspicious," said Mr. Chadwick. "It is not the way in which an honest person would have acted."

Mr. Openshaw kept silence. He was sorely perplexed. But Mrs. Openshaw turned round on Mr. Chadwick with a sudden fierceness no one ever saw in her before.

"You don't know Norah, uncle! She is gone because she is deeply hurt at being suspected. O, I wish I had seen her—that I had spoken to her myself. She would have told me anything." Alice wrung her hands.

"I must confess," continued Mr. Chadwick to his nephew, in a lower voice, "I can't make you out. You used to be a word and a blow, and oftenest the blow first; and now, when there is every cause for suspicion, you just do nought. Your missus is a very good woman, I grant; but she may have been put upon as well as other folk, I suppose. If you don't send for the police, I shall."

"Very well," replied Mr. Openshaw, surlily. "I can't clear Norah. She won't clear herself, as I believe she might if she would. Only I wash my hands of it; for I am sure the woman herself is honest, and she's lived a long time with my wife, and I don't like her to come to shame."

"But she will then be forced to clear herself. That, at any rate, will be a good thing."

"Very well, very well! I am heart-sick of the whole business. Come, Alice, come up to the babies they'll be in a sore way. I tell you, uncle!" he said, turning round once more to Mr. Chadwick, suddenly and sharply, after his eye had fallen on Alice's wan, tearful, anxious face; "I'll have none sending for the police after all. I'll buy my aunt twice as handsome a brooch this very day; but I'll not have Norah suspected, and my missus plagued. There's for you."

He and his wife left the room. Mr. Chadwick quietly waited till he was out of hearing, and then said to his wife; "For all Tom's heroics, I'm just quietly going for a detective, wench. Thou need'st know nought about it."

He went to the police-station, and made a statement of the case. He was gratified by the impression which the evidence against Norah seemed to make. The men all agreed in his opinion, and steps were to be immediately taken to find out where she was. Most probably, as they suggested, she had gone at once to the man, who, to all appearance, was her lover. When Mr. Chadwick asked how they would find her out? they smiled,

142

shook their heads, and spoke of mysterious but infallible ways and means. He returned to his nephew's house with a very comfortable opinion of his own sagacity. He was met by his wife with a penitent face:

"O master, I've found my brooch! It was just sticking by its pin in the flounce of my brown silk, that I wore yesterday. I took it off in a hurry, and it must have caught in it; and I hung up my gown in the closet. Just now, when I was going to fold it up, there was the brooch! I'm very vexed, but I never dreamt but what it was lost!''

Her husband muttering something very like "Confound thee and thy brooch too! I wish I'd never given it thee," snatched up his hat, and rushed back to the station; hoping to be in time to stop the police from searching for Norah. But a detective was already gone off on the errand.

Where was Norah? Half mad with the strain of the fearful secret, she had hardly slept through the night for thinking what must be done. Upon this terrible state of mind had come Ailsie's questions, showing that she had seen the Man, as the unconscious child called her father. Lastly came the suspicion of her honesty. She was little less than crazy as she ran upstairs and dashed on her bonnet and shawl; leaving all else, even her purse, behind her. In that house she would not stay. That was all she knew or was clear about. She would not even see the children again, for fear it should weaken her. She feared above everything Mr. Frank's return to claim his wife. She could not tell what remedy there was for a sorrow so tremendous, for her to stay to witness.

The desire of escaping from the coming event was a stronger motive for her departure than her soreness about the suspicions directed against her; although this last had been the final goad to the course she took. She walked away almost at headlong speed; sobbing as she went, as she had not dared to do during the past night for fear of exciting wonder in those who might hear her. Then she stopped. An idea came into her mind that she would leave London altogether, and betake herself to her native town of Liverpool. She felt in her pocket for her purse, as she drew near the Euston Square station with this intention. She had left it at home. Her poor head aching, her eyes swollen with crying, she had to stand still, and think, as well as she could, where next she should bend her steps. Suddenly the thought flashed into her mind that she would go and find out poor Mr. Frank. She had been hardly kind to him the night before, though her heart had bled for him ever since. She remembered his telling her as she inquired for his address, almost as she had pushed him out of the door, of some hotel in a street not far distant from Euston Square.

Thither she went: with what intention she hardly knew, but to assuage her conscience by telling him how much she pitied him. In her present state she felt herself unfit to counsel, or re-strain, or assist, or do ought else but sympathise and weep. The people of the inn said such a person had been there; had arrived only the day before; had gone out soon after his arrival, leaving his luggage in their care; but had never come back. Norah asked for leave to sit down, and await the gentleman's return. The landlady—pretty secure in the deposit of luggage against any probable injury—showed her into a room, and quietly locked the door on the outside. Norah was utterly worn out, and fell asleep—a shivering, starting, uneasy slumber, which lasted for hours.

The detective, meanwhile, had come up with her some time before she entered the hotel, into which he followed her. Asking the landlady to detain her for an hour or so, without giving any reason beyond showing his authority (which made the landlady applaud herself a good deal for having locked her in), he went back to the police-station to report his proceedings. He could have taken her directly; but his object was, if possible, to trace out the man who was supposed to have committed the robbery. Then he heard of the discovery of the brooch; and consequently did not care to return.

Norah slept till even the summer evening began to close in. Then up. Someone was at the door. It would be Mr. Frank; and she dizzily pushed back her ruffled grey hair, which had fallen over her

eyes, and stood looking to see him. Instead, there came in Mr. Openshaw and a policeman.

"This is Norah Kennedy," said Mr. Openshaw.

"O, sir," said Norah, "I did not touch the brooch; indeed I did not. O, sir, I cannot live to be thought so badly of;" and very sick and faint, she suddenly sank down on the ground. To her surprise, Mr. Openshaw raised her up very tenderly. Even the policeman helped to lay her on the sofa; and, at Mr. Openshaw's desire, he went for some wine and sandwiches; for the poor gaunt woman lay there almost as if dead with weariness and exhaustion.

"Norah!" said Mr. Openshaw, in his kindest voice, "the brooch is found. It was hanging to Mrs. Chadwick's gown. I beg your pardon. Most truly I beg your pardon, for having troubled you about it. My wife is almost broken-hearted. Eat, Norah,—or, stay, first drink this glass of wine," said he, lifting her head, pouring a little down her throat.

As she drank, she remembered where she was, and who she was waiting for. She suddenly pushed Mr. Openshaw away, saying, "O, sir, you must go. You must not stop a minute. If he comes back he will kill you."

"Alas, Norah! I do not know who 'he' is. But someone is gone away who will never come back: someone who knew you, and whom I am afraid you cared for."

"I don't understand you, sir," said Norah, her master's kind and sorrowful manner bewildering her yet more than his words. The policeman had left the room at Mr. Openshaw's desire, and they two were alone.

"You know what I mean, when I say some one is gone who will never come back. I mean that he is dead!"

"Who?" said Norah, trembling all over.

"A poor man has been found in the Thames this morning, drowned."

"Did he drown himself?" asked Norah, solemnly.

"God only knows," replied Mr. Openshaw, in the same tone. "Your name and address at our house, were found in his pocket: that, and his purse, were the only things, that were found upon him. I am sorry to say it, my poor Norah; but you are required to go and identify him."

"To what?" asked Norah.

"To say who it is. It is always done, in order that some reason may be discovered for the suicide—if suicide it was. I make no doubt he was the man who came to see you at our house last night. It is very sad, I know." He made pauses between each little clause, in order to try and bring back her senses; which he feared were wandering—so wild and sad was her look.

"Master Openshaw," said she, at last, "I've a dreadful secret to tell you—only you must never breathe it to anyone, and you and I must hide it away forever. I thought to have done it all by myself, but I see I cannot. Yon poor man—yes! the dead, drowned creature is, I fear, Mr. Frank, my mistress's first husband!"

Mr. Openshaw sate down, as if shot. He did not speak; but, after a while, he signed to Norah to go on.

"He came to me the other night—when—God be thanked-you were all away at Richmond. He asked me if his wife was dead or alive. I was a brute, and thought more of our all coming home than of his sore trial: spoke out sharp, and said she was married again, and very content and happy: I all but turned him away: and now he lies dead and cold!"

"God forgive me!" said Mr. Openshaw.

"God forgive us all!" said Norah. "Yon poor man needs forgiveness perhaps less than anyone among us. He had been among the savages—shipwrecked—I know not what—and he had written letters which had never reached my poor missus."

"He saw his child!"

"He saw her—yes! I took him up, to give his thoughts another start; for I believed he was going mad on my hands. I came to seek him here, as I more than half promised. My mind misgave me when I heard he had never come in. O, sir I it must be him!"

146

Mr. Openshaw rang the bell. Norah was almost too much stunned to wonder at what he did. He asked for writing materials, wrote a letter, and then said to Norah:

"I am writing to Alice, to say I shall be unavoidably absent for a few days; that I have found you; that you are well, and send her your love, and will come home tomorrow. You must go with me to the Police Court; you must identify the body: I will pay high to keep name; and details out of the papers.

"But where are you going, sir?"

He did not answer her directly. Then he said:

"Norah! I must go with you, and look on the face of the man whom I have so injured,—unwittingly, it is true; but it seems to me as if I had killed him. I will lay his head in the grave, as if he were my only brother: and how he must have hated me! I cannot go home to my wife till all that I can do for him is done. Then I go with a dreadful secret on my mind. I shall never speak of it again, after these days are over. I know you will not, either." He shook hands with her: and they never named the subject again, the one to the other.

Norah went home to Alice the next day. Not a word was said on the cause of her abrupt departure a day or two before. Alice had been charged by her husband in his letter not to allude to the supposed theft of the brooch; so she, implicitly obedient to those whom she loved both by nature and habit, was entirely silent on the subject, only treated Norah with the most tender respect, as if to make up for unjust suspicion.

Nor did Alice inquire into the reason why Mr. Openshaw had been absent during his uncle and aunt's visit, after he had once said that it was unavoidable. He came back, grave and quiet; and, from that time forth, was curiously changed. More thoughtful, and perhaps less active; quite as decided in conduct, but with new and different rules for the guidance of that conduct. Towards Alice he could hardly be more kind than he had always been; but he now seemed to look upon her as someone sacred and to be treated with reverence, as well as tenderness. He throve in business, and made a large fortune, one half of which was settled upon her.

Long years after these events,—a few months after her mother died, Ailsie and her "father" (as she always called Mr. Openshaw) drove to a cemetery a little way out of town, and she was carried to a certain mound by her maid, who was then sent back to the carriage. There was a head-stone, with F. W. and a date. That was all. Sitting by the grave, Mr. Openshaw told her the story; and for the sad fate of that poor father whom she had never seen, he shed the only tears she ever saw fall from his eyes.

"A most interesting story, all through," I said, as Jarber folded up the first of his series of discoveries in triumph. "A story that goes straight to the heart—especially at the end. But"—I stopped, and looked at Trottle.

Trottle entered his protest directly in the shape of a cough.

"Well!" I said, beginning to lose my patience. "Don't you see that I want you to speak, and that I don't want you to cough?"

"Quite so, ma'am," said Trottle, in a state of respectful obstinacy which would have upset the temper of a saint. "Relative, I presume, to this story, ma'am?"

"Yes, Yes!" said Jarber. "By all means let us hear what this good man has to say."

"Well, sir," answered Trottle, "I want to know why the House over the way doesn't let, and I don't exactly see how your story answers the question. That's all I have to say, sir."

I should have liked to contradict my opinionated servant, at that moment. But, excellent as the story was in itself, I felt that he had hit on the weak point, so far as Jarber's particular purpose in reading it was concerned.

"And that is what you have to say, is it?" repeated Jarber. "I enter this room announcing that I have a series of discoveries, and you jump instantly to the conclusion that the first of the series exhausts my resources. Have I your permission, dear lady, to enlighten this obtuse person, if possible, by reading Number Two?"

"My work is behindhand, ma'am," said Trottle, moving to the door, the moment I gave Jarber leave to go on.

"Stop where you are," I said, in my most peremptory manner, "and give Mr. Jarber his fair opportunity of answering your objection now you have made it."

Trottle sat down with the look of a martyr, and Jarber began to read with his back turned on the enemy more decidedly than ever.

CHAPTER 3
GOING INTO SOCIETY

At one period of its reverses, the House fell into the occupation of a Showman. He was found registered as its occupier, on the parish books of the time when he rented the House, and there was therefore no need of any clue to his name. But, he himself was less easy to be found; for, he had led a wandering life, and settled people had lost sight of him, and people who plumed themselves on being respectable were shy of admitting that they had ever known anything of him. At last, among the marsh lands near the river's level, that lie about Deptford and the neighbouring market-gardens, a Grizzled Personage in velveteen, with a face so cut up by varieties of weather that he looked as if he had been tattooed, was found smoking a pipe at the door of a wooden house on wheels.

The wooden house was laid up in ordinary for the winter, near the mouth of a muddy creek; and everything near it, the foggy river, the misty marshes, and the steaming market-gardens, smoked in company with the grizzled man. In the midst of this smoking party, the funnel-chimney of the wooden house on wheels was not remiss, but took its pipe with the rest in a companionable manner.

On being asked if it were he who had once rented the House to Let, Grizzled Velveteen looked surprised, and said yes. Then his name was Magsman? That was it, Toby Magsman—which lawfully christened Robert; but called in the line, from a infant, Toby. There was nothing agin Toby Magsman, he believed? If there was suspicion of such—mention it!

There was no suspicion of such, he might rest assured. But,

some inquiries were making about that House, and would he object to say why he left it?

Not at all; why should he? He left it, along of a Dwarf.

Along of a Dwarf?

Mr. Magsman repeated, deliberately and emphatically, Along of a Dwarf.

Might it be compatible with Mr. Magsman's inclination and convenience to enter, as a favour, into a few particulars? Mr. Magsman entered into the following particulars. It was a long time ago, to begin with;—afore lotteries and a deal more was done away with. Mr. Magsman was looking about for a good pitch, and he see that house, and he says to himself, "I'll have you, if you're to be had. If money'll get you, I'll have you."

The neighbours cut up rough, and made complaints; but Mr. Magsman don't know what they *would* have had. It was a lovely thing. First of all, there was the canvass, representin the picter of the Giant, in Spanish trunks and a ruff, who was himself half the height of the house, and was run up with a line and pulley to a pole on the roof, so that his Ed was coeval with the parapet. Then, there was the canvass, representin the picter of the Albina lady, showing her white air to the Army and Navy in correct uniform. Then, there was the canvass, representin the picter of the Wild Indian a scalpin a member of some foreign nation.

Then, there was the canvass, representin the picter of a child of a British Planter, seized by two Boa Constrictors—not that *we* never had no child, nor no Constrictors neither. Similarly, there was the canvass, representin the picter of the Wild Ass of the Prairies—not that *we* never had no wild asses, nor wouldn't have had 'em at a gift. Last, there was the canvass, representin the picter of the Dwarf, and like him too (considerin), with George the Fourth in such a state of astonishment at him as His Majesty couldn't with his utmost politeness and stoutness express.

The front of the House was so covered with canvasses, that there wasn't a spark of daylight ever visible on that side. "*Magsman's Amusements*," fifteen foot long by two foot high, ran over the front door and parlour winders. The passage was a Arbour of green baize and garden-stuff. A barrel-organ performed there unceasing. And as to respectability,—if threepence ain't respectable, what is?

But, the Dwarf is the principal article at present, and he was worth the money. He was wrote up as *Major Tpschoffki, of the Imperial Bulgraderian Brigade*. Nobody couldn't pronounce the name, and it never was intended anybody should. The public always turned it, as a regular rule, into Chopski. In the line he was called Chops; partly on that account, and partly because his real name, if he ever had any real name (which was very dubious), was Stakes.

He was a uncommon small man, he really was. Certainly not so small as he was made out to be, but where *is* your Dwarf as is? He was a most uncommon small man, with a most uncommon large Ed; and what he had inside that Ed, nobody ever knowed but himself: even supposing himself to have ever took stock of it, which it would have been a stiff job for even him to do.

The kindest little man as never growed! Spirited, but not proud. When he travelled with the Spotted Baby—though he knowed himself to be a nat'ral Dwarf, and knowed the Baby's spots to be put upon him artificial, he nursed that Baby like a mother. You never heerd him give a ill-name to a Giant. He *did* allow himself to break out into strong language respectin the Fat Lady from Norfolk; but that was an affair of the 'art; and when a man's 'art has been trifled with by a lady, and the preference giv to a Indian, he ain't master of his actions.

He was always in love, of course; every human nat'ral phenomenon is. And he was always in love with a large woman; I never knowed the Dwarf as could be got to love a small one. Which helps to keep 'em the Curiosities they are.

One sing'ler idea he had in that Ed of his, which must have meant something, or it wouldn't have been there. It was always his opinion that he was entitled to property. He never would put his name to anything. He had been taught to write, by the young man without arms, who got his living with his toes (quite a writing master *he* was, and taught scores in the line), but Chops would have starved to death, afore he'd have gained a bit of bread by putting his hand to a paper. This is the more curious to bear in mind, because *he* had no property, nor hope of property, except his house and a sarser. When I say his house, I mean the box, painted and got up outside like a reg'lar six-roomer, that he used to creep into, with a diamond ring (or quite as good to look at) on his forefinger, and ring a little bell out of what the Public believed to be the Drawing-room winder.

And when I say a sarser, I mean a Chaney sarser in which he made a collection for himself at the end of every Entertainment. His cue for that, he took from me: "Ladies and gentlemen, the little man will now walk three times round the Cairawan, and retire behind the curtain." When he said anything important, in private life, he mostly wound it up with this form of words, and they was generally the last thing he said to me at night afore he went to bed.

He had what I consider a fine mind—a poetic mind. His ideas respectin his property never come upon him so strong as when he sat upon a barrel-organ and had the handle turned. Arter the vibration had run through him a little time, he would screech out, "Toby, I feel my property coming—grind away! I'm counting my guineas by thousands, Toby—grind away! Toby, I shall be a man of fortun! I feel the Mint a jingling in me, Toby, and I'm swelling out into the Bank of England!" Such is the influence of music on a poetic mind. Not that he was partial to any other music but a barrel-organ; on the contrary, hated it.

He had a kind of a everlasting grudge agin the Public: which is a thing you may notice in many phenomenons that get their living out of it. What riled him most in the nater of his occupation was, that it kep him out of Society. He was continiwally saying, "Toby, my ambition is, to go into Society. The curse of my position towards the Public is, that it keeps me hout of Society. This don't signify to a low beast of a Indian; he an't formed for Society. This don't signify to a Spotted Baby; *he* an't formed for Society.—I am."

Nobody never could make out what Chops done with his

money. He had a good salary, down on the drum every Saturday as the day came round, besides having the run of his teeth—and he was a Woodpecker to eat—but all Dwarfs are. The sarser was a little income, bringing him in so many halfpence that he'd carry 'em for a week together, tied up in a pocket-handkercher. And yet he never had money. And it couldn't be the Fat Lady from Norfolk, as was once supposed; because it stands to reason that when you have a animosity towards a Indian, which makes you grind your teeth at him to his face, and which can hardly hold you from Goosing him audible when he's going through his War-Dance—it stands to reason you wouldn't under them circumstances deprive yourself, to support that Indian in the lap of luxury.

Most unexpected, the mystery come out one day at Egham Races. The Public was shy of bein pulled in, and Chops was ringin his little bell out of his drawing-room winder, and was snarlin to me over his shoulder as he kneeled down with his legs out at the back-door—for he couldn't be shoved into his house without kneeling down, and the premises wouldn't accommodate his legs—was snarlin, "Here's a precious Public for you; why the Devil don't they tumble up?" when a man in the crowd holds up a carrier-pigeon, and cries out, "If there's any person here as has got a ticket, the Lottery's just drawed, and the number as has come up for the great prize is three, seven, forty-two! Three, seven, forty-two!"

I was givin the man to the Furies myself, for calling off the Public's attention—for the Public will turn away, at any time, to look at anything in preference to the thing showed 'em; and if you doubt it, get 'em together for any individual purpose on the face of the earth, and send only two people in late, and see if the whole company an't far more interested in takin particular notice of them two than of you—I say, I wasn't best pleased with the man for callin out, and wasn't blessin him in my own mind, when I see Chops's little bell fly out of winder at a old lady, and he gets up and kicks his box over, exposin the whole secret, and he catches hold of the calves of my legs and he says to me,

"Carry me into the wan, Toby, and throw a pail of water over me or I'm a dead man, for I've come into my property!"

Twelve thousand odd hundred pound, was Chops's winnins. He had bought a half-ticket for the twenty-five thousand prize, and it had come up. The first use he made of his property, was, to offer to fight the Wild Indian for five hundred pound a side, him with a poisoned darnin-needle and the Indian with a club; but the Indian being in want of backers to that amount, it went no further. Arter he had been mad for a week—in a state of mind, in short, in which, if I had let him sit on the organ for only two minutes, I believe he would have bust—but we kep the organ from him—Mr. Chops come round, and behaved liberal and beautiful to all. He then sent for a young man he knowed, as had a very genteel appearance and was a Bonnet at a gaming-booth (most respectable brought up, father havin been imminent in the livery stable line but unfort'nate in a commercial crisis, through paintin a old gray, ginger-bay, and sellin him with a Pedigree), and Mr. Chops said to this Bonnet, who said his name was Normandy, which it wasn't:

"Normandy, I'm a goin into Society. Will you go with me?"

Says Normandy: "Do I understand you, Mr. Chops, to hintimate that the 'ole of the expenses of that move will be borne by yourself?"

"Correct," says Mr. Chops. "And you shall have a Princely allowance too."

The Bonnet lifted Mr. Chops upon a chair, to shake hands with him, and replied in poetry, with his eyes seemingly full of tears:

My boat is on the shore,
And my bark is on the sea,
And I do not ask for more,
But I'll Go:—along with thee.

They went into Society, in a chay and four grays with silk jackets. They took lodgings in Pall Mall, London, and they blazed away.

In consequence of a note that was brought to Bartlemy Fair in the autumn of next year by a servant, most wonderful got up in milk-white cords and tops, I cleaned myself and went to Pall Mall, one evening appinted. The gentlemen was at their wine arter dinner, and Mr. Chops's eyes was more fixed in that Ed of his than I thought good for him. There was three of 'em (in company, I mean), and I knowed the third well. When last met, he had on a white Roman shirt, and a bishop's mitre covered with leopard-skin, and played the clarionet all wrong, in a band at a Wild Beast Show.

This gent took on not to know me, and Mr. Chops said: "Gentlemen, this is a old friend of former days:" and Normandy looked at me through a eye-glass, and said, "Magsman, glad to see you!"—which I'll take my oath he wasn't. Mr. Chops, to git him convenient to the table, had his chair on a throne (much of the form of George the Fourth's in the canvass), but he hardly appeared to me to be King there in any other pint of view, for his two gentlemen ordered about like Emperors. They was all dressed like May-Day—gorgeous!—And as to Wine, they swam in all sorts.

I made the round of the bottles, first separate (to say I had done it), and then mixed 'em all together (to say I had done it), and then tried two of 'em as half-and-half, and then t'other two. Altogether, I passed a pleasin evenin, but with a tendency to feel muddled, until I considered it good manners to get up and say, "Mr. Chops, the best of friends must part, I thank you for the variety of foreign drains you have stood so 'ansome, I looks towards you in red wine, and I takes my leave." Mr. Chops replied, "If you'll just hitch me out of this over your right arm, Magsman, and carry me downstairs, I'll see you out." I said I couldn't think of such a thing, but he would have it, so I lifted him off his throne. He smelt strong of Maideary, and I couldn't help thinking as I carried him down that it was like carrying a large bottle full of wine, with a rayther ugly stopper, a good deal out of proportion.

When I set him on the doormat in the hall, he kep me close

to him by holding on to my coat-collar, and he whispers:

"I ain't 'appy, Magsman."

"What's on your mind, Mr. Chops?"

"They don't use me well. They an't grateful to me. They puts me on the mantelpiece when I won't have in more Champagne-wine, and they locks me in the sideboard when I won't give up my property."

"Get rid of 'em, Mr. Chops."

"I can't. We're in Society together, and what would Society say?"

"Come out of Society!" says I.

"I can't. You don't know what you're talking about. When you have once gone into Society, you mustn't come out of it."

"Then if you'll excuse the freedom, Mr. Chops," were my remark, shaking my head grave, "I think it's a pity you ever went in."

Mr. Chops shook that deep ed of his, to a surprisin extent, and slapped it half a dozen times with his hand, and with more vice than I thought were in him. Then, he says, "You're a good fellow, but you don't understand. Goodnight, go along. Magsman, the little man will now walk three times round the Cairawan, and retire behind the curtain." The last I see of him on that occasion was his tryin, on the extremest verge of insensibility, to climb up the stairs, one by one, with his hands and knees. They'd have been much too steep for him, if he had been sober; but he wouldn't be helped.

It warn't long after that, that I read in the newspaper of Mr. Chops's being presented at court. It was printed, "It will be recollected"—and I've noticed in my life, that it is sure to be printed that it will be recollected, whenever it won't—"that Mr. Chops is the individual of small stature, whose brilliant success in the last State Lottery attracted so much attention." Well, I says to myself, Such is Life! He has been and done it in earnest at last. He has astonished George the Fourth!

(On account of which, I had that canvass new-painted, him with a bag of money in his hand, a presentin it to George the

Fourth, and a lady in Ostrich Feathers fallin in love with him in a bag-wig, sword, and buckles correct.)

I took the House as is the subject of present inquiries-though not the honour of bein acquainted—and I run Magsman's Amusements in it thirteen months—sometimes one thing, sometimes another, sometimes nothin particular, but always all the canvasses outside. One night, when we had played the last company out, which was a shy company, through its raining Heavens hard, I was takin a pipe in the one pair back along with the young man with the toes, which I had taken on for a month (though he never drawed—except on paper), and I heard a kickin at the street door. "Halloa!" I says to the young man, "what's up!"

He rubs his eyebrows with his toes, and he says, "I can't imagine, Mr. Magsman"—which he never could imagine nothin, and was monotonous company.

The noise not leavin off, I laid down my pipe, and I took up a candle, and I went down and opened the door. I looked out into the street; but nothin could I see, and nothin was I aware of, until I turned round quick, because some creetur run between my legs into the passage. There was Mr. Chops!

"Magsman," he says, "take me, on the old terms, and you've got me; if it's done, say done!"

I was all of a maze, but I said, "Done, sir."

"Done to your done, and double done!" says he. "Have you got a bit of supper in the house?"

Bearin in mind them sparklin varieties of foreign drains as we'd guzzled away at in Pall Mall, I was ashamed to offer him cold sassages and gin-and-water; but he took 'em both and took 'em free; havin a chair for his table, and sittin down at it on a stool, like hold times. I, all of a maze all the while.

It was arter he had made a clean sweep of the sassages (beef, and to the best of my calculations two pound and a quarter), that the wisdom as was in that little man began to come out of him like prespiration.

"Magsman," he says, "look upon me! You see afore you, One

as has both gone into Society and come out."

"O! You *are* out of it, Mr. Chops? How did you get out, sir?"

"*Sold out!*" says he. You never saw the like of the wisdom as his Ed expressed, when he made use of them two words.

"My friend Magsman, I'll impart to you a discovery I've made. It's vallable; it's cost twelve thousand five hundred pound; it may do you good in life—The secret of this matter is, that it ain't so much that a person goes into Society, as that Society goes into a person."

Not exactly keepin up with his meanin, I shook my head, put on a deep look, and said, "You're right there, Mr. Chops."

"Magsman," he says, twitchin me by the leg, "Society has gone into me, to the tune of every penny of my property."

I felt that I went pale, and though nat'rally a bold speaker, I couldn't hardly say, "Where's Normandy?"

"Bolted. With the plate," said Mr. Chops.

"And t'other one?" meaning him as formerly wore the bishop's mitre.

"Bolted. With the jewels," said Mr. Chops.

I sat down and looked at him, and he stood up and looked at me.

"Magsman," he says, and he seemed to myself to get wiser as he got hoarser; "Society, taken in the lump, is all dwarfs. At the court of St. James's, they was all a doing my old business—all a goin three times round the Cairawan, in the hold court-suits and properties. Elsewheres, they was most of 'em ringin their little bells out of make-believes. Everywheres, the sarser was a goin round. Magsman, the sarser is the universal Institution!"

I perceived, you understand, that he was soured by his misfortunes, and I felt for Mr. Chops.

"As to Fat Ladies," he says, giving his head a tremendious one agin the wall, "there's lots of *them* in Society, and worse than the original. *Hers* was a outrage upon Taste—simply a outrage upon Taste—awakenin contempt—carryin its own punishment in the form of a Indian."

Here he giv himself another tremendious one. "But *theirs,*

Magsman, *theirs* is mercenary outrages. Lay in Cashmeer shawls, buy bracelets, strew 'em and a lot of 'andsome fans and things about your rooms, let it be known that you give away like water to all as come to admire, and the Fat Ladies that don't exhibit for so much down upon the drum, will come from all the pints of the compass to flock about you, whatever you are. They'll drill holes in your 'art, Magsman, like a Cullender. And when you've no more left to give, they'll laugh at you to your face, and leave you to have your bones picked dry by vulturs, like the dead Wild Ass of the Prairies that you deserve to be!" Here he giv himself the most tremendious one of all, and dropped.

I thought he was gone. His Ed was so heavy, and he knocked it so hard, and he fell so stoney, and the sassagerial disturbance in him must have been so immense, that I thought he was gone. But, he soon come round with care, and he sat up on the floor, and he said to me, with wisdom comin out of his eyes, if ever it come:

"Magsman! The most material difference between the two states of existence through which your unhappy friend has passed;" he reache out his poor little hand, and his tears dropped down on the *moustachio* which it was a credit to him to have done his best to grow, but it is not in mortals to command success,—"the difference this. When I was out of Society, I was paid light for being seen. When I went into Society, I paid heavy for being seen. I prefer the former, even if I wasn't forced upon it. Give me out through the trumpet, in the hold way, tomorrow."

Arter that, he slid into the line again as easy as if he had been iled all over. But the organ was kep from him, and no allusions was ever made, when a company was in, to his property. He got wiser every day; his views of Society and the Public was luminous, bewilderin, awful; and his Ed got bigger and bigger as his Wisdom expanded it.

He took well, and pulled 'em in most excellent for nine weeks. At the expiration of that period, when his Ed was a sight, he expressed one evenin, the last Company havin been turned out, and the door shut, a wish to have a little music.

"Mr. Chops," I said (I never dropped the "Mr." with him; the world might do it, but not me); "Mr. Chops, are you sure as you are in a state of mind and body to sit upon the organ?"

His answer was this: "Toby, when next met with on the tramp, I forgive her and the Indian. And I am."

It was with fear and trembling that I began to turn the handle; but he sat like a lamb. I will be my belief to my dying day, that I see his Ed expand as he sat; you may therefore judge how great his thoughts was. He sat out all the changes, and then he come off.

"Toby," he says, with a quiet smile, "the little man will now walk three times round the Cairawan, and retire behind the curtain."

When we called him in the morning, we found him gone into a much better Society than mine or Pall Mall's. I giv Mr. Chops as comfortable a funeral as lay in my power, followed myself as Chief, and had the George the Fourth canvass carried first, in the form of a banner. But, the House was so dismal arterwards, that I giv it up, and took to the Wan again.

"I don't triumph," said Jarber, folding up the second manuscript, and looking hard at Trottle. "I don't triumph over this worthy creature. I merely ask him if he is satisfied now?"

"How can he be anything else?" I said, answering for Trottle, who sat obstinately silent. "This time, Jarber, you have not only read us a delightfully amusing story, but you have also answered the question about the House. Of course it stands empty now. Who would think of taking it after it had been turned into a caravan?" I looked at Trottle, as I said those last words, and Jarber waved his hand indulgently in the same direction.

"Let this excellent person speak," said Jarber. "You were about to say, my good man?"—

"I only wished to ask, sir," said Trottle doggedly, "if you could kindly oblige me with a date or two in connection with that last story?"

"A date!" repeated Jarber. "What does the man want with

dates!"

"I should be glad to know, with great respect," persisted Trottle, "if the person named Magsman was the last tenant who lived in the House. It's my opinion—if I may be excused for giving it—that he most decidedly was not."

With those words, Trottle made a low bow, and quietly left the room.

There is no denying that Jarber, when we were left together, looked sadly discomposed. He had evidently forgotten to inquire about dates; and, in spite of his magnificent talk about his series of discoveries, it was quite as plain that the two stories he had just read, had really and truly exhausted his present stock. I thought myself bound, in common gratitude, to help him out of his embarrassment by a timely suggestion. So I proposed that he should come to tea again, on the next Monday evening, the thirteenth, and should make such inquiries in the meantime, as might enable him to dispose triumphantly of Trottle's objection.

He gallantly kissed my hand, made a neat little speech of acknowledgment, and took his leave. For the rest of the week I would not encourage Trottle by allowing him to refer to the House at all. I suspected he was making his own inquiries about dates, but I put no questions to him.

On Monday evening, the thirteenth, that dear unfortunate Jarber came, punctual to the appointed time. He looked so terribly harassed, that he was really quite a spectacle of feebleness and fatigue. I saw, at a glance, that the question of dates had gone against him, that Mr. Magsman had not been the last tenant of the House, and that the reason of its emptiness was still to seek.

"What I have gone through," said Jarber, "words are not eloquent enough to tell. O Sophonisba, I have begun another series of discoveries! Accept the last two as stories laid on your shrine; and wait to blame me for leaving your curiosity unappeased, until you have heard Number Three."

Number Three looked like a very short manuscript, and I said as much. Jarber explained to me that we were to have some poetry this time. In the course of his investigations he had stepped into the Circulating Library, to seek for information on the one important subject. All the Library-people knew about the House was, that a female relative of the last tenant, as they believed, had, just after that tenant left, sent a little manuscript poem to them which she described as referring to events that had actually passed in the House; and which she wanted the proprietor of the Library to publish. She had written no address on her letter; and the proprietor had kept the manuscript ready to be given back to her (the publishing of poems not being in his line) when she might call for it. She had never called for it; and the poem had been lent to Jarber, at his express request, to read to me.

Before he began, I rang the bell for Trottle; being determined to have him present at the new reading, as a wholesome check on his obstinacy. To my surprise Peggy answered the bell, and told me, that Trottle had stepped out without saying where. I instantly felt the strongest possible conviction that he was at his old tricks: and that his stepping out in the evening, without leave, meant—Philandering.

Controlling myself on my visitor's account, I dismissed Peggy, stifled my indignation, and prepared, as politely as might be, to listen to Jarber.

CHAPTER 4
THREE EVENINGS IN THE HOUSE

Number One.

1

Yes, it look'd dark and dreary
That long and narrow street:
Only the sound of the rain,
And the tramp of passing feet,
The duller glow of the fire,
And gathering mists of night
To mark how slow and weary
The long day's cheerless flight!

2

Watching the sullen fire,
Hearing the dreary rain,
Drop after drop, run down
On the darkening window-pane;
Chill was the heart of Bertha,
Chill as that winter day,—
For the star of her life had risen
Only to fade away.

3

The voice that had been so strong
To bid the snare depart,
The true and earnest will,
And the calm and steadfast heart,
Were now weigh'd down by sorrow,
Were quivering now with pain;
The clear path now seem'd clouded,
And all her grief in vain.

4

Duty, Right, Truth, who promised
To help and save their own,
Seem'd spreading wide their pinions
To leave her there alone.
So, turning from the Present
To well-known days of yore,
She call'd on them to strengthen
And guard her soul once more.

5

She thought how in her girlhood
Her life was given away,
The solemn promise spoken
She kept so well today;
How to her brother Herbert
She had been help and guide,
And how his artist-nature

On her calm strength relied.

6

How through life's fret and turmoil
The passion and fire of art
In him was soothed and quicken'd
By her true sister heart;
How future hopes had always
Been for his sake alone;
And now, what strange new feeling
Possess'd her as its own?

7

Her home; each flower that breathed there;
The wind's sigh, soft and low;
Each trembling spray of ivy;
The river's murmuring flow;
The shadow of the forest;
Sunset, or twilight dim;
Dear as they were, were dearer
By leaving them for him.

8

And each year as it found her
In the dull, feverish town,
Saw self still more forgotten,
And selfish care kept down
By the calm joy of evening
That brought him to her side,
To warn him with wise counsel,
Or praise with tender pride.

9

Her heart, her life, her future,
Her genius, only meant
Another thing to give him,
And be there with content
Today, what words had stirr'd her,
Her soul could not forget?

What dream had fill'd her spirit
With strange and wild regret?

10

To leave him for another:
Could it indeed be so?
Could it have cost such anguish
To bid this vision go?
Was this her faith? Was Herbert
The second in her heart?
Did it need all this struggle
To bid a dream depart?

11

And yet, within her spirit
A far-off land was seen;
A home, which might have held her;
A love, which might have been;
And Life: not the mere being
Of daily ebb and flow,
But Life itself had claim'd her,
And she had let it go!

12

Within her heart there echo'd
Again the well-known tune
That promised this bright future,
And ask'd her for its own:
Then words of sorrow, broken
By half-reproachful pain;
And then a farewell, spoken
In words of cold disdain.

13

Where now was the stern purpose
That nerved her soul so long?
Whence came the words she utter'd,
So hard, so cold, so strong?
What right had she to banish

A hope that God had given?
Why must she choose earth's portion,
And turn aside from Heaven?

14

Today! Was it this morning?
If this long, fearful strife
Was but the work of hours,
What would be years of life?
Why did a cruel Heaven
For such great suffering call?
And why—O, still more cruel!—
Must her own words do all?

15

Did she repent? O Sorrow!
Why do we linger still
To take thy loving message,
And do thy gentle will?
See, her tears fall more slowly;
The passionate murmurs cease,
And back upon her spirit
Flow strength, and love, and peace.

16

The fire burns more brightly,
The rain has passed away,
Herbert will see no shadow
Upon his home today;
Only that Bertha greets him
With doubly tender care,
Kissing a fonder blessing
Down on his golden hair.

Number Two.

1

The studio is deserted,
Palette and brush laid by,
The sketch rests on the easel,

The paint is scarcely dry;
And Silence—who seems always
Within her depths to bear
The next sound that will utter—
Now holds a dumb despair.

2

So Bertha feels it: listening
With breathless, stony fear,
Waiting the dreadful summons
Each minute brings more near:
When the young life, now ebbing,
Shall fail, and pass away
Into that mighty shadow
Who shrouds the house today.

3

But why—when the sick chamber
Is on the upper floor—
Why dares not Bertha enter
Within the close-shut door?
If he—her all—her Brother,
Lies dying in that gloom,
What strange mysterious power
Has sent her from the room?

4

It is not one week's anguish
That can have changed her so;
Joy has not died here lately,
Struck down by one quick blow;
But cruel months have needed
Their long relentless chain,
To teach that shrinking manner
Of helpless, hopeless pain.

5

The struggle was scarce over
Last Christmas Eve had brought:

The fibres still were quivering
Of the one wounded thought,
When Herbert—who, unconscious,
Had guessed no inward strife—
Bade her, in pride and pleasure,
Welcome his fair young wife.

6

Bade her rejoice, and smiling,
Although his eyes were dim,
Thank'd God he thus could pay her
The care she gave to him.
This fresh bright life would bring her
A new and joyous fate—
O Bertha, check the murmur
That cries, Too late! too late!

7

Too late! Could she have known it
A few short weeks before,
That his life was completed,
And needing hers no more,
She might—O sad repining!
What "might have been," forget;
"It was not," should suffice us
To stifle vain regret.

8

He needed her no longer,
Each day it grew more plain;
First with a startled wonder,
Then with a wondering pain.
Love: why, his wife best gave it;
Comfort: durst Bertha speak?
Counsel: when quick resentment
Flush'd on the young wife's cheek.

9

No more long talks by firelight

Of childish times long past,
And dreams of future greatness
Which he must reach at last;
Dreams, where her purer instinct
With truth unerring told
Where was the worthless gilding,
And where refined gold.

10

Slowly, but surely ever,
Dora's poor jealous pride,
Which she call'd love for Herbert,
Drove Bertha from his side;
And, spite of nervous effort
To share their alter'd life,
She felt a check to Herbert,
A burden to his wife.

11

This was the least; for Bertha
Fear'd, dreaded, knew at length,
How much his nature owed her
Of truth, and power, and strength;
And watch'd the daily failing
Of all his nobler part:
Low aims, weak purpose, telling
In lower, weaker art.

12

And now, when he is dying,
The last words she could hear
Must not be hers, but given
The bride of one short year.
The last care is another's;
The last prayer must not be
The one they learnt together
Beside their mother's knee.

13

Summon'd at last: she kisses
The clay-cold stiffening hand;
And, reading pleading efforts
To make her understand,
Answers, with solemn promise,
In clear but trembling tone,
To Dora's life henceforward
She will devote her own.

14

Now all is over. Bertha
Dares not remain to weep,
But soothes the frightened Dora
Into a sobbing sleep.
The poor weak child will need her:
O, who can dare complain,
When God sends a new Duty
To comfort each new Pain!

Number Three.

1

The House is all deserted
In the dim evening gloom,
Only one figure passes
Slowly from room to room;
And, pausing at each doorway,
Seems gathering up again
Within her heart the relics
Of bygone joy and pain.

2

There is an earnest longing
In those who onward gaze,
Looking with weary patience
Towards the coming days.
There is a deeper longing,
More sad, more strong, more keen:
Those know it who look backward,

And yearn for what has been.

3

At every hearth she pauses,
Touches each well-known chair;
Gazes from every window,
Lingers on every stair.
What have these months brought Bertha
Now one more year is past?
This Christmas Eve shall tell us,
The third one and the last.

4

The wilful, wayward Dora,
In those first weeks of grief,
Could seek and find in Bertha
Strength, soothing, and relief.
And Bertha—last sad comfort
True woman-heart can take—
Had something still to suffer
And do for Herbert's sake.

5

Spring, with her western breezes,
From Indian islands bore
To Bertha news that Leonard
Would seek his home once more.
What was it—joy, or sorrow?
What were they—hopes, or fears?
That flush'd her cheeks with crimson,
And fill'd her eyes with tears?

6

He came. And who so kindly
Could ask and hear her tell
Herbert's last hours; for Leonard
Had known and loved him well.
Daily he came; and Bertha,
Poor wear heart, at length,

Weigh'd down by other's weakness,
Could rest upon his strength.

7

Yet not the voice of Leonard
Could her true care beguile,
That turn'd to watch, rejoicing,
Dora's reviving smile.
So, from that little household
The worst gloom pass'd away,
The one bright hour of evening
Lit up the livelong day.

8

Days passed. The golden summer
In sudden heat bore down
Its blue, bright, glowing sweetness
Upon the scorching town.
And sights and sounds of country
Came in the warm soft tune
Sung by the honey'd breezes
Borne on the wings of June.

9

One twilight hour, but earlier
Than usual, Bertha thought
She knew the fresh sweet fragrance
Of flowers that Leonard brought;
Through open'd doors and windows
It stole up through the gloom,
And with appealing sweetness
Drew Bertha from her room.

10

Yes, he was there; and pausing
Just near the open'd door,
To check her heart's quick beating,
She heard—and paused still more—
His low voice Dora's answers—

His pleading—*Yes, she knew*
The tone—the words—the accents:
She once had heard them too.

11

"Would Bertha blame her?" Leonard's
Low, tender answer came:
"Bertha was far too noble
To think or dream of blame."
"And was he sure he loved her?"
"Yes, with the one love given
Once in a lifetime only,
With one soul and one heaven!"

12

Then came a plaintive murmur,—
"Dora had once been told
That he and Bertha—" "Dearest,
Bertha is far too cold
To love; and I, my Dora,
If once I fancied so,
It was a brief delusion,
And over,—long ago."

13

Between the Past and Present,
On that bleak moment's height,
She stood. As some lost traveller
By a quick flash of light
Seeing a gulf before him,
With dizzy, sick despair,
Reels to clutch backward, but to find
A deeper chasm there.

14

The twilight grew still darker,
The fragrant flowers more sweet,
The stars shone out in heaven,
The lamps gleam'd down the street;

And hours pass'd in dreaming
Over their new-found fate,
Ere they could think of wondering
Why Bertha was so late.

15

She came, and calmly listen'd;
In vain they strove to trace
If Herbert's memory shadow'd
In grief upon her face.
No blame, no wonder show'd there,
No feeling could be told;
Her voice was not less steady,
Her manner not more cold.

16

They could not hear the anguish
That broke in words of pain
Through that calm summer midnight,—
"My Herbert—mine again!"
Yes, they have once been parted,
But this day shall restore
The long lost one: she claims him:
"My Herbert—mine once more!"

17

Now Christmas Eve returning,
Saw Bertha stand beside
The altar, greeting Dora,
Again a smiling bride;
And now the gloomy evening
Sees Bertha pale and worn,
Leaving the house for ever,
To wander out forlorn.

18

Forlorn—nay, not so. Anguish
Shall do its work at length;
Her soul, pass'd through the fire,

Shall gain still purer strength.
Somewhere there waits for Bertha
An earnest noble part;
And, meanwhile, God is with her,—
God, and her own true heart!

I could warmly and sincerely praise the little poem, when Jarber had done reading it; but I could not say that it tended in any degree towards clearing up the mystery of the empty House.

Whether it was the absence of the irritating influence of Trottle, or whether it was simply fatigue, I cannot say, but Jarber did not strike me, that evening, as being in his usual spirits. And though he declared that he was not in the least daunted by his want of success thus far, and that he was resolutely determined to make more discoveries, he spoke in a languid absent manner, and shortly afterwards took his leave at rather an early hour.

When Trottle came back, and when I indignantly taxed him with Philandering, he not only denied the imputation, but asserted that he had been employed on my service, and, in consideration of that, boldly asked for leave of absence for two days, and for a morning to himself afterwards, to complete the business, in which he solemnly declared that I was interested. In remembrance of his long and faithful service to me, I did violence to myself, and granted his request. And he, on his side, engaged to explain himself to my satisfaction, in a week's time, on Monday evening the twentieth.

A day or two before, I sent to Jarber's lodgings to ask him to drop in to tea. His landlady sent back an apology for him that made my hair stand on end. His feet were in hot water; his head was in a flannel petticoat; a green shade was over his eyes; the rheumatism was in his legs; and a mustard-poultice was on his chest. He was also a little feverish, and rather distracted in his mind about Manchester Marriages, a Dwarf, and Three Evenings, or Evening Parties—his landlady was not sure which—in an empty House, with the Water Rate unpaid.

Under these distressing circumstances, I was necessarily left alone with Trottle. His promised explanation began, like Jarber's discoveries, with the reading of a written paper. The only difference was that Trottle introduced his manuscript under the name of a Report.

CHAPTER 5
TROTTLE'S REPORT

The curious events related in these pages would, many of them, most likely never have happened, if a person named Trottle had not presumed, contrary to his usual custom, to think for himself.

The subject on which the person in question had ventured, for the first time in his life, to form an opinion purely and entirely his own, was one which had already excited the interest of his respected mistress in a very extraordinary degree. Or, to put it in plainer terms still, the subject was no other than the mystery of the empty House.

Feeling no sort of objection to set a success of his own, if possible, side by side with a failure of Mr. Jarber's, Trottle made up his mind, one Monday evening, to try what he could do, on his own account, towards clearing up the mystery of the empty House. Carefully dismissing from his mind all nonsensical notions of former tenants and their histories, and keeping the one point in view steadily before him, he started to reach it in the shortest way, by walking straight up to the House, and bringing himself face to face with the first person in it who opened the door to him.

It was getting towards dark, on Monday evening, the thirteenth of the month, when Trottle first set foot on the steps of the House. When he knocked at the door, he knew nothing of the matter which he was about to investigate, except that the landlord was an elderly widower of good fortune, and that his name was Forley. A small beginning enough for a man to start from, certainly!

On dropping the knocker, his first proceeding was to look down cautiously out of the corner of his right eye, for any results which might show themselves at the kitchen-window. There appeared at it immediately the figure of a woman, who looked up inquisitively at the stranger on the steps, left the window in a hurry, and came back to it with an open letter in her hand, which she held up to the fading light. After looking over the letter hastily for a moment or so, the woman disappeared once more.

Trottle next heard footsteps shuffling and scraping along the bare hall of the house. On a sudden they ceased, and the sound of two voices—a shrill persuading voice and a gruff resisting voice—confusedly reached his ears. After a while, the voices left off speaking—a chain was undone, a bolt drawn back—the door opened—and Trottle stood face to face with two persons, a woman in advance, and a man behind her, leaning back flat against the wall.

"Wish you good evening, sir," says the woman, in such a sudden way, and in such a cracked voice, that it was quite startling to hear her. "Chilly weather, ain't it, sir? Please to walk in. You come from good Mr. Forley, don't you, sir?"

"Don't you, sir?" chimes in the man hoarsely, making a sort of gruff echo of himself, and chuckling after it, as if he thought he had made a joke.

If Trottle had said, "No," the door would have been probably closed in his face. Therefore, he took circumstances as he found them, and boldly ran all the risk, whatever it might be, of saying, "Yes."

"Quite right sir," says the woman. "Good Mr. Forley's letter told us his particular friend would be here to represent him, at dusk, on Monday the thirteenth—or, if not on Monday the thirteenth, then on Monday the twentieth, at the same time, without fail. And here you are on Monday the thirteenth, ain't you, sir? Mr. Forley's particular friend, and dressed all in black—quite right, sir! Please to step into the dining-room—it's always kep scoured and clean against Mr. Forley comes here—and I'll fetch a candle in half a minute. It gets so dark in the evenings, now, you hardly know where you are, do you, sir? And how is good Mr. Forley in his health? We trust he is better, Benjamin, don't we? We are so sorry not to see him as usual, Benjamin, ain't we? In half a minute, sir, if you don't mind waiting, I'll be back with the candle. Come along, Benjamin."

"Come along, Benjamin," chimes in the echo, and chuckles again as if he thought he had made another joke.

Left alone in the empty front-parlour, Trottle wondered what was coming next, as he heard the shuffling, scraping footsteps go slowly down the kitchen-stairs. The front-door had been carefully chained up and bolted behind him on his entrance; and there was not the least chance of his being able to open it to effect his escape, without betraying himself by making a noise.

Not being of the Jarber sort, luckily for himself, he took his situation quietly, as he found it, and turned his time, while alone, to account, by summing up in his own mind the few particulars which he had discovered thus far. He had found out, first, that Mr. Forley was in the habit of visiting the house regularly. Second, that Mr. Forley being prevented by illness from seeing the people put in charge as usual, had appointed a friend to represent him; and had written to say so. Third, that the friend had a choice of two Mondays, at a particular time in the evening, for doing his errand; and that Trottle had accidentally hit on this time, and on the first of the Mondays, for beginning his own investigations. Fourth, that the similarity between Trottle's black dress, as servant out of livery, and the dress of the messenger (whoever he might be), had helped the error by which Trottle was profiting. So far, so good. But what was the messenger's errand? and what chance was there that he might not come up and knock at the door himself, from minute to minute, on that very evening?

While Trottle was turning over this last consideration in his mind, he heard the shuffling footsteps come up the stairs again, with a flash of candle-light going before them. He waited for the woman's coming in with some little anxiety; for the twilight had been too dim on his getting into the house to allow him to see either her face or the man's face at all clearly.

The woman came in first, with the man she called Benjamin at her heels, and set the candle on the mantel-piece. Trottle takes leave to describe her as an offensively-cheerful old woman, awfully lean and wiry, and sharp all over, at eyes, nose, and chin—devilishly brisk, smiling, and restless, with a dirty false front and a dirty black cap, and short fidgety arms, and long hooked finger-nails—an unnaturally lusty old woman, who walked with a spring in her wicked old feet, and spoke with a smirk on her wicked old face—the sort of old woman (as Trottle thinks) who ought to have lived in the dark ages, and been ducked in a horse-pond, instead of flourishing in the nineteenth century, and taking charge of a Christian house.

"You'll please to excuse my son, Benjamin, won't you, sir?" says this witch without a broomstick, pointing to the man behind her, propped against the bare wall of the dining-room, exactly as he had been propped against the bare wall of the passage. "He's got his inside dreadful bad again, has my son Benjamin. And he won't go to bed, and he will follow me about the house, *upstairs and downstairs, and in my lady's chamber*, as the song says, you know. It's his indigestion, poor dear, that sours his temper and makes him so agravating—and indisgestion is a wearing thing to the best of us, ain't it, sir?"

"Ain't it, sir?" chimes in aggravating Benjamin, winking at the candle-light like an owl at the sunshine.

Trottle examined the man curiously, while his horrid old mother was speaking of him. He found "My son Benjamin" to be little and lean, and buttoned-up slovenly in a frowsy old great-coat that fell down to his ragged carpet-slippers. His eyes were very watery, his cheeks very pale, and his lips very red. His breathing was so uncommonly loud, that it sounded almost like a snore. His head rolled helplessly in the monstrous big collar of his great-coat; and his limp, lazy hands pottered about the wall on either side of him, as if they were groping for a imaginary bottle. In plain English, the complaint of "My son Benjamin" was drunkenness, of the stupid, pig-headed, sottish kind. Drawing this conclusion easily enough, after a moment's observation of the man, Trottle found himself, nevertheless, keeping his eyes fixed much longer than was necessary on the ugly drunken face rolling about in the monstrous big coat collar, and looking at it with a curiosity that he could hardly account for at first. Was there something familiar to him in the man's features? He turned away from them for an instant, and then turned back to him again. After that second look, the notion forced itself into his mind, that he had certainly seen a face somewhere, of which that sot's face appeared like a kind of slovenly copy. "Where?" thinks he to himself, "where did I last see the man whom this agravating Benjamin, here, so very strongly reminds me of?"

It was no time, just then—with the cheerful old woman's eye searching him all over, and the cheerful old woman's tongue talking at him, nineteen to the dozen—for Trottle to be ransacking his memory for small matters that had got into wrong corners of it. He put by in his mind that very curious circumstance respecting Benjamin's face, to be taken up again when a fit opportunity offered itself; and kept his wits about him in prime order for present necessities.

"You wouldn't like to go down into the kitchen, would you?" says the witch without the broomstick, as familiar as if she had been Trottle's mother, instead of Benjamin's. "There's a bit of fire in the grate, and the sink in the back kitchen don't smell to matter much today, and it's uncommon chilly up here when a person's flesh don't hardly cover a person's bones. But you don't look cold, sir, do you? And then, why, Lord bless my soul, our little bit of business is so very, very little, it's hardly worthwhile to go downstairs about it, after all. Quite a game at business, ain't it, sir? Give-and-take that's what I call it—give-and-take!"

With that, her wicked old eyes settled hungrily on the region round about Trottle's waistcoat-pocket, and she began to chuckle like her son, holding out one of her skinny hands, and tapping cheerfully in the palm with the knuckles of the other. Aggravating Benjamin, seeing what she was about, roused up a little, chuckled and tapped in imitation of her, got an idea of his own into his muddled head all of a sudden, and bolted it out charitably for the benefit of Trottle.

"I say!" says Benjamin, settling himself against the wall and nodding his head viciously at his cheerful old mother. "I say! Look out. She'll skin you!"

Assisted by these signs and warnings, Trottle found no difficulty in understanding that the business referred to was the giving and taking of money, and that he was expected to be the giver. It was at this stage of the proceedings that he first felt decidedly uncomfortable, and more than half inclined to wish he was on the street-side of the house-door again.

He was still cudgelling his brains for an excuse to save his pocket, when the silence was suddenly interrupted by a sound in the upper part of the house.

It was not at all loud—it was a quiet, still, scraping sound—so faint that it could hardly have reached the quickest ears, except in an empty house.

"Do you hear that, Benjamin?" says the old woman. "He's at it again, even in the dark, ain't he? P'raps you'd like to see him, sir!" says she, turning on Trottle, and poking her grinning face close to him. "Only name it; only say if you'd like to see him before we do our little bit of business—and I'll show good Forley's friend upstairs, just as if he was good Mr. Forley himself. *My* legs are all right, whatever Benjamin's may be. I get younger and younger, and stronger and stronger, and jollier and jollier, every day—that's what I do! Don't mind the stairs on my account, sir, if you'd like to see him."

"Him?" Trottle wondered whether "him" meant a man, or a boy, or a domestic animal of the male species. Whatever it meant, here was a chance of putting off that uncomfortable give-and-take-business, and, better still, a chance perhaps of finding out one of the secrets of the mysterious House. Trottle's spirits began to rise again and he said "Yes," directly, with the confidence of a man who knew all about it.

Benjamin's mother took the candle at once, and lighted Trottle briskly to the stairs; and Benjamin himself tried to follow as usual. But getting up several flights of stairs, even helped by

181

the banisters, was more, with his particular complaint, than he seemed to feel himself inclined to venture on. He sat down obstinately on the lowest step, with his head against the wall, and the tails of his big great-coat spreading out magnificently on the stairs behind him and above him, like a dirty imitation of a court lady's train.

"Don't sit there, dear," says his affectionate mother, stopping to snuff the candle on the first landing.

"I shall sit here," says Benjamin, aggravating to the last, "till the milk comes in the morning."

The cheerful old woman went on nimbly up the stairs to the first floor, and Trottle followed, with his eyes and ears wide open. He had seen nothing out of the common in the front-parlour, or up the staircase, so far. The House was dirty and dreary and close-smelling—but there was nothing about it to excite the least curiosity, except the faint scraping sound, which was now beginning to get a little clearer—though still not at all loud—as Trottle followed his leader up the stairs to the second floor.

Nothing on the second-floor landing, but cobwebs above and bits of broken plaster below, cracked off from the ceiling. Benjamin's mother was not a bit out of breath, and looked all ready to go to the top of the monument if necessary. The faint scraping sound had got a little clearer still; but Trottle was no nearer to guessing what it might be, than when he first heard it in the parlour downstairs.

On the third, and last, floor, there were two doors; one, which was shut, leading into the front garret; and one, which was ajar, leading into the back garret. There was a loft in the ceiling above the landing; but the cobwebs all over it vouched sufficiently for its not having been opened for some little time. The scraping noise, plainer than ever here, sounded on the other side of the back garret door; and, to Trottle's great relief, that was precisely the door which the cheerful old woman now pushed open.

Trottle followed her in; and, for once in his life, at any rate, was struck dumb with amazement, at the sight which the inside of the room revealed to him.

The garret was absolutely empty of everything in the shape of furniture. It must have been used at one time or other, by somebody engaged in a profession or a trade which required for the practice of it a great deal of light; for the one window in the room, which looked out on a wide open space at the back of the house, was three or four times as large, every way, as a garret-window usually is.

Close under this window, kneeling on the bare boards with his face to the door, there appeared, of all the creatures in the world to see alone at such a place and at such a time, a mere mite of a child—a little, lonely, wizen, strangely-clad boy, who could not at the most, have been more than five years old. He had a greasy old blue shawl crossed over his breast, and rolled up, to keep the ends from the ground, into a great big lump on his back. A strip of something which looked like the remains of a woman's flannel petticoat, showed itself under the shawl, and, below that again, a pair of rusty black stockings, worlds too large for him, covered his legs and his shoeless feet. A pair of old clumsy muffetees, which had worked themselves up on his little frail red arms to the elbows, and a big cotton nightcap that had dropped down to his very eyebrows, finished off the strange dress which the poor little man seemed not half big enough to fill out, and not near strong enough to walk about in.

But there was something to see even more extraordinary than the clothes the child was swaddled up in, and that was the game which he was playing at, all by himself; and which, moreover, explained in the most unexpected manner the faint scraping noise that had found its way downstairs, through the half-opened door, in the silence of the empty house.

It has been mentioned that the child was on his knees in the garret, when Trottle first saw him. He was not saying his prayers, and not crouching down in terror at being alone in the dark. He was, odd and unaccountable as it may appear, doing nothing more or less than playing at a charwoman's or housemaid's business of scouring the floor. Both his little hands had tight hold of a mangy old blacking-brush, with hardly any bristles left in it, which he was rubbing backwards and forwards on the boards, as gravely and steadily as if he had been at scouring-work for years, and had got a large family to keep by it. The coming-in of Trottle and the old woman did not startle or disturb him in the least. He just looked up for a minute at the candle, with a pair of very bright, sharp eyes, and then went on with his work again, as if nothing had happened.

On one side of him was a battered pint saucepan without a handle, which was his make-believe pail; and on the other a morsel of slate-coloured cotton rag, which stood for his flannel to wipe up with. After scrubbing bravely for a minute or two, he took the bit of rag, and mopped up, and then squeezed make-believe water out into his make-believe pail, as grave as any judge that ever sat on a Bench. By the time he thought he had got the floor pretty dry, he raised himself upright on his knees, and blew out a good long breath, and set his little red arms akimbo, and nodded at Trottle.

"There!" says the child, knitting his little downy eyebrows into a frown. "Drat the dirt! I've cleaned up. Where's my beer?"

Benjamin's mother chuckled till Trottle thought she would have choked herself.

"Lord ha' mercy on us!" says she, "just hear the imp. You would never think he was only five years old, would you, sir? Please to tell good Mr. Forley you saw him going on as nicely as ever, playing at being me scouring the parlour floor, and calling for my beer afterwards. That's his regular game, morning, noon, and night—he's never tired of it. Only look how snug we've been and dressed him. That's my shawl a keepin his precious little body warm, and Benjamin's nightcap a keepin his precious little head warm, and Benjamin's stockings, drawed over his trowsers, a keepin his precious little legs warm. He's snug and happy if ever a imp was yet. 'Where's my beer!'—say it again, little dear, say it again!"

If Trottle had seen the boy, with a light and a fire in the room, clothed like other children, and playing naturally with a top, or a box of soldiers, or a bouncing big India-rubber ball, he might have been as cheerful under the circumstances as Benjamin's mother herself. But seeing the child reduced (as he could not help suspecting) for want of proper toys and proper child's company, to take up with the mocking of an old woman at her scouring-work, for something to stand in the place of a game, Trottle, though not a family man, nevertheless felt the sight before him to be, in its way, one of the saddest and the most pitiable that he had ever witnessed.

"Why, my man," says he, "you're the boldest little chap in all England. You don't seem a bit afraid of being up here all by yourself in the dark."

"The big winder," says the child, pointing up to it, "sees in the dark; and I see with the big winder." He stops a bit, and gets up on his legs, and looks hard at Benjamin's mother. "I'm a good 'un," says he, "ain't I? I save candle."

Trottle wondered what else the forlorn little creature had been brought up to do without, besides candle-light; and risked putting a question as to whether he ever got a run in the open air to cheer him up a bit. O, yes, he had a run now and then, out of doors (to say nothing of his runs about the house), the lively little cricket—a run according to good Mr. Forley's instructions, which were followed out carefully, as good Mr. Forley's friend would be glad to hear, to the very letter.

As Trottle could only have made one reply to this, namely, that good Mr. Forley's instructions were, in his opinion, the instructions of an infernal scamp; and as he felt that such an answer would naturally prove the death-blow to all further discoveries on his part, he gulped down his feelings before they got too many for him, and held his tongue, and looked round towards the window again to see what the forlorn little boy was going to amuse himself with next.

The child had gathered up his blacking-brush and bit of rag, and had put them into the old tin saucepan; and was now working his way, as well as his clothes would let him, with his make-believe pail hugged up in his arms, towards a door of communication which led from the back to the front garret.

"I say," says he, looking round sharply over his shoulder, "what are you two stopping here for? I'm going to bed now—and so I tell you!"

With that, he opened the door, and walked into the front room. Seeing Trottle take a step or two to follow him, Benjamin's mother opened her wicked old eyes in a state of great astonishment.

"Mercy on us!" says she, "haven't you seen enough of him yet?"

"No," says Trottle. "I should like to see him go to bed."

Benjamin's mother burst into such a fit of chuckling that the loose extinguisher in the candlestick clattered again with the shaking of her hand. To think of good Mr. Forley's friend taking ten times more trouble about the imp than good Mr. Forley himself! Such a joke as that, Benjamin's mother had not often met with in the course of her life, and she begged to be excused if she took the liberty of having a laugh at it.

Leaving her to laugh as much as she pleased, and coming to a pretty positive conclusion, after what he had just heard, that Mr. Forley's interest in the child was not of the fondest possible kind, Trottle walked into the front room, and Benjamin's mother, enjoying herself immensely, followed with the candle.

There were two pieces of furniture in the front garret. One, an old stool of the sort that is used to stand a cask of beer on; and the other a great big rickety straddling old truckle bedstead. In the middle of this bedstead, surrounded by a dim brown waste of sacking, was a kind of little island of poor bedding—an old bolster, with nearly all the feathers out of it, doubled in three for a pillow; a mere shred of patchwork counter-pane, and a blanket; and under that, and peeping out a little on either side beyond the loose clothes, two faded chair cushions of horsehair, laid along together for a sort of makeshift mattress. When Trottle got into the room, the lonely little boy had scrambled up on the bedstead with the help of the beer-stool, and was kneeling on the outer rim of sacking with the shred of counterpane in his hands, just making ready to tuck it in for himself under the chair cushions.

"I'll tuck you up, my man," says Trottle. "Jump into bed, and let me try."

"I mean to tuck myself up," says the poor forlorn child, "and I don't mean to jump. I mean to crawl, I do—and so I tell you!"

With that, he set to work, tucking in the clothes tight all down the sides of the cushions, but leaving them open at the foot. Then, getting up on his knees, and looking hard at Trottle as much as to say, "What do you mean by offering to help such a handy little chap as me?" he began to untie the big shawl for himself, and did it, too, in less than half a minute. Then, doubling the shawl up loose over the foot of the bed, he says, "I say, look here," and ducks under the clothes, head first, worming his way up and up softly, under the blanket and counterpane, till Trottle saw the top of the large nightcap slowly peep out on the bolster.

This over-sized head-gear of the child's had so shoved itself down in the course of his journey to the pillow, under the clothes, that when he got his face fairly out on the bolster, he was all nightcap down to his mouth. He soon freed himself, however, from this slight encumbrance by turning the ends of the cap up gravely to their old place over his eyebrows—looked at Trottle—said, "Snug, ain't it? Goodbye!"—popped his face under the clothes again—and left nothing to be seen of him but the empty peak of the big nightcap standing up sturdily on end in the middle of the bolster.

"What a young limb it is, ain't it?" says Benjamin's mother, giving Trottle a cheerful dig with her elbow. "Come on! you won't see no more of him tonight!"

"And so I tell you!" sings out a shrill, little voice under the bedclothes, chiming in with a playful finish to the old woman's last words.

If Trottle had not been, by this time, positively resolved to follow the wicked secret which accident had mixed him up with, through all its turnings and windings, right on to the end, he would have probably snatched the boy up then and there, and carried him off from his garret prison, bed-clothes and all. As it was, he put a strong check on himself, kept his eye on future possibilities, and allowed Benjamin's mother to lead him downstairs again.

"Mind them top bannisters," says she, as Trottle laid his hand on them. "They are as rotten as medlars every one of 'em."

"When people come to see the premises," says Trottle, trying to feel his way a little farther into the mystery of the House, "you don't bring many of them up here, do you?"

"Bless your heart alive!" says she, "nobody ever comes now. The outside of the house is quite enough to warn them off. Mores the pity, as I say. It used to keep me in spirits, staggering 'em all, one after another, with the frightful high rent—specially the women, drat 'em. 'What's the rent of this house?'—'Hundred and twenty pound a-year!'—

"'Hundred and twenty? why, there ain't a house in the street as lets for more than eighty!'—Likely enough, ma'am; other landlords may lower their rents if they please; but this here landlord sticks to his rights, and means to have as much for his house as his father had before him!'—

"'But the neighbourhood's gone off since then!'—'Hundred and twenty pound, ma'am.'—

"'The landlord must be mad!'—'Hundred and twenty pound, ma'am.'—

"'Open the door you impertinent woman!' Lord! what a happiness it was to see 'em bounce out, with that awful rent a-ringing in their ears all down the street!"

She stopped on the second-floor landing to treat herself to another chuckle, while Trottle privately posted up in his memory what he had just heard. "Two points made out," he thought to himself: "the house is kept empty on purpose, and the way it's done is to ask a rent that nobody will pay."

"Ah, deary me!" says Benjamin's mother, changing the subject on a sudden, and twisting back with a horrid, greedy quickness to those awkward money-matters which she had broached down in the parlour. "What we've done, one way and another for Mr. Forley, it isn't in words to tell! That nice little bit of business of ours ought to be a bigger bit of business, considering the trouble we take, Benjamin and me, to make the imp upstairs as happy as the day is long. If good Mr. Forley would only please to think a little more of what a deal he owes to Benjamin and me—"

"That's just it," says Trottle, catching her up short in desperation, and seeing his way, by the help of those last words of hers, to slipping cleverly through her fingers. "What should you say, if I told you that Mr. Forley was nothing like so far from thinking about that little matter as you fancy? You would be disappointed, now, if I told you that I had come today without the money?"- (her lank old jaw fell, and her villainous old eyes glared, in a perfect state of panic, at that!)—"But what should you say, if I told you that Mr. Forley was only waiting for my report, to send me here next Monday, at dusk, with a bigger bit of business for us two to do together than ever you think for? What should you say to that?"

The old wretch came so near to Trottle, before she answered, and jammed him up confidentially so close into the corner of the landing, that his throat, in a manner, rose at her.

"Can you count it off, do you think, on more than that?" says she, holding up her four skinny fingers and her long crooked thumb, all of a tremble, right before his face.

"What do you say to two hands, instead of one?" says he, pushing past her, and getting downstairs as fast as he could.

What she said Trottle thinks it best not to report, seeing that the old hypocrite, getting next door to light-headed at the golden prospect before her, took such liberties with unearthly names and persons which ought never to have approached her lips, and rained down such an awful shower of blessings on Trottle's head, that his hair almost stood on end to hear her. He went on downstairs as fast as his feet would carry him, till he was brought up all standing, as the sailors say, on the last flight, by aggravating Benjamin, lying right across the stair, and fallen off, as might have been expected, into a heavy drunken sleep.

189

The sight of him instantly reminded Trottle of the curious half likeness which he had already detected between the face of Benjamin and the face of another man, whom he had seen at a past time in very different circumstances. He determined, before leaving the House, to have one more look at the wretched muddled creature; and accordingly shook him up smartly, and propped him against the staircase wall, before his mother could interfere.

"Leave him to me; I'll freshen him up," says Trottle to the old woman, looking hard in Benjamin's face, while he spoke.

The fright and surprise of being suddenly woke up, seemed, for about a quarter of a minute, to sober the creature. When he first opened his eyes, there was a new look in them for a moment, which struck home to Trottle's memory as quick and as clear as a flash of light. The old maudlin sleepy expression came back again in another instant, and blurred out all further signs and tokens of the past. But Trottle had seen enough in the moment before it came; and he troubled Benjamin's face with no more inquiries.

"Next Monday, at dusk," says he, cutting short some more of the old woman's palaver about Benjamin's indisgestion. "I've got no more time to spare, ma'am, tonight: please to let me out."

With a few last blessings, a few last dutiful messages to good Mr. Forley, and a few last friendly hints not to forget next Monday at dusk, Trottle contrived to struggle through the sickening business of leave-taking; to get the door opened; and to find himself, to his own indescribable relief, once more on the outer side of the House To Let.

CHAPTER 6

LET AT LAST

"There, ma'am!" said Trottle, folding up the manuscript from which he had been reading, and setting it down with a smart tap of triumph on the table. "May I venture to ask what you think of that plain statement, as a guess on my part (and not on Mr. Jarber's) at the riddle of the empty House?"

For a minute or two I was unable to say a word. When I recovered a little, my first question referred to the poor forlorn little boy.

"Today is Monday the twentieth," I said. "Surely you have not let a whole week go by without trying to find out something more?"

"Except at bedtime, and meals, ma'am," answered Trottle, "I have not let an hour go by. Please to understand that I have only come to an end of what I have written, and not to an end of what I have done. I wrote down those first particulars, ma'am, because they are of great importance, and also because I was determined to come forward with my written documents, seeing that Mr. Jarber chose to come forward, in the first instance, with his. I am now ready to go on with the second part of my story as shortly and plainly as possible, by word of mouth.

"The first thing I must clear up, if you please, is the matter of Mr. Forley's family affairs. I have heard you speak of them, ma'am, at various times; and I have understood that Mr. Forley had two children only by his deceased wife, both daughters. The eldest daughter married, to her father's entire satisfaction, one Mr. Bayne, a rich man, holding a high government situation in Canada. She is now living there with her husband, and her only child, a little girl of eight or nine years old. Right so far, I think, ma'am?"

"Quite right," I said.

"The second daughter," Trottle went on, "and Mr. Forley's favourite, set her father's wishes and the opinions of the world at flat defiance, by running away with a man of low origin—a mate of a merchant-vessel, named Kirkland. Mr. Forley not only never forgave that marriage, but vowed that he would visit the scandal of it heavily in the future on husband and wife. Both escaped his vengeance, whatever he meant it to be. The husband was drowned on his first voyage after his marriage, and the wife died in child-bed. Right again, I believe, ma'am?"

"Again quite right."

"Having got the family matter all right, we will now go back, ma'am, to me and my doings. Last Monday, I asked you for leave of absence for two days; I employed the time in clearing up the matter of Benjamin's face. Last Saturday I was out of the way when you wanted me. I played truant, ma'am, on that occasion, in company with a friend of mine, who is managing clerk in a lawyer's office; and we both spent the morning at Doctors' Commons, over the last will and testament of Mr. Forley's father. Leaving the will-business for a moment, please to follow me first, if you have no objection, into the ugly subject of Benjamin's face. About six or seven years ago (thanks to your kindness) I had a week's holiday with some friends of mine who live in the town of Pendlebury.

"One of those friends (the only one now left in the place) kept a chemist's shop, and in that shop I was made acquainted with one of the two doctors in the town, named Barsham. This Barsham was a first-rate surgeon, and might have got to the top of his profession, if he had not been a first-rate blackguard. As it was, he both drank and gambled; nobody would have anything to do with him in Pendlebury; and, at the time when I was made known to him in the chemist's shop, the other doctor, Mr. Dix, who was not to be compared with him for surgical skill, but who was a respectable man, had got all the practice; and Barsham and his old mother were living together in such a condition of utter poverty, that it was a marvel to everybody how they kept out of the parish workhouse."

"Benjamin and Benjamin's mother!"

"Exactly, ma'am. Last Thursday morning (thanks to your kindness, again) I went to Pendlebury to my friend the chemist, to ask a few questions about Barsham and his mother. I was told that they had both left the town about five years since. When I inquired into the circumstances, some strange particulars came out in the course of the chemist's answer. You know I have no doubt, ma'am, that poor Mrs. Kirkland was confined while her husband was at sea, in lodgings at a village called Flatfield, and that she died and was buried there. But what you may not know is, that Flatfield is only three miles from Pendlebury; that the doctor who attended on Mrs. Kirkland was Barsham; that the nurse who took care of her was Barsham's mother; and that the person who called them both in, was Mr. Forley.

"Whether his daughter wrote to him, or whether he heard of it in some other way, I don't know; but he was with her (though he had sworn never to see her again when she married) a month or more before her confinement, and was backwards and forwards a good deal between Flatfield and Pendlebury. How he managed matters with the Barshams cannot at present be discovered; but it is a fact that he contrived to keep the drunken doctor sober, to everybody's amazement. It is a fact that Barsham went to the poor woman with all his wits about him.

"It is a fact that he and his mother came back from Flatfield after Mrs. Kirkland's death, packed up what few things they had, and left the town mysteriously by night. And, lastly, it is also a fact that the other doctor, Mr. Dix, was not called in to help, till a week after the birth *and burial* of the child, when the mother was sinking from exhaustion—exhaustion (to give the vagabond, Barsham, his due) not produced, in Mr. Dix's opinion, by improper medical treatment, but by the bodily weakness of the poor woman herself—"

"Burial of the child?" I interrupted, trembling all over. "Trottle! you spoke that word 'burial' in a very strange way—you are fixing your eyes on me now with a very strange look—"

Trottle leaned over close to me, and pointed through the window to the empty house.

"The child's death is registered, at Pendlebury," he said, "on Barsham's certificate, under the head of Male Infant, Still-Born. The child's coffin lies in the mother's grave, in Flatfield churchyard. The child himself—as surely as I live and breathe, is living and breathing now—a castaway and a prisoner in that villainous house!"

I sank back in my chair.

"It's guess-work, so far, but it is borne in on my mind, for all that, as truth. Rouse yourself, ma'am, and think a little. The last I hear of Barsham, he is attending Mr. Forley's disobedient daughter. The next I see of Barsham, he is in Mr. Forley's house, trusted with a secret. He and his mother leave Pendlebury suddenly and suspiciously five years back; and he and his mother have got a child of five years old, hidden away in the house. Wait! please to wait—I have not done yet. The will left by Mr. Forley's father, strengthens the suspicion. The friend I took with me to Doctors' Commons, made himself master of the contents of that will; and when he had done so, I put these two questions to him. 'Can Mr. Forley leave his money at his own discretion to anybody he pleases?'

" 'No,' my friend says, 'his father has left him with only a life interest in it.'

"'Suppose one of Mr. Forley's married daughters has a girl, and the other a boy, how would the money go?'

"'It would all go,' my friend says, 'to the boy, and it would be charged with the payment of a certain annual income to his female cousin. After her death, it would go back to the male descendant, and to his heirs.'

"Consider that, ma'am! The child of the daughter whom Mr. Forley hates, whose husband has been snatched away from his vengeance by death, takes his whole property in defiance of him; and the child of the daughter whom he loves, is left a pensioner on her low-born boy-cousin for life! There was good-too good reason—why that child of Mrs. Kirkland's should be registered stillborn. And if, as I believe, the register is founded on a false certificate, there is better, still better reason, why the existence of the child should be hidden, and all trace of his parentage blotted out, in the garret of that empty house."

He stopped, and pointed for the second time to the dim, dust-covered garret-windows opposite. As he did so, I was startled—a very slight matter sufficed to frighten me now—by a knock at the door of the room in which we were sitting.

My maid came in, with a letter in her hand. I took it from her. The mourning card, which was all the envelope enclosed, dropped from my hands.

George Forley was no more. He had departed this life three

days since, on the evening of Friday.

"Did our last chance of discovering the truth," I asked, "rest with *him*? Has it died with *his* death?"

"Courage, ma'am! I think not. Our chance rests on our power to make Barsham and his mother confess; and Mr. Forley's death, by leaving them helpless, seems to put that power into our hands. With your permission, I will not wait till dusk today, as I at first intended, but will make sure of those two people at once. With a policeman in plain clothes to watch the house, in case they try to leave it; with this card to vouch for the fact of Mr. Forley's death; and with a bold acknowledgment on my part of having got possession of their secret, and of being ready to use it against them in case of need, I think there is little doubt of bringing Barsham and his mother to terms.

"In case I find it impossible to get back here before dusk, please to sit near the window, ma'am, and watch the house, a little before they light the street-lamps. If you see the front-door open and close again, will you be good enough to put on your bonnet, and come across to me immediately? Mr. Forley's death may, or may not, prevent his messenger from coming as arranged. But, if the person does come, it is of importance that you, as a relative of Mr. Forley's should be present to see him, and to have that proper influence over him which I cannot pretend to exercise."

The only words I could say to Trottle as he opened the door and left me, were words charging him to take care that no harm happened to the poor forlorn little boy.

Left alone, I drew my chair to the window; and looked out with a beating heart at the guilty house. I waited and waited through what appeared to me to be an endless time, until I heard the wheels of a cab stop at the end of the street. I looked in that direction, and saw Trottle get out of the cab alone, walk up to the house, and knock at the door. He was let in by Barsham's mother. A minute or two later, a decently-dressed man sauntered past the house, looked up at it for a moment, and sauntered on to the corner of the street close by. Here he leant against the post, and lighted a cigar, and stopped there smoking in an idle way, but keeping his face always turned in the direction of the house-door.

I waited and waited still. I waited and waited, with my eyes riveted to the door of the house. At last I thought I saw it open in the dusk, and then felt sure I heard it shut again softly. Though I tried hard to compose myself, I trembled so that I was obliged to call for Peggy to help me on with my bonnet and cloak, and was forced to take her arm to lean on, in crossing the street.

Trottle opened the door to us, before we could knock. Peggy went back, and I went in. He had a lighted candle in his hand.

"It has happened, ma'am, as I thought it would," he whispered, leading me into the bare, comfortless, empty parlour. "Barsham and his mother have consulted their own interests, and have come to terms. My guess-work is guess-work no longer. It is now what I felt it was—Truth!"

Something strange to me—something which women who are mothers must often know—trembled suddenly in my heart, and brought the warm tears of my youthful days thronging back into my eyes. I took my faithful old servant by the hand, and asked him to let me see Mrs. Kirkland's child, for his mother's sake.

"If you desire it, ma'am," said Trottle, with a gentleness of manner that I had never noticed in him before. "But pray don't think me wanting in duty and right feeling, if I beg you to try and wait a little. You are agitated already, and a first meeting with the child will not help to make you so calm, as you would wish to be, if Mr. Forley's messenger comes. The little boy is safe up-stairs. Pray think first of trying to compose yourself for a meeting with a stranger; and believe me you shall not leave the house afterwards without the child."

I felt that Trottle was right, and sat down as patiently as I could in a chair he had thoughtfully placed ready for me. I was so horrified at the discovery of my own relation's wickedness that when Trottle proposed to make me acquainted with the confession wrung from Barsham and his mother, I begged him to spare me all details, and only to tell me what was necessary about George Forley.

"All that can be said for Mr. Forley, ma'am, is, that he was just scrupulous enough to hide the child's existence and blot out its parentage here, instead of consenting, at the first, to its death, or afterwards, when the boy grew up, to turning him adrift, absolutely helpless in the world. The fraud has been managed, ma'am, with the cunning of Satan himself. Mr. Forley had the hold over the Barshams, that they had helped him in his villainy, and that they were dependent on him for the bread they eat. He brought them up to London to keep them securely under his own eye. He put them into this empty house (taking it out of the agent's hands previously, on pretence that he meant to manage the letting of it himself); and by keeping the house empty, made it the surest of all hiding places for the child.

"Here, Mr. Forley could come, whenever he pleased, to see that the poor lonely child was not absolutely starved; sure that his visits would only appear like looking after his own property. Here the child was to have been trained to believe himself Barsham's child, till he should be old enough to be provided for in some situation, as low and as poor as Mr. Forley's uneasy conscience would let him pick out. He may have thought of atonement on his death-bed; but not before—I am only too certain of it—not before!"

A low, double knock startled us.

"The messenger!" said Trottle, under his breath. He went out instantly to answer the knock; and returned, leading in a respectable-looking elderly man, dressed like Trottle, all in black, with a white cravat, but otherwise not at all resembling him.

"I am afraid I have made some mistake," said the stranger.

Trottle, considerately taking the office of explanation into his own hands, assured the gentleman that there was no mistake; mentioned to him who I was; and asked him if he had not come on business connected with the late Mr. Forley. Looking greatly astonished, the gentleman answered, "Yes." There was an awkward moment of silence, after that. The stranger seemed to be not only startled and amazed, but rather distrustful and fearful of committing himself as well. Noticing this, I thought it best to request Trottle to put an end to further embarrassment, by stating all particulars truthfully, as he had stated them to me; and I begged the gentleman to listen patiently for the late Mr. Forley's sake. He bowed to me very respectfully, and said he was prepared to listen with the greatest interest.

It was evident to me—and, I could see, to Trottle also—that we were not dealing, to say the least, with a dishonest man.

"Before I offer any opinion on what I have heard," he said, earnestly and anxiously, after Trottle had done, "I must be allowed, in justice to myself, to explain my own apparent connection with this very strange and very shocking business. I was the confidential legal adviser of the late Mr. Forley, and I am left his executor. Rather more than a fortnight back, when Mr. Forley was confined to his room by illness, he sent for me, and charged me to call and pay a certain sum of money here, to a man and woman whom I should find taking charge of the house. He said he had reasons for wishing the affair to be kept a secret.

"He begged me so to arrange my engagements that I could call at this place either on Monday last, or today, at dusk; and he mentioned that he would write to warn the people of my coming, without mentioning my name (Dalcott is my name), as he did not wish to expose me to any future importunities on the part of the man and woman. I need hardly tell you that this commission struck me as being a strange one; but, in my position with Mr. Forley, I had no resource but to accept it without asking questions, or to break off my long and friendly connection with my client. I chose the first alternative. Business prevented me from doing my errand on Monday last—and if I am here today, notwithstanding Mr. Forley's unexpected death, it is emphatically because I understood nothing of the matter, on knocking at this door; and therefore felt myself bound, as executor, to clear it up. That, on my word of honour, is the whole truth, so far as I am personally concerned."

"I feel quite sure of it, sir," I answered.

"You mentioned Mr. Forley's death, just now, as unexpected. May I inquire if you were present, and if he has left any last instructions?"

"Three hours before Mr. Forley's death," said Mr. Dalcott, "his medical attendant left him apparently in a fair way of recovery. The change for the worse took place so suddenly, and was accompanied by such severe suffering, to prevent him from communicating his last wishes to anyone. When I reached his house, he was insensible. I have since examined his papers. Not one of them refers to the present time or to the serious matter which now occupies us. In the absence of instructions I must act cautiously on what you have told me; but I will be rigidly fair and just at the same time.

"The first thing to be done," he continued, addressing himself to Trottle, "is to hear what the man and woman, downstairs, have to say. If you can supply me with writing-materials, I will take their declarations separately on the spot, in your presence, and in the presence of the policeman who is watching the house. Tomorrow I will send copies of those declarations, accompanied by a full statement of the case, to Mr. and Mrs. Bayne in Canada (both of whom know me well as the late Mr. Forley's legal adviser); and I will suspend all proceedings, on my part, until I hear from them, or from their solicitor in London. In the present posture of affairs this is all I can safely do."

We could do no less than agree with him, and thank him for his frank and honest manner of meeting us. It was arranged that I should send over the writing-materials from my lodgings; and, to my unutterable joy and relief, it was also readily acknowledged that the poor little orphan boy could find no fitter refuge than my old arms were longing to offer him, and no safer protection for the night than my roof could give. Trottle hastened away upstairs, as actively as if he had been a young man, to fetch the child down.

And he brought him down to me without another moment of delay, and I went on my knees before the poor little Mite, and embraced him, and asked him if he would go with me to where

I lived? He held me away for a moment, and his wan, shrewd little eyes looked sharp at me. Then he clung close to me all at once, and said:

"I'm a-going along with you, I am—and so I tell you!"

For inspiring the poor neglected child with this trust in my old self, I thanked Heaven, then, with all my heart and soul, and I thank it now!

I bundled the poor darling up in my own cloak, and I carried him in my own arms across the road. Peggy was lost in speechless amazement to behold me trudging out of breath upstairs, with a strange pair of poor little legs under my arm; but, she began to cry over the child the moment she saw him, like a sensible woman as she always was, and she still cried her eyes out over him in a comfortable manner, when he at last lay fast asleep, tucked up by my hands in Trottle's bed.

"And Trottle, bless you, my dear man," said I, kissing his hand, as he looked on: "the forlorn baby came to this refuge through you, and he will help you on your way to Heaven."

Trottle answered that I was his dear mistress, and immediately went and put his head out at an open window on the landing, and looked into the back street for a quarter of an hour.

That very night, as I sat thinking of the poor child, and of another poor child who is never to be thought about enough at Christmas-time, the idea came into my mind which I have lived to execute, and in the realisation of which I am the happiest of women this day.

"The executor will sell that House, Trottle?" said I.

"Not a doubt of it, ma'am, if he can find a purchaser."

"I'll buy it."

I have often seen Trottle pleased; but, I never saw him so perfectly enchanted as he was when I confided to him, which I did, then and there, the purpose that I had in view.

To make short of a long story—and what story would not be long, coming from the lips of an old woman like me, unless it was made short by main force!—I bought the House. Mrs. Bayne had her father's blood in her; she evaded the opportunity of forgiving and generous reparation that was offered her, and disowned the child; but, I was prepared for that, and loved him all the more for having no one in the world to look to, but me.

I am getting into a flurry by being over-pleased, and I dare say I am as incoherent as need be. I bought the House, and I altered it from the basement to the roof, and I turned it into a Hospital for Sick Children.

Never mind by what degrees my little adopted boy came to the knowledge of all the sights and sounds in the streets, so familiar to other children and so strange to him; never mind by what degrees he came to be pretty, and childish, and winning, and companionable, and to have pictures and toys about him, and suitable playmates. As I write, I look across the road to my Hospital, and there is the darling (who has gone over to play) nodding at me out of one of the once lonely windows, with his dear chubby face backed up by Trottle's waistcoat as he lifts my pet for "Grandma" to see.

Many an Eye I see in that House now, but it is never in solitude, never in neglect. Many an Eye I see in that House now, that is more and more radiant every day with the light of returning health. As my precious darling has changed beyond description for the brighter and the better, so do the not less precious darlings of poor women change in that House every day in the year. For which I humbly thank that Gracious Being whom the restorer of the Widow's son and of the Ruler's daughter, instructed all mankind to call their Father.

A Madman's Manuscript

'Yes!—a madman's! How that word would have struck to my heart, many years ago! How it would have roused the terror that used to come upon me sometimes, sending the blood hissing and tingling through my veins, till the cold dew of fear stood in large drops upon my skin, and my knees knocked together with fright! I like it now though. It's a fine name. Show me the monarch whose angry frown was ever feared like the glare of a madman's eye—whose cord and axe were ever half so sure as a madman's gripe. Ho! ho! It's a grand thing to be mad! to be peeped at like a wild lion through the iron bars—to gnash one's teeth and howl, through the long still night, to the merry ring of a heavy chain and to roll and twine among the straw, transported with such brave music. Hurrah for the madhouse! Oh, it's a rare place!

'I remember days when I was afraid of being mad; when I used to start from my sleep, and fall upon my knees, and pray to be spared from the curse of my race; when I rushed from the sight of merriment or happiness, to hide myself in some lonely place, and spend the weary hours in watching the progress of the fever that was to consume my brain. I knew that madness was mixed up with my very blood, and the marrow of my bones! that one generation had passed away without the pestilence appearing among them, and that I was the first in whom it would revive. I knew it must be so: that so it always had been, and so it ever would be: and when I cowered in some obscure corner of a crowded room, and saw men whisper, and point, and turn their eyes towards me, I knew they were telling each other of the doomed madman; and I slunk away again to mope in solitude.

'I did this for years; long, long years they were. The nights here are long sometimes—very long; but they are nothing to the restless nights, and dreadful dreams I had at that time. It makes me cold to remember them. Large dusky forms with sly and jeering faces crouched in the corners of the room, and bent over my bed at night, tempting me to madness. They told me in low whispers, that the floor of the old house in which my father died, was stained with his own blood, shed by his own hand in raging madness. I drove my fingers into my ears, but they screamed into my head till the room rang with it, that in one generation before him the madness slumbered, but that his grandfather had lived for years with his hands fettered to the ground, to prevent his tearing himself to pieces. I knew they told the truth—I knew it well. I had found it out years before, though they had tried to keep it from me. Ha! ha! I was too cunning for them, madman as they thought me.

'At last it came upon me, and I wondered how I could ever have feared it. I could go into the world now, and laugh and shout with the best among them. I knew I was mad, but they did not even suspect it. How I used to hug myself with delight, when I thought of the fine trick I was playing them after their old pointing and leering, when I was not mad, but only dreading that I might one day become so! And how I used to laugh for joy, when I was alone, and thought how well I kept my secret, and how quickly my kind friends would have fallen from me, if they had known the truth. I could have screamed with ecstasy when I dined alone with some fine roaring fellow, to think how pale he would have turned, and how fast he would have run, if he had known that the dear friend who sat close to him, sharpening a bright, glittering knife, was a madman with all the power, and half the will, to plunge it in his heart. Oh, it was a merry life!

'Riches became mine, wealth poured in upon me, and I rioted in pleasures enhanced a thousandfold to me by the consciousness of my well–kept secret. I inherited an estate. The law—the eagle–eyed law itself—had been deceived, and had handed over disputed thousands to a madman's hands. Where was the wit of the sharp–sighted men of sound mind? Where the dexterity of the lawyers, eager to discover a flaw? The madman's cunning had overreached them all.

'I had money. How I was courted! I spent it profusely. How I was praised! How those three proud, overbearing brothers humbled themselves before me! The old, white–headed father, too—such deference—such respect—such devoted friendship—he worshipped me! The old man had a daughter, and the young men a sister; and all the five were poor. I was rich; and when I married the girl, I saw a smile of triumph play upon the faces of her needy relatives, as they thought of their well–planned scheme, and their fine prize. It was for me to smile. To smile! To laugh outright, and tear my hair, and roll upon the ground with shrieks of merriment. They little thought they had married her to a madman.

'Stay. If they had known it, would they have saved her? A sister's happiness against her husband's gold. The lightest feather I blow into the air, against the gay chain that ornaments my body!

'In one thing I was deceived with all my cunning. If I had not been mad—for though we madmen are sharp–witted enough, we get bewildered sometimes—I should have known that the girl would rather have been placed, stiff and cold in a dull leaden coffin, than borne an envied bride to my rich, glittering house. I should have known that her heart was with the dark–eyed boy whose name I once heard her breathe in her troubled sleep; and that she had been sacrificed to me, to relieve the poverty of the old, white–headed man and the haughty brothers.

'I don't remember forms or faces now, but I know the girl was beautiful. I know she was; for in the bright moonlight nights, when I start up from my sleep, and all is quiet about me, I see, standing still and motionless in one corner of this cell, a slight and wasted figure with long black hair, which, streaming down her back, stirs with no earthly wind, and eyes that fix their gaze on me, and never wink or close. Hush! the blood chills at my heart as I write it down—that form is *hers*; the face is very pale, and the eyes are glassy bright; but I know them well. That figure never moves; it never frowns and mouths as others do, that fill this place sometimes; but it is much more dreadful to me, even than the spirits that tempted me many years ago—it comes fresh from the grave; and is so very death–like.

'For nearly a year I saw that face grow paler; for nearly a year I saw the tears steal down the mournful cheeks, and never knew the cause. I found it out at last though. They could not keep it from me long. She had never liked me; I had never thought she did: she despised my wealth, and hated the splendour in which she lived; but I had not expected that. She loved another. This I had never thought of. Strange feelings came over me, and thoughts, forced upon me by some secret power, whirled round and round my brain. I did not hate her, though I hated the boy she still wept for. I pitied—yes, I pitied—the wretched life to which her cold and selfish relations had doomed her. I knew that she could not live long; but the thought that before her death she might give birth to some ill–fated being, destined to hand down madness to its offspring, determined me. I resolved to kill her.

'For many weeks I thought of poison, and then of drowning, and then of fire. A fine sight, the grand house in flames, and the madman's wife smouldering away to cinders. Think of the jest of a large reward, too, and of some sane man swinging in the wind for a deed he never did, and all through a madman's cunning! I thought often of this, but I gave it up at last. Oh! the pleasure of stropping the razor day after day, feeling the sharp edge, and thinking of the gash one stroke of its thin, bright edge would make! 'At last the old spirits who had been with me so often before whispered in my ear that the time was come, and thrust the open razor into my hand. I grasped it firmly, rose softly from the bed, and leaned over my sleeping wife. Her face was buried in her hands. I withdrew them softly, and they fell listlessly on her bosom. She had been weeping; for the traces of the tears were still wet upon her cheek. Her face was calm and placid; and even as I looked upon it, a tranquil smile lighted up her pale features. I laid my hand softly on her shoulder. She started—it was only a passing dream. I leaned forward again. She screamed, and woke.

'One motion of my hand, and she would never again have uttered cry or sound. But I was startled, and drew back. Her eyes were fixed on mine. I knew not how it was, but they cowed and frightened me; and I quailed beneath them. She rose from the bed, still gazing fixedly and steadily on me. I trembled; the razor was in my hand, but I could not move. She made towards the door. As she neared it, she turned, and withdrew her eyes from my face. The spell was broken. I bounded forward, and clutched her by the arm. Uttering shriek upon shriek, she sank upon the ground.

'Now I could have killed her without a struggle; but the house was alarmed. I heard the tread of footsteps on the stairs. I replaced the razor in its usual drawer, unfastened the door, and called loudly for assistance.

'They came, and raised her, and placed her on the bed. She lay bereft of animation for hours; and when life, look, and speech returned, her senses had deserted her, and she raved wildly and furiously.

'Doctors were called in—great men who rolled up to my door in easy carriages, with fine horses and gaudy servants. They were at her bedside for weeks. They had a great meeting and consulted together in low and solemn voices in another room. One, the cleverest and most celebrated among them, took me aside, and bidding me prepare for the worst, told me—me, the madman!—that my wife was mad. He stood close beside me at an open window, his eyes looking in my face, and his hand laid upon my arm. With one effort, I could have hurled him into the street beneath. It would have been rare sport to have done it; but my secret was at stake, and I let him go. A few days after, they told me I must place her under some restraint: I must provide a keeper for her. I! I went into the open fields where none could hear me, and laughed till the air resounded with my shouts!

'She died next day. The white–headed old man followed her to the grave, and the proud brothers dropped a tear over the insensible corpse of her whose sufferings they had regarded in her lifetime with muscles of iron. All this was food for my secret mirth, and I laughed behind the white handkerchief which I held up to my face, as we rode home, till the tears came into my eyes.

'But though I had carried my object and killed her, I was restless and disturbed, and I felt that before long my secret must be known. I could not hide the wild mirth and joy which boiled within me, and made me when I was alone, at home, jump up and beat my hands together, and dance round and round, and roar aloud. When I went out, and saw the busy crowds hurrying about the streets; or to the theatre, and heard the sound of music, and beheld the people dancing, I felt such glee, that I could have rushed among them, and torn them to pieces limb from limb, and howled in transport. But I ground my teeth, and struck my feet upon the floor, and drove my sharp nails into my hands. I kept it down; and no one knew I was a madman yet.

'I remember—though it's one of the last things I can re-member: for now I mix up realities with my dreams, and having so much to do, and being always hurried here, have no time to separate the two, from some strange confusion in which they get involved —I remember how I let it out at last. Ha! ha! I think I see their frightened looks now, and feel the ease with which I flung them from me, and dashed my clenched fist into their white faces, and then flew like the wind, and left them scream-ing and shouting far behind. The strength of a giant comes upon me when I think of it. There—see how this iron bar bends be-neath my furious wrench. I could snap it like a twig, only there are long galleries here with many doors—I don't think I could find my way along them; and even if I could, I know there are iron gates below which they keep locked and barred. They know what a clever madman I have been, and they are proud to have me here, to show.

'Let me see: yes, I had been out. It was late at night when I reached home, and found the proudest of the three proud brothers waiting to see me—urgent business he said: I recollect it well. I hated that man with all a madman's hate. Many and many a time had my fingers longed to tear him. They told me he was there. I ran swiftly upstairs. He had a word to say to me. I dismissed the servants. It was late, and we were alone together—for the first time.

'I kept my eyes carefully from him at first, for I knew what he little thought—and I gloried in the knowledge—that the light of madness gleamed from them like fire. We sat in silence for a few minutes. He spoke at last. My recent dissipation, and strange remarks, made so soon after his sister's death, were an insult to her memory. Coupling together many circumstances which had at first escaped his observation, he thought I had not treated her well. He wished to know whether he was right in inferring that I meant to cast a reproach upon her memory, and a disrespect upon her family. It was due to the uniform he wore, to demand this explanation.

'This man had a commission in the army—a commission, purchased with my money, and his sister's misery! This was the man who had been foremost in the plot to ensnare me, and grasp my wealth. This was the man who had been the main instrument in forcing his sister to wed me; well knowing that her heart was given to that puling boy. Due to his uniform! The livery of his degradation! I turned my eyes upon him—I could not help it—but I spoke not a word.

'I saw the sudden change that came upon him beneath my gaze. He was a bold man, but the colour faded from his face, and he drew back his chair. I dragged mine nearer to him; and I laughed—I was very merry then—I saw him shudder. I felt the madness rising within me. He was afraid of me.

'"You were very fond of your sister when she was alive," I said.—"Very."

'He looked uneasily round him, and I saw his hand grasp the back of his chair; but he said nothing.

"'You villain,' said I, "I found you out: I discovered your hellish plots against me; I know her heart was fixed on someone else before you compelled her to marry me. I know it—I know it."

'He jumped suddenly from his chair, brandished it aloft, and bid me stand back—for I took care to be getting closer to him all the time I spoke.

'I screamed rather than talked, for I felt tumultuous passions eddying through my veins, and the old spirits whispering and taunting me to tear his heart out.

"'Damn you,' said I, starting up, and rushing upon him; "I killed her. I am a madman. Down with you. Blood, blood! I will have it!"

'I turned aside with one blow the chair he hurled at me in his terror, and closed with him; and with a heavy crash we rolled upon the floor together. 'It was a fine struggle that; for he was a tall, strong man, fighting for his life; and I, a powerful madman, thirsting to destroy him. I knew no strength could equal mine, and I was right. Right again, though a madman! His struggles grew fainter. I knelt upon his chest, and clasped his brawny throat firmly with both hands. His face grew purple; his eyes were starting from his head, and with protruded tongue, he seemed to mock me. I squeezed the tighter. 'The door was suddenly burst open with a loud noise, and a crowd of people rushed forward, crying aloud to each other to secure the madman.

'My secret was out; and my only struggle now was for liberty and freedom. I gained my feet before a hand was on me, threw myself among my assailants, and cleared my way with my strong arm, as if I bore a hatchet in my hand, and hewed them down before me. I gained the door, dropped over the banisters, and in an instant was in the street.

'Straight and swift I ran, and no one dared to stop me. I heard the noise of the feet behind, and redoubled my speed. It grew fainter and fainter in the distance, and at length died away altogether; but on I bounded, through marsh and rivulet, over fence and wall, with a wild shout which was taken up by the strange beings that flocked around me on every side, and swelled the sound, till it pierced the air. I was borne upon the arms of demons who swept along upon the wind, and bore down bank and hedge before them, and spun me round and round with a rustle and a speed that made my head swim, until at last they threw me from them with a violent shock, and I fell heavily upon the earth. When I woke I found myself here—here in this gray cell, where the sunlight seldom comes, and the moon steals in, in rays which only serve to show the dark shadows about me, and that silent figure in its old corner. When I lie awake, I can sometimes hear strange shrieks and cries from distant parts of this large place. What they are, I know not; but they neither come from that pale form, nor does it regard them. For from the first shades of dusk till the earliest light of morning, it still stands motionless in the same place, listening to the music of my iron chain, and watching my gambols on my straw bed.'

At the end of the manuscript was written, in another hand, this note:—

[The unhappy man whose ravings are recorded above, was a melancholy instance of the baneful results of energies misdirect-ed in early life, and excesses prolonged until their consequences could never be repaired. The thoughtless riot, dissipation, and debauchery of his younger days produced fever and delirium. The first effects of the latter was the strange delusion, founded upon a well–known medical theory, strongly contended for by some, and as strongly contested by others, that an hereditary madness existed in his family. This produced a settled gloom, which in time developed a morbid insanity, and finally termi-nated in raving madness. There is every reason to believe that the events he detailed, though distorted in the description by his diseased imagination, really happened. It is only matter of won-der to those who were acquainted with the vices of his early ca-reer, that his passions, when no longer controlled by reason, did not lead him to the commission of still more frightful deeds.]

The Queer Chair

One winter's evening, about five o'clock, just as it began to grow dusk, a man in a gig might have been seen urging his tired horse along the road which leads across Marlborough Downs, in the direction of Bristol. I say he might have been seen, and I have no doubt he would have been, if anybody but a blind man had happened to pass that way; but the weather was so bad, and the night so cold and wet, that nothing was out but the water, and so the traveller jogged along in the middle of the road, lonesome and dreary enough.

If any bagman of that day could have caught sight of the little neck-or-nothing sort of gig, with a clay-coloured body and red wheels, and the vixenish, ill tempered, fast-going bay mare, that looked like a cross between a butcher's horse and a twopenny post-office pony, he would have known at once, that this traveller could have been no other than Tom Smart, of the great house of Bilson and Slum, Cateaton Street, City. However, as there was no bagman to look on, nobody knew anything at all about the matter; and so Tom Smart and his clay-coloured gig with the red wheels, and the vixenish mare with the fast pace, went on together, keeping the secret among them, and nobody was a bit the wiser.

There are many pleasanter places even in this dreary world, than Marlborough Downs when it blows hard; and if you throw in beside, a gloomy winter's evening, a miry and sloppy road, and a pelting fall of heavy rain, and try the effect, by way of experiment, in your own proper person, you will experience the full force of this observation.

The wind blew—not up the road or down it, though that's bad enough, but sheer across it, sending the rain slanting down like the lines they used to rule in the copy-books at school, to make the boys slope well. For a moment it would die away, and the traveller would begin to delude himself into the belief that, exhausted with its previous fury, it had quietly laid itself down to rest, when, whoo! he could hear it growling and whistling in the distance, and on it would come rushing over the hilltops, and sweeping along the plain, gathering sound and strength as it drew nearer, until it dashed with a heavy gust against horse and man, driving the sharp rain into their ears, and its cold damp breath into their very bones; and past them it would scour, far, far away, with a stunning roar, as if in ridicule of their weakness, and triumphant in the consciousness of its own strength and power.

The bay mare splashed away, through the mud and water, with drooping ears; now and then tossing her head as if to express her disgust at this very ungentlemanly behaviour of the elements, but keeping a good pace notwithstanding, until a gust of wind, more furious than any that had yet assailed them, caused her to stop suddenly and plant her four feet firmly against the ground, to prevent her being blown over. It's a special mercy that she did this, for if she *had* been blown over, the vixenish mare was so light, and the gig was so light, and Tom Smart such a light weight into the bargain, that they must infallibly have all gone rolling over and over together, until they reached the confines of earth, or until the wind fell; and in either case the probability is, that neither the vixenish mare, nor the clay-coloured gig with the red wheels, nor Tom Smart, would ever have been fit for service again.

"Well, damn my straps and whiskers," says Tom Smart (Tom sometimes had an unpleasant knack of swearing)—"damn my straps and whiskers," says Tom, "if this ain't pleasant, blow me!"

You'll very likely ask me why, as Tom Smart had been pretty well blown already, he expressed this wish to be submitted to the same process again. I can't say—all I know is, that Tom Smart said so—or at least he always told my uncle he said so, and it's just the same thing.

"Blow me," says Tom Smart; and the mare neighed as if she were precisely of the same opinion.

"Cheer up, old girl," said Tom, patting the bay mare on the neck with the end of his whip. "It won't do pushing on, such a night as this; the first house we come to we'll put up at, so the faster you go the sooner it's over. Soho, old girl—gently—gently."

Whether the vixenish mare was sufficiently well acquainted with the tones of Tom's voice to comprehend his meaning, or whether she found it colder standing still than moving on, of course I can't say. But I can say that Tom had no sooner finished speaking, than she pricked up her ears, and started forward at a speed which made the clay-coloured gig rattle until you would have supposed every one of the red spokes were going to fly out on the turf of Marlborough Downs; and even Tom, whip as he was, couldn't stop or check her pace, until she drew up of her own accord, before a roadside inn on the right-hand side of the way, about half a quarter of a mile from the end of the Downs.

'Tom cast a hasty glance at the upper part of the house as he threw the reins to the hostler, and stuck the whip in the box. It was a strange old place, built of a kind of shingle, inlaid, as it were, with cross-beams, with gabled-topped windows projecting completely over the pathway, and a low door with a dark porch, and a couple of steep steps leading down into the house, instead of the modern fashion of half a dozen shallow ones leading up to it. It was a comfortable-looking place though, for there was a strong, cheerful light in the bar window, which shed a bright ray across the road, and even lighted up the hedge on the other side; and there was a red flickering light in the opposite window, one moment but faintly discernible, and the next gleaming strongly through the drawn curtains, which intimated that a rousing fire was blazing within. Marking these little evidences with the eye of an experienced traveller, Tom dismounted with as much agility as his half-frozen limbs would permit, and entered the house.

In less than five minutes' time, Tom was ensconced in the room opposite the bar—the very room where he had imagined the fire blazing—before a substantial, matter-of-fact, roaring fire, composed of something short of a bushel of coals, and wood enough to make half a dozen decent gooseberry bushes, piled half-way up the chimney, and roaring and crackling with a sound that of itself would have warmed the heart of any reasonable man. This was comfortable, but this was not all; for a smartly-dressed girl, with a bright eye and a neat ankle, was laying a very clean white cloth on the table; and as Tom sat with his slippered feet on the fender, and his back to the open door, he saw a charming prospect of the bar reflected in the glass over the chimney-piece, with delightful rows of green bottles and gold labels, together with jars of pickles and preserves, and cheeses and boiled hams, and rounds of beef, arranged on shelves in the most tempting and delicious array.

Well, this was comfortable too; but even this was not all—for in the bar, seated at tea at the nicest possible little table, drawn close up before the brightest possible little fire, was a buxom widow of somewhere about eight-and-forty or thereabouts, with a face as comfortable as the bar, who was evidently the landlady of the house, and the supreme ruler over all these agreeable possessions. There was only one drawback to the beauty of the whole picture, and that was a tall man—a very tall man—in a brown coat and bright basket buttons, and black whiskers and wavy black hair, who was seated at tea with the widow, and who it required no great penetration to discover was in a fair way of persuading her to be a widow no longer, but to confer upon him the privilege of sitting down in that bar, for and during the whole remainder of the term of his natural life.

Tom Smart was by no means of an irritable or envious disposition, but somehow or other the tall man with the brown coat and the bright basket buttons did rouse what little gall he had in his composition, and did make him feel extremely indignant, the more especially as he could now and then observe, from his seat before the glass, certain little affectionate familiarities passing between the tall man and the widow, which sufficiently denoted that the tall man was as high in favour as he was in size. Tom was fond of hot punch—I may venture to say he was VERY fond of hot punch—and after he had seen the vixenish mare well fed and well littered down, and had eaten every bit of the nice little hot dinner which the widow tossed up for him with her own hands, he just ordered a tumbler of it by way of experiment.

Now, if there was one thing in the whole range of domestic art, which the widow could manufacture better than another, it was this identical article; and the first tumbler was adapted to Tom Smart's taste with such peculiar nicety, that he ordered a second with the least possible delay. Hot punch is a pleasant thing, gentlemen—an extremely pleasant thing under any circumstances —but in that snug old parlour, before the roaring fire, with the wind blowing outside till every timber in the old house creaked again, Tom Smart found it perfectly delightful. He ordered another tumbler, and then another—I am not quite certain whether he didn't order another after that—but the more he drank of the hot punch, the more he thought of the tall man.

"Confound his impudence!" said Tom to himself, "what business has he in that snug bar? Such an ugly villain too!" said Tom. "If the widow had any taste, she might surely pick up some better fellow than that." Here Tom's eye wandered from the glass on the chimney-piece to the glass on the table; and as he felt himself becoming gradually sentimental, he emptied the fourth tumbler of punch and ordered a fifth.

Tom Smart, gentlemen, had always been very much attached to the public line. It had been long his ambition to stand in a bar of his own, in a green coat, knee-cords, and tops. He had a great notion of taking the chair at convivial dinners, and he had often thought how well he could preside in a room of his own in the talking way, and what a capital example he could set to his customers in the drinking department. All these things passed rapidly through Tom's mind as he sat drinking the hot punch by the roaring fire, and he felt very justly and properly indignant that the tall man should be in a fair way of keeping such an excellent house, while he, Tom Smart, was as far off from it as ever. So, after deliberating over the two last tumblers, whether he hadn't a perfect right to pick a quarrel with the tall man for having contrived to get into the good graces of the buxom widow, Tom Smart at last arrived at the satisfactory conclusion that he was a very ill-used and persecuted individual, and had better go to bed.

Up a wide and ancient staircase the smart girl preceded Tom, shading the chamber candle with her hand, to protect it from the currents of air which in such a rambling old place might have found plenty of room to disport themselves in, without blowing the candle out, but which did blow it out nevertheless—thus affording Tom's enemies an opportunity of asserting that it was he, and not the wind, who extinguished the candle, and that while he pretended to be blowing it alight again, he was in fact kissing the girl. Be this as it may, another light was obtained, and Tom was conducted through a maze of rooms, and a labyrinth of passages, to the apartment which had been prepared for his reception, where the girl bade him good-night and left him alone.

It was a good large room with big closets, and a bed which might have served for a whole boarding-school, to say nothing of a couple of oaken presses that would have held the baggage of a small army; but what struck Tom's fancy most was a strange, grim-looking, high backed chair, carved in the most fantastic manner, with a flowered damask cushion, and the round knobs at the bottom of the legs carefully tied up in red cloth, as if it had got the gout in its toes. Of any other queer chair, Tom would only have thought it was a queer chair, and there would have been an end of the matter; but there was something about this particular chair, and yet he couldn't tell what it was, so odd and so unlike any other piece of furniture he had ever seen, that it seemed to fascinate him. He sat down before the fire, and stared at the old chair for half an hour.—Damn the chair, it was such a strange old thing, he couldn't take his eyes off it.

"Well," said Tom, slowly undressing himself, and staring at the old chair all the while, which stood with a mysterious aspect by the bedside, "I never saw such a rum concern as that in my days. Very odd," said Tom, who had got rather sage with the hot punch—'very odd." Tom shook his head with an air of profound wisdom, and looked at the chair again. He couldn't make anything of it though, so he got into bed, covered himself up warm, and fell asleep.

In about half an hour, Tom woke up with a start, from a confused dream of tall men and tumblers of punch; and the first object that presented itself to his waking imagination was the queer chair.

"I won't look at it anymore," said Tom to himself, and he squeezed his eyelids together, and tried to persuade himself he was going to sleep again. No use; nothing but queer chairs danced before his eyes, kicking up their legs, jumping over each other's backs, and playing all kinds of antics.

"I may as well see one real chair, as two or three complete sets of false ones," said Tom, bringing out his head from under the bedclothes. There it was, plainly discernible by the light of the fire, looking as provoking as ever.

Tom gazed at the chair; and, suddenly as he looked at it, a most extraordinary change seemed to come over it. The carving of the back gradually assumed the lineaments and expression of an old, shrivelled human face; the damask cushion became an antique, flapped waistcoat; the round knobs grew into a couple of feet, encased in red cloth slippers; and the whole chair looked like a very ugly old man, of the previous century, with his arms akimbo. Tom sat up in bed, and rubbed his eyes to dispel the illusion. No. The chair was an ugly old gentleman; and what was more, he was winking at Tom Smart.

Tom was naturally a headlong, careless sort of dog, and he had had five tumblers of hot punch into the bargain; so, although he was a little startled at first, he began to grow rather indignant when he saw the old gentleman winking and leering at him with such an impudent air. At length he resolved that he wouldn't stand it; and as the old face still kept winking away as fast as ever, Tom said, in a very angry tone—

"What the devil are you winking at me for?"

"Because I like it, Tom Smart," said the chair; or the old gentleman, whichever you like to call him. He stopped winking though, when Tom spoke, and began grinning like a superannuated monkey.

"How do you know my name, old nut-cracker face?" inquired Tom Smart, rather staggered; though he pretended to carry it off so well.

"Come, come, Tom," said the old gentleman, "that's not the way to address solid Spanish mahogany. Damme, you couldn't treat me with less respect if I was veneered." When the old gentleman said this, he looked so fierce that Tom began to grow frightened.

"I didn't mean to treat you with any disrespect, Sir," said Tom, in a much humbler tone than he had spoken in at first.

"Well, well," said the old fellow, "perhaps not—perhaps not. Tom—"

"sir—"

"I know everything about you, Tom; everything. You're very poor, Tom."

"I certainly am," said Tom Smart. "But how came you to know that?"

"Never mind that," said the old gentleman; "you're much too fond of punch, Tom."

Tom Smart was just on the point of protesting that he hadn't tasted a drop since his last birthday, but when his eye encountered that of the old gentleman he looked so knowing that Tom blushed, and was silent.

"Tom," said the old gentleman, "the widow's a fine woman—remarkably fine woman—eh, Tom?" Here the old fellow screwed up his eyes, cocked up one of his wasted little legs, and looked altogether so unpleasantly amorous, that Tom was quite disgusted with the levity of his behaviour—at his time of life, too!

"I am her guardian, Tom," said the old gentleman.

"Are you?" inquired Tom Smart.

"I knew her mother, Tom," said the old fellow: "and her grandmother. She was very fond of me—made me this waistcoat, Tom."

"Did she?" said Tom Smart.

"And these shoes," said the old fellow, lifting up one of the red cloth mufflers; "but don't mention it, Tom. I shouldn't like to have it known that she was so much attached to me. It might occasion some unpleasantness in the family." When the old rascal said this, he looked so extremely impertinent, that, as Tom Smart afterwards declared, he could have sat upon him without remorse.

"I have been a great favourite among the women in my time, Tom," said the profligate old debauchee; "hundreds of fine women have sat in my lap for hours together. What do you think of that, you dog, eh!" The old gentleman was proceeding to recount some other exploits of his youth, when he was seized with such a violent fit of creaking that he was unable to proceed.

"Just serves you right, old boy," thought Tom Smart; but he didn't say anything.

"Ah!" said the old fellow, "I am a good deal troubled with this now. I am getting old, Tom, and have lost nearly all my rails. I have had an operation performed, too—a small piece let into my back—and I found it a severe trial, Tom."

"I dare say you did, Sir," said Tom Smart.

"However," said the old gentleman, "that's not the point. Tom! I want you to marry the widow."

"Me, Sir!" said Tom.

"You," said the old gentleman.

"Bless your reverend locks," said Tom (he had a few scattered horse-hairs left)—"bless your reverend locks, she wouldn't have me." And Tom sighed involuntarily, as he thought of the bar.

"Wouldn't she?" said the old gentleman firmly.

"No, no," said Tom; "there's somebody else in the wind. A tall man—a confoundedly tall man—with black whiskers."

"Tom," said the old gentleman; "she will never have him."

"Won't she?" said Tom. "If you stood in the bar, old gentleman, you'd tell another story." "'Pooh, pooh," said the old gentleman. "I know all about that. "

"About what?" said Tom.

"The kissing behind the door, and all that sort of thing, Tom," said the old gentleman. And here he gave another impudent look, which made Tom very wroth, because as you all know, gentlemen, to hear an old fellow, who ought to know better, talking about these things, is very unpleasant—nothing more so.

"I know all about that, Tom," said the old gentleman. "I have seen it done very often in my time, Tom, between more people than I should like to mention to you; but it never came to anything after all."

"You must have seen some queer things," said Tom, with an inquisitive look.

"You may say that, Tom," replied the old fellow, with a very complicated wink. "I am the last of my family, Tom," said the old gentleman, with a melancholy sigh.

"Was it a large one?" inquired Tom Smart.

"There were twelve of us, Tom," said the old gentleman; "fine, straight-backed, handsome fellows as you'd wish to see. None of your modern abortions—all with arms, and with a degree of polish, though I say it that should not, which it would have done your heart good to behold."

"And what's become of the others, Sir?" asked Tom Smart—

The old gentleman applied his elbow to his eye as he replied, "Gone, Tom, gone. We had hard service, Tom, and they hadn't all my constitution. They got rheumatic about the legs and arms, and went into kitchens and other hospitals; and one of 'em, with long service and hard usage, positively lost his senses—he got so crazy that he was obliged to be burnt. Shocking thing that, Tom."

"Dreadful!" said Tom Smart.

The old fellow paused for a few minutes, apparently struggling with his feelings of emotion, and then said—

"However, Tom, I am wandering from the point. This tall man, Tom, is a rascally adventurer. The moment he married the widow, he would sell off all the furniture, and run away. What would be the consequence? She would be deserted and reduced to ruin, and I should catch my death of cold in some broker's shop."

"Yes, but—"

"Don't interrupt me," said the old gentleman. "Of you, Tom, I entertain a very different opinion; for I well know that if you once settled yourself in a public-house, you would never leave it, as long as there was anything to drink within its walls."

"I am very much obliged to you for your good opinion, Sir," said Tom Smart.

"Therefore," resumed the old gentleman, in a dictatorial tone, "you shall have her, and he shall not."

"'What is to prevent it?" said Tom Smart eagerly.

"'This disclosure," replied the old gentleman; "he is already married."

"How can I prove it?" said Tom, starting half out of bed.

The old gentleman untucked his arm from his side, and having pointed to one of the oaken presses, immediately replaced it, in its old position.

"He little thinks," said the old gentleman, "that in the right-hand pocket of a pair of trousers in that press, he has left a letter, entreating him to return to his disconsolate wife, with six—mark me, Tom—six babes, and all of them small ones."

As the old gentleman solemnly uttered these words, his features grew less and less distinct, and his figure more shadowy. A film came over Tom Smart's eyes. The old man seemed gradually blending into the chair, the damask waistcoat to resolve into a cushion, the red slippers to shrink into little red cloth bags. The light faded gently away, and Tom Smart fell back on his pillow, and dropped asleep.

Morning aroused Tom from the lethargic slumber, into which he had fallen on the disappearance of the old man. He sat up in bed, and for some minutes vainly endeavoured to recall the events of the preceding night. Suddenly they rushed upon him. He looked at the chair; it was a fantastic and grim-looking piece of furniture, certainly, but it must have been a remarkably ingenious and lively imagination, that could have discovered any resemblance between it and an old man.

"How are you, old boy?" said Tom. He was bolder in the daylight—most men are.

The chair remained motionless, and spoke not a word.

"Miserable morning," said Tom. No. The chair would not be drawn into conversation.

"Which press did you point to?—you can tell me that," said Tom. Devil a word, gentlemen, the chair would say.

"It's not much trouble to open it, anyhow," said Tom, getting out of bed very deliberately. He walked up to one of the presses. The key was in the lock; he turned it, and opened the door. There was a pair of trousers there. He put his hand into the pocket, and drew forth the identical letter the old gentleman had described!

"Queer sort of thing, this," said Tom Smart, looking first at the chair and then at the press, and then at the letter, and then at the chair again. "Very queer," said Tom. But, as there was nothing in either, to lessen the queerness, he thought he might as well dress himself, and settle the tall man's business at once—just to put him out of his misery.

Tom surveyed the rooms he passed through, on his way downstairs, with the scrutinising eye of a landlord; thinking it not impossible, that before long, they and their contents would be his property. The tall man was standing in the snug little bar, with his hands behind him, quite at home. He grinned vacantly at Tom. A casual observer might have supposed he did it, only to show his white teeth; but Tom Smart thought that a consciousness of triumph was passing through the place where the tall man's mind would have been, if he had had any. Tom laughed in his face; and summoned the landlady.

"Good-morning ma'am," said Tom Smart, closing the door of the little parlour as the widow entered.

"Good-morning, Sir," said the widow. "What will you take for breakfast, sir?"

Tom was thinking how he should open the case, so he made no answer.

"There's a very nice ham," said the widow, "and a beautiful cold larded fowl. Shall I send 'em in, Sir?"

These words roused Tom from his reflections. His admiration of the widow increased as she spoke. Thoughtful creature! Comfortable provider!

"Who is that gentleman in the bar, ma'am?" inquired Tom.

"His name is Jinkins, Sir," said the widow, slightly blushing.

"He's a tall man," said Tom.

"He is a very fine man, Sir," replied the widow, "and a very nice gentleman."

"Ah!" said Tom.

"Is there anything more you want, Sir?" inquired the widow, rather puzzled by Tom's manner. "'Why, yes,' said Tom. "My dear ma'am, will you have the kindness to sit down for one moment?"

The widow looked much amazed, but she sat down, and Tom sat down too, close beside her. I don't know how it happened, gentlemen—indeed my uncle used to tell me that Tom Smart said he didn't know how it happened either—but somehow or other the palm of Tom's hand fell upon the back of the widow's hand, and remained there while he spoke.

"'My dear ma'am,' said Tom Smart—he had always a great notion of committing the amiable—"my dear ma'am, you deserve a very excellent husband—you do indeed."

"Lor, Sir!" said the widow—as well she might; Tom's mode of commencing the conversation being rather unusual, not to say startling; the fact of his never having set eyes upon her before the previous night being taken into consideration. "Lor, Sir!"

"I scorn to flatter, my dear ma'am," said Tom Smart. "You

deserve a very admirable husband, and whoever he is, he'll be a very lucky man." As Tom said this, his eye involuntarily wandered from the widow's face to the comfort around him.

The widow looked more puzzled than ever, and made an effort to rise. Tom gently pressed her hand, as if to detain her, and she kept her seat. Widows, gentlemen, are not usually timorous, as my uncle used to say.

"I am sure I am very much obliged to you, Sir, for your good opinion," said the buxom landlady, half laughing; "and if ever I marry again—"

"*If*," said Tom Smart, looking very shrewdly out of the right-hand corner of his left eye. "*If*—"

"Well," said the widow, laughing outright this time, "*When* I do, I hope I shall have as good a husband as you describe."

"Jinkins, to wit," said Tom.

"Lor, sir!" exclaimed the widow.

"Oh, don't tell me," said Tom, "I know him."

"I am sure nobody who knows him, knows anything bad of him," said the widow, bridling up at the mysterious air with which Tom had spoken.

"Hem!" said Tom Smart.

The widow began to think it was high time to cry, so she took out her handkerchief, and inquired whether Tom wished to insult her, whether he thought it like a gentleman to take away the character of another gentleman behind his back, why, if he had got anything to say, he didn't say it to the man, like a man, instead of terrifying a poor weak woman in that way; and so forth.

"I'll say it to him fast enough," said Tom, "only I want you to hear it first."

"What is it?" inquired the widow, looking intently in Tom's countenance.

"I'll astonish you," said Tom, putting his hand in his pocket.

"If it is, that he wants money," said the widow, "I know that already, and you needn't trouble yourself."

"Pooh, nonsense, that's nothing," said Tom Smart, "I want

money. 'Tain't that."

"Oh, dear, what can it be?" exclaimed the poor widow.

"Don't be frightened," said Tom Smart. He slowly drew forth the letter, and unfolded it. "You won't scream?" said Tom doubtfully.

"No, no," replied the widow; "let me see it."

"You won't go fainting away, or any of that nonsense?" said Tom.

"No, no," returned the widow hastily.

"And don't run out, and blow him up," said Tom; "because I'll do all that for you. You had better not exert yourself."

"Well, well," said the widow, "let me see it."

"I will," replied Tom Smart; and, with these words, he placed the letter in the widow's hand.

Gentlemen, I have heard my uncle say, that Tom Smart said the widow's lamentations when she heard the disclosure would have pierced a heart of stone. Tom was certainly very tender- hearted, but they pierced his, to the very core. The widow rocked herself to and fro, and wrung her hands.

"Oh, the deception and villainy of the man!" said the widow.

"Frightful, my dear ma'am; but compose yourself," said Tom Smart.

"Oh, I can't compose myself," shrieked the widow. "I shall never find anyone else I can love so much!"

"Oh, yes you will, my dear soul," said Tom Smart, letting fall a shower of the largest-sized tears, in pity for the widow's misfortunes. Tom Smart, in the energy of his compassion, had put his arm round the widow's waist; and the widow, in a passion of grief, had clasped Tom's hand. She looked up in Tom's face, and smiled through her tears. Tom looked down in hers, and smiled through his.

I never could find out, gentlemen, whether Tom did or did not kiss the widow at that particular moment. He used to tell my uncle he didn't, but I have my doubts about it. Between ourselves, gentlemen, I rather think he did.

At all events, Tom kicked the very tall man out at the front door half an hour later, and married the widow a month after. And he used to drive about the country, with the clay-coloured gig with the red wheels, and the vixenish mare with the fast pace, till he gave up business many years afterwards, and went to France with his wife; and then the old house was pulled down.

The Baron of Grogzwig

aka Baron Koeldwethout's Apparition

The Baron Von Koeldwethout, of Grogzwig in Germany, was as likely a young baron as you would wish to see. I needn't say that he lived in a castle, because that's of course; neither need I say that he lived in an old castle; for what German baron ever lived in a new one? There were many strange circumstances connected with this venerable building, among which, not the least startling and mysterious were, that when the wind blew, it rumbled in the chimneys, or even howled among the trees in the neighbouring forest; and that when the moon shone, she found her way through certain small loopholes in the wall, and actually made some parts of the wide halls and galleries quite light, while she left others in gloomy shadow.

I believe that one of the baron's ancestors, being short of money, had inserted a dagger in a gentleman who called one night to ask his way, and it *was* supposed that these miraculous occurrences took place in consequence. And yet I hardly know how that could have been, either, because the baron's ancestor, who was an amiable man, felt very sorry afterwards for having been so rash, and laying violent hands upon a quantity of stone and timber which belonged to a weaker baron, built a chapel as an apology, and so took a receipt from Heaven, in full of all demands.

Talking of the baron's ancestor puts me in mind of the baron's great claims to respect, on the score of his pedigree. I am afraid to say, I am sure, how many ancestors the baron had; but I know that he had a great many more than any other man of his time; and I only wish that he had lived in these latter days, that he might have had more. It is a very hard thing upon the great men of past centuries, that they should have come into the world so soon, because a man who was born three or four hundred years ago, cannot reasonably be expected to have had as many relations before him, as a man who is born now. The last man, whoever he is—and he may be a cobbler or some low vulgar dog for aught we know—will have a longer pedigree than the greatest nobleman now alive; and I contend that this is not fair.

Well, but the Baron Von Koeldwethout of Grogzwig! He was a fine swarthy fellow, with dark hair and large *moustachios*, who rode a-hunting in clothes of Lincoln green, with russet boots on his feet, and a bugle slung over his shoulder like the guard of a long stage. When he blew this bugle, four-and-twenty other gentlemen of inferior rank, in Lincoln green a little coarser, and russet boots with a little thicker soles, turned out directly: and away galloped the whole train, with spears in their hands like lacquered area railings, to hunt down the boars, or perhaps encounter a bear: in which latter case the baron killed him first, and greased his whiskers with him afterwards.

This was a merry life for the Baron of Grogzwig, and a merrier still for the baron's retainers, who drank Rhine wine every night till they fell under the table, and then had the bottles on the floor, and called for pipes. Never were such jolly, roystering, rollicking, merry-making blades, as the jovial crew of Grogzwig.

But the pleasures of the table, or the pleasures of under the table, require a little variety; especially when the same five-and-twenty people sit daily down to the same board, to discuss the same subjects, and tell the same stories. The baron grew weary, and wanted excitement. He took to quarrelling with his gentlemen, and tried kicking two or three of them every day after dinner. This was a pleasant change at first; but it became monotonous after a week or so, and the baron felt quite out of sorts, and cast about, in despair, for some new amusement.

One night, after a day's sport in which he had outdone Nimrod or Gillingwater, and slaughtered "another fine bear," and brought him home in triumph, the Baron Von Koeldwethout sat moodily at the head of his table, eyeing the smoky roof of the hall with a discontented aspect. He swallowed huge bumpers of wine, but the more he swallowed, the more he frowned. The gentlemen who had been honoured with the dangerous distinction of sitting on his right and left, imitated him to a miracle in the drinking, and frowned at each other.

"I will!" cried the baron suddenly, smiting the table with his right hand, and twirling his moustache with his left. "Fill to the Lady of Grogzwig!"

The four-and-twenty Lincoln greens turned pale, with the exception of their four-and-twenty noses, which were unchangeable.

"I said to the Lady of Grogzwig," repeated the baron, looking round the board.

"To the Lady of Grogzwig!" shouted the Lincoln greens; and down their four-and-twenty throats went four-and-twenty imperial pints of such rare old hock, that they smacked their eight-and-forty lips, and winked again.

"The fair daughter of the Baron Von Swillenhausen," said Koeldwethout, condescending to explain. "We will demand her in marriage of her father, ere the sun goes down tomorrow. If he refuse our suit, we will cut off his nose."

A hoarse murmur arose from the company; every man touched, first the hilt of his sword, and then the tip of his nose, with appalling significance.

What a pleasant thing filial piety is to contemplate! If the daughter of the Baron Von Swillenhausen had pleaded a preoccupied heart, or fallen at her father's feet and corned them in salt tears, or only fainted away, and complimented the old gentleman in frantic ejaculations, the odds are a hundred to one but Swillenhausen Castle would have been turned out at window, or rather the baron turned out at window, and the castle demolished. The damsel held her peace, however, when an early messenger bore the request of Von Koeldwethout next morning, and modestly retired to her chamber, from the casement of which she watched the coming of the suitor and his retinue. She was no sooner assured that the horseman with the large moustachios was her proffered husband, than she hastened to her father's presence, and expressed her readiness to sacrifice herself to secure his peace. The venerable baron caught his child to his arms, and shed a wink of joy.

There was great feasting at the castle, that day. The four-and-twenty Lincoln greens of Von Koeldwethout exchanged vows of eternal friendship with twelve Lincoln greens of Von Swillenhausen, and promised the old baron that they would drink his wine "Till all was blue"—meaning probably until their whole countenances had acquired the same tint as their noses. Everybody slapped everybody else's back, when the time for parting came; and the Baron Von Koeldwethout and his followers rode gaily home.

For six mortal weeks, the bears and boars had a holiday. The houses of Koeldwethout and Swillenhausen were united; the spears rusted; and the baron's bugle grew hoarse for lack of blowing.

Those were great times for the four-and-twenty; but, alas! their high and palmy days had taken boots to themselves, and were already walking off.

"My dear," said the baroness.

"My love," said the baron.

"Those coarse, noisy men—"

"Which, ma'am?" said the baron, starting.

The baroness pointed, from the window at which they stood, to the courtyard beneath, where the unconscious Lincoln greens were taking a copious stirrup-cup, preparatory to issuing forth after a boar or two.

"My hunting train, ma'am," said the baron.

"Disband them, love," murmured the baroness.

"Disband them!" cried the baron, in amazement.

"To please me, love," replied the baroness.

"To please the devil, ma'am," answered the baron.

Whereupon the baroness uttered a great cry, and swooned away at the baron's feet.

What could the baron do? He called for the lady's maid, and roared for the doctor; and then, rushing into the yard, kicked the two Lincoln greens who were the most used to it, and cursing the others all round, bade them go—but never mind where. I don't know the German for it, or I would put it delicately that way.

It is not for me to say by what means, or by what degrees, some wives manage to keep down some husbands as they do, although I may have my private opinion on the subject, and may think that no Member of Parliament ought to be married, inasmuch as three married members out of every four, must vote according to their wives' consciences (if there be such things), and not according to their own. All I need say, just now, is, that the Baroness Von Koeldwethout somehow or other acquired great control over the Baron Von Koeldwethout, and that, little by little, and bit by bit, and day by day, and year by year, the baron got the worst of some disputed question, or was slyly unhorsed from some old hobby; and that by the time he was a fat hearty fellow of forty-eight or thereabouts, he had no feasting, no revelry, no hunting train, and no hunting—nothing in short that he liked, or used to have; and that, although he was as fierce as a lion, and as bold as brass, he was decidedly snubbed and put down, by his own lady, in his own castle of Grogzwig.

Nor was this the whole extent of the baron's misfortunes. About a year after his nuptials, there came into the world a lusty young baron, in whose honour a great many fireworks were let off, and a great many dozens of wine drunk; but next year there came a young baroness, and next year another young baron, and so on, every year, either a baron or baroness (and one year both together), until the baron found himself the father of a small family of twelve.

Upon every one of these anniversaries, the venerable Baroness Von Swillenhausen was nervously sensitive for the well-being of her child the Baroness Von Koeldwethout; and although it was not found that the good lady ever did anything material towards contributing to her child's recovery, still she made it a point of duty to be as nervous as possible at the castle of Grogzwig, and to divide her time between moral observations on the baron's housekeeping, and bewailing the hard lot of her unhappy daughter. And if the Baron of Grogzwig, a little hurt and irritated at this, took heart, and ventured to suggest that his wife was at least no worse off than the wives of other barons, the Baroness Von Swillenhausen begged all persons to take notice, that nobody but she, sympathised with her dear daughter's sufferings; upon which, her relations and friends remarked, that to be sure she did cry a great deal more than her son-in-law, and that if there were a hard-hearted brute alive, it was that Baron of Grogzwig.

The poor baron bore it all as long as he could, and when he could bear it no longer lost his appetite and his spirits, and sat himself gloomily and dejectedly down. But there were worse troubles yet in store for him, and as they came on, his melancholy and sadness increased. Times changed. He got into debt. The Grogzwig coffers ran low, though the Swillenhausen family had looked upon them as inexhaustible; and just when the baroness was on the point of making a thirteenth addition to the family pedigree, Von Koeldwethout discovered that he had no means of replenishing them.

"I don't see what is to be done," said the baron. "I think I'll kill myself."

This was a bright idea. The baron took an old hunting-knife from a cupboard hard by, and having sharpened it on his boot, made what boys call "an offer" at his throat.

"Hem!" said the baron, stopping short. "Perhaps it's not sharp enough."

The baron sharpened it again, and made another offer, when his hand was arrested by a loud screaming among the young barons and baronesses, who had a nursery in an upstairs tower with iron bars outside the window, to prevent their tumbling out into the moat.

"If I had been a bachelor," said the baron sighing, "I might have done it fifty times over, without being interrupted. Hallo! Put a flask of wine and the largest pipe in the little vaulted room behind the hall."

One of the domestics, in a very kind manner, executed the baron's order in the course of half an hour or so, and Von Koeldwethout being apprised thereof, strode to the vaulted room, the walls of which, being of dark shining wood, gleamed in the light of the blazing logs which were piled upon the hearth. The bottle and pipe were ready, and, upon the whole, the place looked very comfortable.

"Leave the lamp," said the baron.

"Anything else, my lord?" inquired the domestic.

"The room," replied the baron. The domestic obeyed, and the baron locked the door.

"I'll smoke a last pipe," said the baron, "and then I'll be off." So, putting the knife upon the table till he wanted it, and tossing off a goodly measure of wine, the Lord of Grogzwig threw himself back in his chair, stretched his legs out before the fire, and puffed away.

He thought about a great many things—about his present troubles and past days of bachelorship, and about the Lincoln greens, long since dispersed up and down the country, no one knew whither: with the exception of two who had been unfortunately beheaded, and four who had killed themselves with drinking. His mind was running upon bears and boars, when, in the process of draining his glass to the bottom, he raised his eyes, and saw, for the first time and with unbounded astonishment, that he was not alone.

No, he was not; for, on the opposite side of the fire, there sat with folded arms a wrinkled hideous figure, with deeply sunk and bloodshot eyes, and an immensely long cadaverous face, shadowed by jagged and matted locks of coarse black hair. He wore a kind of tunic of a dull bluish colour, which, the baron observed, on regarding it attentively, was clasped or ornamented down the front with coffin handles. His legs, too, were encased in coffin plates as though in armour; and over his left shoulder he wore a short dusky cloak, which seemed made of a remnant of some pall. He took no notice of the baron, but was intently eyeing the fire.

"Halloa!" said the baron, stamping his foot to attract attention.

"Halloa!" replied the stranger, moving his eyes towards the baron, but not his face or himself "What now?"

"What now!" replied the baron, nothing daunted by his hollow voice and lustreless eyes. "I should ask that question. How did you get here?"

"Through the door," replied the figure.

"What are you?" says the baron.

"A man," replied the figure.

"I don't believe it," says the baron.

"Disbelieve it then," says the figure.

"I will," rejoined the baron.

The figure looked at the bold Baron of Grogzwig for some time, and then said familiarly,

"There's no coming over you, I see. I'm not a man!"

"What are you then?" asked the baron.

"A genius," replied the figure.

"You don't look much like one," returned the baron scornfully.

"I am the Genius of Despair and Suicide," said the apparition. "Now you know me."

With these words the apparition turned towards the baron, as if composing himself for a talk—and, what was very remarkable, was, that he threw his cloak aside, and displaying a stake, which was run through the centre of his body, pulled it out with a jerk, and laid it on the table, as composedly as if it had been a walking-stick.

"Now," said the figure, glancing at the hunting-knife, "are you ready for me?"

"Not quite," rejoined the baron; "I must finish this pipe

234

first."

"Look sharp then," said the figure.

"You seem in a hurry," said the baron.

"Why, yes, I am," answered the figure; "they're doing a pretty brisk business in my way, over in England and France just now, and my time is a good deal taken up."

"Do you drink?" said the baron, touching the bottle with the bowl of his pipe.

"Nine times out of ten, and then very hard," rejoined the figure, drily.

"Never in moderation?" asked the baron.

"Never," replied the figure, with a shudder, "that breeds cheerfulness."

The baron took another look at his new friend, whom he thought an uncommonly queer customer, and at length inquired whether he took any active part in such little proceedings as that which he had in contemplation.

"No," replied the figure evasively; "but I am always present."

"Just to see fair, I suppose?" said the baron.

"Just that," replied the figure, playing with his stake, and examining the ferule. "Be as quick as you can, will you, for there's a young gentleman who is afflicted with too much money and leisure wanting me now, I find."

"Going to kill himself because he has too much money!" exclaimed the baron, quite tickled. "Ha! ha! that's a good one." (This was the first time the baron had laughed for many a long day.)

"I say," expostulated the figure, looking very much scared; "don't do that again."

"Why not?" demanded the baron.

"Because it gives me pain all over," replied the figure. "Sigh as much as you please: that does me good."

The baron sighed mechanically at the mention of the word; the figure, brightening up again, handed him the hunting-knife with most winning politeness.

"It's not a bad idea though," said the baron, feeling the edge of the weapon; "a man killing himself because he has too much money."

"Pooh!" said the apparition, petulantly, "no better than a man's killing himself because he has none or little."

Whether the genius unintentionally committed himself in saying this, or whether he thought the baron's mind was so thoroughly made up that it didn't matter what he said, I have no means of knowing. I only know that the baron stopped his hand, all of a sudden, opened his eyes wide, and looked as if quite a new light had come upon him for the first time.

"Why, certainly," said Von Koeldwethout, "nothing is too bad to be retrieved."

"Except empty coffers," cried the genius.

"Well; but they may be one day filled again," said the baron.

"Scolding wives," snarled the genius.

"Oh! They may be made quiet," said the baron.

"Thirteen children," shouted the genius.

"Can't all go wrong, surely," said the baron.

The genius was evidently growing very savage with the baron, for holding these opinions all at once; but he tried to laugh it off, and said if he would let him know when he had left off joking he should feel obliged to him.

"But I am not joking; I was never farther from it," remonstrated the baron.

"Well, I am glad to hear that," said the genius, looking very grim, "because a joke, without any figure of speech, IS the death of me. Come! Quit this dreary world at once."

"I don't know," said the baron, playing with the knife; "it's a dreary one certainly, but I don't think yours is much better, for you have not the appearance of being particularly comfortable. That puts me in mind—what security have I, that I shall be any the better for going out of the world after all!" he cried, starting up; "I never thought of that."

"Dispatch," cried the figure, gnashing his teeth.

"Keep off!" said the baron. 'I'll brood over miseries no longer, but put a good face on the matter, and try the fresh air and the bears again; and if that don't do, I'll talk to the baroness soundly, and cut the Von Swillenhausens dead.' With this the baron fell into his chair, and laughed so loud and boisterously, that the room rang with it.

The figure fell back a pace or two, regarding the baron meanwhile with a look of intense terror, and when he had ceased, caught up the stake, plunged it violently into its body, uttered a frightful howl, and disappeared.

Von Koeldwethout never saw it again. Having once made up his mind to action, he soon brought the baroness and the Von Swillenhausens to reason, and died many years afterwards: not a rich man that I am aware of, but certainly a happy one: leaving behind him a numerous family, who had been carefully educated in bear and boar-hunting under his own personal eye. And my advice to all men is, that if ever they become hipped and melancholy from similar causes (as very many men do), they look at both sides of the question, applying a magnifying-glass to the best one; and if they still feel tempted to retire without leave, that they smoke a large pipe and drink a full bottle first, and profit by the laudable example of the Baron of Grogzwig.

Captain Murderer and
the Devil's Bargain

There are not many places that I find it more agreeable to revisit when I am in an idle mood, than some places to which I have never been. For, my acquaintance with those spots is of such long standing, and has ripened into an intimacy of so affectionate a nature, that I take a particular interest in assuring myself that they are unchanged.

I never was in Robinson Crusoe's Island, yet I frequently return there. The colony he established on it soon faded away, and it is uninhabited by any descendants of the grave and courteous Spaniards, or of Will Atkins and the other mutineers, and has relapsed into its original condition. Not a twig of its wicker houses remains, its goats have long run wild again, its screaming parrots would darken the sun with a cloud of many flaming colours if a gun were fired there, no face is ever reflected in the waters of the little creek which Friday swam across when pursued by his two brother cannibals with sharpened stomachs.

After comparing notes with other travellers who have similarly revisited the Island and conscientiously inspected it, I have satisfied myself that it contains no vestige of Mr. Atkins's domesticity or theology, though his track on the memorable evening of his landing to set his captain ashore, when he was decoyed about and round about until it was dark, and his boat was stove, and his strength and spirits failed him, is yet plainly to be traced.

So is the hilltop on which Robinson was struck dumb with joy when the reinstated captain pointed to the ship, riding within half a mile of the shore, that was to bear him away, in the nine-and-twentieth year of his seclusion in that lonely place. So is the sandy beach on which the memorable footstep was impressed, and where the savages hauled up their canoes when they came ashore for those dreadful public dinners, which led to a dancing worse than speech-making.

So is the cave where the flaring eyes of the old goat made such a goblin appearance in the dark. So is the site of the hut where Robinson lived with the dog and the parrot and the cat, and where he endured those first agonies of solitude, which—strange to say—never involved any ghostly fancies; a circumstance so very remarkable, that perhaps he left out something in writing his record? Round hundreds of such objects, hidden in the dense tropical foliage, the tropical sea breaks evermore; and over them the tropical sky, saving in the short rainy season, shines bright and cloudless.

Neither, was I ever belated among wolves, on the borders of France and Spain; nor, did I ever, when night was closing in and the ground was covered with snow, draw up my little company among some felled trees which served as a breastwork, and there fire a train of gunpowder so dexterously that suddenly we had three or four score blazing wolves illuminating the darkness around us.

Nevertheless, I occasionally go back to that dismal region and perform the feat again; when indeed to smell the singeing and the frying of the wolves afire, and to see them setting one another alight as they rush and tumble, and to behold them rolling in the snow vainly attempting to put themselves out, and to hear their howlings taken up by all the echoes as well as by all the unseen wolves within the woods, makes me tremble.

I was never in the robbers' cave, where Gil Blas lived, but I often go back there and find the trap-door just as heavy to raise as it used to be, while that wicked old disabled Black lies everlastingly cursing in bed. I was never in Don Quixote's study, where he read his books of chivalry until he rose and hacked at imaginary giants, and then refreshed himself with great draughts of water, yet you couldn't move a book in it without my knowledge, or with my consent.

I was never (thank Heaven) in company with the little old woman who hobbled out of the chest and told the merchant Abudah to go in search of the Talisman of Oromanes, yet I make it my business to know that she is well preserved and as intolerable as ever. I was never at the school where the boy Horatio Nelson got out of bed to steal the pears: not because he wanted any, but because every other boy was afraid: yet I have several times been back to this Academy, to see him let down out of window with a sheet.

So with Damascus, and Bagdad, and Brobingnag (which has the curious fate of being usually misspelt when written), and Lilliput, and Laputa, and the Nile, and Abyssinia, and the Ganges, and the North Pole, and many hundreds of places—I was never at them, yet it is an affair of my life to keep them intact, and I am always going back to them.

But, when I was in Dullborough one day, revisiting the associations of my childhood as recorded in previous pages of these notes, my experience in this wise was made quite inconsiderable and of no account, by the quantity of places and people—utterly impossible places and people, but none the less alarmingly real—that I found I had been introduced to by my nurse before I was six years old, and used to be forced to go back to at night without at all wanting to go.

If we all knew our own minds (in a more enlarged sense than the popular acceptation of that phrase), I suspect we should find our nurses responsible for most of the dark corners we are forced to go back to, against our wills.

The first diabolical character who intruded himself on my peaceful youth was a certain Captain Murderer. This wretch must have been an offshoot of the Blue Beard family, but I had no suspicion of the consanguinity in those times. His warning name would seem to have awakened no general prejudice against him, for he was admitted into the best society and possessed immense wealth. Captain Murderer's mission was matrimony, and the gratification of a cannibal appetite with tender brides. On his marriage morning, he always caused both sides of the way to church to be planted with curious flowers; and when his bride said, "Dear Captain Murderer, I never saw flowers like these before: what are they called?" he answered, "They are called Garnish for house-lamb," and laughed at his ferocious practical joke in a horrid manner, disquieting the minds of the noble bridal company, with a very sharp show of teeth, then displayed for the first time.

He made love in a coach and six, and married in a coach and twelve, and all his horses were milk-white horses with one red spot on the back which he caused to be hidden by the harness. For, the spot *would* come there, though every horse was milk-white when Captain Murderer bought him. And the spot was young bride's blood. (*To this terrific point I am indebted for my personal experience of a shudder and cold beads on the forehead.*) When Captain Murderer had made an end of feasting and revelry, and had dismissed the noble guests, and was alone with his wife on the day month after their marriage, it was his whimsical custom to produce a golden rolling-pin and a silver pie-board. Now, there was this special feature in the Captain's courtships, that he always asked if the young lady could make pie-crust; and if she couldn't by nature or education, she was taught.

Well. When the bride saw Captain Murderer produce the golden rolling-pin and silver pie-board, she remembered this, and turned up her laced-silk sleeves to make a pie. The Captain brought out a silver pie-dish of immense capacity, and the Captain brought out flour and butter and eggs and all things needful, except the inside of the pie; of materials for the staple of the pie itself, the Captain brought out none. Then said the lovely bride, "Dear Captain Murderer, what pie is this to be?"

He replied, "A meat pie."

Then said the lovely bride, "Dear Captain Murderer, I see no meat."

The Captain humorously retorted, "Look in the glass."

She looked in the glass, but still she saw no meat, and then the Captain roared with laughter, and suddenly frowning and drawing his sword, bade her roll out the crust. So she rolled out the crust, dropping large tears upon it all the time because he was so cross, and when she had lined the dish with crust and had cut the crust all ready to fit the top, the Captain called out, "*I* see the meat in the glass!"

And the bride looked up at the glass, just in time to see the Captain cutting her head off; and he chopped her in pieces, and peppered her, and salted her, and put her in the pie, and sent it to the baker's, and ate it all, and picked the bones.

Captain Murderer went on in this way, prospering exceedingly, until he came to choose a bride from two twin sisters, and at first didn't know which to choose. For, though one was fair and the other dark, they were both equally beautiful. But the fair twin loved him, and the dark twin hated him, so he chose the fair one. The dark twin would have prevented the marriage if she could, but she couldn't; however, on the night before it, much suspecting Captain Murderer, she stole out and climbed his garden wall, and looked in at his window through a chink in the shutter, and saw him having his teeth filed sharp.

Next day she listened all day, and heard him make his joke about the house-lamb. And that day month, he had the paste rolled out, and cut the fair twin's head off, and chopped her in pieces, and peppered her, and salted her, and put her in the pie, and sent it to the baker's, and ate it all, and picked the bones.

Now, the dark twin had had her suspicions much increased by the filing of the Captain's teeth, and again by the house-lamb joke. Putting all things together when he gave out that her sister was dead, she divined the truth, and determined to be revenged. So, she went up to Captain Murderer's house, and knocked at the knocker and pulled at the bell, and when the Captain came to the door, said: "Dear Captain Murderer, marry me next for I always loved you and was jealous of my sister."

The Captain took it as a compliment, and made a polite answer, and the marriage was quickly arranged. On the night before it, the bride again climbed to his window, and again saw him having his teeth filed sharp. At this sight she laughed such a terrible laugh at the chink in the shutter, that the Captain's blood curdled, and he said: "I hope nothing has disagreed with me!" At that, she laughed again, a still more terrible laugh, and the shutter was opened and search made, but she was nimbly gone, and there was no one. Next day they went to church in a coach and twelve, and were married. And that day month, she rolled the pie-crust out, and Captain Murderer cut her head off, and chopped her in pieces, and peppered her, and salted her, and put her in the pie, and sent it to the baker's, and ate it all, and picked the bones.

But before she began to roll out the paste she had taken a deadly poison of a most awful character, distilled from toads' eyes and spiders' knees; and Captain Murderer had hardly picked her last bone, when he began to swell, and to turn blue, and to be all over spots, and to scream. And he went on swelling and turning bluer, and being more all over spots and screaming, until he reached from floor to ceiling and from wall to wall; and then, at one o'clock in the morning, he blew up with a loud explosion. At the sound of it, all the milk-white horses in the stables broke their halters and went mad, and then they galloped over everybody in Captain Murderer's house (beginning with the family blacksmith who had filed his teeth) until the whole were dead, and then they galloped away.

Hundreds of times did I hear this legend of Captain Murderer, in my early youth, and added hundreds of times was there a mental compulsion upon me in bed, to peep in at his window as the dark twin peeped, and to revisit his horrible house, and look at him in his blue and spotty and screaming stage, as he reached from floor to ceiling and from wall to wall.

The young woman who brought me acquainted with Captain Murderer had a fiendish enjoyment of my terrors, and used to begin, I remember—as a sort of introductory overture—by clawing the air with both hands, and uttering a long low hollow groan. So acutely did I suffer from this ceremony in combination with this infernal Captain, that I sometimes used to plead I thought I was hardly strong enough and old enough to hear the story again just yet.

But, she never spared me one word of it, and indeed commanded the awful chalice to my lips as the only preservative known to science against 'The Black Cat'—a weird and glaring-eyed supernatural Tom, who was reputed to prowl about the world by night, sucking the breath of infancy, and who was endowed with a special thirst (as I was given to understand) for mine.

This female bard—may she have been repaid my debt of obligation to her in the matter of nightmares and perspirations!-reappears in my memory as the daughter of a shipwright. Her name was Mercy, though she had none on me. There was something of a shipbuilding flavour in the following story. As it always recurs to me in a vague association with calomel pills, I believe it to have been reserved for dull nights when I was low with medicine.

There was once a shipwright, and he wrought in a Government Yard, and his name was Chips. And his father's name before him was Chips, and *his* father's name before *him* was Chips, and they were all Chipses. And Chips the father had sold himself to the Devil for an iron pot and a bushel of tenpenny nails and half a ton of copper and a rat that could speak; and Chips the grandfather had sold himself to the Devil for an iron pot and a bushel of tenpenny nails and half a ton of copper and a rat that could speak; and Chips the great-grandfather had disposed of himself in the same direction on the same terms; and the bargain had run in the family for a long, long time. So, one day, when young Chips was at work in the Dock Slip all alone, down in the dark hold of an old Seventy-four that was haled up for repairs, the Devil presented himself, and remarked:

A Lemon has pips,
And a Yard has ships,
And I'll have Chips!

(I don't know why, but this fact of the Devil's expressing

himself in rhyme was peculiarly trying to me.) Chips looked up when he heard the words, and there he saw the Devil with saucer eyes that squinted on a terrible great scale, and that struck out sparks of blue fire continually. And whenever he winked his eyes, showers of blue sparks came out, and his eyelashes made a clattering like flints and steels striking lights. And hanging over one of his arms by the handle was an iron pot, and under that arm was a bushel of tenpenny nails, and under his other arm was half a ton of copper, and sitting on one of his shoulders was a rat that could speak. So, the Devil said again:

A Lemon has pips,
And a Yard has ships,
And I'll have Chips!

(The invariable effect of this alarming tautology on the part of the Evil Spirit was to deprive me of my senses for some moments.) So, Chips answered never a word, but went on with his work. 'What are you doing, Chips?' said the rat that could speak.

'I am putting in new planks where you and your gang have eaten old away,' said Chips.

'But we'll eat them too,' said the rat that could speak; 'and we'll let in the water and drown the crew, and we'll eat them too.'

Chips, being only a shipwright, and not a Man-of-war's man, said, 'You are welcome to it.' But he couldn't keep his eyes off the half a ton of copper or the bushel of tenpenny nails; for nails and copper are a shipwright's sweethearts, and shipwrights will run away with them whenever they can.

So, the Devil said, 'I see what you are looking at, Chips. You had better strike the bargain. You know the terms. Your father before you was well acquainted with them, and so were your grandfather and great-grandfather before him.'

Says Chips, 'I like the copper, and I like the nails, and I don't mind the pot, but I don't like the rat.' Says the Devil, fiercely, 'You can't have the metal without him--and HE'S a curiosity.

I'm going.' Chips, afraid of losing the half a ton of copper and the bushel of nails, then said, 'Give us hold!' So, he got the copper and the nails and the pot and the rat that could speak, and the Devil vanished.

Chips sold the copper, and he sold the nails, and he would have sold the pot; but whenever he offered it for sale, the rat was in it, and the dealers dropped it, and would have nothing to say to the bargain. So, Chips resolved to kill the rat, and, being at work in the Yard one day with a great kettle of hot pitch on one side of him and the iron pot with the rat in it on the other, he turned the scalding pitch into the pot, and filled it full. Then, he kept his eye upon it till it cooled and hardened, and then he let it stand for twenty days, and then he heated the pitch again and turned it back into the kettle, and then he sank the pot in water for twenty days more, and then he got the smelters to put it in the furnace for twenty days more, and then they gave it him out, red hot, and looking like red-hot glass instead of iron—yet there was the rat in it, just the same as ever! And the moment it caught his eye, it said with a jeer:

A Lemon has pips,
And a Yard has ships,
And I'll have Chips!

(For this Refrain I had waited since its last appearance, with inexpressible horror, which now culminated.) Chips now felt certain in his own mind that the rat would stick to him; the rat, answering his thought, said, 'I will—like pitch!'

Now, as the rat leaped out of the pot when it had spoken, and made off, Chips began to hope that it wouldn't keep its word. But, a terrible thing happened next day. For, when dinner-time came, and the Dock-bell rang to strike work, he put his rule into the long pocket at the side of his trousers, and there he found a rat—not that rat, but another rat. And in his hat, he found another; and in his pocket-handkerchief, another; and in the sleeves of his coat, when he pulled it on to go to dinner, two more.

And from that time he found himself so frightfully intimate with all the rats in the Yard, that they climbed up his legs when he was at work, and sat on his tools while he used them. And they could all speak to one another, and he understood what they said. And they got into his lodging, and into his bed, and into his teapot, and into his beer, and into his boots.

And he was going to be married to a corn-chandler's daughter; and when he gave her a workbox he had himself made for her, a rat jumped out of it; and when he put his arm round her waist, a rat clung about her; so the marriage was broken off, though the banns were already twice put up—which the parish clerk well remembers, for, as he handed the book to the clergyman for the second time of asking, a large fat rat ran over the leaf. (By this time a special cascade of rats was rolling down my back, and the whole of my small listening person was overrun with them. At intervals ever since, I have been morbidly afraid of my own pocket, lest my exploring hand should find a specimen or two of those vermin in it.)

You may believe that all this was very terrible to Chips; but even all this was not the worst. He knew besides, what the rats were doing, wherever they were. So, sometimes he would cry aloud, when he was at his club at night, 'Oh! Keep the rats out of the convicts' burying-ground! Don't let them do that!'

Or, 'There's one of them at the cheese downstairs!'

Or, 'There's two of them smelling at the baby in the garret!'

Or, other things of that sort. At last, he was voted mad, and lost his work in the Yard, and could get no other work. But, King George wanted men, so before very long he got pressed for a sailor. And so he was taken off in a boat one evening to his ship, lying at Spithead, ready to sail. And so the first thing he made out in her as he got near her, was the figure-head of the old Seventy-four, where he had seen the Devil.

She was called the *Argonaut*, and they rowed right under the bowsprit where the figure-head of the *Argonaut*, with a sheep-skin in his hand and a blue gown on, was looking out to sea; and sitting staring on his forehead was the rat who could speak, and his exact words were these: 'Chips ahoy! Old boy! We've pretty well eat them too, and we'll drown the crew, and will eat them too!' (Here I always became exceedingly faint, and would have asked for water, but that I was speechless.)

The ship was bound for the Indies; and if you don't know where that is, you ought to it, and angels will never love you. (Here I felt myself an outcast from a future state.) The ship set sail that very night, and she sailed, and sailed, and sailed. Chips's feelings were dreadful. Nothing ever equalled his terrors. No wonder. At last, one day he asked leave to speak to the Admiral. The Admiral giv' leave.

Chips went down on his knees in the Great State Cabin. 'Your Honour, unless your Honour, without a moment's loss of time, makes sail for the nearest shore, this is a doomed ship, and her name is the Coffin!'

'Young man, your words are a madman's words.'

'Your Honour no; they are nibbling us away.'

'They?'

'Your Honour, them dreadful rats. Dust and hollowness where solid oak ought to be! Rats nibbling a grave for every man on board! Oh! Does your Honour love your Lady and your pretty children?'

'Yes, my man, to be sure.'

'Then, for God's sake, make for the nearest shore, for at this present moment the rats are all stopping in their work, and are all looking straight towards you with bare teeth, and are all saying to one another that you shall never, never, never, never, see your Lady and your children more.'

'My poor fellow, you are a case for the doctor. Sentry, take care of this man!'

So, he was bled and he was blistered, and he was this and that, for six whole days and nights. So, then he again asked leave to speak to the Admiral. The Admiral giv' leave. He went down on his knees in the Great State Cabin. 'Now, Admiral, you must die! You took no warning; you must die! The rats are never wrong in their calculations, and they make out that they'll be through, at twelve tonight. So, you must die!—With me and all the rest!'

And so at twelve o'clock there was a great leak reported in the ship, and a torrent of water rushed in and nothing could stop it, and they all went down, every living soul. And what the rats—being water-rats—left of Chips, at last floated to shore, and sitting on him was an immense overgrown rat, laughing, that dived when the corpse touched the beach and never came up. And there was a deal of seaweed on the remains. And if you get thirteen bits of seaweed, and dry them and burn them in the fire, they will go off like in these thirteen words as plain as plain can be:

A Lemon has pips,
And a Yard has ships,
And I've got Chips!

The same female bard—descended, possibly, from those terrible old Scalds who seem to have existed for the express purpose of addling the brains of mankind when they begin to investigate languages—made a standing pretence which greatly assisted in forcing me back to a number of hideous places that I would by all means have avoided. This pretence was, that all her ghost stories had occurred to her own relations. Politeness towards a meritorious family, therefore, forbade my doubting them, and they acquired an air of authentication that impaired my digestive powers for life.

There was a narrative concerning an unearthly animal foreboding death, which appeared in the open street to a parlour-maid who 'went to fetch the beer' for supper: first (as I now recall it) assuming the likeness of a black dog, and gradually rising on its hind-legs and swelling into the semblance of some quadruped greatly surpassing a hippopotamus: which apparition—not because I deemed it in the least improbable, but because I felt it to be really too large to bear—I feebly endeavoured to explain away. But, on Mercy's retorting with wounded dignity that the parlour-maid was her own sister-in-law, I perceived there was no hope, and resigned myself to this zoological phenomenon as one of my many pursuers.

There was another narrative describing the apparition of a young woman who came out of a glass-case and haunted another young woman until the other young woman questioned it and elicited that its bones (Lord! To think of its being so particular about its bones!) were buried under the glass-case, whereas she required them to be interred, with every Undertaking solemnity up to twenty-four pound ten, in another particular place. This narrative I considered—I had a personal interest in disproving, because we had glass-cases at home, and how, otherwise, was I to be guaranteed from the intrusion of young women requiring *me to* bury them up to twenty-four pound ten, when I had only twopence a week? But my remorseless nurse cut the ground from under my tender feet, by informing me that She was the other young woman; and I couldn't say 'I don't believe you;' it was not possible.

Such are a few of the uncommercial journeys that I was forced to make, against my will, when I was very young and unreasoning. And really, as to the latter part of them, it is not so very long ago—now I come to think of it—that I was asked to undertake them once again, with a steady countenance.

Mr Testator's Visitation

Mr. Testator took a set of chambers in Lyons Inn when he had but very scanty furniture for his bedroom, and none for his sitting-room. He had lived some wintry months in this condition, and had found it very bare and cold. One night, past midnight, when he sat writing and still had writing to do that must be done before he went to bed, he found himself out of coals. He had coals downstairs, but had never been to his cellar; however the cellar-key was on his mantelshelf, and if he went down and opened the cellar it fitted, he might fairly assume the coals in that cellar to be his. As to his laundress, she lived among the coal-wagons and Thames watermen—for there were Thames watermen at that time—in some unknown rat-hole by the river, down lanes and alleys on the other side of the Strand.

As to any other person to meet him or obstruct him, Lyons Inn was dreaming, drunk, maudlin, moody, betting, brooding over bill-discounting or renewing—asleep or awake, minding its own affairs. Mr. Testator took his coal-scuttle in one hand, his candle and key in the other, and descended to the dismallest underground dens of Lyons Inn, where the late vehicles in the streets became thunderous, and all the water-pipes in the neighbourhood seemed to have Macbeth's Amen sticking in their throats, and to be trying to get it out.

After groping here and there among low doors to no purpose, Mr. Testator at length came to a door with a rusty padlock which his key fitted. Getting the door open with much trouble, and looking in, he found, no coals, but a confused pile of furniture. Alarmed by this intrusion on another man's property, he locked the door again, found his own cellar, filled his scuttle, and returned upstairs.

But the furniture he had seen, ran on castors across and across Mr. Testator's mind incessantly, when, in the chill hour of five in the morning, he got to bed. He particularly wanted a table to write at, and a table expressly made to be written at, had been the piece of furniture in the foreground of the heap. When his laundress emerged from her burrow in the morning to make his kettle boil, he artfully led up to the subject of cellars and furniture; but the two ideas had evidently no connexion in her mind.

When she left him, and he sat at his breakfast, thinking about the furniture, he recalled the rusty state of the padlock, and inferred that the furniture must have been stored in the cellars for a long time—was perhaps forgotten—owner dead, perhaps? After thinking it over, a few days, in the course of which he could pump nothing out of Lyons Inn about the furniture, he became desperate, and resolved to borrow that table. He did so, that night. He had not had the table long, when he determined to borrow an easy-chair; he had not had that long, when he made up his mind to borrow a bookcase; then, a couch; then, a carpet and rug. By that time, he felt he was 'in furniture stepped in so far,' as that it could be no worse to borrow it all.

Consequently, he borrowed it all, and locked up the cellar for good. He had always locked it, after every visit. He had carried up every separate article in the dead of the night, and, at the best, had felt as wicked as a Resurrection Man. Every article was blue and furry when brought into his rooms, and he had had, in a murderous and guilty sort of way, to polish it up while London slept.

Mr. Testator lived in his furnished chambers two or three years, or more, and gradually lulled himself into the opinion that the furniture was his own. This was his convenient state of mind when, late one night, a step came up the stairs, and a hand passed over his door feeling for his knocker, and then one deep and solemn rap was rapped that might have been a spring in Mr. Testator's easy-chair to shoot him out of it; so promptly was it attended with that effect.

With a candle in his hand, Mr. Testator went to the door, and found there, a very pale and very tall man; a man who stooped; a man with very high shoulders, a very narrow chest, and a very red nose; a shabby-genteel man. He was wrapped in a long thread-bare black coat, fastened up the front with more pins than buttons, and under his arm he squeezed an umbrella without a handle, as if he were playing bagpipes. He said, 'I ask your pardon, but can you tell me—' and stopped; his eyes resting on some object within the chambers.

'Can I tell you what?' asked Mr. Testator, noting his stoppage with quick alarm.

'I ask your pardon,' said the stranger, 'but—this is not the inquiry I was going to make—*Do* I see in there, any small article of property belonging to *me*?'

Mr. Testator was beginning to stammer that he was not aware—when the visitor slipped past him, into the chambers. There, in a goblin way which froze Mr. Testator to the marrow, he examined, first, the writing-table, and said, 'Mine;' then, the easy-chair, and said, 'Mine;' then, the bookcase, and said, 'Mine;' then, turned up a corner of the carpet, and said, 'Mine!' in a word, inspected every item of furniture from the cellar, in succession, and said, 'Mine!' Towards the end of this investigation, Mr. Testator perceived that he was sodden with liquor, and that the liquor was gin. He was not unsteady with gin, either in his speech or carriage; but he was stiff with gin in both particulars.

Mr. Testator was in a dreadful state, for (according to his making out of the story) the possible consequences of what he had done in recklessness and hardihood, flashed upon him in their fullness for the first time. When they had stood gazing at one another for a little while, he tremulously began:

'Sir, I am conscious that the fullest explanation, compensation, and restitution, are your due. They shall be yours. Allow me to entreat that, without temper, without even natural irritation on your part, we may have a little—'

'Drop of something to drink,' interposed the stranger. 'I am agreeable.'

Mr. Testator had intended to say, 'a little quiet conversation,' but with great relief of mind adopted the amendment. He produced a decanter of gin, and was bustling about for hot water and sugar, when he found that his visitor had already drunk half of the decanter's contents. With hot water and sugar the visitor drank the remainder before he had been an hour in the chambers by the chimes of the church of St. Mary in the Strand; and during the process he frequently whispered to himself, 'Mine!'

The gin gone, and Mr. Testator wondering what was to follow it, the visitor rose and said, with increased stiffness, 'At what hour of the morning, sir, will it be convenient?'

Mr. Testator hazarded, 'At ten?'

'Sir,' said the visitor, 'at ten, to the moment, I shall be here.'

He then contemplated Mr. Testator somewhat at leisure, and said, 'God bless you! How is your wife?'

Mr. Testator (who never had a wife) replied with much feeling, 'Deeply anxious, poor soul, but otherwise well.'

The visitor thereupon turned and went away, and fell twice in going downstairs. From that hour he was never heard of. Whether he was a ghost, or a spectral illusion of conscience, or a drunken man who had no business there, or the drunken rightful owner of the furniture, with a transitory gleam of memory; whether he got safe home, or had no time to get to; whether he died of liquor on the way, or lived in liquor ever afterwards; he never was heard of more. This was the story, received with the furniture and held to be as substantial, by its second possessor in an upper set of chambers in grim Lyons Inn.

The Black Veil

One winter's evening, towards the close of the year 1800, or within a year or two of that time, a young medical practitioner, recently established in business, was seated by a cheerful fire in his little parlour, listening to the wind which was beating the rain in pattering drops against the window, or rumbling dismally in the chimney. The night was wet and cold; he had been walking through mud and water the whole day, and was now comfortably reposing in his dressing-gown and slippers, more than half asleep and less than half awake, revolving a thousand matters in his wandering imagination. First, he thought how hard the wind was blowing, and how the cold, sharp rain would be at that moment beating in his face, if he were not comfortably housed at home.

Then, his mind reverted to his annual Christmas visit to his native place and dearest friends; he thought how glad they would all be to see him, and how happy it would make Rose if he could only tell her that he had found a patient at last, and hoped to have more, and to come down again, in a few months' time, and marry her, and take her home to gladden his lonely fireside, and stimulate him to fresh exertions. Then, he began to wonder when his first patient would appear, or whether he was destined, by a special dispensation of Providence, never to have any patients at all; and then, he thought about Rose again, and dropped to sleep and dreamed about her, till the tones of her sweet merry voice sounded in his ears, and her soft tiny hand rested on his shoulder.

There *was* a hand upon his shoulder, but it was neither soft nor tiny; its owner being a corpulent round-headed boy, who, in consideration of the sum of one shilling per week and his food, was let out by the parish to carry medicine and messages. As there was no demand for the medicine, however, and no necessity for the messages, he usually occupied his unemployed hours—averaging fourteen a day—in abstracting peppermint drops, taking animal nourishment, and going to sleep.

'A lady, sir—a lady!' whispered the boy, rousing his master with a shake.

'What lady?' cried our friend, starting up, not quite certain that his dream was an illusion, and half expecting that it might be Rose herself.—'What lady? Where?'

'*There*, sir!' replied the boy, pointing to the glass door leading into the surgery, with an expression of alarm which the very unusual apparition of a customer might have tended to excite.

The surgeon looked towards the door, and started himself, for an instant, on beholding the appearance of his unlooked-for visitor.

It was a singularly tall woman, dressed in deep mourning, and standing so close to the door that her face almost touched the glass. The upper part of her figure was carefully muffled in a black shawl, as if for the purpose of concealment; and her face was shrouded by a thick black veil. She stood perfectly erect, her figure was drawn up to its full height, and though the surgeon felt that the eyes beneath the veil were fixed on him, she stood perfectly motionless, and evinced, by no gesture whatever, the slightest consciousness of his having turned towards her.

'Do you wish to consult me?' he inquired, with some hesitation, holding open the door. It opened inwards, and therefore the action did not alter the position of the figure, which still remained motionless on the same spot.

She slightly inclined her head, in token of acquiescence.

'Pray walk in,' said the surgeon.

The figure moved a step forward; and then, turning its head in the direction of the boy—to his infinite horror—appeared to hesitate.

'Leave the room, Tom,' said the young man, addressing the boy, whose large round eyes had been extended to their utmost width during this brief interview. 'Draw the curtain, and shut the door.'

The boy drew a green curtain across the glass part of the door, retired into the surgery, closed the door after him, and immediately applied one of his large eyes to the keyhole on the other side.

The surgeon drew a chair to the fire, and motioned the visitor to a seat. The mysterious figure slowly moved towards it. As the blaze shone upon the black dress, the surgeon observed that the bottom of it was saturated with mud and rain.

'You are very wet,' he said.

'I am,' said the stranger, in a low deep voice.

'And you are ill?' added the surgeon, compassionately, for the tone was that of a person in pain.

'I am,' was the reply—'very ill; not bodily, but mentally. It is not for myself, or on my own behalf,' continued the stranger, 'that I come to you. If I laboured under bodily disease, I should not be out, alone, at such an hour, or on such a night as this; and if I were afflicted with it, twenty-four hours hence, God knows how gladly I would lie down and pray to die. It is for another that I beseech your aid, sir. I may be mad to ask it for him—I think I am; but, night after night, through the long dreary hours of watching and weeping, the thought has been ever present to my mind; and though even *I* see the hopelessness of human assistance availing him, the bare thought of laying him in his grave without it makes my blood run cold!' And a shudder, such as the surgeon well knew art could not produce, trembled through the speaker's frame.

There was a desperate earnestness in this woman's manner, that went to the young man's heart. He was young in his profession, and had not yet witnessed enough of the miseries which are daily presented before the eyes of its members, to have grown comparatively callous to human suffering.

'If,' he said, rising hastily, 'the person of whom you speak, be in so hopeless a condition as you describe, not a moment is to be lost. I will go with you instantly. Why did you not obtain medical advice before?'

'Because it would have been useless before—because it is useless even now,' replied the woman, clasping her hands passionately.

The surgeon gazed, for a moment, on the black veil, as if to ascertain the expression of the features beneath it: its thickness, however, rendered such a result impossible.

'You *are* ill,' he said, gently, 'although you do not know it. The fever which has enabled you to bear, without feeling it, the fatigue you have evidently undergone, is burning within you now. Put that to your lips,' he continued, pouring out a glass of water—'compose yourself for a few moments, and then tell me, as calmly as you can, what the disease of the patient is, and how long he has been ill. When I know what it is necessary I should know, to render my visit serviceable to him, I am ready to accompany you.'

The stranger lifted the glass of water to her mouth, without raising the veil; put it down again untasted; and burst into tears.

'I know,' she said, sobbing aloud, 'that what I say to you now, seems like the ravings of fever. I have been told so before, less kindly than by you. I am not a young woman; and they do say, that as life steals on towards its final close, the last short remnant, worthless as it may seem to all beside, is dearer to its possessor than all the years that have gone before, connected though they be with the recollection of old friends long since dead, and young ones—children perhaps—who have fallen off from, and forgotten one as completely as if they had died too.

'My natural term of life cannot be many years longer, and should be dear on that account; but I would lay it down without a sigh—with cheerfulness—with joy—if what I tell you now, were only false, or imaginary. Tomorrow morning he of whom I speak will be, I *know*, though I would fain think otherwise, beyond the reach of human aid; and yet, to night, though he is in deadly peril, you must not see, and could not serve, him.'

'I am unwilling to increase your distress,' said the surgeon, after a short pause, 'by making any comment on what you have just said, or appearing desirous to investigate a subject you are so anxious to conceal; but there is an inconsistency in your statement which I cannot reconcile with probability. This person is dying to-night, and I cannot see him when my assistance might possibly avail; you apprehend it will be useless tomorrow, and yet you would have me see him then! If he be, indeed, as dear to you, as your words and manner would imply, why not try to save his life before delay and the progress of his disease render it impracticable?'

'God help me!' exclaimed the woman, weeping bitterly, 'how can I hope strangers will believe what appears incredible, even to myself? You will *not* see him then, sir?' she added, rising suddenly.

'I did not say that I declined to see him,' replied the surgeon; 'but I warn you, that if you persist in this extraordinary procrastination, and the individual dies, a fearful responsibility rests with you.'

'The responsibility will rest heavily somewhere,' replied the stranger bitterly. 'Whatever responsibility rests with me, I am content to bear, and ready to answer.'

'As I incur none,' continued the surgeon, 'by acceding to your request, I will see him in the morning, if you leave me the address. At what hour can he be seen?'

'*Nine*,' replied the stranger.

'You must excuse my pressing these inquiries,' said the surgeon. 'But is he in your charge now?'

'He is not,' was the rejoinder.

'Then, if I gave you instructions for his treatment through the night, you could not assist him?'

The woman wept bitterly, as she replied, 'I could not.'

Finding that there was but little prospect of obtaining more information by prolonging the interview; and anxious to spare the woman's feelings, which, subdued at first by a violent effort, were now irrepressible and most painful to witness; the surgeon repeated his promise of calling in the morning at the appointed hour. His visitor, after giving him a direction to an obscure part of Walworth, left the house in the same mysterious manner in which she had entered it.

It will be readily believed that so extraordinary a visit produced a considerable impression on the mind of the young surgeon; and that he speculated a great deal and to very little purpose on the possible circumstances of the case. In common with the generality of people, he had often heard and read of singular instances, in which a presentiment of death, at a particular day, or even minute, had been entertained and realised.

At one moment he was inclined to think that the present might be such a case; but, then, it occurred to him that all the anecdotes of the kind he had ever heard, were of persons who had been troubled with a foreboding of their own death. This woman, however, spoke of another person—a man; and it was impossible to suppose that a mere dream or delusion of fancy would induce her to speak of his approaching dissolution with such terrible certainty as she had spoken. It could not be that the man was to be murdered in the morning, and that the woman, originally a consenting party, and bound to secrecy by an oath, had relented, and, though unable to prevent the commission of some outrage on the victim, had determined to prevent his death if possible, by the timely interposition of medical aid?

The idea of such things happening within two miles of the metropolis appeared too wild and preposterous to be entertained beyond the instant. Then, his original impression that the woman's intellects were disordered, recurred; and, as it was the only mode of solving the difficulty with any degree of satisfaction, he obstinately made up his mind to believe that she was mad. Certain misgivings upon this point, however, stole upon his thoughts at the time, and presented themselves again and again through the long dull course of a sleepless night; during which, in spite of all his efforts to the contrary, he was unable to banish the black veil from his disturbed imagination.

The back part of Walworth, at its greatest distance from town, is a straggling miserable place enough, even in these days; but, five-and-thirty years ago, the greater portion of it was little better than a dreary waste, inhabited by a few scattered people of questionable character, whose poverty prevented their living in any better neighbourhood, or whose pursuits and mode of life rendered its solitude desirable. Very many of the houses which have since sprung up on all sides, were not built until some years afterwards; and the great majority even of those which were sprinkled about, at irregular intervals, were of the rudest and most miserable description.

The appearance of the place through which he walked in the morning, was not calculated to raise the spirits of the young surgeon, or to dispel any feeling of anxiety or depression which the singular kind of visit he was about to make, had awakened. Striking off from the high road, his way lay across a marshy common, through irregular lanes, with here and there a ruinous and dismantled cottage fast falling to pieces with decay and neglect. A stunted tree, or pool of stagnant water, roused into a sluggish action by the heavy rain of the preceding night, skirted the path occasionally; and, now and then, a miserable patch of garden-ground, with a few old boards knocked together for a summer-house, and old palings imperfectly mended with stakes pilfered from the neighbouring hedges, bore testimony, at once to the poverty of the inhabitants, and the little scruple they entertained in appropriating the property of other people to their own use.

Occasionally, a filthy-looking woman would make her appearance from the door of a dirty house, to empty the contents of some cooking utensil into the gutter in front, or to scream after a little slip-shod girl, who had contrived to stagger a few yards from the door under the weight of a sallow infant almost as big as herself; but, scarcely anything was stirring around: and so much of the prospect as could be faintly traced through the cold damp mist which hung heavily over it, presented a lonely and dreary appearance perfectly in keeping with the objects we have described.

After plodding wearily through the mud and mire; making many inquiries for the place to which he had been directed; and receiving as many contradictory and unsatisfactory replies in return; the young man at length arrived before the house which had been pointed out to him as the object of his destination. It was a small low building, one story above the ground, with even a more desolate and unpromising exterior than any he had yet passed. An old yellow curtain was closely drawn across the window upstairs, and the parlour shutters were closed, but not fastened. The house was detached from any other, and, as it stood at an angle of a narrow lane, there was no other habitation in sight.

When we say that the surgeon hesitated, and walked a few paces beyond the house, before he could prevail upon himself to lift the knocker, we say nothing that need raise a smile upon the face of the boldest reader. The police of London were a very different body in that day; the isolated position of the suburbs, when the rage for building and the progress of improvement had not yet begun to connect them with the main body of the city and its environs, rendered many of them (and this in particular) a place of resort for the worst and most depraved characters. Even the streets in the gayest parts of London were imperfectly lighted, at that time; and such places as these, were left entirely to the mercy of the moon and stars.

The chances of detecting desperate characters, or of tracing them to their haunts, were thus rendered very few, and their offences naturally increased in boldness, as the consciousness of comparative security became the more impressed upon them by daily experience. Added to these considerations, it must be remembered that the young man had spent some time in the public hospitals of the metropolis; and, although neither Burke nor Bishop had then gained a horrible notoriety, his own observation might have suggested to him how easily the atrocities to which the former has since given his name, might be committed.

Be this as it may, whatever reflection made him hesitate, he *did* hesitate: but, being a young man of strong mind and great personal courage, it was only for an instant;—he stepped briskly back and knocked gently at the door.

A low whispering was audible, immediately afterwards, as if some person at the end of the passage were conversing stealthily with another on the landing above. It was succeeded by the noise of a pair of heavy boots upon the bare floor. The door-chain was softly unfastened; the door opened; and a tall, ill-favoured man, with black hair, and a face, as the surgeon often declared afterwards, as pale and haggard, as the countenance of any dead man he ever saw, presented himself.

'Walk in, sir,' he said in a low tone.

The surgeon did so, and the man having secured the door again, by the chain, led the way to a small back parlour at the extremity of the passage.

'Am I in time?'

'Too soon!' replied the man. The surgeon turned hastily round, with a gesture of astonishment not unmixed with alarm, which he found it impossible to repress.

'If you'll step in here, sir,' said the man, who had evidently noticed the action—'if you'll step in here, sir, you won't be detained five minutes, I assure you.'

The surgeon at once walked into the room. The man closed the door, and left him alone.

It was a little cold room, with no other furniture than two deal chairs, and a table of the same material. A handful of fire, unguarded by any fender, was burning in the grate, which brought out the damp if it served no more comfortable purpose, for the unwholesome moisture was stealing down the walls, in long slug-like tracks. The window, which was broken and patched in many places, looked into a small enclosed piece of ground, almost covered with water. Not a sound was to be heard, either within the house, or without. The young surgeon sat down by the fireplace, to await the result of his first professional visit.

He had not remained in this position many minutes, when

the noise of some approaching vehicle struck his ear. It stopped; the street-door was opened; a low talking succeeded, accompanied with a shuffling noise of footsteps, along the passage and on the stairs, as if two or three men were engaged in carrying some heavy body to the room above. The creaking of the stairs, a few seconds afterwards, announced that the new-comers having completed their task, whatever it was, were leaving the house. The door was again closed, and the former silence was restored.

Another five minutes had elapsed, and the surgeon had resolved to explore the house, in search of someone to whom he might make his errand known, when the room-door opened, and his last night's visitor, dressed in exactly the same manner, with the veil lowered as before, motioned him to advance. The singular height of her form, coupled with the circumstance of her not speaking, caused the idea to pass across his brain for an instant, that it might be a man disguised in woman's attire. The hysteric sobs which issued from beneath the veil, and the convulsive attitude of grief of the whole figure, however, at once exposed the absurdity of the suspicion; and he hastily followed.

The woman led the way upstairs to the front room, and paused at the door, to let him enter first. It was scantily furnished with an old deal box, a few chairs, and a tent bedstead, without hangings or cross-rails, which was covered with a patchwork counterpane. The dim light admitted through the curtain which he had noticed from the outside, rendered the objects in the room so indistinct, and communicated to all of them so uniform a hue, that he did not, at first, perceive the object on which his eye at once rested when the woman rushed frantically past him, and flung herself on her knees by the bedside.

Stretched upon the bed, closely enveloped in a linen wrapper, and covered with blankets, lay a human form, stiff and motionless. The head and face, which were those of a man, were uncovered, save by a bandage which passed over the head and under the chin. The eyes were closed. The left arm lay heavily across the bed, and the woman held the passive hand.

The surgeon gently pushed the woman aside, and took the hand in his.

'My God!' he exclaimed, letting it fall involuntarily—'the man is dead!'

The woman started to her feet and beat her hands together.

'Oh! don't say so, sir,' she exclaimed, with a burst of passion, amounting almost to frenzy. 'Oh! don't say so, sir! I can't bear it! Men have been brought to life, before, when unskilful people have given them up for lost; and men have died, who might have been restored, if proper means had been resorted to. Don't let him lie here, sir, without one effort to save him! This very moment life may be passing away. Do try, sir,—do, for Heaven's sake!'—And while speaking, she hurriedly chafed, first the forehead, and then the breast, of the senseless form before her; and then, wildly beat the cold hands, which, when she ceased to hold them, fell listlessly and heavily back on the coverlet.

'It is of no use, my good woman,' said the surgeon, soothingly, as he withdrew his hand from the man's breast. 'Stay—undraw that curtain!'

'Why?' said the woman, starting up.

'Undraw that curtain!' repeated the surgeon in an agitated tone.

'I darkened the room on purpose,' said the woman, throwing herself before him as he rose to undraw it.—'Oh! sir, have pity on me! If it can be of no use, and he is really dead, do not expose that form to other eyes than mine!'

'This man died no natural or easy death,' said the surgeon. 'I *must* see the body!' With a motion so sudden, that the woman hardly knew that he had slipped from beside her, he tore open the curtain, admitted the full light of day, and returned to the bedside.

'There has been violence here,' he said, pointing towards the body, and gazing intently on the face, from which the black veil was now, for the first time, removed. In the excitement of a minute before, the female had thrown off the bonnet and veil, and now stood with her eyes fixed upon him. Her features were those of a woman about fifty, who had once been handsome. Sorrow and weeping had left traces upon them which not time itself would ever have produced without their aid; her face was deadly pale; and there was a nervous contortion of the lip, and an unnatural fire in her eye, which showed too plainly that her bodily and mental powers had nearly sunk, beneath an accumulation of misery.

'There has been violence here,' said the surgeon, preserving his searching glance.

'There has!' replied the woman.

'This man has been murdered.'

'That I call God to witness he has,' said the woman, passionately; 'pitilessly, inhumanly murdered!'

'By whom?' said the surgeon, seizing the woman by the arm.

'Look at the butchers' marks, and then ask me!' she replied.

The surgeon turned his face towards the bed, and bent over the body which now lay full in the light of the window. The throat was swollen, and a livid mark encircled it. The truth flashed suddenly upon him.

'This is one of the men who were hanged this morning!' he exclaimed, turning away with a shudder.

'It is,' replied the woman, with a cold, unmeaning stare.

'Who was he?' inquired the surgeon.

'*My son*,' rejoined the woman; and fell senseless at his feet.

It was true. A companion, equally guilty with himself, had been acquitted for want of evidence; and this man had been left for death, and executed. To recount the circumstances of the case, at this distant period, must be unnecessary, and might give pain to some persons still alive. The history was an everyday one. The mother was a widow without friends or money, and had denied herself necessaries to bestow them on her orphan boy. That boy, unmindful of her prayers, and forgetful of the sufferings she had endured for him—incessant anxiety of mind, and voluntary starvation of body—had plunged into a career of dissipation and crime. And this was the result; his own death by the hangman's hands, and his mother's shame, and incurable insanity.

For many years after this occurrence, and when profitable and arduous avocations would have led many men to forget that such a miserable being existed, the young surgeon was a daily visitor at the side of the harmless mad woman; not only soothing her by his presence and kindness, but alleviating the rigour of her condition by pecuniary donations for her comfort and support, bestowed with no sparing hand.

In the transient gleam of recollection and consciousness which preceded her death, a prayer for his welfare and protection, as fervent as mortal ever breathed, rose from the lips of this poor friendless creature. That prayer flew to Heaven, and was heard. The blessings he was instrumental in conferring, have been repaid to him a thousand-fold; but, amid all the honours of rank and station which have since been heaped upon him, and which he has so well earned, he can have no reminiscence more gratifying to his heart than that connected with The Black Veil.

The Goodwood Ghost

My wife's sister, Mrs M——, was left a widow at the age of thirty-five, with two children, girls, of whom she was passionately fond. She carried on the draper's business at Bognor, established by her husband. Being still a very handsome woman, there were several suitors for her hand. The only favoured one amongst them was a Mr Barton. My wife never liked this Mr Barton, and made no secret of her feelings to her sister, whom she frequently told that Mr Barton only wanted to be master of the little haberdashery shop in Bognor. He was a man in poor circumstances, and had no other motive in his proposal of marriage, so my wife thought, than to better himself.

On the 23rd of August 1831 Mrs M—— arranged to go with Barton to a picnic party at Goodwood Park, the seat of the Duke of Richmond, who had kindly thrown open his grounds to the public for the day. My wife, a little annoyed at her going out with this man, told her she had much better remain at home to look after her children and attend to the business. Mrs M——, however, bent on going, made arrangements about leaving the shop, and got my wife to promise to see to her little girls while she was away.

The party set out in a four-wheeled phaeton, with a pair of ponies driven by Mrs M——, and a gig for which I lent the horse.

Now we did not expect them to come back till nine or ten o'clock, at any rate. I mention this particularly to show that there could be no expectation of their earlier return in the mind of my wife, to account for what follows.

At six o'clock that bright summer's evening my wife went out into the garden to call the children. Not finding them, she went all round the place in her search till she came to the empty stable; thinking they might have run in there to play, she pushed open the door; there, standing in the darkest corner, she saw Mrs M——. My wife was surprised to see her, certainly; for she did not expect her return so soon; but, oddly enough, it did not strike her as being singular to see her there.

Vexed as she had felt with her all day for going, and rather glad, in her woman's way, to have something entirely different from the genuine casus belli to hang a retort upon, my wife said: "Well, Harriet, I should have thought another dress would have done quite as well for your picnic as that best black silk you have on." My wife was the elder of the twain, and had always assumed a little of the air of counsellor to her sister. Black silks were thought a great deal more of at that time than they are just now, and silk of any kind was held particularly inconsistent wear for Wesleyan Methodists, to which denomination we belonged.

Receiving no answer, my wife said: "Oh, well, Harriet, if you can't take a word of reproof without being sulky, I'll leave you to yourself"; and then she came into the house to tell me the party had returned and that she had seen her sister in the stable, not in the best of tempers. At the moment it did not seem extraordinary to me that my wife should have met her sister in the stable.

I waited indoors some time, expecting them to return my horse. Mrs M—— was my neighbour, and, being always on most friendly terms, I wondered that none of the party had come in to tell us about the day's pleasure. I thought I would just run in and see how they had got on. To my great surprise the servant told me they had not returned. I began, then, to feel anxiety about the result. My wife, however, having seen Harriet in the stable, refused to believe the servant's assertion; and said there was no doubt of their return, but that they had probably left word to say they were not come back, in order to offer a plausible excuse for taking a further drive, and detaining my horse for another hour or so.

At eleven o'clock Mr Pinnock, my brother-in-law, who had been one of the party, came in, apparently much agitated. As soon as she saw him, and before he had time to speak, my wife seemed to know what he had to say.

"What is the matter?" she said; "something has happened to Harriet, I know!"

"Yes" replied Mr Pinnock; "if you wish to see her alive, you must come with me directly to Goodwood."

From what he said it appeared that one of the ponies had never been properly broken in; that the man from whom the turn-out was hired for the day had cautioned Mrs M—— respecting it before they started; and that he had lent it reluctantly, being the only pony to match in the stable at the time, and would not have lent it at all had he not known Mrs M—— to be a remarkably good whip.

On reaching Goodwood, it seems, the gentlemen of the party had got out, leaving the ladies to take a drive round the park in the phaeton. One or both of the ponies must then have taken fright at something in the road, for Mrs M—— had scarcely taken the reins when the ponies shied. Had there been plenty of room she would readily have mastered the difficulty; but it was in a narrow road, where a gate obstructed the way. Some men rushed to open the gate—too late.

The three other ladies jumped out at the beginning of the accident; but Mrs M—— still held on to the reins, seeking to control her ponies, until, finding it was impossible for the men to get the gate open in time, she too sprang forward; and at the same instant the ponies came smash on to the gate. She had made her spring too late, and fell heavily to the ground on her head. The heavy, old-fashioned comb of the period, with which her hair was looped up, was driven into her skull by the force of the fall.

The Duke of Richmond, a witness to the accident, ran to her assistance, lifted her up, and rested her head upon his knees.

The only words Mrs M—— had spoken were uttered at the time: "Good God, my children!" By direction of the Duke she was immediately conveyed to a neighbouring inn, where every assistance, medical and otherwise, that forethought or kindness could suggest was afforded her.

At six o'clock in the evening, the time at which my wife had gone into the stable and seen what we now knew had been her spirit, Mrs M——, in her sole interval of returning consciousness, had made a violent but unsuccessful attempt to speak. From her glance having wandered round the room, in solemn awful wistfulness, it had been conjectured she wished to see some relative or friend not then present. I went to Goodwood in the gig with Mr Pinnock, and arrived in time to see my sister-in-law die at two o'clock in the morning. Her only conscious moments had been those in which she laboured unsuccessfully to speak, which had occurred at six o'clock. She wore a black silk dress.

When we came to dispose of her business, and to wind up her affairs, there was scarcely anything left for the two orphan girls. Mrs M——'s father, however, being well-to-do, took them to bring up. At his death, which happened soon afterwards, his property went to his eldest son, who speedily dissipated the inheritance. During a space of two years the children were taken as visitors by various relations in turn, and lived an unhappy life with no settled home.

For some time I had been debating with myself how to help these children, having many boys and girls of my own to provide for. I had almost settled to take them myself, bad as trade was with me, at the time, and bring them up with my own family, when one day business called me to Brighton. The business was so urgent that it necessitated my travelling at night.

I set out from Bognor in a close-headed gig on a beautiful moonlight winter's night, when the crisp frozen snow lay deep over the earth, and its fine glistening dust was whirled about in little eddies on the bleak night-wind—driven now and then in stinging powder against my tingling cheek, warm and glowing in the sharp air. I had taken my great "Bose" (short for "Boatswain") for company. He lay, blinking wakefully, sprawled out on the spare seat of the gig beneath a mass of warm rugs.

Between Littlehampton and Worthing is a lonely piece of road, long and dreary, through bleak and bare open country, where the snow lay knee-deep, sparkling in the moonlight. It was so cheerless that I turned round to speak to my dog, more for the sake of hearing the sound of a voice than anything else. "Good Bose," I said, patting him, "there's a good dog!" Then suddenly I noticed he shivered, and shrank underneath the wraps. Then the horse required my attention, for he gave a start, and was going wrong, and had nearly taken me into the ditch.

Then I looked up. Walking at my horse's head, dressed in a sweeping robe, so white that it shone dazzling against the white snow, I saw a lady, her back turned to me, her head bare; her hair dishevelled and strayed, showing sharp and black against her white dress.

I was at first so much surprised at seeing a lady, so dressed, exposed to the open night, and such a night as this, that I scarcely knew what to do. Recovering myself, I called out to know if I could render assistance—if she wished to ride? No answer. I drove faster, the horse blinking, and shying, and trembling the while, his ears laid back in abject terror. Still the figure maintained its position close to my horse's head. Then I thought that what I saw was no woman, but perchance a man disguised for the purpose of robbing me, seeking an opportunity to seize the bridle and stop the horse. Filled with this idea, I said, "Good Bose! hi! look at it, boy!" but the dog only shivered as if in fright. Then we came to a place where four cross-roads meet.

Determined to know the worst, I pulled up the horse. I fetched Bose, unwilling, out by the ears. He was a good dog at anything from a rat to a man, but he slunk away that night into the hedge, and lay there, his head between his paws, whining and howling. I walked straight up to the figure, still standing by the horse's head. As I walked, the figure turned, and I saw Harriet's face as plainly as I see you now—white and calm—placid, as idealised and beautified by death.

I must own that, though not a nervous man, in that instant I felt sick and faint. Harriet looked me full in the face with a long, eager, silent look. I knew then it was her spirit, and felt a strange calm come over me, for I knew it was nothing to harm me. When I could speak, I asked what troubled her. She looked at me still, never changing that cold fixed stare. Then I felt in my mind it was her children, and I said:

"Harriet! is it for your children you are troubled?"

No answer.

"Harriet," I continued, "if for these you are troubled, be assured they shall never want while I have power to help them. Rest in peace!"

Still no answer.

I put up my hand to wipe from my forehead the cold perspiration which had gathered there. When I took my hand away from shading my eyes, the figure was gone. I was alone on the bleak snow-covered ground. The breeze, that had been hushed before, breathed coolly and gratefully on my face, and the cold stars glimmered and sparkled sharply in the far blue heavens. My dog crept up to me and furtively licked my hand, as who would say, "Good master, don't be angry. I have served you in all but this."

I took the children and brought them up till they could help themselves.

Lying Awake

My uncle lay with his eyes half closed, and his nightcap drawn almost down to his nose. His fancy was already wandering, and began to mingle up the present scene with the crater of Vesuvius, the French Opera, the Coliseum at Rome, Dolly's Chop-house in London, and all the farrago of noted places with which the brain of a traveller is crammed; in a word, he was just falling asleep.

Thus, that delightful writer, WASHINGTON IRVING, in his *Tales of a Traveller*. But, it happened to me the other night to be lying: not with my eyes half closed, but with my eyes wide open; not with my nightcap drawn almost down to my nose, for on sanitary principles I never wear a nightcap: but with my hair pitch-forked and tousled all over the pillow; not just falling asleep by any means, but glaringly, persistently, and obstinately, broad awake. Perhaps, with no scientific intention or invention, I was illustrating the theory of the Duality of the Brain; perhaps one part of my brain, being wakeful, sat up to watch the other part which was sleepy. Be that as it may, something in me was as desirous to go to sleep as it possibly could be, but something else in me WOULD NOT go to sleep, and was as obstinate as George the Third.

Thinking of George the Third—for I devote this paper to my train of thoughts as I lay awake: most people lying awake sometimes, and having some interest in the subject—put me in mind of BENJAMIN FRANKLIN, and so Benjamin Franklin's paper on the art of procuring pleasant dreams, which would seem necessarily to include the art of going to sleep, came into my head.

Now, as I often used to read that paper when I was a very small boy, and as I recollect everything I read then as perfectly as I forget everything I read now, I quoted

'Get out of bed, beat up and turn your pillow, shake the bed-clothes well with at least twenty shakes, then throw the bed open and leave it to cool; in the meanwhile, continuing undrest, walk about your chamber. When you begin to feel the cold air unpleasant, then return to your bed, and you will soon fall asleep, and your sleep will be sweet and pleasant.

Not a bit of it! I performed the whole ceremony, and if it were possible for me to be more saucer-eyed than I was before, that was the only result that came of it.

Except Niagara. The two quotations from Washington Irving and Benjamin Franklin may have put it in my head by an American association of ideas; but there I was, and the Horse-shoe Fall was thundering and tumbling in my eyes and ears, and the very rainbows that I left upon the spray when I really did last look upon it, were beautiful to see. The night-light being quite as plain, however, and sleep seeming to be many thousand miles further off than Niagara, I made up my mind to think a little about Sleep; which I no sooner did than I whirled off in spite of myself to Drury Lane Theatre, and there saw a great actor and dear friend of mine (whom I had been thinking of in the day) playing Macbeth, and heard him apostrophising 'the death of each day's life,' as I have heard him many a time, in the days that are gone.

But, Sleep. I WILL think about Sleep. I am determined to think (this is the way I went on) about Sleep. I must hold the word Sleep, tight and fast, or I shall be off at a tangent in half a second. I feel myself unaccountably straying, already, into Clare Market. Sleep. It would be curious, as illustrating the equality of sleep, to inquire how many of its phenomena are common to all classes, to all degrees of wealth and poverty, to every grade of education and ignorance. Here, for example, is her Majesty Queen Victoria in her palace, this present blessed night, and here is Winking Charley, a sturdy vagrant, in one of her Majesty's jails. Her Majesty has fallen, many thousands of times, from that same Tower, which I claim a right to tumble off now and then. So has Winking Charley. Her Majesty in her sleep has opened or prorogued Parliament, or has held a Drawing Room, attired in some very scanty dress, the deficiencies and improprieties of which have caused her great uneasiness.

I, in my degree, have suffered unspeakable agitation of mind from taking the chair at a public dinner at the London Tavern in my night-clothes, which not all the courtesy of my kind friend and host MR. BATHE could persuade me were quite adapted to the occasion. Winking Charley has been repeatedly tried in a worse condition. Her Majesty is no stranger to a vault or firmament, of a sort of floor-cloth, with an indistinct pattern distantly resembling eyes, which occasionally obtrudes itself on her repose. Neither am I. Neither is Winking Charley.

It is quite common to all three of us to skim along with airy strides a little above the ground; also to hold, with the deepest interest, dialogues with various people, all represented by ourselves; and to be at our wit's end to know what they are going to tell us; and to be indescribably astonished by the secrets they disclose. It is probable that we have all three committed murders and hidden bodies. It is pretty certain that we have all desperately wanted to cry out, and have had no voice; that we have all gone to the play and not been able to get in; that we have all dreamed much more of our youth than of our later lives; that—I have lost it! The thread's broken.

And up I go. I, lying here with the night-light before me, up I go, for no reason on earth that I can find out, and drawn by no links that are visible to me, up the Great Saint Bernard! I have lived in Switzerland, and rambled among the mountains; but, why I should go there now, and why up the Great Saint Bernard in preference to any other mountain, I have no idea.

As I lie here broad awake, and with every sense so sharpened that I can distinctly hear distant noises inaudible to me at another time, I make that journey, as I really did, on the same summer day, with the same happy party—ah! two since dead, I grieve to think—and there is the same track, with the same black wooden arms to point the way, and there are the same storm-refuges here and there; and there is the same snow falling at the top, and there are the same frosty mists, and there is the same intensely cold convent with its menagerie smell, and the same breed of dogs fast dying out, and the same breed of jolly young monks whom I mourn to know as humbugs, and the same convent parlour with its piano and the sitting round the fire, and the same supper, and the same lone night in a cell, and the same bright fresh morning when going out into the highly rarefied air was like a plunge into an icy bath. Now, see here what comes along; and why does this thing stalk into my mind on the top of a Swiss mountain!

It is a figure that I once saw, just after dark, chalked upon a door in a little back lane near a country church—my first church. How young a child I may have been at the time I don't know, but it horrified me so intensely—in connexion with the churchyard, I suppose, for it smokes a pipe, and has a big hat with each of its ears sticking out in a horizontal line under the brim, and is not in itself more oppressive than a mouth from ear to ear, a pair of goggle eyes, and hands like two bunches of carrots, five in each, can make it—that it is still vaguely alarming to me to recall (as I have often done before, lying awake) the running home, the looking behind, the horror, of its following me; though whether disconnected from the door, or door and all, I can't say, and perhaps never could. It lays a disagreeable train. I must resolve to think of something on the voluntary principle.

The balloon ascents of this last season. They will do to think about, while I lie awake, as well as anything else. I must hold them tight though, for I feel them sliding away, and in their stead are the Mannings, husband and wife, hanging on the top of Horsemonger Lane Jail. In connexion with which dismal spectacle, I recall this curious fantasy of the mind. That, having beheld that execution, and having left those two forms dangling on the top of the entrance gateway—the man's, a limp, loose suit of clothes as if the man had gone out of them; the woman's, a fine shape, so elaborately corseted and artfully dressed, that it was quite unchanged in its trim appearance as it slowly swung from side to side—I never could, by my uttermost efforts, for some weeks, present the outside of that prison to myself (which the terrible impression I had received continually obliged me to do) without presenting it with the two figures still hanging in the morning air. Until, strolling past the gloomy place one night, when the street was deserted and quiet, and actually seeing that the bodies were not there, my fancy was persuaded, as it were, to take them down and bury them within the precincts of the jail, where they have lain ever since.

The balloon ascents of last season. Let me reckon them up. There were the horse, the bull, the parachute,—and the tumbler hanging on—chiefly by his toes, I believe—below the car. Very wrong, indeed, and decidedly to be stopped. But, in connexion with these and similar dangerous exhibitions, it strikes me that that portion of the public whom they entertain, is unjustly reproached. Their pleasure is in the difficulty overcome. They are a public of great faith, and are quite confident that the gentleman will not fall off the horse, or the lady off the bull or out of the parachute, and that the tumbler has a firm hold with his toes.

They do not go to see the adventurer vanquished, but triumphant. There is no parallel in public combats between men and beasts, because nobody can answer for the particular beast—unless it were always the same beast, in which case it would be a mere stage-show, which the same public would go in the same state of mind to see, entirely believing in the brute being beforehand safely subdued by the man. That they are not accustomed to calculate hazards and dangers with any nicety, we may know from their rash exposure of themselves in overcrowded steamboats, and unsafe conveyances and places of all kinds.

And I cannot help thinking that instead of railing, and attributing savage motives to a people naturally well disposed and humane, it is better to teach them, and lead them argumentatively and reasonably—for they are very reasonable, if you will discuss a matter with them—to more considerate and wise conclusions.

This is a disagreeable intrusion! Here is a man with his throat cut, dashing towards me as I lie awake! A recollection of an old story of a kinsman of mine, who, going home one foggy winter night to Hampstead, when London was much smaller and the road lonesome, suddenly encountered such a figure rushing past him, and presently two keepers from a madhouse in pursuit. A very unpleasant creature indeed, to come into my mind unbidden, as I lie awake.

The balloon ascents of last season. I must return to the balloons. Why did the bleeding man start out of them? Never mind; if I inquire, he will be back again. The balloons. This particular public have inherently a great pleasure in the contemplation of physical difficulties overcome; mainly, as I take it, because the lives of a large majority of them are exceedingly monotonous and real, and further, are a struggle against continual difficulties, and further still, because anything in the form of accidental injury, or any kind of illness or disability is so very serious in their own sphere. I will explain this seeming paradox of mine.

Take the case of a Christmas Pantomime. Surely nobody supposes that the young mother in the pit who falls into fits of laughter when the baby is boiled or sat upon, would be at all diverted by such an occurrence off the stage. Nor is the decent workman in the gallery, who is transported beyond the ignorant present by the delight with which he sees a stout gentleman pushed out of a two pair of stairs window, to be slandered by the suspicion that he would be in the least entertained by such a spectacle in any street in London, Paris, or New York.

It always appears to me that the secret of this enjoyment lies in the temporary superiority to the common hazards and mischances of life; in seeing casualties, attended when they really occur with bodily and mental suffering, tears, and poverty, happen through a very rough sort of poetry without the least harm being done to anyone—the pretence of distress in a pantomime being so broadly humorous as to be no pretence at all. Much as in the comic fiction I can understand the mother with a very vulnerable baby at home, greatly relishing the invulnerable baby on the stage, so in the Cremorne reality I can understand the mason who is always liable to fall off a scaffold in his working jacket and to be carried to the hospital, having an infinite admiration of the radiant personage in spangles who goes into the clouds upon a bull, or upside down, and who, he takes it for granted—not reflecting upon the thing—has, by uncommon skill and dexterity, conquered such mischances as those to which he and his acquaintance are continually exposed.

I wish the Morgue in Paris would not come here as I lie awake, with its ghastly beds, and the swollen saturated clothes hanging up, and the water dripping, dripping all day long, upon that other swollen saturated something in the corner, like a heap of crushed over-ripe figs that I have seen in Italy! And this detestable Morgue comes back again at the head of a procession of forgotten ghost stories. This will never do. I must think of something else as I lie awake; or, like that sagacious animal in the United States who recognised the colonel who was such a dead shot, I am a gone 'Coon'. What shall I think of? The late brutal assaults. Very good subject. The late brutal assaults.

(Though whether, supposing I should see, here before me as I lie awake, the awful phantom described in one of those ghost stories, who, with a head-dress of shroud, was always seen looking in through a certain glass door at a certain dead hour—whether, in such a case it would be the least consolation to me to know on philosophical grounds that it was merely my imagination, is a question I can't help asking myself by the way.)

The late brutal assaults. I strongly question the expediency of advocating the revival of whipping for those crimes. It is a natural and generous impulse to be indignant at the perpetration of inconceivable brutality, but I doubt the whipping panacea gravely. Not in the least regard or pity for the criminal, whom I hold in far lower estimation than a mad wolf, but in consideration for the general tone and feeling, which is very much improved since the whipping times.

It is bad for a people to be familiarised with such punishments. When the whip went out of Bridewell, and ceased to be flourished at the carts tail and at the whipping-post, it began to fade out of madhouses, and workhouses, and schools and families, and to give place to a better system everywhere, than cruel driving. It would be hasty, because a few brutes may be inadequately punished, to revive, in any aspect, what, in so many aspects, society is hardly yet happily rid of. The whip is a very contagious kind of thing, and difficult to confine within one set of bounds. Utterly abolish punishment by fine—a barbarous device, quite as much out of date as wager by battle, but particularly connected in the vulgar mind with this class of offence—at least quadruple the term of imprisonment for aggravated assaults—and above all let us, in such cases, have no Pet Prisoning, vain glorifying, strong soup, and roasted meats, but hard work, and one unchanging and uncompromising dietary of bread and water, well or ill; and we shall do much better than by going down into the dark to grope for the whip among the rusty fragments of the rack, and the branding iron, and the chains and gibbet from the public roads, and the weights that pressed men to death in the cells of Newgate.

I had proceeded thus far, when I found I had been lying awake so long that the very dead began to wake too, and to crowd into my thoughts most sorrowfully. Therefore, I resolved to lie awake no more, but to get up and go out for a night walk—which resolution was an acceptable relief to me, as I dare say it may prove now to a great many more.

The Drunkard's Death

We will be bold to say, that there is scarcely a man in the constant habit of walking, day after day, through any of the crowded thoroughfares of London, who cannot recollect among the people whom he 'knows by sight,' to use a familiar phrase, some being of abject and wretched appearance whom he remembers to have seen in a very different condition, whom he has observed sinking lower and lower, by almost imperceptible degrees, and the shabbiness and utter destitution of whose appearance, at last, strike forcibly and painfully upon him, as he passes by.

Is there any man who has mixed much with society, or whose avocations have caused him to mingle, at one time or other, with a great number of people, who cannot call to mind the time when some shabby, miserable wretch, in rags and filth, who shuffles past him now in all the squalor of disease and poverty, with a respectable tradesman, or clerk, or a man following some thriving pursuit, with good prospects, and decent means?—or cannot any of our readers call to mind from among the list of their quondam acquaintance, some fallen and degraded man, who lingers about the pavement in hungry misery—from whom every one turns coldly away, and who preserves himself from sheer starvation, nobody knows how?

Alas! such cases are of too frequent occurrence to be rare items in any man's experience; and but too often arise from one cause—drunkenness—that fierce rage for the slow, sure poison, that oversteps every other consideration; that casts aside wife, children, friends, happiness, and station; and hurries its victims madly on to degradation and death.

Some of these men have been impelled, by misfortune and misery, to the vice that has degraded them. The ruin of worldly expectations, the death of those they loved, the sorrow that slowly consumes, but will not break the heart, has driven them wild; and they present the hideous spectacle of madmen, slowly dying by their own hands. But by far the greater part have wilfully, and with open eyes, plunged into the gulf from which the man who once enters it never rises more, but into which he sinks deeper and deeper down, until recovery is hopeless.

Such a man as this once stood by the bedside of his dying wife, while his children knelt around, and mingled loud bursts of grief with their innocent prayers. The room was scantily and meanly furnished; and it needed but a glance at the pale form from which the light of life was fast passing away, to know that grief, and want, and anxious care, had been busy at the heart for many a weary year.

An elderly woman, with her face bathed in tears, was supporting the head of the dying woman—her daughter—on her arm. But it was not towards her that the face was turned; it was not her hand that the cold and trembling fingers clasped; they pressed the husband's arm; the eyes so soon to be closed in death rested on his face, and the man shook beneath their gaze. His dress was slovenly and disordered, his face inflamed, his eyes bloodshot and heavy. He had been summoned from some wild debauch to the bed of sorrow and death.

A shaded lamp by the bedside cast a dim light on the figures around, and left the remainder of the room in thick, deep shadow. The silence of night prevailed without the house, and the stillness of death was in the chamber. A watch hung over the mantelshelf; its low ticking was the only sound that broke the profound quiet, but it was a solemn one, for well they knew, who heard it, that before it had recorded the passing of another hour, it would beat the knell of a departed spirit.

It is a dreadful thing to wait and watch for the approach of death; to know that hope is gone, and recovery impossible; and to sit and count the dreary hours through long, long nights-such nights as only watchers by the bed of sickness know. It chills the blood to hear the dearest secrets of the heart—the pent-up, hidden secrets of many years—poured forth by the unconscious, helpless being before you; and to think how little the reserve and cunning of a whole life will avail, when fever and delirium tear off the mask at last.

Strange tales have been told in the wanderings of dying men; tales so full of guilt and crime, that those who stood by the sick person's couch have fled in horror and affright, lest they should be scared to madness by what they heard and saw; and many a wretch has died alone, raving of deeds the very name of which has driven the boldest man away.

But no such ravings were to be heard at the bedside by which the children knelt. Their half-stifled sobs and moaning alone broke the silence of the lonely chamber. And when at last the mother's grasp relaxed, and, turning one look from the children to the father, she vainly strove to speak, and fell backward on the pillow, all was so calm and tranquil that she seemed to sink to sleep. They leant over her; they called upon her name, softly at first, and then in the loud and piercing tones of desperation. But there was no reply. They listened for her breath, but no sound came. They felt for the palpitation of the heart, but no faint throb responded to the touch. That heart was broken, and she was dead!

The husband sunk into a chair by the bedside, and clasped his hands upon his burning forehead. He gazed from child to child, but when a weeping eye met his, he quailed beneath its look. No word of comfort was whispered in his ear, no look of kindness lighted on his face. All shrunk from and avoided him; and when at last he staggered from the room, no one sought to follow or console the widower.

The time had been when many a friend would have crowded round him in his affliction, and many a heartfelt condolence would have met him in his grief. Where were they now? One by one, friends, relations, the commonest acquaintance even, had fallen off from and deserted the drunkard. His wife alone had clung to him in good and evil, in sickness and poverty, and how had he rewarded her? He had reeled from the tavern to her bed-side in time to see her die.

He rushed from the house, and walked swiftly through the streets. Remorse, fear, shame, all crowded on his mind. Stupe-fied with drink, and bewildered with the scene he had just wit-nessed, he re-entered the tavern he had quitted shortly before. Glass succeeded glass. His blood mounted, and his brain whirled round. Death! Everyone must die, and why not SHE? She was too good for him; her relations had often told him so. Curses on them! Had they not deserted her, and left her to whine away the time at home? Well—she was dead, and happy perhaps. It was better as it was. Another glass—one more! Hurrah! It was a merry life while it lasted; and he would make the most of it.

Time went on; the three children who were left to him, grew up, and were children no longer. The father remained the same—poorer, shabbier, and more dissolute-looking, but the same confirmed and irreclaimable drunkard. The boys had, long ago, run wild in the streets, and left him; the girl alone remained, but she worked hard, and words or blows could always procure him something for the tavern. So he went on in the old course, and a merry life he led.

One night, as early as ten o'clock—for the girl had been sick for many days, and there was, consequently, little to spend at the public-house—he bent his steps homeward, bethinking himself that if he would have her able to earn money, it would be as well to apply to the parish surgeon, or, at all events, to take the trou-ble of inquiring what ailed her, which he had not yet thought it worthwhile to do. It was a wet December night; the wind blew piercing cold, and the rain poured heavily down. He begged a few halfpence from a passer-by, and having bought a small loaf (for it was his interest to keep the girl alive, if he could), he shuf-fled onwards as fast as the wind and rain would let him.

At the back of Fleet-street, and lying between it and the wa-terside, are several mean and narrow courts, which form a portion of Whitefriars: it was to one of these that he directed his steps.

The alley into which he turned, might, for filth and misery, have competed with the darkest corner of this ancient sanctuary in its dirtiest and most lawless time. The houses, varying from two stories in height to four, were stained with every indescribable hue that long exposure to the weather, damp, and rottenness can impart to tenements composed originally of the roughest and coarsest materials. The windows were patched with paper, and stuffed with the foulest rags; the doors were falling from their hinges; poles with lines on which to dry clothes, projected from every casement, and sounds of quarrelling or drunkenness issued from every room.

The solitary oil lamp in the centre of the court had been blown out, either by the violence of the wind or the act of some inhabitant who had excellent reasons for objecting to his residence being rendered too conspicuous; and the only light which fell upon the broken and uneven pavement, was derived from the miserable candles that here and there twinkled in the rooms of such of the more fortunate residents as could afford to indulge in so expensive a luxury. A gutter ran down the centre of the alley—all the sluggish odours of which had been called forth by the rain; and as the wind whistled through the old houses, the doors and shutters creaked upon their hinges, and the windows shook in their frames, with a violence which every moment seemed to threaten the destruction of the whole place.

The man whom we have followed into this den, walked on in the darkness, sometimes stumbling into the main gutter, and at others into some branch repositories of garbage which had been formed by the rain, until he reached the last house in the court. The door, or rather what was left of it, stood ajar, for the convenience of the numerous lodgers; and he proceeded to grope his way up the old and broken stair, to the attic story.

He was within a step or two of his room door, when it opened, and a girl, whose miserable and emaciated appearance was only to be equalled by that of the candle which she shaded with her hand, peeped anxiously out.

'Is that you, father?' said the girl.

'Who else should it be?' replied the man gruffly. 'What are you trembling at? It's little enough that I've had to drink today, for there's no drink without money, and no money without work. What the devil's the matter with the girl?'

'I am not well, father—not at all well,' said the girl, bursting into tears.

'Ah!' replied the man, in the tone of a person who is compelled to admit a very unpleasant fact, to which he would rather remain blind, if he could. 'You must get better somehow, for we must have money. You must go to the parish doctor, and make him give you some medicine. They're paid for it, damn 'em. What are you standing before the door for? Let me come in, can't you?'

'Father,' whispered the girl, shutting the door behind her, and placing herself before it, 'William has come back.'

'Who!' said the man with a start.

'Hush,' replied the girl, 'William; brother William.'

'And what does he want?' said the man, with an effort at composure—'money? meat? drink? He's come to the wrong shop for that, if he does. Give me the candle—give me the candle, fool—I ain't going to hurt him.' He snatched the candle from her hand, and walked into the room.

Sitting on an old box, with his head resting on his hand, and his eyes fixed on a wretched cinder fire that was smouldering on the hearth, was a young man of about two-and-twenty, miserably clad in an old coarse jacket and trousers. He started up when his father entered.

'Fasten the door, Mary,' said the young man hastily—'Fasten the door. You look as if you didn't know me, father. It's long enough, since you drove me from home; you may well forget me.'

'And what do you want here, now?' said the father, seating himself on a stool, on the other side of the fireplace. 'What do you want here, now?'

'Shelter,' replied the son. 'I'm in trouble: that's enough. If I'm caught I shall swing; that's certain. Caught I shall be, unless I stop here; that's AS certain. And there's an end of it.'

'You mean to say, you've been robbing, or murdering, then?' said the father.

'Yes, I do,' replied the son. 'Does it surprise you, father?' He looked steadily in the man's face, but he withdrew his eyes, and bent them on the ground.

'Where's your brothers?' he said, after a long pause.

'Where they'll never trouble you,' replied his son: 'John's gone to America, and Henry's dead.'

'Dead!' said the father, with a shudder, which even he could not express.

'Dead,' replied the young man. 'He died in my arms—shot like a dog, by a gamekeeper. He staggered back, I caught him, and his blood trickled down my hands. It poured out from his side like water. He was weak, and it blinded him, but he threw himself down on his knees, on the grass, and prayed to God, that if his mother was in heaven, He would hear her prayers for pardon for her youngest son. "I was her favourite boy, Will," he said, "and I am glad to think, now, that when she was dying, though I was a very young child then, and my little heart was almost bursting, I knelt down at the foot of the bed, and thanked God for having made me so fond of her as to have never once done anything to bring the tears into her eyes. O Will, why was she taken away, and father left?" There's his dying words, father,' said the young man; 'make the best you can of 'em. You struck him across the face, in a drunken fit, the morning we ran away; and here's the end of it.'

The girl wept aloud; and the father, sinking his head upon his knees, rocked himself to and fro.

'If I am taken,' said the young man, 'I shall be carried back into the country, and hung for that man's murder. They cannot trace me here, without your assistance, father. For aught I know, you may give me up to justice; but unless you do, here I stop, until I can venture to escape abroad.'

For two whole days, all three remained in the wretched room, without stirring out. On the third evening, however, the girl was worse than she had been yet, and the few scraps of food they had were gone. It was indispensably necessary that somebody should go out; and as the girl was too weak and ill, the father went, just at nightfall.

He got some medicine for the girl, and a trifle in the way of pecuniary assistance. On his way back, he earned sixpence by holding a horse; and he turned homewards with enough money to supply their most pressing wants for two or three days to come. He had to pass the public-house. He lingered for an instant, walked past it, turned back again, lingered once more, and finally slunk in. Two men whom he had not observed, were on the watch. They were on the point of giving up their search in despair, when his loitering attracted their attention; and when he entered the public-house, they followed him.

'You'll drink with me, master,' said one of them, proffering him a glass of liquor.

'And me too,' said the other, replenishing the glass as soon as it was drained of its contents.

The man thought of his hungry children, and his son's danger. But they were nothing to the drunkard. He DID drink; and his reason left him.

'A wet night, Warden,' whispered one of the men in his ear, as he at length turned to go away, after spending in liquor one-half of the money on which, perhaps, his daughter's life depended.

'The right sort of night for our friends in hiding, Master Warden,' whispered the other.

'Sit down here,' said the one who had spoken first, drawing him into a corner. 'We have been looking arter the young un. We came to tell him, it's all right now, but we couldn't find him 'cause we hadn't got the precise direction. But that ain't strange, for I don't think he know'd it himself, when he come to London, did he?'

'No, he didn't,' replied the father.

The two men exchanged glances.

'There's a vessel down at the docks, to sail at midnight, when it's high water,' resumed the first speaker, 'and we'll put him on board. His passage is taken in another name, and what's better than that, it's paid for. It's lucky we met you.'

'Very,' said the second.

'Capital luck,' said the first, with a wink to his companion.

'Great,' replied the second, with a slight nod of intelligence.

'Another glass here; quick'—said the first speaker. And in five minutes more, the father had unconsciously yielded up his own son into the hangman's hands.

Slowly and heavily the time dragged along, as the brother and sister, in their miserable hiding-place, listened in anxious suspense to the slightest sound. At length, a heavy footstep was heard upon the stair; it approached nearer; it reached the landing; and the father staggered into the room.

The girl saw that he was intoxicated, and advanced with the candle in her hand to meet him; she stopped short, gave a loud scream, and fell senseless on the ground. She had caught sight of the shadow of a man reflected on the floor. They both rushed in, and in another instant the young man was a prisoner, and handcuffed.

'Very quietly done,' said one of the men to his companion, 'thanks to the old man. Lift up the girl, Tom—come, come, it's no use crying, young woman. It's all over now, and can't be helped.'

The young man stooped for an instant over the girl, and then turned fiercely round upon his father, who had reeled against the wall, and was gazing on the group with drunken stupidity.

'Listen to me, father,' he said, in a tone that made the drunkard's flesh creep. 'My brother's blood, and mine, is on your head: I never had kind look, or word, or care, from you, and alive or dead, I never will forgive you. Die when you will, or how, I will be with you. I speak as a dead man now, and I warn you, father, that as surely as you must one day stand before your Maker, so surely shall your children be there, hand in hand, to cry for judgment against you.' He raised his manacled hands in a threatening attitude, fixed his eyes on his shrinking parent, and slowly left the room; and neither father nor sister ever beheld him more, on this side of the grave.

When the dim and misty light of a winter's morning penetrated into the narrow court, and struggled through the begrimed window of the wretched room, Warden awoke from his heavy sleep, and found himself alone. He rose, and looked round him; the old flock mattress on the floor was undisturbed; everything was just as he remembered to have seen it last: and there were no signs of any one, save himself, having occupied the room during the night. He inquired of the other lodgers, and of the neighbours; but his daughter had not been seen or heard of. He rambled through the streets, and scrutinised each wretched face among the crowds that thronged them, with anxious eyes. But his search was fruitless, and he returned to his garret when night came on, desolate and weary.

For many days he occupied himself in the same manner, but no trace of his daughter did he meet with, and no word of her reached his ears. At length he gave up the pursuit as hopeless. He had long thought of the probability of her leaving him, and endeavouring to gain her bread in quiet, elsewhere. She had left him at last to starve alone. He ground his teeth, and cursed her!

He begged his bread from door to door. Every halfpenny he could wring from the pity or credulity of those to whom he addressed himself, was spent in the old way. A year passed over his head; the roof of a jail was the only one that had sheltered him for many months. He slept under archways, and in brickfields-anywhere, where there was some warmth or shelter from the cold and rain. But in the last stage of poverty, disease, and houseless want, he was a drunkard still.

At last, one bitter night, he sunk down on a doorstep faint and ill. The premature decay of vice and profligacy had worn him to the bone. His cheeks were hollow and livid; his eyes were sunken, and their sight was dim. His legs trembled beneath his weight, and a cold shiver ran through every limb.

And now the long-forgotten scenes of a misspent life crowded thick and fast upon him. He thought of the time when he had a home—a happy, cheerful home—and of those who peopled it, and flocked about him then, until the forms of his elder children seemed to rise from the grave, and stand about him—so plain, so clear, and so distinct they were that he could touch and feel them. Looks that he had long forgotten were fixed upon him once more; voices long since hushed in death sounded in his ears like the music of village bells. But it was only for an instant. The rain beat heavily upon him; and cold and hunger were gnawing at his heart again.

He rose, and dragged his feeble limbs a few paces further. The street was silent and empty; the few passengers who passed by, at that late hour, hurried quickly on, and his tremulous voice was lost in the violence of the storm. Again that heavy chill struck through his frame, and his blood seemed to stagnate beneath it. He coiled himself up in a projecting doorway, and tried to sleep.

But sleep had fled from his dull and glazed eyes. His mind wandered strangely, but he was awake, and conscious. The well-known shout of drunken mirth sounded in his ear, the glass was at his lips, the board was covered with choice rich food—they were before him: he could see them all, he had but to reach out his hand, and take them—and, though the illusion was reality itself, he knew that he was sitting alone in the deserted street, watching the raindrops as they pattered on the stones; that death was coming upon him by inches—and that there were none to care for or help him.

Suddenly he started up, in the extremity of terror. He had heard his own voice shouting in the night air, he knew not what, or why. Hark! A groan!—another! His senses were leaving him: half-formed and incoherent words burst from his lips; and his hands sought to tear and lacerate his flesh. He was going mad, and he shrieked for help till his voice failed him.

He raised his head, and looked up the long dismal street. He recollected that outcasts like himself, condemned to wander day and night in those dreadful streets, had sometimes gone distracted with their own loneliness. He remembered to have heard many years before that a homeless wretch had once been found in a solitary corner, sharpening a rusty knife to plunge into his own heart, preferring death to that endless, weary, wandering to and fro. In an instant his resolve was taken, his limbs received new life; he ran quickly from the spot, and paused not for breath until he reached the riverside.

He crept softly down the steep stone stairs that lead from the commencement of Waterloo Bridge, down to the water's level. He crouched into a corner, and held his breath, as the patrol passed. Never did prisoner's heart throb with the hope of liberty and life half so eagerly as did that of the wretched man at the prospect of death. The watch passed close to him, but he remained unobserved; and after waiting till the sound of footsteps had died away in the distance, he cautiously descended, and stood beneath the gloomy arch that forms the landing-place from the river.

The tide was in, and the water flowed at his feet. The rain had ceased, the wind was lulled, and all was, for the moment, still and quiet—so quiet, that the slightest sound on the opposite bank, even the rippling of the water against the barges that were moored there, was distinctly audible to his ear. The stream stole languidly and sluggishly on. Strange and fantastic forms rose to the surface, and beckoned him to approach; dark gleaming eyes peered from the water, and seemed to mock his hesitation, while hollow murmurs from behind, urged him onwards. He retreated a few paces, took a short run, desperate leap, and plunged into the river.

Not five seconds had passed when he rose to the water's surface—but what a change had taken place in that short time, in all his thoughts and feelings! Life—life in any form, poverty, misery, starvation—anything but death. He fought and struggled with the water that closed over his head, and screamed in agonies of terror. The curse of his own son rang in his ears. The shore—but one foot of dry ground—he could almost touch the step. One hand's breadth nearer, and he was saved—but the tide bore him onward, under the dark arches of the bridge, and he sank to the bottom.

Again he rose, and struggled for life. For one instant—for one brief instant—the buildings on the river's banks, the lights on the bridge through which the current had borne him, the black water, and the fast-flying clouds, were distinctly visible—once more he sunk, and once again he rose. Bright flames of fire shot up from earth to heaven, and reeled before his eyes, while the water thundered in his ears, and stunned him with its furious roar.

A week afterwards the body was washed ashore, some miles down the river, a swollen and disfigured mass. Unrecognised and unpitied, it was borne to the grave; and there it has long since mouldered away!

The Long Voyage

When the wind is blowing and the sleet or rain is driving against the dark windows, I love to sit by the fire, thinking of what I have read in books of voyage and travel. Such books have had a strong fascination for my mind from my earliest childhood; and I wonder it should have come to pass that I never have been round the world, never have been shipwrecked, ice-environed, tomahawked, or eaten.

Sitting on my ruddy hearth in the twilight of New Year's Eve, I find incidents of travel rise around me from all the latitudes and longitudes of the globe. They observe no order or sequence, but appear and vanish as they will—'come like shadows, so depart.' Columbus, alone upon the sea with his disaffected crew, looks over the waste of waters from his high station on the poop of his ship, and sees the first uncertain glimmer of the light, 'rising and falling with the waves, like a torch in the bark of some fisherman,' which is the shining star of a new world.

Bruce is caged in Abyssinia, surrounded by the gory horrors which shall often startle him out of his sleep at home when years have passed away. Franklin, come to the end of his unhappy overland journey—would that it had been his last!—lies perishing of hunger with his brave companions: each emaciated figure stretched upon its miserable bed without the power to rise: all, dividing the weary days between their prayers, their remembrances of the dear ones at home, and conversation on the pleasures of eating; the last-named topic being ever present to them, likewise, in their dreams.

All the African travellers, wayworn, solitary and sad, submit themselves again to drunken, murderous, man-selling despots, of the lowest order of humanity; and Mungo Park, fainting under a tree and succoured by a woman, gratefully remembers how his Good Samaritan has always come to him in woman's shape, the wide world over.

A shadow on the wall in which my mind's eye can discern some traces of a rocky sea-coast, recalls to me a fearful story of travel derived from that unpromising narrator of such stories, a parliamentary blue-book. A convict is its chief figure, and this man escapes with other prisoners from a penal settlement. It is an island, and they seize a boat, and get to the main land. Their way is by a rugged and precipitous sea-shore, and they have no earthly hope of ultimate escape, for the party of soldiers despatched by an easier course to cut them off, must inevitably arrive at their distant bourne long before them, and retake them if by any hazard they survive the horrors of the way.

Famine, as they all must have foreseen, besets them early in their course. Some of the party die and are eaten; some are murdered by the rest and eaten. This one awful creature eats his fill, and sustains his strength, and lives on to be recaptured and taken back. The unrelateable experiences through which he has passed have been so tremendous, that he is not hanged as he might be, but goes back to his old chained-gang work. A little time, and he tempts one other prisoner away, seizes another boat, and flies once more—necessarily in the old hopeless direction, for he can take no other.

He is soon cut off, and met by the pursuing party face to face, upon the beach. He is alone. In his former journey he acquired an inappeasable relish for his dreadful food. He urged the new man away, expressly to kill him and eat him. In the pockets on one side of his coarse convict-dress, are portions of the man's body, on which he is regaling; in the pockets on the other side is an untouched store of salted pork (stolen before he left the island) for which he has no appetite. He is taken back, and he is hanged. But I shall never see that sea-beach on the wall or in the fire, without him, solitary monster, eating as he prowls along, while the sea rages and rises at him.

Captain Bligh (a worse man to be entrusted with arbitrary power there could scarcely be) is handed over the side of the Bounty, and turned adrift on the wide ocean in an open boat, by order of Fletcher Christian, one of his officers, at this very minute. Another flash of my fire, and 'Thursday October Christian,' five-and-twenty years of age, son of the dead and gone Fletcher by a savage mother, leaps aboard His Majesty's ship Briton, hove-to off Pitcairn's Island; says his simple grace before eating, in good English; and knows that a pretty little animal on board is called a dog, because in his childhood he had heard of such strange creatures from his father and the other mutineers, grown grey under the shade of the bread-fruit trees, speaking of their lost country far away.

See the Halsewell, East Indiaman outward bound, driving madly on a January night towards the rocks near Seacombe, on the island of Purbeck! The captain's two dear daughters are aboard, and five other ladies. The ship has been driving many hours, has seven feet water in her hold, and her mainmast has been cut away. The description of her loss, familiar to me from my early boyhood, seems to be read aloud as she rushes to her destiny.

> About two in the morning of Friday the sixth of January, the ship still driving, and approaching very fast to the shore, Mr. Henry Meriton, the second mate, went again into the cuddy, where the captain then was. Another conversation taking place, Captain Pierce expressed extreme anxiety for the preservation of his beloved daughters, and earnestly asked the officer if he could devise any method of saving them. On his answering with great concern, that he feared it would be impossible, but that their only chance would be to wait for morning, the captain lifted up his hands in silent and distressful ejaculation.
>
> At this dreadful moment, the ship struck, with such violence as to dash the heads of those standing in the cuddy

against the deck above them, and the shock was accompanied by a shriek of horror that burst at one instant from every quarter of the ship.

Many of the seamen, who had been remarkably inattentive and remiss in their duty during great part of the storm, now poured upon deck, where no exertions of the officers could keep them, while their assistance might have been useful. They had actually skulked in their hammocks, leaving the working of the pumps and other necessary labours to the officers of the ship, and the soldiers, who had made uncommon exertions. Roused by a sense of their danger, the same seamen, at this moment, in frantic exclamations, demanded of heaven and their fellow-sufferers that succour which their own efforts, timely made, might possibly have procured.

The ship continued to beat on the rocks; and soon bilging, fell with her broadside towards the shore. When she struck, a number of the men climbed up the ensign-staff, under an apprehension of her immediately going to pieces.

Mr. Meriton, at this crisis, offered to these unhappy beings the best advice which could be given; he recommended that all should come to the side of the ship lying lowest on the rocks, and singly to take the opportunities which might then offer, of escaping to the shore.

Having thus provided, to the utmost of his power, for the safety of the desponding crew, he returned to the round-house, where, by this time, all the passengers and most of the officers had assembled. The latter were employed in offering consolation to the unfortunate ladies; and, with unparalleled magnanimity, suffering their compassion for the fair and amiable companions of their misfortunes to prevail over the sense of their own danger.

In this charitable work of comfort, Mr. Meriton now joined, by assurances of his opinion, that, the ship would hold together till the morning, when all would be safe. Captain Pierce, observing one of the young gentlemen loud in his exclamations of terror, and frequently cry that the ship was parting, cheerfully bid him be quiet, remarking that though the ship should go to pieces, he would not, but would be safe enough.

It is difficult to convey a correct idea of the scene of this deplorable catastrophe, without describing the place where it happened. The Haleswell struck on the rocks at a part of the shore where the cliff is of vast height, and rises almost perpendicular from its base. But at this particular spot, the foot of the cliff is excavated into a cavern of ten or twelve yards in depth, and of breadth equal to the length of a large ship. The sides of the cavern are so nearly upright, as to be of extremely difficult access; and the bottom is strewed with sharp and uneven rocks, which seem, by some convulsion of the earth, to have been detached from its roof.

The ship lay with her broadside opposite to the mouth of this cavern, with her whole length stretched almost from side to side of it. But when she struck, it was too dark for the unfortunate persons on board to discover the real magnitude of the danger, and the extreme horror of such a situation.

In addition to the company already in the round-house, they had admitted three black women and two soldiers' wives; who, with the husband of one of them, had been allowed to come in, though the seamen, who had tumultuously demanded entrance to get the lights, had been opposed and kept out by Mr. Rogers and Mr. Brimer, the third and fifth mates. The numbers there were, therefore, now increased to near fifty. Captain Pierce sat on a chair, a cot, or some other moveable, with a daughter on each side, whom he alternately pressed to his affectionate breast. The rest of the melancholy assembly were seated on the deck, which was strewed with musical instruments, and the wreck of furniture and other articles.

Here also Mr. Meriton, after having cut several wax-candles in pieces, and stuck them up in various parts of the round-house, and lighted up all the glass lanthorns he could find, took his seat, intending to wait the approach of dawn; and then assist the partners of his dangers to escape. But, observing that the poor ladies appeared parched and exhausted, he brought a basket of oranges and prevailed on some of them to refresh themselves by sucking a little of the juice. At this time they were all tolerably composed, except Miss Mansel, who was in hysteric fits on the floor of the deck of the round-house.

But on Mr. Meriton's return to the company, he perceived a considerable alteration in the appearance of the ship; the sides were visibly giving way; the deck seemed to be lifting, and he discovered other strong indications that she could not hold much longer together. On this account, he attempted to go forward to look out, but immediately saw that the ship had separated in the middle, and that the forepart having changed its position, lay rather further out towards the sea. In such an emergency, when the next moment might plunge him into eternity, he determined to seize the present opportunity, and follow the example of the crew and the soldiers, who were now quitting the ship in numbers, and making their way to the shore, though quite ignorant of its nature and description.

Among other expedients, the ensign-staff had been unshipped, and attempted to be laid between the ship's side and some of the rocks, but without success, for it snapped asunder before it reached them. However, by the light of a lanthorn, which a seaman handed through the skylight of the round-house to the deck, Mr. Meriton discovered a spar which appeared to be laid from the ship's side to the rocks, and on this spar he resolved to attempt his escape.

Accordingly, lying down upon it, he thrust himself forward; however, he soon found that it had no communication with the rock; he reached the end of it, and then slipped off, receiving a very violent bruise in his fall, and before he could recover his legs, he was washed off by the surge. He now supported himself by swimming, until a returning wave dashed him against the back part of the cavern. Here he laid hold of a small projection in the rock, but was so much benumbed that he was on the point of quitting it, when a seaman, who had already gained a footing, extended his hand, and assisted him until he could secure himself a little on the rock; from which he clambered on a shelf still higher, and out of the reach of the surf.

Mr. Rogers, the third mate, remained with the captain and the unfortunate ladies and their companions nearly twenty minutes after Mr. Meriton had quitted the ship. Soon after the latter left the round-house, the captain asked what was become of him, to which Mr. Rogers replied, that he was gone on deck to see what could be done. After this, a heavy sea breaking over the ship, the ladies exclaimed, "Oh, poor Meriton! He is drowned; had he stayed with us he would have been safe!" and they all, particularly Miss Mary Pierce, expressed great concern at the apprehension of his loss.

The sea was now breaking in at the fore part of the ship, and reached as far as the mainmast. Captain Pierce gave Mr. Rogers a nod, and they took a lamp and went together into the stern-gallery, where, after viewing the rocks for some time, Captain Pierce asked Mr. Rogers if he thought there was any possibility of saving the girls; to which he replied, he feared there was none; for they could only discover the black face of the perpendicular rock, and not the cavern which afforded shelter to those who escaped. They then returned to the round-house, where Mr. Rogers hung up the lamp, and Captain Pierce sat down between his two daughters.

The sea continuing to break in very fast, Mr. Macmanus, a midshipman, and Mr. Schutz, a passenger, asked Mr. Rogers what they could do to escape. "Follow me," he replied, and they all went into the stern-gallery, and from thence to the upper-quarter-gallery on the poop. While there, a very heavy sea fell on board, and the round-house gave way; Mr. Rogers heard the ladies shriek at intervals, as if the water reached them; the noise of the sea at other times drowning their voices.

Mr. Brimer had followed him to the poop, where they remained together about five minutes, when on the breaking of this heavy sea, they jointly seized a hen-coop. The same wave which proved fatal to some of those below, carried him and his companion to the rock, on which they were violently dashed and miserably bruised.

Here on the rock were twenty-seven men; but it now being low water, and as they were convinced that on the flowing of the tide all must be washed off, many attempted to get to the back or the sides of the cavern, beyond the reach of the returning sea. Scarcely more than six, besides Mr. Rogers and Mr. Brimer, succeeded.

Mr. Rogers, on gaining this station, was so nearly exhausted, that had his exertions been protracted only a few minutes longer, he must have sunk under them. He was now prevented from joining Mr. Meriton, by at least twenty men between them, none of whom could move, without the imminent peril of his life.

They found that a very considerable number of the crew, seamen and soldiers, and some petty officers, were in the same situation as themselves, though many who had reached the rocks below, perished in attempting to ascend. They could yet discern some part of the ship, and in their dreary station solaced themselves with the hopes of its remaining entire until daybreak; for, in the midst of their own distress, the sufferings of the females on board affected them with the most poignant anguish; and every sea that broke inspired them with terror for their safety.

But, alas, their apprehensions were too soon realised! Within a very few minutes of the time that Mr. Rogers gained the rock, an universal shriek, which long vibrated in their ears, in which the voice of female distress was lamentably distinguished, announced the dreadful catastrophe. In a few moments all was hushed, except the roaring of the winds and the dashing of the waves; the wreck was buried in the deep, and not an atom of it was ever afterwards seen.'

The most beautiful and affecting incident I know, associated with a shipwreck, succeeds this dismal story for a winter night. The Grosvenor, East Indiaman, homeward bound, goes ashore on the coast of Caffraria. It is resolved that the officers, passengers, and crew, in number one hundred and thirty-five souls, shall endeavour to penetrate on foot, across trackless deserts, infested by wild beasts and cruel savages, to the Dutch settlements at the Cape of Good Hope. With this forlorn object before them, they finally separate into two parties—never more to meet on earth.

There is a solitary child among the passengers—a little boy of seven years old who has no relation there; and when the first party is moving away he cries after some member of it who has been kind to him. The crying of a child might be supposed to be a little thing to men in such great extremity; but it touches them, and he is immediately taken into that detachment.

From which time forth, this child is sublimely made a sacred charge. He is pushed, on a little raft, across broad rivers by the swimming sailors; they carry him by turns through the deep sand and long grass (he patiently walking at all other times); they share with him such putrid fish as they find to eat; they lie down and wait for him when the rough carpenter, who becomes his especial friend, lags behind. Beset by lions and tigers, by savages, by thirst, by hunger, by death in a crowd of ghastly shapes, they never—O Father of all mankind, thy name be blessed for it!— forget this child.

The captain stops exhausted, and his faithful coxswain goes back and is seen to sit down by his side, and neither of the two shall be any more beheld until the great last day; but, as the rest go on for their lives, they take the child with them. The carpenter dies of poisonous berries eaten in starvation; and the steward, succeeding to the command of the party, succeeds to the sacred guardianship of the child.

God knows all he does for the poor baby; how he cheerfully carries him in his arms when he himself is weak and ill; how he feeds him when he himself is griped with want; how he folds his ragged jacket round him, lays his little worn face with a woman's tenderness upon his sunburnt breast, soothes him in his sufferings, sings to him as he limps along, unmindful of his own parched and bleeding feet. Divided for a few days from the rest, they dig a grave in the sand and bury their good friend the cooper—these two companions alone in the wilderness—and then the time comes when they both are ill, and beg their wretched partners in despair, reduced and few in number now, to wait by them one day. They wait by them one day, they wait by them two days. On the morning of the third, they move very softly about, in making their preparations for the resumption of their journey; for, the child is sleeping by the fire, and it is agreed with one consent that he shall not be disturbed until the last moment. The moment comes, the fire is dying—and the child is dead.

His faithful friend, the steward, lingers but a little while behind him. His grief is great, he staggers on for a few days, lies down in the desert, and dies. But he shall be re-united in his immortal spirit—who can doubt it!—with the child, when he and the poor carpenter shall be raised up with the words, *Inasmuch as ye have done it unto the least of these, ye have done it unto Me.*

As I recall the dispersal and disappearance of nearly all the participators in this once famous shipwreck (a mere handful being recovered at last), and the legends that were long afterwards revived from time to time among the English officers at the Cape, of a white woman with an infant, said to have been seen weeping outside a savage hut far in the interior, who was whisperingly associated with the remembrance of the missing ladies saved from the wrecked vessel, and who was often sought but never found, thoughts of another kind of travel came into my mind.

Thoughts of a voyager unexpectedly summoned from home, who travelled a vast distance, and could never return. Thoughts of this unhappy wayfarer in the depths of his sorrow, in the bitterness of his anguish, in the helplessness of his self-reproach, in the desperation of his desire to set right what he had left wrong, and do what he had left undone.

For, there were many, many things he had neglected. Little matters while he was at home and surrounded by them, but things of mighty moment when he was at an immeasurable distance. There were many many blessings that he had inadequately felt, there were many trivial injuries that he had not forgiven, there was love that he had but poorly returned, there was friendship that he had too lightly prized: there were a million kind words that he might have spoken, a million kind looks that he might have given, uncountable slight easy deeds in which he might have been most truly great and good. O for a day (he would exclaim), for but one day to make amends! But the sun never shone upon that happy day, and out of his remote captivity he never came.

Why does this traveller's fate obscure, on New Year's Eve, the other histories of travellers with which my mind was filled but now, and cast a solemn shadow over me! Must I one day make his journey? Even so. Who shall say, that I may not then be tortured by such late regrets: that I may not then look from my exile on my empty place and undone work? I stand upon a sea-shore, where the waves are years. They break and fall, and I may little heed them; but, with every wave the sea is rising, and I know that it will float me on this traveller's voyage at last.

Well-Authenticated Rappings

A.k.a. The Rapping Spirits

The writer, who is about to record three spiritual experiences of his own in the present truthful article, deems it essential to state that, down to the time of his being favoured therewith, he had not been a believer in rappings, or tippings. His vulgar notions of the spiritual world, represented its inhabitants as probably advanced, even beyond the intellectual supremacy of Peckham or New York; and it seemed to him, considering the large amount of ignorance, presumption, and folly with which this earth is blessed, so very unnecessary to call in immaterial Beings to gratify mankind with bad spelling and worse nonsense, that the presumption was strongly against those respected films taking the trouble to come here, for no better purpose than to make supererogatory idiots of themselves.

This was the writer's gross and fleshy state of mind at so late a period as the twenty-sixth of December last. On that memorable morning, at about two hours after daylight—that is to say, at twenty minutes before ten by the writer's watch, which stood on a table at his bedside, and which can be seen at the publishing-office, and identified as a demi-chronometer made by Bautte of Geneva, and numbered 67,700 on that memorable morning, at about two hours after daylight, the writer, starting up in bed with his hand to his forehead, distinctly felt seventeen heavy throbs or beats in that region They were accompanied by a feeling of pain in the locality, and by a general sensation not unlike that which is usually attendant on biliousness. Yielding to a sudden impulse, the writer asked, 'What is this?'

The answer immediately returned (in throbs or beats upon the forehead) was, 'Yesterday.'

The writer then demanded, being as yet but imperfectly awake, 'What was yesterday?'

Answer: 'Christmas Day.'

The writer, being now quite come to himself, inquired, 'Who is the Medium in this case?'

Answer: 'Clarkins.'

Question: 'Mrs Clarkins, or Mr Clarkins?'

Answer. 'Both.'

Question: 'By Mr, do you mean Old Clarkins, or Young Clarkins?'

Answer: 'Both.'

Now, the writer had dined with his friend Clarkins (who can be appealed to, at the State Paper Office) on the previous day, and spirits had actually been discussed at that dinner, under various aspects. It was in the writer's remembrance, also, that both Clarkins Senior and Clarkins Junior had been very active in such discussion, and had rather pressed it on the company. Mrs Clarkins too had joined in it with animation, and had observed, in a joyous if not an exuberant tone, that it was 'only once a year'.

Convinced by these tokens that the rapping was of spiritual origin, the writer proceeded as follows, 'Who are you?'

The rapping on the forehead was resumed, but in a most incoherent manner. It was for some time impossible to make sense of it. After a pause, the writer (holding his head) repeated the inquiry in a solemn voice, accompanied with a groan, 'Who *are* you?'

Incoherent rappings were still the response.

The writer then asked, solemnly as before, and with another groan, 'What is your name?'

The reply was conveyed in a sound exactly resembling a loud hiccough. It afterwards appeared that this spiritual voice was distinctly heard by Alexander Pumpion, the writer's footboy (seventh son of Widow Pumpion, mangler), in an adjoining chamber.

Question: 'Your name cannot be Hiccough? Hiccough is not a proper name.'

No answer being returned, the writer said, 'I solemnly charge you, by our joint knowledge of Clarkins the Medium—of Clarkins Senior, Clarkins Junior, and Clarkins Mrs—to reveal your name!'

The reply rapped out with extreme unwillingness, was 'Sloe-Juice, Logwood, Blackberry.'

This appeared to the writer sufficiently like a parody on Cobweb, Moth, and Mustard-seed, in the *Midsummer Night's Dream,* to justify the retort, *"That* is not your name?'

The rapping spirit admitted, 'No.'

'Then what do they generally call you?'

A Pause.

'I ask you, what do they generally call you?'

The spirit, evidently under coercion, responded, in a most solemn manner, 'Port!'

This awful communication caused the writer to lie prostrate, on the verge of insensibility, for a quarter of an hour: during which the rappings were continued with violence, and a host of spiritual appearances passed before his eyes, of a black hue, and greatly resembling tadpoles endowed with the power of occasionally spinning themselves out into musical notes as they swam down into space. After contemplating a vast legion of these appearances, the writer demanded of the rapping spirit, 'How am I to present you to myself? What, upon the whole, is most like you?'

The terrific reply was, 'Blacking.'

As soon as the writer could command his emotion, which was now very great, he inquired, 'Had I better take something?'

Answer: 'Yes.'

Question: 'Can I write something?'

Answer: 'Yes.'

A pencil and a slip of paper which were on the table at the bedside immediately bounded into the writer's hand, and he found himself forced to write (in a curiously unsteady character and all downhill, whereas his own writing is remarkably plain and straight), the following spiritual note.

Mr C.D.S. Pooney presents his compliments to Messrs Bell and Company, Pharmaceutical Chemists, Oxford Street, opposite to Portland Street, and begs them to have the goodness to send him by bearer a five-grain genuine blue pill and a genuine black draught of corresponding power.

But, before entrusting this document to Alexander Pumpion (who unfortunately lost it on his return, if he did not even lay himself open to the suspicion of having wilfully inserted it into one of the holes of a perambulating chestnut-roaster, to see how it would flare), the writer resolved to test the rapping spirit with one conclusive question. He therefore asked, in a slow and impressive voice, 'Will these remedies make my stomach ache?'

It is impossible to describe the prophetic confidence of the reply. 'Yes.' The assurance was fully borne out by the result, as the writer will long remember; and after this experience it were needless to observe that he could no longer doubt.

The next communication of a deeply interesting character with which the writer was favoured, occurred on one of the leading lines of railway. The circumstances under which the revelation was made to him—on the second day of January in the present year—were these: He had recovered from the effects of the previous remarkable visitation, and had again been partaking of the compliments of the season. The preceding day had been passed in hilarity. He was on his way to a celebrated town, a well-known commercial emporium where he had business to transact, and had lunched in a somewhat greater hurry than is usual on railways, in consequence of the train being behind time. His lunch had been very reluctantly administered to him by a young lady behind a counter. She had been much occupied at the time with the arrangement of her hair and dress, and her expressive countenance had denoted disdain. It will be seen that this young lady proved to be a powerful medium.

The writer had returned to the first-class carriage in which he chanced to be travelling alone, the train had resumed its motion, he had fallen into a doze, and the unimpeachable watch already mentioned recorded forty-five minutes to have elapsed since his interview with the medium, when he was aroused by a very singular musical instrument. This instrument, he found to his admiration not unmixed with alarm, was performing in his inside. Its tones were of a low and rippling character, difficult to describe; but, if such a comparison may be admitted, resembling a melodious heartburn. Be this as it may, they suggested that humble sensation to the writer.

Concurrently with his becoming aware of the phenomenon in question, the writer perceived that his attention was being solicited by a hurried succession of angry raps in the stomach, and a pressure on the chest. A sceptic no more, he immediately communed with the spirit. The dialogue was as follows:

Question: 'Do I know your name?'

Answer: '*I* should think so!'

Question: 'Does it begin with a P?'

Answer (second time): '*I* should think so!'

Question: 'Have you two names, and does each begin with a P?'

Answer (third time): '*I* should think so!'

Question: 'I charge you to lay aside this levity, and inform me what you are called.'

The spirit, after reflecting for a few seconds, spelt out P.O.R.K. The musical instrument then performed a short and fragmentary strain. The spirit then recommenced, and spelt out the word 'P.I.E.'

Now, this precise article of pastry, this particular viand or comestible, actually had formed—let the scoffer know—the staple of the writer's lunch, and actually had been handed to him by the young lady whom he now knew to be a powerful medium! Highly gratified by the conviction thus forced upon his mind that the knowledge with which he conversed was not of this world, the writer pursued the dialogue.

Question: "They call you pork pie?'

Answer: 'Yes.'

Question (which the writer timidly put, after struggling with some natural reluctance): 'Are you in fact, pork pie?'

Answer: 'Yes.'

It were vain to attempt a description of the mental comfort and relief which the writer derived from this important answer. He proceeded:

Question: 'Let us understand each other. A part of you is pork, and a part of you is pie?'

Answer: 'Exactly so.'

Question: 'What is your pie-part made of?'

Answer: 'Lard.' Then came a sorrowful strain from the musical instrument. Then the word, 'Dripping.'

Question: 'How am I to present you to my mind? What are you most like?'

Answer (very quickly): 'Lead.'

A sense of despondency overcame the writer at this point. When he had in some measure conquered it, he resumed:

Question: 'Your other nature is a porky nature. What has that nature been chiefly sustained upon?'

Answer (in a sprightly manner): 'Pork, to be sure!'

Question: 'Not so. Pork is not fed upon pork?'

Answer: 'Isn't it, though!'

A strange internal feeling, resembling a flight of pigeons, seized upon the writer. He then became illuminated in a surprising manner, and said, 'Do I understand you to hint that the human race, incautiously attacking the indigestible fortresses called by your name, and not having time to storm them, owing to the great solidity of their almost impregnable walls, are in the habit of leaving much of their contents in the hands of the mediums, who with such pig nourish the pigs of the future pies?'

Answer: 'That's it!'

Question: 'Then to paraphrase the words of our immortal bard—'

Answer (interrupting): *'The same pork in its time, makes many pies, It's least being seven pasties.'*

The writer's emotion was profound. But, again desirous still further to try the spirit, and to ascertain whether, in the poetic phraseology of the advanced seers of the United States, it hailed from one of the inner and more elevated circles, he tested its knowledge with the following:

Question: 'In the wild harmony of the musical instrument within me, of which I am again conscious, what other substances are there airs of, besides those you have mentioned?'

Answer: 'Cape, Gamboge. Camomile. Treacle. Spirits of wine. Distilled potatoes.'

Question: 'Nothing else?'

Answer: 'Nothing worth mentioning.'

Let the scorner tremble and do homage; let the feeble sceptic blush! The writer at his lunch had demanded of the powerful medium, a glass of sherry, and likewise a small glass of brandy. Who can doubt that the articles of commerce indicated by the spirit were supplied to him from that source under those two names?

One other instance may suffice to prove that experiences of the foregoing nature are no longer to be questioned, and that it ought to be made capital to attempt to explain them away. It is an exquisite case of tipping.

The writer's destiny had appointed him to entertain a hope-less affection for Miss L. B., of Bungay, in the county of Suffolk. Miss L. B. had not, at the period of the occurrence of the tipping, openly rejected the writer's offer of his hand and heart; but it has since seemed probable that she had been withheld from doing so, by filial fear of her father, Mr B., who was favourable to the writer's pretensions. Now, mark the tipping.

A young man, obnoxious to all well-constituted minds (since married to Miss L. B.), was visiting at the house. Young B. was also home from school. The writer was present. The family party were assembled about a round table. It was the spiritual time of twilight in the month of July. Objects could not be discerned with any degree of distinctness. Suddenly, Mr B., whose senses had been lulled to repose, infused terror into all our breasts, by

uttering a passionate roar or ejaculation. His words (his education was neglected in his youth) were exactly these: 'Damn, here's
somebody a shoving of a letter into my hand, under my own
mahogany!'

Consternation seized the assembled group. Mrs B. augment-
ed the prevalent dismay by declaring that somebody had been
softly treading on her toes, at intervals, for half an hour. Greater
consternation seized the assembled group. Mr B. called for lights.
Now, mark the tipping.

Young B. cried (I quote his expressions accurately), 'It's the
spirits, father! They've been at it with me this last fortnight.'

Mr B. demanded with irascibility, 'What do you mean, sir?
What have they been at?'

Young B. replied, 'Wanting to make a regular Post-Office of
me, father. They're always handing impalpable letters to me, father. A letter must have come creeping round to you by mistake.
I must be a medium, father. O here's a go!' cried young B. 'If I
ain't a jolly medium!'

The boy now became violently convulsed, sputtering exceedingly, and jerking out his legs and arms in a manner calculated to
cause me (and which did cause me) serious inconvenience; for,
I was supporting his respected mother within range of his boots,
and he conducted himself like a telegraph before the invention
of the electric one. All this time Mr B. was looking about under
the table for the letter, while the obnoxious young man, since
married to Miss L. B., protected that young lady in an obnoxious
manner.

'O here's a go!' Young B. continued to cry without intermis-
sion. 'If I an't a jolly medium, father! Here's a go! There'll be a
tipping presently, father. Look out for the table!'

Now mark the tipping. The table tipped so violently as to strike
Mr B. a good half-dozen times on his bald head while he was
looking under it; which caused Mr B. to come out with great
agility, and rub it with much tenderness (I refer to his head), and
to imprecate it with much violence (I refer to the table).

I observed that the tipping of the table was uniformly in the direction of the magnetic current; that is to say, from south to north, or from young B. to Mr B. I should have made some further observations on this deeply interesting point, but that the table suddenly revolved, and tipped over on myself, bearing me to the ground with a force increased by the momentum imparted to it by young B., who came over with it in a state of mental exaltation, and could not be displaced for some time. In the interval, I was aware of being crushed by his weight and the table's, and also of his constantly calling out to his sister and the obnoxious young man, that he foresaw there would be another tipping presently.

None such, however, took place. He recovered after taking a short walk with them in the dark, and no worse effects of the very beautiful experience with which we had been favoured, were perceptible in him during the rest of the evening, than a slight tendency to hysterical laughter, and a noticeable attraction (I might almost term it fascination) of his left hand, in the direction of his heart or waistcoat-pocket.

Was this, or was it not a case of tipping? Will the sceptic and the scoffer reply?

Christmas Ghosts

I like to come home at Christmas. We all do, or we all *should*. We ought to come home for a holiday—the longer the better—from the great boarding school where we are forever working at our arithmetical slates, to take and give a rest.

We travel home across a winter prospect; by low-lying mist grounds, through fens and fogs, up long hills, winding dark as caverns between thick plantations, almost shutting out the sparkling stars; so, out on broad heights, until we stop at last, with sudden silence, at an avenue. The gate bell has a deep, half-awful sound in the frosty air; the gate swings open on its hinges; and, as we drive up to a great house, the glancing lights grow larger in the windows, and the opposing rows of trees seem to fall solemnly back on either side, to give us place.

At intervals, all day, a frightened hare has shot across this whitened turf; or the distant clatter of a herd of deer trampling the hard frost has, for the minute, crushed the silence too. Their watchful eyes beneath the fern may be shining now, if we could see them, like the icy dewdrops on the leaves; but they are still, and all is still. And so, the lights growing larger, and the trees falling back before us, and closing up again behind us, as if to forbid retreat, we come to the house.

There is probably a smell of roasted chestnuts and other good comfortable things all the time, for we are telling Winter Stories—Ghost Stories, or more shame for us—round the Christmas fire; and we have never stirred, except to draw a little nearer to it. But, no matter for that. We come to the house, and it is an old house, full of great chimneys where wood is burnt on ancient dogs upon the hearth, and grim portraits (some of them with grim legends, too) lower distrustfully from the oaken panels of the walls. We are a middle-aged nobleman, and we make a generous supper with our host and hostess and their guests—it being Christmas-time, and the old house full of company—and then we go to bed.

Our room is a very old room. It is hung with tapestry. We don't like the portrait of a cavalier in green, over the fireplace. There are great black beams in the ceiling, and there is a great black bedstead, supported at the foot by two great black figures, who seem to have come off a couple of tombs in the old baronial church in the park, for our particular accommodation. But, we are not a superstitious nobleman, and we don't mind. Well! we dismiss our servant, lock the door, and sit before the fire in our dressing-gown, musing about a great many things.

At length we go to bed. Well! we can't sleep. We toss and tumble, and can't sleep. The embers on the hearth burn fitfully, and make the room look ghostly. We can't help peeping out, over the counterpane, at the two black figures and the cavalier—that wicked-looking cavalier in green. In the flickering light they seem to advance and retire: which, though we are not by any means a superstitious nobleman, is not agreeable. Well! we get nervous— more and more nervous. We say, 'This is very foolish, but we can't stand this; we'll pretend to be ill, and knock up somebody.' Well! we are just going to do it, when the locked door opens, and there comes in a young woman, deadly pale, and with long fair hair, who glides to the fire, and sits down in the chair we have left there, wringing her hands.

Then, we notice that her clothes are wet. Our tongue cleaves to the roof of our mouth, and we can't speak; but, we observe her accurately. Her clothes are wet; her long hair is dabbled with moist mud; she is dressed in the fashion of two hundred years ago; and she has at her girdle a bunch of rusty keys. Well! there she sits, and we can't even faint, we are in such a state about it. Presently she gets up, and tries all the locks in the room with the rusty keys, which won't fit one of them; then, she fixes her eyes on the portrait of the cavalier in green, and says, in a low, terrible voice, 'The stags know it!'

After that, she wrings her hands again, passes the bedside, and goes out at the door. We hurry on our dressing-gown, seize our pistols (we always travel with pistols), and are following, when we find the door locked. We turn the key, look out into the dark gallery; no one there. We wander away, and try to find our servant. Can't be done. We pace the gallery till daybreak; then return to our deserted room, fall asleep, and are awakened by our servant (nothing ever haunts *him*) and the shining sun. Well! we make a wretched breakfast, and all the company say we look queer.

After breakfast, we go over the house with our host, and then we take him to the portrait of the cavalier in green, and then it all comes out. He was false to a young housekeeper once attached to that family, and famous for her beauty, who drowned herself in a pond, and whose body was discovered, after a long time, because the stags refused to drink the water.

Since which, it has been whispered that she traverses the house at midnight (but goes especially to that room, where the cavalier in green was wont to sleep), trying the old locks with the rusty keys. Well! we tell our host of what we have seen, and a shade comes over his features, and he begs it may be hushed up; and so it is. But, it's all true; and we said so, before we died (we are dead now), to many responsible people.

There is no end to the old houses, with resounding galleries, and dismal state bedchambers, and haunted wings shut up for many years, through which we may ramble, with an agreeable creeping up our back, and encounter any number of ghosts, but (it is worthy of remark perhaps) reducible to a very few general types and classes; for, ghosts have little originality, and 'walk' in a beaten track. Thus, it comes to pass that a certain room in a certain old hall, where a certain bad lord, baronet, knight, or gentleman shot himself, has certain planks in the floor from which the blood *will not* be taken out.

You may scrape and scrape, as the present owner has done,

or plane and plane, as his father did, or scrub and scrub, as his grandfather did, or burn and burn with strong acids, as his great-grandfather did, but there the blood will still be—no redder and no paler—no more and no less—always just the same. Thus, in such another house there is a haunted door that never will keep open; or another door that never will keep shut; or a haunted sound of a spinning-wheel, or a hammer, or a footstep, or a cry, or a sigh, or a horse's tramp, or the rattling of a chain. Or else there is a turret clock, which, at the midnight hour, strikes thirteen when the head of the family is going to die; or a shadowy, immovable black carriage which at such a time is always seen by somebody, waiting near the great gates in the stable-yard.

Or thus, it came to pass how Lady Mary went to pay a visit at a large wild house in the Scottish Highlands, and, being fatigued with her long journey, retired to bed early, and innocently said, next morning, at the breakfast-table, 'How odd to have so late a party last night in this remote place, and not to tell me of it before I went to bed!' Then, every one asked Lady Mary what she meant. Then, Lady Mary replied, 'Why, all night long, the carriages were driving round and round the terrace, underneath my window!'

Then, the owner of the house turned pale, and so did his Lady, and Charles Macdoodle of Macdoodle signed to Lady Mary to say no more, and everyone was silent. After breakfast, Charles Macdoodle told Lady Mary that it was a tradition in the family that those rumbling carriages on the terrace betokened death. And so it proved, for, two months afterwards, the Lady of the mansion died. And Lady Mary, who was a Maid of Honour at Court, often told this story to the old Queen Charlotte; by this token, that the old King always said, 'Eh, eh? What, what? Ghosts, ghosts? No such thing, no such thing!' And never left off saying so until he went to bed.

Or, a friend of somebody's, whom most of us know, when he was a young man at college, had a particular friend, with whom he made the compact that, if it were possible for the Spirit to return to this earth after its separation from the body, he of the twain who first died should reappear to the other. In course of time this compact was forgotten by our friend; the two young men having progressed in life, and taken diverging paths that were wide asunder.

But one night, many years afterwards, our friend being in the North of England, and staying for the night in an inn on the Yorkshire Moors, happened to look out of bed; and there, in the moonlight, leaning on a bureau near the window, steadfastly regarding him, saw his old college friend! The appearance being solemnly addressed, replied, in a kind of whisper, but very audibly, 'Do not come near me. I am dead. I am here to redeem my promise. I come from another world, but may not disclose its secrets!' Then, the whole form becoming paler, melted, as it were, into the moonlight, and faded away.

Or, there was the daughter of the first occupier of the picturesque Elizabethan house, so famous in our neighbourhood. You have heard about her? No! Why, *she* went out one summer evening at twilight, when she was a beautiful girl, just seventeen years of age, to gather flowers in the garden; and presently came running, terrified, into the hall to her father, saying, 'Oh, dear father, I have met myself!'

He took her in his arms, and told her it was fancy, but she said, 'Oh no! I met myself in the broad walk, and I was pale and gathering withered flowers, and I turned my head, and held them up!' And, that night, she died; and a picture of her story was begun, though never finished, and they say it is somewhere in the house to this day, with its face to the wall.

Or, the uncle of my brother's wife was riding home on horseback, one mellow evening at sunset, when, in a green lane close to his own house, he saw a man standing before him, in the very centre of the narrow way. 'Why does that man in the cloak stand there?' he thought. 'Does he want me to ride over him?' But the figure never moved. He felt a strange sensation at seeing it so still, but slackened his trot and rode forward.

When he was so close to it as almost to touch it with his stirrup, his horse shied, and the figure glided up the bank in a curious, unearthly manner— backward, and without seeming to use its feet—and was gone. The uncle of my brother's wife exclaiming, 'Good Heaven! It's my cousin Harry, from Bombay!' put spurs to his horse, which was suddenly in a profuse sweat, and, wondering at such strange behaviour, dashed round to the front of his house. There, he saw the same figure, just passing in at the long French window of the drawing-room opening on the ground. He threw his bridle to a servant, and hastened in after it. His sister was sitting there alone.

'Alice, where's my cousin Harry?'

'Your cousin Harry, John?'

'Yes. From Bombay. I met him in the lane just now, and saw him enter here this instant.'

Not a creature had been seen by any one; and in that hour and minute, as it afterwards appeared, this cousin died in India.

Or, it was a certain sensible old maiden lady, who died at ninety-nine, and retained her faculties to the last, who really did see the Orphan Boy; a story which has often been incorrectly told, but of which the real truth is this—because it is, in fact, a story belonging to our family—and she was a connection of our family. When she was about forty years of age, and still an uncommonly fine woman (her lover died young, which was the reason why she never married, though she had many offers), she went to stay at a place in Kent, which her brother, an Indian merchant, had newly bought.

There was a story that this place had once been held in trust by the guardian of a young boy; who was himself the next heir, and who killed the young boy by harsh and cruel treatment. She knew nothing of that. It has been said that there was a cage in her bedroom, in which the guardian used to put the boy. There was no such thing. There was only a closet. She went to bed, made no alarm whatever in the night, and in the morning said composedly to her maid, when she came in, 'Who is the pretty forlorn-looking child who has been peeping out of that closet all night?'

The maid replied by giving a loud scream, and instantly decamping. She was surprised; but, she was a woman of remarkable strength of mind, and she dressed herself and went downstairs, and closeted herself with her brother. 'Now, Walter,' she said, 'I have been disturbed all night by a pretty, forlorn-looking boy, who has been constantly peeping out of that closet in my room, which I can't open. This is some trick.'

'I am afraid not, Charlotte,' said he, 'for it is the legend of the house. It is the Orphan Boy. What did he do?'

'He opened the door softly,' said she, 'and peeped out.

Sometimes, he came a step or two into the room. Then, I called to him, to encourage him, and he shrunk, and shuddered, and crept in again, and shut the door.'

'The closet has no communication, Charlotte,' said her brother, 'with any other part of the house, and it's nailed up.'

This was undeniably true, and it took two carpenters a whole forenoon to get it open for examination. Then, she was satisfied that she had seen the Orphan Boy. But the wild and terrible part of the story is, that he was also seen by three of her brother's sons in succession, who all died young.

On the occasion of each child being taken ill, he came home in a heat, twelve hours before, and said, Oh, mamma, he had been playing under a particular oak-tree, in a certain meadow, with a strange boy—a pretty, forlorn-looking boy, who was very timid, and made signs! From fatal experience, the parents came to know that this was the Orphan Boy, and that the course of that child whom he chose for his little playmate was surely run.

Prince Bull

Once upon a time, and of course it was in the Golden Age, and I hope you may know when that was, for I am sure I don't, though I have tried hard to find out, there lived in a rich and fertile country, a powerful Prince whose name was BULL. He had gone through a great deal of fighting, in his time, about all sorts of things, including nothing; but, had gradually settled down to be a steady, peaceable, good-natured, corpulent, rather sleepy Prince.

This Puissant Prince was married to a lovely Princess whose name was Fair Freedom. She had brought him a large fortune, and had borne him an immense number of children, and had set them to spinning, and farming, and engineering, and soldiering, and sailoring, and doctoring, and lawyering, and preaching, and all kinds of trades. The coffers of Prince Bull were full of treasure, his cellars were crammed with delicious wines from all parts of the world, the richest gold and silver plate that ever was seen adorned his sideboards, his sons were strong, his daughters were handsome, and in short you might have supposed that if there ever lived upon earth a fortunate and happy Prince, the name of that Prince, take him for all in all, was assuredly Prince Bull.

But, appearances, as we all know, are not always to be trusted—far from it; and if they had led you to this conclusion respecting Prince Bull, they would have led you wrong as they often have led me.

For, this good Prince had two sharp thorns in his pillow, two hard knobs in his crown, two heavy loads on his mind, two un-bridled nightmares in his sleep, two rocks ahead in his course. He could not by any means get servants to suit him, and he had a tyrannical old godmother, whose name was Tape.

She was a Fairy, this Tape, and was a bright red all over. She was disgustingly prim and formal, and could never bend herself a hair's breadth this way or that way, out of her naturally crooked shape. But, she was very potent in her wicked art. She could stop the fastest thing in the world, change the strongest thing into the weakest, and the most useful into the most useless. To do this she had only to put her cold hand upon it, and repeat her own name, Tape. Then it withered away.

At the Court of Prince Bull—at least I don't mean literally at his court, because he was a very genteel Prince, and readily yielded to his godmother when she always reserved that for his hereditary Lords and Ladies—in the dominions of Prince Bull, among the great mass of the community who were called in the language of that polite country the Mobs and the Snobs, were a number of very ingenious men, who were always busy with some invention or other, for promoting the prosperity of the Prince's subjects, and augmenting the Prince's power.

But, whenever they submitted their models for the Prince's approval, his godmother stepped forward, laid her hand upon them, and said 'Tape.' Hence it came to pass, that when any par-ticularly good discovery was made, the discoverer usually car-ried it off to some other Prince, in foreign parts, who had no old godmother who said Tape. This was not on the whole an advantageous state of things for Prince Bull, to the best of my understanding.

The worst of it was, that Prince Bull had in course of years lapsed into such a state of subjection to this unlucky godmother, that he never made any serious effort to rid himself of her tyr-anny. I have said this was the worst of it, but there I was wrong, because there is a worse consequence still, behind. The Prince's numerous family became so downright sick and tired of Tape, that when they should have helped the Prince out of the difficulties into which that evil creature led him, they fell into a dangerous habit of moodily keeping away from him in an impassive and indifferent manner, as though they had quite forgotten that no harm could happen to the Prince their father, without its inevitably affecting themselves.

Such was the aspect of affairs at the court of Prince Bull, when this great Prince found it necessary to go to war with Prince Bear. He had been for some time very doubtful of his servants, who, besides being indolent and addicted to enriching their families at his expense, domineered over him dreadfully; threatening to discharge themselves if they were found the least fault with, pretending that they had done a wonderful amount of work when they had done nothing, making the most unmeaning speeches that ever were heard in the Prince's name, and uniformly showing themselves to be very inefficient indeed.

Though, that some of them had excellent characters from previous situations is not to be denied. Well; Prince Bull called his servants together, and said to them one and all, 'Send out my army against Prince Bear. Clothe it, arm it, feed it, provide it with all necessaries and contingencies, and I will pay the piper! Do your duty by my brave troops,' said the Prince, 'and do it well, and I will pour my treasure out like water, to defray the cost. Who ever heard ME complain of money well laid out!' Which indeed he had reason for saying, inasmuch as he was well known to be a truly generous and munificent Prince.

When the servants heard those words, they sent out the army against Prince Bear, and they set the army tailors to work, and the army provision merchants, and the makers of guns both great and small, and the gunpowder makers, and the makers of ball, shell, and shot; and they bought up all manner of stores and ships, without troubling their heads about the price, and appeared to be so busy that the good Prince rubbed his hands, and (using a favourite expression of his), said, 'It's all right!'

But, while they were thus employed, the Prince's godmother, who was a great favourite with those servants, looked in upon them continually all day long, and whenever she popped in her head at the door said, How do you do, my children? What are you doing here?' 'Official business, godmother.' 'Oho!' says this wicked Fairy. '—Tape!' And then the business all went wrong, whatever it was, and the servants' heads became so addled and muddled that they thought they were doing wonders.

Now, this was very bad conduct on the part of the vicious old nuisance, and she ought to have been strangled, even if she had stopped here; but, she didn't stop here, as you shall learn. For, a number of the Prince's subjects, being very fond of the Prince's army who were the bravest of men, assembled together and provided all manner of eatables and drinkables, and books to read, and clothes to wear, and tobacco to smoke, and candies to burn, and nailed them up in great packing-cases, and put them aboard a great many ships, to be carried out to that brave army in the cold and inclement country where they were fighting Prince Bear.

Then, up comes this wicked Fairy as the ships were weighing anchor, and says, 'How do you do, my children? What are you doing here?'

'We are going with all these comforts to the army, godmother.'

'Oho!' says she. 'A pleasant voyage, my darlings.—Tape!'

And from that time forth, those enchanting ships went sailing, against wind and tide and rhyme and reason, round and round the world, and whenever they touched at any port were ordered off immediately, and could never deliver their cargoes anywhere.

This, again, was very bad conduct on the part of the vicious old nuisance, and she ought to have been strangled for it if she had done nothing worse; but, she did something worse still, as you shall learn. For, she got astride of an official broomstick, and muttered as a spell these two sentences, 'On Her Majesty's service,' and 'I have the honour to be, sir, your most obedient servant,' and presently alighted in the cold and inclement country where the army of Prince Bull were encamped to fight the army of Prince Bear. On the sea-shore of that country, she found piled together, a number of houses for the army to live in, and a quantity of provisions for the army to live upon, and a quantity of clothes for the army to wear: while, sitting in the mud gazing at them, were a group of officers as red to look at as the wicked old woman herself.

So, she said to one of them, 'Who are you, my darling, and how do you do?'

'I am the Quartermaster General's Department, godmother, and I am pretty well.'

Then she said to another, 'Who are YOU, my darling, and how do YOU do?'

'I am the Commissariat Department, godmother, and I am pretty well!'

Then she said to another, 'Who are YOU, my darling, and how do YOU do?'

'I am the Head of the Medical Department, godmother, and I am pretty well.'

Then, she said to some gentlemen scented with lavender, who kept themselves at a great distance from the rest, 'And who are YOU, my pretty pets, and how do YOU do?'

And they answered, 'We-aw-are-the-aw-Staff-aw-Department, godmother, and we are very well indeed.'

'I am delighted to see you all, my beauties,' says this wicked old Fairy, '—Tape!'

Upon that, the houses, clothes, and provisions, all mouldered away; and the soldiers who were sound, fell sick; and the soldiers who were sick, died miserably: and the noble army of Prince Bull perished.

When the dismal news of his great loss was carried to the Prince, he suspected his godmother very much indeed; but, he knew that his servants must have kept company with the malicious beldame, and must have given way to her, and therefore he resolved to turn those servants out of their places. So, he called to him a Roebuck who had the gift of speech, and he said, 'Good Roebuck, tell them they must go.'

So, the good Roebuck delivered his message, so like a man

that you might have supposed him to be nothing but a man, and they were turned out—but, not without warning, for that they had had a long time.

And now comes the most extraordinary part of the history of this Prince. When he had turned out those servants, of course he wanted others. What was his astonishment to find that in all his dominions, which contained no less than twenty-seven millions of people, there were not above five-and-twenty servants altogether! They were so lofty about it, too, that instead of discussing whether they should hire themselves as servants to Prince Bull, they turned things topsy-turvy, and considered whether as a favour they should hire Prince Bull to be their master!

While they were arguing this point among themselves quite at their leisure, the wicked old red Fairy was incessantly going up and down, knocking at the doors of twelve of the oldest of the five-and-twenty, who were the oldest inhabitants in all that country, and whose united ages amounted to one thousand, saying, 'Will YOU hire Prince Bull for your master?—Will YOU hire Prince Bull for your master?'

To which one answered, 'I will if next door will;' and another, 'I won't if over the way does;' and another, 'I can't if he, she, or they, might, could, would, or should.' And all this time Prince Bull's affairs were going to rack and ruin.

At last, Prince Bull in the height of his perplexity assumed a thoughtful face, as if he were struck by an entirely new idea. The wicked old Fairy, seeing this, was at his elbow directly, and said, 'How do you do, my Prince, and what are you thinking of?'—'I am thinking, godmother,' says he, 'that among all the seven-and-twenty millions of my subjects who have never been in service, there are men of intellect and business who have made me very famous both among my friends and enemies.'

'Aye, truly?' says the Fairy.

'Aye, truly,' says the Prince.

'And what then?' says the Fairy.

'Why, then,' says he, 'since the regular old class of servants do so ill, are so hard to get, and carry it with so high a hand, perhaps

I might try to make good servants of some of these.'

The words had no sooner passed his lips than she returned, chuckling, 'You think so, do you? Indeed, my Prince?—Tape!'

Thereupon he directly forgot what he was thinking of, and cried out lamentably to the old servants, 'O, do come and hire your poor old master! Pray do! On any terms!'

And this, for the present, finishes the story of Prince Bull. I wish I could wind it up by saying that he lived happy ever afterwards, but I cannot in my conscience do so; for, with Tape at his elbow, and his estranged children fatally repelled by her from coming near him, I do not, to tell you the plain truth, believe in the possibility of such an end to it.

The Signal-Man

A.k.a. No. 1 Branch Line, The Signalman

"Halloa! Below there!"

When he heard a voice thus calling to him, he was standing at the door of his box, with a flag in his hand, furled round its short pole. One would have thought, considering the nature of the ground, that he could not have doubted from what quarter the voice came; but instead of looking up to where I stood on the top of the steep cutting nearly over his head, he turned himself about, and looked down the Line. There was something remarkable in his manner of doing so, though I could not have said for my life what. But I know it was remarkable enough to attract my notice, even though his figure was foreshortened and shadowed, down in the deep trench, and mine was high above him, so steeped in the glow of an angry sunset, that I had shaded my eyes with my hand before I saw him at all.

"Halloa! Below!"

From looking down the Line, he turned himself about again, and, raising his eyes, saw my figure high above him.

"Is there any path by which I can come down and speak to you?"

He looked up at me without replying, and I looked down at him without pressing him too soon with a repetition of my idle question. Just then there came a vague vibration in the earth and air, quickly changing into a violent pulsation, and an oncoming rush that caused me to start back, as though it had force to draw me down. When such vapour as rose to my height from this rapid train had passed me, and was skimming away over the landscape, I looked down again, and saw him refurling the flag he had shown while the train went by.

I repeated my inquiry. After a pause, during which he seemed to regard me with fixed attention, he motioned with his rolled-up flag towards a point on my level, some two or three hundred yards distant. I called down to him, "All right!" and made for that point. There, by dint of looking closely about me, I found a rough zigzag descending path notched out, which I followed.

The cutting was extremely deep, and unusually precipitate. It was made through a clammy stone, that became oozier and wetter as I went down. For these reasons, I found the way long enough to give me time to recall a singular air of reluctance or compulsion with which he had pointed out the path.

When I came down low enough upon the zigzag descent to see him again, I saw that he was standing between the rails on the way by which the train had lately passed, in an attitude as if he were waiting for me to appear. He had his left hand at his chin, and that left elbow rested on his right hand, crossed over his breast. His attitude was one of such expectation and watch-fulness that I stopped a moment, wondering at it.

I resumed my downward way, and stepping out upon the level of the railroad, and drawing nearer to him, saw that he was a dark sallow man, with a dark beard and rather heavy eyebrows. His post was in as solitary and dismal a place as ever I saw. On either side, a dripping-wet wall of jagged stone, excluding all view but a strip of sky; the perspective one way only a crooked prolongation of this great dungeon; the shorter perspective in the other direction terminating in a gloomy red light, and the gloomier entrance to a black tunnel, in whose massive architec-ture there was a barbarous, depressing, and forbidding air. So lit-tle sunlight ever found its way to this spot, that it had an earthy, deadly smell; and so much cold wind rushed through it, that it struck chill to me, as if I had left the natural world.

Before he stirred, I was near enough to him to have touched him. Not even then removing his eyes from mine, he stepped back one step, and lifted his hand.

This was a lonesome post to occupy (I said), and it had riveted my attention when I looked down from up yonder. A visitor was a rarity, I should suppose; not an unwelcome rarity, I hoped? In me, he merely saw a man who had been shut up within narrow limits all his life, and who, being at last set free, had a newly-awakened interest in these great works. To such purpose I spoke to him; but I am far from sure of the terms I used; for, besides that I am not happy in opening any conversation, there was something in the man that daunted me.

He directed a most curious look towards the red light near the tunnel's mouth, and looked all about it, as if something were missing from it, and then looked at me.

That light was part of his charge? Was it not?

He answered in a low voice,—"Don't you know it is?"

The monstrous thought came into my mind, as I perused the fixed eyes and the saturnine face, that this was a spirit, not a man. I have speculated since, whether there may have been infection in his mind.

In my turn, I stepped back. But in making the action, I detected in his eyes some latent fear of me. This put the monstrous thought to flight.

"You look at me," I said, forcing a smile, "as if you had a dread of me."

"I was doubtful," he returned, "whether I had seen you before."

"Where?"

He pointed to the red light he had looked at.

"There?" I said.

Intently watchful of me, he replied (but without sound), "Yes."

"My good fellow, what should I do there? However, be that as it may, I never was there, you may swear."

"I think I may," he rejoined. "Yes; I am sure I may."

His manner cleared, like my own. He replied to my remarks with readiness, and in well-chosen words. Had he much to do there? Yes; that was to say, he had enough responsibility to bear; but exactness and watchfulness were what was required of him, and of actual work—manual labour—he had next to none. To change that signal, to trim those lights, and to turn this iron handle now and then, was all he had to do under that head. Regarding those many long and lonely hours of which I seemed to make so much, he could only say that the routine of his life had shaped itself into that form, and he had grown used to it. He had taught himself a language down here,—if only to know it by sight, and to have formed his own crude ideas of its pronunciation, could be called learning it.

He had also worked at fractions and decimals, and tried a little algebra; but he was, and had been as a boy, a poor hand at figures. Was it necessary for him when on duty always to remain in that channel of damp air, and could he never rise into the sunshine from between those high stone walls? Why, that depended upon times and circumstances. Under some conditions there would be less upon the Line than under others, and the same held good as to certain hours of the day and night. In bright weather, he did choose occasions for getting a little above these lower shadows; but, being at all times liable to be called by his electric bell, and at such times listening for it with redoubled anxiety, the relief was less than I would suppose.

He took me into his box, where there was a fire, a desk for an official book in which he had to make certain entries, a telegraphic instrument with its dial, face, and needles, and the little bell of which he had spoken. On my trusting that he would excuse the remark that he had been well educated, and (I hoped I might say without offence) perhaps educated above that station, he observed that instances of slight incongruity in such wise would rarely be found wanting among large bodies of men; that he had heard it was so in workhouses, in the police force, even in that last desperate resource, the army; and that he knew it was so, more or less, in any great railway staff. He had been, when young (if I could believe it, sitting in that hut,—he scarcely could), a student of natural philosophy, and had attended lectures; but he had run wild, misused his opportunities, gone down, and never risen again. He had no complaint to offer about that. He had made his bed, and he lay upon it. It was far too late to make another.

All that I have here condensed he said in a quiet manner, with his grave dark regards divided between me and the fire. He threw in the word, "Sir," from time to time, and especially when he referred to his youth,—as though to request me to understand that he claimed to be nothing but what I found him. He was several times interrupted by the little bell, and had to read off messages, and send replies. Once he had to stand without the door, and display a flag as a train passed, and make some verbal communication to the driver. In the discharge of his duties, I observed him to be remarkably exact and vigilant, breaking off his discourse at a syllable, and remaining silent until what he had to do was done.

In a word, I should have set this man down as one of the safest of men to be employed in that capacity, but for the circumstance that while he was speaking to me he twice broke off with a fallen colour, turned his face towards the little bell when it did *not* ring, opened the door of the hut (which was kept shut to exclude the unhealthy damp), and looked out towards the red light near the mouth of the tunnel. On both of those occasions, he came back to the fire with the inexplicable air upon him which I had remarked, without being able to define, when we were so far asunder.

Said I, when I rose to leave him, "You almost make me think that I have met with a contented man."

(I am afraid I must acknowledge that I said it to lead him on.)

"I believe I used to be so," he rejoined, in the low voice in which he had first spoken; "but I am troubled, sir, I am troubled."

He would have recalled the words if he could. He had said them, however, and I took them up quickly.

"With what? What is your trouble?"

"It is very difficult to impart, sir. It is very, very difficult to speak of. If ever you make me another visit, I will try to tell you."

"But I expressly intend to make you another visit. Say, when shall it be?"

"I go off early in the morning, and I shall be on again at ten tomorrow night, sir."

"I will come at eleven."

He thanked me, and went out at the door with me. "I'll show my white light, sir," he said, in his peculiar low voice, "till you have found the way up. When you have found it, don't call out! And when you are at the top, don't call out!"

His manner seemed to make the place strike colder to me, but I said no more than, "Very well."

"And when you come down to-morrow night, don't call out! Let me ask you a parting question. What made you cry, 'Halloa! Below there!' tonight?"

"Heaven knows," said I. "I cried something to that effect—"

"Not to that effect, sir. Those were the very words. I know them well."

"Admit those were the very words. I said them, no doubt, because I saw you below."

"For no other reason?"

"What other reason could I possibly have?"

"You had no feeling that they were conveyed to you in any supernatural way?"

"No."

He wished me goodnight, and held up his light. I walked by the side of the down Line of rails (with a very disagreeable sensation of a train coming behind me) until I found the path. It was easier to mount than to descend, and I got back to my inn without any adventure.

Punctual to my appointment, I placed my foot on the first notch of the zigzag next night, as the distant clocks were striking eleven. He was waiting for me at the bottom, with his white light on. "I have not called out," I said, when we came close together; "may I speak now?"

"By all means, sir."

"Goodnight, then, and here's my hand."

"Goodnight, sir, and here's mine." With that we walked side by side to his box, entered it, closed the door, and sat down by the fire.

"I have made up my mind, sir," he began, bending forward as soon as we were seated, and speaking in a tone but a little above a whisper, "that you shall not have to ask me twice what troubles me. I took you for someone else yesterday evening. That troubles me."

"That mistake?"

"No. That someone else."

"Who is it?"

"I don't know."

"Like me?"

"I don't know. I never saw the face. The left arm is across the face, and the right arm is waved,—violently waved. This way."

I followed his action with my eyes, and it was the action of an arm gesticulating, with the utmost passion and vehemence, "For God's sake, clear the way!"

"One moonlight night," said the man, "I was sitting here, when I heard a voice cry, 'Halloa! Below there!' I started up, looked from that door, and saw this Someone else standing by the red light near the tunnel, waving as I just now showed you. The voice seemed hoarse with shouting, and it cried, 'Look out! Look out!' And then again, 'Halloa! Below there! Look out!' I caught up my lamp, turned it on red, and ran towards the figure, calling, 'What's wrong? What has happened? Where?' It stood just outside the blackness of the tunnel. I advanced so close upon it that I wondered at its keeping the sleeve across its eyes. I ran right up at it, and had my hand stretched out to pull the sleeve away, when it was gone."

"Into the tunnel?" said I.

"No. I ran on into the tunnel, five hundred yards. I stopped, and held my lamp above my head, and saw the figures of the measured distance, and saw the wet stains stealing down the walls and trickling through the arch. I ran out again faster than I had run in (for I had a mortal abhorrence of the place upon me), and I looked all round the red light with my own red light, and I went up the iron ladder to the gallery atop of it, and I came down again, and ran back here. I telegraphed both ways, 'An alarm has been given. Is anything wrong?' The answer came back, both ways, 'All well.'"

Resisting the slow touch of a frozen finger tracing out my spine, I showed him how that this figure must be a deception of his sense of sight; and how that figures, originating in disease of the delicate nerves that minister to the functions of the eye, were known to have often troubled patients, some of whom had become conscious of the nature of their affliction, and had even proved it by experiments upon themselves. "As to an imaginary cry," said I, "do but listen for a moment to the wind in this un-natural valley while we speak so low, and to the wild harp it makes of the telegraph wires."

That was all very well, he returned, after we had sat listening for a while, and he ought to know something of the wind and the wires,—he who so often passed long winter nights there, alone and watching. But he would beg to remark that he had not finished.

I asked his pardon, and he slowly added these words, touching my arm,—

"Within six hours after the Appearance, the memorable accident on this Line happened, and within ten hours the dead and wounded were brought along through the tunnel over the spot where the figure had stood."

A disagreeable shudder crept over me, but I did my best against it. It was not to be denied, I rejoined, that this was a remarkable coincidence, calculated deeply to impress his mind. But it was unquestionable that remarkable coincidences did continually occur, and they must be taken into account in dealing with such a subject. Though to be sure I must admit, I added (for I thought I saw that he was going to bring the objection to bear upon me), men of common sense did not allow much for coincidences in making the ordinary calculations of life.

He again begged to remark that he had not finished.

I again begged his pardon for being betrayed into interruptions.

"This," he said, again laying his hand upon my arm, and glancing over his shoulder with hollow eyes, "was just a year ago. Six or seven months passed, and I had recovered from the surprise and shock, when one morning, as the day was breaking, I, standing at the door, looked towards the red light, and saw the spectre again." He stopped, with a fixed look at me.

"Did it cry out?"

"No. It was silent."

"Did it wave its arm?"

"No. It leaned against the shaft of the light, with both hands before the face. Like this."

Once more I followed his action with my eyes. It was an action of mourning. I have seen such an attitude in stone figures on tombs.

"Did you go up to it?"

"I came in and sat down, partly to collect my thoughts, partly because it had turned me faint. When I went to the door again, daylight was above me, and the ghost was gone."

"But nothing followed? Nothing came of this?"

He touched me on the arm with his forefinger twice or thrice giving a ghastly nod each time:—

"That very day, as a train came out of the tunnel, I noticed, at a carriage window on my side, what looked like a confusion of hands and heads, and something waved. I saw it just in time to signal the driver, Stop! He shut off, and put his brake on, but the train drifted past here a hundred and fifty yards or more. I ran after it, and, as I went along, heard terrible screams and cries. A beautiful young lady had died instantaneously in one of the compartments, and was brought in here, and laid down on this floor between us."

Involuntarily I pushed my chair back, as I looked from the

boards at which he pointed to himself.

"True, sir. True. Precisely as it happened, so I tell it you."

I could think of nothing to say, to any purpose, and my mouth was very dry. The wind and the wires took up the story with a long lamenting wail.

He resumed. "Now, sir, mark this, and judge how my mind is troubled. The spectre came back a week ago. Ever since, it has been there, now and again, by fits and starts."

"At the light?"

"At the Danger-light."

"What does it seem to do?"

He repeated, if possible with increased passion and vehemence, that former gesticulation of, "For God's sake, clear the way!"

Then he went on. "I have no peace or rest for it. It calls to me, for many minutes together, in an agonised manner, 'Below there! Look out! Look out!' It stands waving to me. It rings my little bell—"

I caught at that. "Did it ring your bell yesterday evening when I was here, and you went to the door?"

"Twice."

"Why, see," said I, "how your imagination misleads you. My eyes were on the bell, and my ears were open to the bell, and if I am a living man, it did *not* ring at those times. No, nor at any other time, except when it was rung in the natural course of physical things by the station communicating with you."

He shook his head. "I have never made a mistake as to that yet, sir. I have never confused the spectre's ring with the man's. The ghost's ring is a strange vibration in the bell that it derives from nothing else, and I have not asserted that the bell stirs to the eye. I don't wonder that you failed to hear it. But I heard it."

"And did the spectre seem to be there, when you looked out?"

"It *was* there."'

"Both times?"

He repeated firmly: "Both times."

"Will you come to the door with me, and look for it now?"

He bit his under lip as though he were somewhat unwilling, but arose. I opened the door, and stood on the step, while he stood in the doorway. There was the Danger-light. There was the dismal mouth of the tunnel. There were the high, wet stone walls of the cutting. There were the stars above them.

"Do you see it?" I asked him, taking particular note of his face. His eyes were prominent and strained, but not very much more so, perhaps, than my own had been when I had directed them earnestly towards the same spot.

"No," he answered. "It is not there."

"Agreed," said I.

We went in again, shut the door, and resumed our seats. I was thinking how best to improve this advantage, if it might be called one, when he took up the conversation in such a matter-of-course way, so assuming that there could be no serious question of fact between us, that I felt myself placed in the weakest of positions.

"By this time you will fully understand, sir," he said, "that what troubles me so dreadfully is the question, What does the spectre mean?"

I was not sure, I told him, that I did fully understand.

"What is its warning against?" he said, ruminating, with his eyes on the fire, and only by times turning them on me. "What is the danger? Where is the danger? There is danger overhanging somewhere on the Line. Some dreadful calamity will happen. It is not to be doubted this third time, after what has gone before. But surely this is a cruel haunting of me. What can I do?"

He pulled out his handkerchief, and wiped the drops from his heated forehead.

"If I telegraph Danger, on either side of me, or on both, I can give no reason for it," he went on, wiping the palms of his hands. "I should get into trouble, and do no good. They would think I was mad. This is the way it would work,—Message: 'Danger! Take care!' Answer: 'What Danger? Where?' Message: 'Don't know. But, for God's sake, take care!' They would displace me. What else could they do?"

His pain of mind was most pitiable to see. It was the mental torture of a conscientious man, oppressed beyond endurance by an unintelligible responsibility involving life.

"When it first stood under the Danger-light," he went on, putting his dark hair back from his head, and drawing his hands outward across and across his temples in an extremity of feverish distress, "why not tell me where that accident was to happen,- if it must happen? Why not tell me how it could be averted,—if it could have been averted? When on its second coming it hid its face, why not tell me, instead, 'She is going to die. Let them keep her at home'? If it came, on those two occasions, only to show me that its warnings were true, and so to prepare me for the third, why not warn me plainly now? And I, Lord help me! A mere poor signal-man on this solitary station! Why not go to somebody with credit to be believed, and power to act?"

When I saw him in this state, I saw that for the poor man's sake, as well as for the public safety, what I had to do for the time was to compose his mind. Therefore, setting aside all question of reality or unreality between us, I represented to him that whoever thoroughly discharged his duty must do well, and that at least it was his comfort that he understood his duty, though he did not understand these confounding Appearances. In this effort I succeeded far better than in the attempt to reason him out of his conviction. He became calm; the occupations incidental to his post as the night advanced began to make larger demands on his attention: and I left him at two in the morning. I had offered to stay through the night, but he would not hear of it.

That I more than once looked back at the red light as I ascended the pathway, that I did not like the red light, and that I should have slept but poorly if my bed had been under it, I see no reason to conceal. Nor did I like the two sequences of the accident and the dead girl. I see no reason to conceal that either.

But what ran most in my thoughts was the consideration how ought I to act, having become the recipient of this disclosure? I had proved the man to be intelligent, vigilant, painstaking, and exact; but how long might he remain so, in his state of mind? Though in a subordinate position, still he held a most important trust, and would I (for instance) like to stake my own life on the chances of his continuing to execute it with precision?

Unable to overcome a feeling that there would be something treacherous in my communicating what he had told me to his superiors in the Company, without first being plain with himself and proposing a middle course to him, I ultimately resolved to offer to accompany him (otherwise keeping his secret for the present) to the wisest medical practitioner we could hear of in those parts, and to take his opinion. A change in his time of duty would come round next night, he had apprised me, and he would be off an hour or two after sunrise, and on again soon after sunset. I had appointed to return accordingly.

Next evening was a lovely evening, and I walked out early to enjoy it. The sun was not yet quite down when I traversed the field-path near the top of the deep cutting. I would extend my walk for an hour, I said to myself, half an hour on and half an hour back, and it would then be time to go to my signal-man's box.

Before pursuing my stroll, I stepped to the brink, and me-chanically looked down, from the point from which I had first seen him. I cannot describe the thrill that seized upon me, when, close at the mouth of the tunnel, I saw the appearance of a man, with his left sleeve across his eyes, passionately waving his right arm.

The nameless horror that oppressed me passed in a moment, for in a moment I saw that this appearance of a man was a man indeed, and that there was a little group of other men, standing at a short distance, to whom he seemed to be rehearsing the gesture he made. The Danger-light was not yet lighted. Against its shaft, a little low hut, entirely new to me, had been made of some wooden supports and tarpaulin. It looked no bigger than a bed.

With an irresistible sense that something was wrong,—with a

flashing self-reproachful fear that fatal mischief had come of my leaving the man there, and causing no one to be sent to overlook or correct what he did,—I descended the notched path with all the speed I could make.

"What is the matter?" I asked the men.

"Signal-man killed this morning, sir."

"Not the man belonging to that box?"

"Yes, sir."

"Not the man I know?"

"You will recognise him, sir, if you knew him," said the man who spoke for the others, solemnly uncovering his own head, and raising an end of the tarpaulin, "for his face is quite composed."

"O, how did this happen, how did this happen?" I asked, turning from one to another as the hut closed in again.

"He was cut down by an engine, sir. No man in England knew his work better. But somehow he was not clear of the outer rail. It was just at broad day. He had struck the light, and had the lamp in his hand. As the engine came out of the tunnel, his back was towards her, and she cut him down. That man drove her, and was showing how it happened. Show the gentleman, Tom."

The man, who wore a rough dark dress, stepped back to his former place at the mouth of the tunnel.

"Coming round the curve in the tunnel, sir," he said, "I saw him at the end, like as if I saw him down a perspective-glass. There was no time to check speed, and I knew him to be very careful. As he didn't seem to take heed of the whistle, I shut it off when we were running down upon him, and called to him as loud as I could call."

"What did you say?"

"I said, 'Below there! Look out! Look out! For God's sake, clear the way!'"

I started.

"Ah! it was a dreadful time, sir. I never left off calling to him. I put this arm before my eyes not to see, and I waved this arm to the last; but it was no use."

Without prolonging the narrative to dwell on any one of its curious circumstances more than on any other, I may, in closing it, point out the coincidence that the warning of the Engine-Driver included, not only the words which the unfortunate Signal-man had repeated to me as haunting him, but also the words which I myself—not he—had attached, and that only in my own mind, to the gesticulation he had imitated.

The Martyr Medium

"After the valets, the master!" is Mr. Fechter's rallying cry in the picturesque romantic drama which attracts all London to the Lyceum Theatre. After the worshippers and puffers of Mr. Daniel Dunglas Home, the spirit medium, comes Mr. Daniel Dunglas Home himself, in one volume. And we must, for the honour of Literature, plainly express our great surprise and regret that he comes arm-in-arm with such good company as Messrs. Longman and Company.

We have already summed up Mr. Home's demands on the public capacity of swallowing, as sounded through the war-denouncing trumpet of Mr. Howitt, and it is not our intention to revive the strain as performed by Mr. Home on his own melodious instrument. We notice, by the way, that in that part of the Fantasia where the hand of the first Napoleon is supposed to be reproduced, recognised, and kissed, at the Tuileries, Mr. Home subdues the florid effects one might have expected after Mr. Howitt's execution, and brays in an extremely general manner.

And yet we observe Mr. Home to be in other things very reliant on Mr. Howitt, of whom he entertains as gratifying an opinion as Mr. Howitt entertains of him: dwelling on his "deep researches into this subject", and of his "great work now ready for the press", and of his "eloquent and forcible" advocacy, and eke of his "elaborate and almost exhaustive work", which Mr. Home trusts will be "extensively read".

But, indeed, it would seem to be the most reliable characteristic of the Dear Spirits, though very capricious in other particulars, that they always form their circles into what may be described, in worldly terms, as A Mutual Admiration and Complimentation Company (Limited).

Mr. Home's book is entitled *Incidents in My Life*. We will extract a dozen sample passages from it, as variations on and phrases of harmony in, the general strain for the Trumpet, which we have promised not to repeat.

1. MR. HOME IS SUPERNATURALLY NURSED

"I cannot remember when first I became subject to the curious phenomena which have now for so long attended me, but my aunt and others have told me that when I was a baby my cradle was frequently rocked, as if some kind guardian spirit was attending me in my slumbers."

2. DISRESPECTFUL CONDUCT OF MR. HOME'S AUNT NEVERTHELESS

"In her uncontrollable anger she seized a chair and threw it at me."

3. PUNISHMENT OF MR. HOME'S AUNT

"Upon one occasion as the table was being thus moved about of itself, my aunt brought the family Bible, and placing it on the table, said, 'There, that will soon drive the devils away'; but to her astonishment the table only moved in a more lively manner, as if pleased to bear such a burden." (We believe this is constantly observed in pulpits and church reading desks, which are invariably lively.) "Seeing this she was greatly incensed, and determined to stop it, she angrily placed her whole weight on the table, and was actually lifted up with it bodily from the floor."

4. TRIUMPHANT EFFECT OF THIS DISCIPLINE ON MR. HOME'S AUNT

"And she felt it a duty that I should leave her house, and which I did."

5. MR. HOME'S MISSION

It was communicated to him by the spirit of his mother, in

the following terms: "Daniel, fear not, my child, God is with you, and who shall be against you? Seek to do good: be truthful and truth-loving, and you will prosper, my child. Yours is a glorious mission—you will convince the infidel, cure the sick, and console the weeping."

It is a coincidence that another eminent man, with several missions, heard a voice from the Heavens blessing him, when he also was a youth, and saying, "You will be rewarded, my son, in time". This Medium was the celebrated Baron Munchausen, who relates the experience in the opening of the second chapter of the incidents in HIS life.

6. MODEST SUCCESS OF MR. HOME'S MISSION

"Certainly these phenomena, whether from God or from the devil, have in ten years caused more converts to the great truths of immortality and angel communion, with all that flows from these great facts, than all the sects in Christendom have made during the same period."

7. WHAT THE FIRST COMPOSERS SAY
OF THE SPIRIT-MUSIC, TO MR. HOME

"As to the music, it has been my good fortune to be on intimate terms with some of the first composers of the day, and more than one of them have said of such as they have heard, that it is such music as only angels could make, and no man could write it."

These "first composers" are not more particularly named. We shall therefore be happy to receive and file at the office of this Journal, the testimonials in the foregoing terms of Dr. Sterndale Bennett, Mr. Balfe, Mr. Macfarren, Mr. Benedict, Mr. Vincent Wallace, Signor Costa, M. Auber, M. Gounod, Signor Rossini, and Signor Verdi. We shall also feel obliged to Mr. Alfred Mellon, who is no doubt constantly studying this wonderful music, under the Medium's auspices, if he will note on paper, from memory, say a single sheet of the same.

Signor Giulio Regondi will then perform it, as correctly as a mere mortal can, on the Accordion, at the next ensuing concert of the Philharmonic Society; on which occasion the before-mentioned testimonials will be conspicuously displayed in the front of the orchestra.

8. MR. HOME'S MIRACULOUS INFANT

"On the 26th April, old style, or 8th May, according to our style, at seven in the evening, and as the snow was fast falling, our little boy was born at the town house, situate on the Gagarines Quay, in St. Petersburg, where we were still staying. A few hours after his birth, his mother, the nurse, and I heard for several hours the warbling of a bird as if singing over him. Also that night, and for two or three nights afterwards, a bright starlike light, which was clearly visible from the partial darkness of the room, in which there was only a night-lamp burning, appeared several times directly over its head, where it remained for some moments, and then slowly moved in the direction of the door, where it disappeared.

"This was also seen by each of us at the same time. The light was more condensed than those which have been so often seen in my presence upon previous and subsequent occasions. It was brighter and more distinctly globular. I do not believe that it came through my mediumship, but rather through that of the child, who has manifested on several occasions the presence of the gift. I do not like to allude to such a matter, but as there are more strange things in Heaven and earth than are dreamt of, even in my philosophy, I do not feel myself at liberty to omit stating, that during the latter part of my wife's pregnancy, we thought it better that she should not join in Seances, because it was found that whenever the rappings occurred in the room, a simultaneous movement of the child was distinctly felt, perfectly in unison with the sounds.

"When there were three sounds, three movements were felt, and so on, and when five sounds were heard, which is generally the call for the alphabet, she felt the five internal movements, and she would frequently, when we were mistaken in the latter, correct us from what the child indicated."

We should ask pardon of our readers for sullying our paper with this nauseous matter, if without it they could adequately understand what Mr. Home's book is.

9. CAGLIOSTRO'S SPIRIT CALLS ON MR. HOME

Prudently avoiding the disagreeable question of his giving himself, both in this state of existence and in his spiritual circle, a name to which he never had any pretensions whatever, and likewise prudently suppressing any reference to his amiable weakness as a swindler and an infamous trafficker in his own wife, the guileless Mr. Balsamo delivered, in a "distinct voice", this distinct celestial utterance—unquestionably punctuated in a supernatural manner: "My power was that of a mesmerist, but all-misunderstood by those about me, my biographers have even done me injustice, but I care not for the untruths of earth".

10. ORACULAR STATE OF MR. HOME

"After various manifestations, Mr. Home went into the trance, and addressing a person present, said, 'You ask what good are such trivial manifestations, such as rapping, table-moving, etc.? God is a better judge than we are what is fitted for humanity, immense results may spring from trivial things. The steam from a kettle is a small thing, but look at the locomotive! The electric spark from the back of a cat is a small thing, but see the wonders of electricity! The raps are small things, but their results will lead you to the Spirit-World, and to eternity! Why should great results spring from such small causes? Christ was born in a manger, he was not born a King. When you tell me why he was born in a manger, I will tell you why these manifestations, so trivial, so undignified as they appear to you, have been appointed to convince the world of the truth of spiritualism.'"

Wonderful! Clearly direct Inspiration!—And yet, perhaps, hardly worth the trouble of going "into the trance" for, either. Amazing as the revelation is, we seem to have heard something like it from more than one personage who was wide awake. A quack doctor, in an open barouche (attended by a barrel-organ and two footmen in brass helmets), delivered just such another address within our hearing, outside a gate of Paris, not two months ago.

11. THE TESTIMONY OF MR. HOME'S BOOTS

"The lady of the house turned to me and said abruptly, 'Why, you are sitting in the air'; and on looking, we found that the chair remained in its place, but that I was elevated two or three inches above it, and my feet not touching the floor. This may show how utterly unconscious I am at times to the sensation of levitation. As is usual, when I had not got above the level of the heads of those about me, and when they change their position much—as they frequently do in looking wistfully at such a phenomenon—I came down again, but not till I had remained so raised about half a minute from the time of its being first seen. I was now impressed to leave the table, and was soon carried to the lofty ceiling.

"The Count de B—— left his place at the table, and coming under where I was, said, 'Now, young Home, come and let me touch your feet.' I told him I had no volition in the matter, but perhaps the spirits would kindly allow me to come down to him. They did so, by floating me down to him, and my feet were soon in his outstretched hands. He seized my boots, and now I was again elevated, he holding tightly, and pulling at my feet, till the boots I wore, which had elastic sides, came off and remained in his hands."

12. THE UNCOMBATIVE NATURE OF MR. HOME

As there is a maudlin complaint in this book, about men of Science being hard upon "the 'Orphan' Home", and as the "gentle and uncombative nature" of this Medium in a martyred point of view is pathetically commented on by the anonymous literary friend who supplies him with an introduction and appendix—rather at odds with Mr. Howitt, who is so mightily triumphant about the same Martyr's reception by crowned heads, and about the competence he has become endowed with—we cull from Mr. Home's book one or two little illustrative flowers.

Sir David Brewster (a pestilent unbeliever) "has come before the public in few matters which have brought more shame upon him than his conduct and assertions on this occasion, in which he manifested not only a disregard for truth, but also a disloyalty to scientific observation, and to the use of his own eyesight and natural faculties".

The same unhappy Sir David Brewster's "character may be the better known, not only for his untruthful dealing with this subject, but also in his own domain of science in which the same unfaithfulness to truth will be seen to be the characteristic of his mind.." Again, he "is really not a man over whom victory is any honour." Again, "not only he, but Professor Faraday have had time and ample leisure to regret that they should have so foolishly pledged themselves", etc.

A Faraday a fool in the sight of a Home! That unjust judge and whited wall, Lord Brougham, has his share of this Martyr Medium's uncombativeness. "In order that he might not be compelled to deny Sir David's statements, he found it necessary that he should be silent, and I have some reason to complain that his Lordship preferred sacrificing me to his desire not to immolate his friend."

M. Arago also came off with very doubtful honours from a wrestle with the uncombative Martyr; who is perfectly clear (and so are we, let us add) that scientific men are not the men for his purpose. Of course, he is the butt of "utter and acknowledged ignorance", and of "the most gross and foolish statements", and of "the unjust and dishonest", and of "the press-gang", and of crowds of other alien and combative adjectives, participles, and substantives.

Nothing is without its use, and even this odious book may do some service. Not because it coolly claims for the writer and his disciples such powers as were wielded by the Saviour and the Apostles; not because it sees no difference between twelve table rappers in these days, and "twelve fishermen" in those; not because it appeals for precedents to statements extracted from the most ignorant and wretched of mankind, by cruel torture, and constantly withdrawn when the torture was withdrawn; not because it sets forth such a strange confusion of ideas as is presented by one of the faithful when, writing of a certain sprig of geranium handed by an invisible hand, he adds in ecstasies, *"which we have planted and it is growing, so that it is no delusion, no fairy money turned into dross or leaves"*—as if it followed that the conjuror's half-crowns really did become invisible and in that state fly, because he afterwards cuts them out of a real orange; or as if the conjuror's pigeon, being after the discharge of his gun, a real live pigeon fluttering on the target, must therefore conclusively be a pigeon, fired, whole, living and unshattered, out of the gun!—not because of the exposure of any of these weaknesses, or a thousand such, are these moving incidents in the life of the Martyr Medium, and similar productions, likely to prove useful, but because of their uniform abuse of those who go to test the reality of these alleged phenomena, and who come away incredulous.

There is an old homely proverb concerning pitch and its adhesive character, which we hope this significant circumstance may impress on many minds. The writer of these lines has lately heard overmuch touching young men of promise in the imaginative arts, "towards whom" Martyr Mediums assisting at evening parties feel themselves "drawn." It may be a hint to such young men to stick to their own drawing, as being of a much better kind, and to leave Martyr Mediums alone in their glory.

As there is a good deal in these books about "lying spirits", we will conclude by putting a hypothetical case. Supposing that a Medium (Martyr or otherwise) were established for a time in the house of an English gentleman abroad; say, somewhere in Italy. Supposing that the more marvellous the Medium became, the more suspicious of him the lady of the house became.

Supposing that the lady, her distrust once aroused, were particularly struck by the Medium's exhibiting a persistent desire to commit her, somehow or other, to the disclosure of the manner of the death, to him unknown, of a certain person. Supposing that she at length resolved to test the Medium on this head, and, therefore, on a certain evening mentioned a wholly suppositi-tious manner of death (which was not the real manner of death, nor anything at all like it) within the range of his listening ears.

And supposing that a spirit presently afterwards rapped out its presence, claiming to be the spirit of that deceased person, and claiming to have departed this life in that suppositious way. Would that be a lying spirit? Or would it be a something else, tainting all that Medium's statements and suppressions, even if they were not in themselves of a manifestly outrageous charac-ter?

Four Ghost Stories

A Note From the Publisher

It has rarely been the Leonaur practice to prelude the fiction books it publishes with introductions—lengthy or otherwise. Leonaur does not represent its versions of these kinds of collections as either absolutely definitive or as academic works. Furthermore, the Leonaur editors reason, the original editions of almost all of the books collected carried no such introductions, so at one time, someone—the author in particular—did not think they were absolutely necessary for the enjoyment of his or her penmanship. Of course, on those occasions where there has been an original introduction it has also appeared in the Leonaur edition. In the majority of instances, however, the author's audience was simply required to read the book. Since that was occasionally sufficient to bestow ever-lasting accolades on both work and author it seems doubtful that such introductions were (or are) considered essential given the objective was simply to provide 'a good read.' It is acknowledged that some Leonaur readers would certainly disagree with our view and some have gone so far as to tell us so. Nevertheless, that remains the Leonaur position and that should be borne in mind by readers in the light of what follows.

All that said, it may seem to some readers strange that an introduction is appearing here before a single story—'Four Ghost Stories' in a Leonaur edition. The reason, perhaps ironically has nothing to do with the story itself, but with the business of introductions.

The late Peter Haining compiled a substantial anthology of the supernatural fiction of Charles Dickens entitled, 'The Complete Ghost Stories of Charles Dickens', (Michael Joseph 1982). No one interested in stories of the ghostly and macabre could (or should) undervalue Peter

Haining's contribution to the genre as an authority, editor, compiler and author. Nevertheless, it is a reasonable point of view that his Dickens collection was not 'complete'—and this was not the only statement concerning the book which became contentious.

Haining wrote a substantial introduction to his book and he addressed this story, 'Four Ghost Stories' particularly. He had sound reasons for identifying Dickens as the author of this story irrespective of any view regarding it prior to that time—negatively or positively. It was not unusual that on its original publication a story appeared without a clear attribution as to its authorship, because it was commonplace in magazines of the period to include stories written by anonymous authors. Haining gave a well reasoned verdict as to why he was certain 'Four Ghost Stories' was a Dickens story, not least that the tale is written in what he considered to be Dickens' clearly recognisable style. Furthermore, within his introduction he included part of a piece of correspondence that appears to suggest Dickens himself was acknowledging proprietorship of it. On that basis one would expect to find 'Four Ghost Stories' within any anthology of Dickens' supernatural fiction—indeed here it is!

Richard Dalby is a contemporary expert on the fiction of the supernatural and has also compiled some excellent and highly regarded anthologies of the genre. His own introductions to these works are recognised as scholarship of the highest order. Dalby has established that the author of 'Four Ghost Stories' is not Dickens but one Amelia Edwards.

Amelia Edwards was certainly a highly regarded author of ghostly tales and before she gave up the writing of fiction produced three excellent collections of supernatural short stories and a number of uncollected tales including those for magazines of the period. Subsequently she became a dauntless traveller—particularly in Africa with a special interest in Egypt and Egyptology. She remained an author, but of non-fiction and particularly of books concerning her travels.

On the basis of Dalby's evidence one would therefore not expect to find 'Four Ghost Stories' in this Dickens collection, so the reader may reasonably enquire, why then does it appear here? Is Leonaur weighing into the debate? **No** is the short answer. We are reporting—we trust reasonably fairly—only what others far more qualified than are we—have written. We have no opinion or indeed knowledge of the matter.

Perhaps irreverently, the Leonaur view is that it seemed a shame not to include a tale that had so much interesting history concerning Dickens and this genre in particular. Certainly, for some time there was little doubt in the minds of almost everybody who considered the matter that this was a Dickens story and in a Leonaur edition that is a more than sufficient reason to earn it a place. Given its background the Leonaur editors reason that readers would want to enjoy it as would we ourselves in a similar position.

There is another reason which we believe is even more convincing. This story has a sequel, 'The Portrait Painter's Story' which, unsurprisingly, follows it in this collection. It would seem very strange indeed to publish the sequel—the provenance of which, as a Dickens work, is not so far as we know in question—without the story that inspired it! Perhaps selfishly we also seek to avert a raft of correspondence from those who might object to the presence of 'Four Ghost Stories' without some qualification to support it.

If the reader of this Leonaur book has arrived at this point in a substantial collection of tales of the macabre and chilling, perhaps the Leonaur editors might be excused for assuming that a good ghost story has a certain appeal. In that event—here is another good one—please enjoy it!

The Leonaur Editors

1

Some few years ago a well-known English artist received commission from Lady F. to paint a portrait of her husband It was settled that he should execute the commission at F. Hall, in the country, because his engagements were too many to permit his entering upon a fresh work till the London season should be over. As he happened to be on terms of intimate acquaintance with his employers, the arrangement was satisfactory to all concerned, and on the 13th of September he set out in good heart to perform his engagement.

He took the train for the station nearest to F. Hall, and found himself, when first starting, alone in a carriage. His solitude did not, however, continue long. At the first station out of London, a young lady entered the carriage, and took the corner opposite to him. She was very delicate-looking, with a remarkable blending of sweetness and sadness in her countenance, which did not fail to attract the notice of a man of observation and sensibility. For some time neither uttered a syllable. But at length the gentleman made the remarks usual under such circumstances, on the weather and the country, and, the ice being broken, they entered into conversation.

They spoke of painting. The artist was much surprised by the intimate knowledge the young lady seemed to have of himself and his doings. He was quite certain that he had never seen her before. His surprise was by no means lessened when she suddenly inquired whether he could make, from recollection, the likeness of a person whom he had seen only once, or at most twice? He was hesitating what to reply, when she added, 'Do you think, for example, that you could paint me from recollection?'

He replied that he was not quite sure, but that perhaps he could.

'Well,' she said, 'look at me again. You may have to take a likeness of me.'

He complied with this odd request, and she asked, rather eagerly, 'Now, do you think you could?'

'I think so,' he replied; 'but I cannot say for certain.'

At this moment the train stopped. The young lady rose from her seat, smiled in a friendly manner on the painter, and bade him goodbye; adding, as she quitted the carriage, 'We shall meet again soon.' The train rattled off, and Mr H. (the artist) was left to his own reflections.

The station was reached in due time, and Lady F.'s carriage was there, to meet the expected guest. It carried him to the place of his destination, one of 'the stately homes of England', after a pleasant drive, and deposited him at the hall door, where his host and hostess were standing to receive him. A kind greeting passed, and he was shown to his room: for the dinner-hour was close at hand.

Having completed his toilet, and descended to the drawing-room, Mr H. was much surprised, and much pleased, to see, seated on one of the ottomans, his young companion of the railway carriage. She greeted him with a smile and a bow of recognition. She sat by his side at dinner, spoke to him two or three times, mixed in the general conversation, and seemed perfectly at home. Mr H. had no doubt of her being an intimate friend of his hostess. The evening passed away pleasantly. The conversation turned a good deal upon the fine arts in general, and on painting in particular, and Mr H. was entreated to show some of the sketches he had brought down with him from London. He readily produced them, and the young lady was much interested in them.

At a late hour the party broke up, and retired to their several apartments.

Next morning, early, Mr H. was tempted by the bright sunshine to leave his room, and stroll out into the park. The drawing-room opened into the garden; passing through it, he inquired of a servant who was busy arranging the furniture, whether the young lady had come down yet?

'What young lady, sir?' asked the man, with an appearance of surprise.

'The young lady who dined here last night.'

'No young lady dined here last night, sir,' replied the man, looking fixedly at him.

The painter said no more: thinking within himself that the servant was either very stupid or had a very bad memory. So, leaving the room, he sauntered out into the park.

He was returning to the house, when his host met him, and the usual morning salutations passed between them.

'Your fair young friend has left you?' observed the artist.

'What young friend?' inquired the lord of the manor.

'The young lady who dined here last night,' returned Mr H.

'I cannot imagine to whom you refer,' replied the gentleman, very greatly surprised.

'Did not a young lady dine and spend the evening here yesterday?' persisted Mr H., who in his turn was beginning to wonder.

'No,' replied his host; 'most certainly not. There was no one at table but yourself, my lady, and I.'

The subject was never reverted to after this occasion, yet our artist could not bring himself to believe that he was labouring under a delusion. If the whole were a dream, it was a dream in two parts. As surely as the young lady had been his companion in the railway carriage, so surely she had sat beside him at the dinner-table. Yet she did not come again; and everybody in the house, except himself, appeared to be ignorant of her existence.

He finished the portrait on which he was engaged, and returned to London.

For two whole years he followed up his profession: growing in reputation, and working hard. Yet he never all the while forgot a single lineament in the fair young face of his fellow-traveller. He had no clue by which to discover where she had come from, or who she was. He often thought of her, but spoke to no one about her. There was a mystery about the matter which imposed silence on him. It was wild, strange, utterly unaccountable.

Mr H. was called by business to Canterbury. An old friend of his—whom I will call Mr Wylde—resided there. Mr H., being anxious to see him, and having only a few hours at his disposal, wrote as soon as he reached the hotel, begging Mr Wylde to call upon him there. At the time appointed the door of his room opened, and Mr Wylde was announced. He was a complete stranger to the artist; and the meeting between the two was a little awkward.

It appeared, on explanation, that Mr H.'s friend had left Canterbury some time; that the gentleman now face to face with the artist was another Mr Wylde; that the note intended for the absentee had been given to him; and that he had obeyed the summons, supposing some business matter to be the cause of it.

The first coldness and surprise dispelled, the two gentlemen entered into a more friendly conversation; for Mr H. had mentioned his name, and it was not a strange one to his visitor. When they had conversed a little while, Mr Wylde asked Mr H. whether he had ever painted, or could undertake to paint, a portrait from mere description? Mr H. replied, never.

'I ask you this strange question,' said Mr Wylde, 'because, about two years ago, I lost a dear daughter. She was my only child, and I loved her dearly. Her loss was a heavy affliction to me, and my regrets are the deeper that I have no likeness of her. You are a man of unusual genius. If you could paint me a portrait of my child, I should be very grateful.'

Mr Wylde then described the features and appearance of his daughter, and the colour of her eyes and hair, and tried to give an idea of the expression of her face. Mr H. listened attentively, and, feeling great sympathy with his grief, made a sketch. He had no thought of its being like, but hoped the bereaved father might possibly think it so. But the father shook his head on seeing the sketch, and said, 'No, it was not at all like.' Again the artist tried, and again he failed. The features were pretty well, but the expression was not hers; and the father turned away from it, thanking Mr H. For his kind endeavours, but quite hopeless of any successful result.

Suddenly a thought struck the painter; he took another sheet of paper, made a rapid and vigorous sketch, and handed it to his companion. Instantly, a bright look of recognition and pleasure lighted up the father's face, and he exclaimed, 'That is she! Surely you must have seen my child, or you never could have made so perfect a likeness!'

'When did your daughter die?' inquired the painter, with agitation.

'Two years ago; on the 13th of September. She died in the afternoon, after a few days' illness.'

Mr H. pondered, but said nothing. The image of that fair young face was engraven on his memory as with a diamond's point, and her strangely prophetic words were now fulfilled.

A few weeks after, having completed a beautiful full-length portrait of the young lady, he sent it to her father, and the likeness was declared, by all who had ever seen her, to be perfect.

2

Among the friends of my family was a young Swiss lady, who, with an only brother, had been left an orphan in her childhood. She was brought up, as well as her brother, by an aunt; and the children, thus thrown very much upon each other, became very strongly attached. At the age of twenty-two the youth got some appointment in India, and the terrible day drew near when they must part. I need not describe the agony of persons so circumstanced. But the mode in which these two sought to mitigate the anguish of separation was singular. They agreed that if either should die before the young man's return, the dead should appear to the living.

The youth departed. The young lady by-and-by married a Scotch gentleman, and quitted her home, to be the light and ornament of his. She was a devoted wife, but she never forgot her brother. She corresponded with him regularly, and her brightest days in all the year were those which brought letters from India.

One cold winter's day, two or three years after her marriage, she was seated at work near a large bright fire, in her own bedroom upstairs. It was about midday, and the room was full of light. She was very busy, when some strange impulse caused her to raise her head and look round. The door was slightly open, and, near the large antique bed, stood a figure, which she, at a glance, recognised as that of her brother.

With a cry of delight she started up, and ran forward to meet him, exclaiming, 'Oh, Henry! How could you surprise me so! You never told me you were coming!' But he waved his hand sadly, in a way that forbade approach, and she remained rooted to the spot. He advanced a step towards her, and said, in a low soft voice, 'Do you remember our agreement? I have come to fulfil it'; and approaching nearer he laid his hand on her wrist. It was icy cold, and the touch made her shiver. Her brother smiled, a faint sad smile, and, again waving his hand, turned and left the room.

When the lady recovered from a long swoon there was a mark on her wrist, which never left it to her dying day. The next mail from India brought a letter, informing her that her brother had died on the very day, and at the very hour, when he presented himself to her in her room.

Overhanging the waters of the Firth of Forth there lived, a good many years ago, a family of old standing in the kingdom of Fife: frank, hospitable, and hereditary Jacobites. It consisted of the squire, or laird—a man well advanced in years—his wife, three sons, and four daughters. The sons were sent out into the world, but not into the service of the reigning family. The daughters were all young and unmarried, and the eldest and the youngest were much attached to each other. They slept in the same room, shared the same bed, and had no secrets one from the other.

It chanced that among the visitors to the old house there came a young naval officer, whose gun-brig often put in to the neighbouring harbours. He was well received, and between him and the elder of the two sisters a tender attachment sprang up.

But the prospect of such an alliance did not quite please the lady's mother, and, without being absolutely told that it should never take place, the lovers were advised to separate. The plea urged, was, that they could not then afford to marry, and that they must wait for better times. Those were times when parental authority—at all events in Scotland— was like the decree of fate, and the lady felt that she had nothing left to do, but to say farewell to her lover. Not so he. He was a fine gallant fellow, and, taking the old lady at her word, he determined to do his utmost to push his worldly fortunes.

There was war at that time with some northern power—I think with Prussia—and the lover, who had interest at the Admiralty, applied to be sent to the Baltic. He obtained his wish. Nobody interfered to prevent the young people from taking a tender farewell of each other, and, he full of hope, and she desponding, they parted. It was settled that he should write by every opportunity; and twice a week—on the post days at the neighbouring village—the younger sister would mount her pony and ride in for letters.

There was much hidden joy over every letter that arrived. And often and often the sisters would sit at the window a whole winter's night listening to the roar of the sea among the rocks, and hoping and praying that each light, as it shone far away, might be the signal-lamp hung at the mast-head to apprise them that the gun-brig was coming. So weeks stole on in hope deferred, and there came a lull in the correspondence. Post-day after post-day brought no letters from the Baltic, and the agony of the sisters, especially of the betrothed, became almost unbearable.

They slept, as I have said, in the same room, and their window looked down well-nigh into the waters of the Firth. One night, the younger sister was awakened by the heavy moanings of the elder. They had taken to burning a candle in their room, and placing it in the window: thinking, poor girls, that it would serve as a beacon to the brig. She saw by its light that her sister was tossing about, and was greatly disturbed in her sleep. After some hesitation she determined to awaken the sleeper, who sprang up with a wild cry, and, pushing back her long hair with her hands, exclaimed, 'What have you done, what have you done!' Her sister tried to soothe her, and asked tenderly if anything had alarmed her. 'Alarmed!' she answered, still very wildly, 'no! But I saw him! He entered at that door, and came near the foot of the bed. He looked very pale, and his hair was wet. He was just going to speak to me, when you drove him away. O what have you done, what have you done!'

I do not believe that her lover's ghost really appeared, but the fact is certain that the next mail from the Baltic brought intelligence that the gun-brig had gone down in a gale of wind, with all on board.

4

When my mother was a girl about eight or nine years old, and living in Switzerland, the Count R. of Holstein, coming to Switzerland for his health, took a house at Vevay, with the intention of remaining there for two or three years. He soon became acquainted with my mother's parents, and between him and them acquaintance ripened into friendship. They met constantly, and liked each other more and more.

Knowing the count's intentions respecting his stay in Switzerland, my grandmother was much surprised by receiving from him one morning a short hurried note, informing her that urgent and unexpected business obliged him to return that very day to Germany. He added, that he was very sorry to go, but that he must go; and he ended by bidding her farewell, and hoping they might meet again someday. He quitted Vevay that evening, and nothing more was heard of him or his mysterious business.

A few years after this departure, my grandmother and one of her sons went to spend some time at Hamburg. Count R., hearing that they were there, went to see them, and brought them to his castle at Breitenburg, where they were to stay a few days. It was a wild but beautiful district, and the castle, a huge pile, was a relic of the feudal times, which, like most old places of the sort, was said to be haunted. Never having heard the story upon which this belief was founded, my grandmother entreated the count to tell it.

After some little hesitation and demur, he consented: 'There is a room in this house,' he began, 'in which no one is ever able to sleep. Noises are heard in it continually, which have never been accounted for, and which sound like the ceaseless turning over and upsetting of furniture. I have had the room emptied, I have had the old floor taken up and a new one laid down, but nothing would stop the noises. At last, in despair, I had it walled up. The story attached to the room is this.'

Some hundreds of years ago, there lived in this castle a countess, whose charity to the poor and kindness to all people were unbounded. She was known far and wide as 'the good Countess R.' and everybody loved her. The room in question was her room. One night, she was awakened from her sleep by a voice near her; and looking out of bed, she saw, by the faint light of her lamp, a little tiny man, about a foot in height, standing near her bedside. She was greatly surprised, but he spoke, and said, 'Good Countess of R., I have come to ask you to be godmother to my child. Will you consent?' She said she would, and he told her that he would come and fetch her in a few days, to attend the christening; with those words he vanished out of the room.

Next morning, recollecting the incidents of the night, the countess came to the conclusion that she had had an odd dream, and thought no more of the matter. But, about a fortnight afterwards, when she had well-nigh forgotten the dream, she was again roused at the same hour and by the same small individual, who said he had come to claim the fulfilment of her promise. She rose, dressed herself, and followed her tiny guide down the stairs of the castle. In the centre of the courtyard there was, and still is, a large square well, very deep, and stretching underneath the building nobody knew how far.

Having reached the side of this well, the little man blindfolded the countess, and bidding her not fear, but follow him, descended some unknown stairs. This was for the countess a strange and novel position, and she felt uncomfortable; but she determined at all hazards to see the adventure to the end, and descended bravely. They reached the bottom, and when her guide removed the bandage from her eyes, she found herself in a room full of small people like himself. The christening was performed, the countess stood godmother, and at the conclusion of the ceremony, as the lady was about to say goodbye, the mother of the baby took a handful of wood shavings which lay in a corner, and put them into her visitor's apron.

'You have been very kind, good Countess of R.,' she said, 'in coming to be godmother to my child, and your kindness shall not go unrewarded. When you rise tomorrow, these shavings will have turned into metal, and out of them you must immediately get made, two fishes and thirty *silberlingen* (a German coin). When you get them back, take great care of them, for so long as they all remain in your family everything will prosper with you; but, if one of them ever gets lost, then you will have troubles without end.'

The countess thanked her, and bade them all farewell. Having again covered her eyes, the little man led her out of the well, and landed her safe in her own courtyard, where he removed the bandage, and she never saw him more.

Next morning the countess awoke with a confused notion of

some extraordinary dream. While at her toilet, she recollected all the incidents quite plainly, and racked her brain for some cause which might account for it. She was so employed when, stretching out her hand for her apron, she was astounded to find it tied up, and, within the folds, a number of metal shavings. How came they there? Was it a reality? Had she not dreamed of the little man and the christening? She told the story to the members of her family at breakfast, who all agreed that whatever the token might mean, it should not be disregarded.

It was therefore settled that the fishes and the *silberlingen* should be made, and carefully kept among the archives of the family. Time passed; everything prospered with the house of R. The King of Denmark loaded them with honours and benefits, and gave the count high office in his household. For many years all went well with them.

Suddenly, to the consternation of the family, one of the fishes disappeared, and, though strenuous efforts were made to discover what had become of it, they all failed. From this time everything went wrong. The count then living, had two sons; while out hunting together, one killed the other; whether accidentally or not, is uncertain, but, as the youths were known to be perpetually disagreeing, the case seemed doubtful. This was the beginning of sorrows.

The king, hearing what had occurred, thought it necessary to deprive the count of the office he held. Other misfortunes followed. The family fell into discredit. Their lands were sold, or forfeited to the crown; till little was left but the old castle of Breitenburg and the narrow domain which surrounded it. This deteriorating process went on through two or three generations, and, to add to all other misfortunes, there was always in the family one mad member.

'And now,' continued the count, 'comes the strange part of the mystery. I had never placed much faith in these mysterious little relics, and I regarded the story in connexion with them as a fable. I should have continued in this belief, but for a very extraordinary circumstance. You remember my sojourn in Switzerland a few years ago, and how abruptly it terminated? Well. Just before leaving Holstein, I had received a curious wild letter from some knight in Norway, saying that he was very ill, but that he could not die without first seeing and conversing with me. I thought the man mad, because I had never heard of him before, and he could have no possible business to transact with me. So, throwing the letter aside, I did not give it another thought.

'My correspondent, however, was not satisfied. He wrote again. My agent, who in my absence opened and answered my letters, told him that I was in Switzerland for my health, and that, if he had anything to say, he had better say it in writing, as I could not possibly travel so far as Norway.

'This, however, did not satisfy the knight. He wrote a third time, beseeching me to come to him, and declaring that what he had to tell me was of the utmost importance to us both. My agent was so struck by the earnest tone of the letter, that he forwarded it to me: at the same time advising me not to refuse the entreaty. This was the cause of my sudden departure from Vevay, and I shall never cease to rejoice that I did not persist in my refusal.

'I had a long and weary journey, and once or twice I felt sorely tempted to stop short, but some strange impulse kept me going. I had to traverse well-nigh the whole of Norway; often for days on horseback, riding over wild moorland, heathery bogs, mountains and crags and lonely places, and ever at my left the rocky coast, lashed and torn by the surging waters.

'At last, after some fatigue and hardship, I reached the village named in the letter, on the northern coast of Norway. The knight's castle—a large round tower—was built on a small island off the coast, and communicated with the land by a drawbridge. I arrived there, late at night, and must admit that I felt misgivings when I crossed the bridge by the lurid glare of torchlight, and heard the dark waters surging under me.

'The gate was opened by a man, who, as soon as I entered, closed it behind me. My horse was taken from me, and I was led up to the knight's room. It was a small circular apartment, nearly at the top of the tower, and scantily furnished. There, on a bed, lay the old knight, evidently at the point of death. He tried to rise as I entered, and gave me such a look of gratitude and relief that it repaid me for my pains.

"'I cannot thank you sufficiently, Count of R.," said he, "for granting my request. Had I been in a state to travel I should have gone to you; but that was impossible, and I could not die without first seeing you. My business is short, though important. Do you know this?" And he drew from under his pillow, my long-lost fish. Of course I knew it; and he went on. "How long it has been in this house, I do not know, nor by what means it came here, nor, till quite lately, was I at all aware to whom it rightfully belonged. It did not come here in my time, nor in my father's time, and who brought it is a mystery. When I fell ill, and my recovery was pronounced to be impossible, I heard one night, a voice telling me that I should not die till I had restored the fish to the Count R. of Breitenburg. I did not know you; I had never heard of you; and at first I took no heed of the voice. But it came again, every night, until at length in despair I wrote to you. Then the voice stopped. Your answer came, and again I heard the warning, that I must not die till you arrived. At last I heard that you were coming, and I have no language in which to thank you for your kindness. I feel sure I could not have died without seeing you."

'That night the old man died. I waited to bury him, and then returned home, bringing my recovered treasure with me. It was carefully restored to its place. That same year, my eldest brother, whom you know to have been the inmate of a lunatic asylum for years, died, and I became the owner of this place. Last year, to my great surprise, I received a kind letter from the King of Denmark, restoring to me the office which my fathers once held. This year, I have been named governor to his eldest son, and the king has returned a great part of the confiscated property; so that the sun of prosperity seems to shine once more upon the house of Breitenburg.

Not long ago, I sent one of the *silberlingen* to Paris, and another to Vienna, in order that they might be analysed, and the metal of which they are composed made known to me; but no one is able to decide that point.'

Thus ended the Count of R.'s story, after which he led his eager listener to the place where these precious articles were kept, and showed them to her.

The Portrait-Painter's Story

There was lately published in these pages a paper entitled 'Four Ghost Stories'. The first of those stories related the strange experience of 'a well-known English artist, Mr H.' On the publication of that account, Mr H. himself addressed the Editor of this journal—to his great surprise—and forwarded to him his own narrative of the occurrences in question. As Mr H. wrote, without any concealment, in his own name in full, and from his own studio in London, and as there was no possible doubt of his being a real existing person and a responsible gentleman, it became a duty to read his communication attentively. And great injustice having been unconsciously done to it, in the version published as the first of the Four Ghost Stories, it follows here exactly as received. It is, of course, published with the sanction and authority of Mr H., and Mr H. has himself corrected the proofs. Entering on no theory of our own towards the explanation of any part of this remarkable narrative, we have prevailed on Mr H. to present it without any introductory remarks whatever. It only remains to add, that no one has for a moment stood between us and Mr H. in this matter. The whole communication is at first hand. On seeing the article, Four Ghost Stories, Mr H. frankly and good humouredly wrote, I am the Mr H., the living man, of whom mention is made; how my story has been picked up, I do not know, but it is correctly told. I have it by me, written by myself, and here it is.'

I am a painter. One morning in May, 1858, I was seated in my studio at my usual occupation. At an earlier hour than that at which visits are usually made, I received one from a friend whose acquaintance I had made some year or two previously in Richmond Barracks, Dublin. My acquaintance was a captain in the 3rd West York Militia, and from the hospitable manner in which I had been received while a guest with that regiment, as well as from the intimacy that existed between us personally, it was incumbent on me to offer my visitor suitable refreshments; consequently, two o'clock found us well occupied in conversation, cigars, and a decanter of sherry.

About that hour a ring at the bell reminded me of an engagement I had made with a model, or a young person who, having a pretty face and neck, earned a livelihood by sitting for artists. Not being in the humour for work, I arranged with her to come on the following day, promising, of course, to remunerate her for her loss of time, and she went away. In about five minutes she returned, and, speaking to me privately, stated that she had looked forward to the money for the day's sitting, and would be inconvenienced by the want of it; would I let her have a part? There being no difficulty on this point, she again went.

Close to the street in which I live there is another of a very similar name, and persons who are not familiar with my address often go to it by mistake. The model's way lay directly through it, and, on arriving there, she was accosted by a lady and gentleman, who asked if she could inform them where I lived? They had forgotten my right address, and were endeavouring to find me by inquiring of persons whom they met; in a few more minutes they were shown into my room.

My new visitors were strangers to me. They had seen a portrait I had painted, and wished for likenesses of themselves and their children. The price I named did not deter them, and they asked to look round the studio to select the style and size they should prefer. My friend of the 3rd West York, with infinite address and humour, took upon himself the office of showman, dilating on the merits of the respective works in a manner that the diffidence that is expected in a professional man when speaking of his own productions would not have allowed me to adopt. The inspection proving satisfactory, they asked whether I could paint the pictures at their house in the country, and there being no difficulty on this point, an engagement was made for the following autumn, subject to my writing to fix the time when I might be able to leave town for the purpose. This being adjusted, the gentleman gave me his card, and they left.

Shortly afterwards my friend went also, and on looking for the first time at the card left by the strangers, I was somewhat disappointed to find that though it contained the name of Mr and Mrs Kirkbeck, there was no address. I tried to find it by looking at the Court Guide, but it contained no such name, so I put the card in my writing-desk, and forgot for a time the entire transaction.

Autumn came, and with it a series of engagements I had made in the north of England. Towards the end of September, 1858, I was one of a dinner-party at a country-house on the confines of Yorkshire and Lincolnshire. Being a stranger to the family, it was by a mere accident that I was at the house at all. I had arranged to pass a day and a night with a friend in the neighbourhood who was intimate at the house, and had received an invitation, and the dinner occurring on the evening in question, I had been asked to accompany him.

The party was a numerous one, and as the meal approached its termination, and was about to subside into the dessert, the conversation became general. I should here mention that my hearing is defective; at some times more so than at others, and on this particular evening I was extra deaf—so much so, that the conversation only reached me in the form of a continued din. At one instant, however, I heard a word distinctly pronounced, though it was uttered by a person at a considerable distance from me, and that word was Kirkbeck. In the business of the London season I had forgotten all about the visitors of the spring, who had left their card without the address. The word reaching me under such circumstances, arrested my attention, and immediately recalled the transaction to my remembrance. On the first opportunity that offered, I asked a person whom I was conversing with if a family of the name in question was resident in the neighbourhood. I was told in reply, that a Mr Kirkbeck lived at A——, at the farther end of the county.

The next morning I wrote to this person, saying that I believed he called at my studio in the spring, and had made an arrangement with me, which I was prevented fulfilling by there being no address on his card; furthermore, that I should shortly be in his neighbourhood on my return from the north, but should I be mistaken in addressing him, I begged he would not trouble himself to reply to my note. I gave as my address, The Post Office, York.

On applying there three days afterwards, I received a note from Mr Kirkbeck, stating that he was very glad he had heard from me, and that if I would call on my return, he would arrange about the pictures; he also told me to write a day before I proposed coming, that he might not otherwise engage himself. It was ultimately arranged that I should go to his house the succeeding Saturday, stay till Monday morning, transact afterwards what matters I had to attend to in London, and return in a fortnight to execute the commissions.

The day having arrived for my visit, directly after breakfast I took my place in the morning train from York to London. The train would stop at Doncaster, and after that at Retford junction, where I should have to get out in order to take the line through Lincoln to A———. The day was cold, wet, foggy, and in every way as disagreeable as I have ever known a day to be in an English October. The carriage in which I was seated had no other occupant than myself, but at Doncaster a lady got in.

My place was back to the engine and next to the door. As that is considered the ladies' seat, I offered it to her; she, however, very graciously declined it, and took the corner opposite, saying, in a very agreeable voice, that she liked to feel the breeze on her cheek. The next few minutes were occupied in locating herself. There was the cloak to be spread under her, the skirts of the dress to be arranged, the gloves to be tightened, and such other trifling arrangements of plumage as ladies are wont to make before settling themselves comfortably at church or elsewhere, the last and most important being the placing back over her hat the veil that concealed her features. I could then see that the lady was young, certainly not more than two- or three-and-twenty; but being moderately tall, rather robust in make, and decided in expression, she might have been two or three years younger.

I suppose that her complexion would be termed a medium one; her hair being of a bright brown, or auburn, while her eyes and rather decidedly marked eyebrows were nearly black. The colour of her cheek was of that pale transparent hue that sets off to such advantage large expressive eyes, and an equable firm expression of mouth. On the whole, the ensemble was rather handsome than beautiful, her expression having that agreeable depth and harmony about it that rendered her face and features, though not strictly regular, infinitely more attractive than if they had been modelled upon the strictest rules of symmetry.

It is no small advantage on a wet day and a dull long journey to have an agreeable companion, one who can converse, and whose conversation has sufficient substance in it to make one forget the length and the dreariness of the journey. In this respect I had no deficiency to complain of, the lady being decidedly and agreeably conversational. When she had settled herself to her satisfaction, she asked to be allowed to look at my Bradshaw, and not being a proficient in that difficult work, she requested my aid in ascertaining at what time the train passed through Retford again on its way back from London to York.

The conversation turned afterwards on general topics, and, somewhat to my surprise, she led it into such particular subjects as I might be supposed to be more especially familiar with; indeed, I could not avoid remarking that her entire manner, while it was anything but forward, was that of one who had either known me personally or by report. There was in her manner a kind of confidential reliance when she listened to me that is not usually accorded to a stranger, and sometimes she actually seemed to refer to different circumstances with which I had been connected in times past.

After about three-quarters of an hour's conversation the train arrived at Retford, where I was to change carriages. On my alighting and wishing her good morning, she made a slight movement of the hand as if she meant me to shake it, and on my doing so she said, by way of *adieu*, 'I dare say we shall meet again;' to which I replied, 'I hope that we shall all meet again,' and so parted, she going on the line towards London, and I through Lincolnshire to A———. The remainder of the journey was cold, wet, and dreary.

I missed the agreeable conversation, and tried to supply its place with a book I had brought with me from York, and the *Times* newspaper, which I had procured at Retford. But the most disagreeable journey comes to an end at last, and half-past five in the evening found me at the termination of mine. A carriage was waiting for me at the station, where Mr Kirkbeck was also expected by the same train, but as he did not appear it was concluded he would come by the next—half an hour later; accordingly, the carriage drove away with myself only.

The family being from home at the moment, and the dinner hour being seven, I went at once to my room to unpack and to dress; having completed these operations, I descended to the drawing-room. It probably wanted some time to the dinner hour, as the lamps were not lighted, but in their place a large blazing fire threw a flood of light into every corner of the room, and more especially over a lady who, dressed in deep black, was standing by the chimney-piece warming a very handsome foot on the edge of the fender.

Her face being turned away from the door by which I had entered, I did not at first see her features; on my advancing into the middle of the room, however, the foot was immediately withdrawn, and she turned round to accost me, when, to my profound astonishment, I perceived that it was none other than my companion in the railway carriage. She betrayed no surprise at seeing me; on the contrary, with one of those agreeable joyous expressions that make the plainest woman appear beautiful, she accosted me with, I said we should meet again.'

My bewilderment at the moment almost deprived me of utterance. I knew of no railway or other means by which she could have come. I had certainly left her in a London train, and had seen it start, and the only conceivable way in which she could have come was by going on to Peterborough and then returning by a branch to A——, a circuit of about ninety miles. As soon as my surprise enabled me to speak, I said that I wished I had come by the same conveyance as herself.

'That would have been rather difficult,' she rejoined.

At this moment the servant came with the lamps, and informed me that his master had just arrived and would be down in a few minutes.

The lady took up a book containing some engravings, and having singled one out (a portrait of Lady ———), asked me to look at it well and tell her whether I thought it like her.

I was engaged trying to get up an opinion, when Mr and Mrs Kirkbeck entered, and shaking me heartily by the hand, apologised for not being at home to receive me; the gentleman ending by requesting me to take Mrs Kirkbeck in to dinner.

The lady of the house having taken my arm, we marched on. I certainly hesitated a moment to allow Mr Kirkbeck to pass on first with the mysterious lady in black, but Mrs Kirkbeck not seeming to understand it, we passed on at once. The dinner-party consisting of us four only, we fell into our respective places at the table without difficulty, the mistress and master of the house at the top and bottom, the lady in black and myself on each side.

The dinner passed much as is usual on such occasions. I, having to play the guest, directed my conversation principally, if not exclusively, to my host and hostess, and I cannot call to mind that I or anyone else once addressed the lady opposite. Seeing this, and remembering something that looked like a slight want of attention to her on coming into the dining-room, I at once concluded that she was the governess. I observed, however, that she made an excellent dinner; she seemed to appreciate both the beef and the tart as well as a glass of claret afterwards; probably she had had no luncheon, or the journey had given her an appetite.

The dinner ended, the ladies retired, and after the usual port, Mr Kirkbeck and I joined them in the drawing-room. By this time, however, a much larger party had assembled. Brothers and sisters-in-laws had come in from their residences in the neighbourhood, and several children, with Miss Hardwick, their governess, were also introduced to me. I saw at once that my supposition as to the lady in black being the governess was incorrect.

After passing the time necessarily occupied in complimenting the children, and saying something to the different persons to whom I was introduced, I found myself again engaged in conversation with the lady of the railway carriage, and as the topic of the evening had referred principally to portrait-painting, she continued the subject.

'Do you think you could paint my portrait?' the lady inquired.

'Yes, I think I could, if I had the opportunity.'

'Now, look at my face well; do you think you should recollect my features?'

'Yes, I am sure I should never forget your features.'

'Of course I might have expected you to say that; but do you think you could do me from recollection?'

'Well, if it be necessary, I will try; but can't you give me any sittings?'

'No, quite impossible; it could not be. It is said that the print I showed to you before dinner is like me; do you think so?'

'Not much,' I replied; 'it has not your expression. If you can give me only one sitting, it would be better than none.'

'No; I don't see how it could be.'

The evening being by this time rather far advanced, and the chamber candles being brought in, on the plea of being rather tired, she shook me heartily by the hand, and wished me good night. My mysterious acquaintance caused me no small pondering during the night. I had never been introduced to her, I had not seen her speak to any one during the entire evening, not even to wish them good night—how she got across the country was an inexplicable mystery. Then, why did she wish me to paint her from memory, and why could she not give me even one sitting? Finding the difficulties of a solution to these questions rather increase upon me, I made up my mind to defer further consideration of them till breakfast-time, when I supposed the matter would receive some elucidation.

The breakfast now came, but with it no lady in black. The breakfast over, we went to church, came home to luncheon, and so on through the day, but still no lady, neither any reference to her. I then concluded that she must be some relative, who had gone away early in the morning to visit another member of the family living close by. I was much puzzled, however, by no reference whatever being made to her, and finding no opportunity of leading any part of my conversation with the family towards the subject, I went to bed the second night more puzzled than ever. On the servant coming in in the morning, I ventured to ask him the name of the lady who dined at the table on the Saturday evening, to which he answered: 'A lady, sir? No lady, only Mrs Kirkbeck, sir.'

'Yes, the lady that sat opposite me dressed in black?'

'Perhaps, Miss Hardwick, the governess, sir?'

'No, not Miss Hardwick; she came down afterwards.'

'No lady as I see, sir.'

'Oh dear me, yes, the lady dressed in black that was in the drawing-room when I arrived, before Mr Kirkbeck came home?'

The man looked at me with surprise as if he doubted my sanity, and only answered, 'I never see any lady, sir,' and then left.

The mystery now appeared more impenetrable than ever—I thought it over in every possible aspect, but could come to no conclusion upon it. Breakfast was early that morning, in order to allow of my catching the morning train to London. The same cause also slightly hurried us, and allowed no time for conversation beyond that having direct reference to the business that brought me there; so, after arranging to return to paint the portraits on that day three weeks, I made my *adieus*, and took my departure for town.

It is only necessary for me to refer to my second visit to that house, in order to state that I was assured most positively, both by Mr and Mrs Kirkbeck, that no fourth person dined at the table on the Saturday evening in question. Their recollection was clear on the subject, as they had debated whether they should ask Miss Hardwick, the governess, to take the vacant seat, but had decided not to do so; neither could they recall to mind any such person as I described in the whole circle of their acquaintance.

Some weeks passed. It was close upon Christmas. The light of a short winter day was drawing to a close, and I was seated at my table, writing letters for the evening post. My back was towards the folding-doors leading into the room in which my visitors usually waited. I had been engaged some minutes in writing, when, without hearing or seeing anything, I became aware that a person had come through the folding-doors, and was then standing beside me. I turned, and beheld the lady of the railway carriage. I suppose that my manner indicated that I was somewhat startled, as the lady, after the usual salutation, said, 'Pardon me for disturbing you. You did not hear me come in.'

Her manner, though it was more quiet and subdued than I had known it before, was hardly to be termed grave, still less sorrowful. There was a change, but it was that kind of change only which may often be observed from the frank impulsiveness of an intelligent young lady, to the composure of self-possession of that same young lady when she is either betrothed or has recently become a matron. She asked me whether I had made any attempt at a likeness of her. I was obliged to confess that I had not. She regretted it much, as she wished one for her father.

She had brought an engraving (a portrait of Lady M. A.) with her that she thought would assist me. It was like the one she had asked my opinion upon at the house in Lincolnshire. It had always been considered very like her, and she would leave it with me. Then (putting her hand impressively on my arm) she added, 'She really would be most thankful and grateful to me if I would do it' (and, if I recollect rightly, she added), *'as much depended on it.'*

Seeing she was so much in earnest, I took up my sketch-book, and by the dim light that was still remaining began to make a rapid pencil sketch of her. On observing my doing so, however, instead of giving me what assistance she was able, she turned away under pretence of looking at the pictures around the room, occasionally passing from one to another so as to enable me to catch a momentary glimpse of her features.

In this manner I made two hurried but rather expressive sketches of her, which being all that the declining light would allow me to do, I shut my book, and she prepared to leave. This time, instead of the usual 'Good morning,' she wished me an impressively pronounced 'Goodbye,' firmly holding rather than shaking my hand while she said it. I accompanied her to the door, outside of which she seemed rather to fade into the darkness than to pass through it. But I refer this impression to my own fancy.

I immediately inquired of the servant why she had not announced the visitor to me. She stated that she was not aware there had been one, and that anyone who had entered must have done so when she had left the street door open about half an hour previously, while she went across the road for a moment.

Soon after this occurred I had to fulfil an engagement at a house near Bosworth Field, in Leicestershire. I left town on a Friday, having sent some pictures, that were too large to take with me, by the luggage train a week previously, in order that they might be at the house on my arrival, and occasion me no loss of time in waiting for them.

On getting to the house, however, I found that they had not been heard of, and on inquiring at the station, it was stated that a case similar to the one I described had passed through and gone on to Leicester, where it probably still was. It being Friday, and past the hour for the post, there was no possibility of getting a letter to Leicester before Monday morning, as the luggage office would be closed there on the Sunday; consequently, I could in no case expect the arrival of the pictures before the succeeding Tuesday or Wednesday.

The loss of three days would be a serious one; therefore, to avoid it, I suggested to my host that I should leave immediately to transact some business in South Staffordshire, as I should be obliged to attend to it before my return to town, and if I could see about it in the vacant interval thus thrown upon my hands, it would be saving me the same amount of time after my visit to his house was concluded. This arrangement meeting with his ready assent, I hastened to the Atherstone station on the Trent Valley Railway. By reference to Bradshaw, I found that my route lay through L——, where I was to change carriages, to S——, in Staffordshire.

I was just in time for the train that would put me down at L—— at eight in the evening, and a train was announced to start from L—— for S—— at ten minutes after eight, answering, as I concluded, to the train in which I was about to travel. I therefore saw no reason to doubt but that I should get to my journey's end the same night; but on my arriving at L—— I found my plans entirely frustrated. The train arrived punctually, and I got out intending to wait on the platform for the arrival of the carriages for the other line.

I found, however, that though the two lines crossed at L——, they did not communicate with each other, the L—— station on the Trent Valley line being on one side of the town, and the L—— station on the South Staffordshire line on the other. I also found that there was not time to get to the other station so as to catch the train the same evening; indeed, the train had just that moment passed on a lower level beneath my feet, and to get to the other side of the town, where it would stop for two minutes only, was out of the question.

There was, therefore, nothing for it but to put up at the Swan Hotel for the night. I have an especial dislike to passing an evening at an hotel in a country town. Dinner at such places I never take, as I had rather go without than have such as I am likely to get. Books are never to be had, the country newspapers do not interest me. *The Times* I have spelt through on my journey. The society I am likely to meet have few ideas in common with myself. Under such circumstances, I usually resort to a meat tea to while away the time, and when that is over, occupy myself in writing letters.

This was the first time I had been in L——, and while waiting for the tea, it occurred to me how, on two occasions within the past six months, I had been on the point of coming to that very place, at one time to execute a small commission for an old acquaintance, resident there, and another, to get the materials for a picture I proposed painting of an incident in the early life of Dr Johnson. I should have come on each of these occasions had not other arrangements diverted my purpose and caused me to postpone the journey indefinitely.

The thought, however, would occur to me, 'How strange! Here I am at L——, by no intention of my own, though I have twice tried to get here and been balked.' When I had done tea, I thought I might as well write to an acquaintance I had known some years previously, and who lived in the cathedral close, asking him to come and pass an hour or two with me. Accordingly, I rang for the waitress and asked, 'Does Mr Lute live in Lichfield?'

'Yes, sir.'

'Cathedral close?'

'Yes, sir.'

'Can I send a note to him?'

'Yes, sir.'

I wrote the note, saying where I was, and asking if he would come for an hour or two and talk over old matters. The note was taken; in about twenty minutes a person of gentlemanly appearance, and what might be termed the advanced middle age, entered the room with my note in his hand, saying that I had sent him a letter, he presumed, by mistake, as he did not know my name. Seeing instantly that he was not the person I intended to write to, I apologised, and asked whether there was not another Mr Lute living in L——?

'No, there was none other.'

'Certainly,' I rejoined, 'my friend must have given me his right address, for I had written to him on other occasions here. He was a fair young man, he succeeded to an estate in consequence of his uncle having been killed while hunting with the Quorn hounds, and he married about two years since a lady of the name of Fairbairn.'

The stranger very composedly replied, 'You are speaking of Mr Clyne; he did live in the cathedral close, but he has now gone away.'

The stranger was right, and in my surprise I exclaimed, 'Oh dear, to be sure, that is the name; what could have made me address you instead? I really beg your pardon; my writing to you, and unconsciously guessing your name, is one of the most extraordinary and unaccountable things I ever did. Pray pardon me.'

He continued very quietly, "There is no need of apology; it happens that you are the very person I most wished to see. You are a painter, and I want you to paint a portrait of my daughter; can you come to my house immediately for the purpose?'

I was rather surprised at finding myself known by him, and the turn matters had taken being so entirely unexpected, I did not at the moment feel inclined to undertake the business; I therefore explained how I was situate, stating that I had only the next day and Monday at my disposal. He, however, pressed me so earnestly, that I arranged to do what I could for him in those two days, and having put up my baggage, and arranged other matters, I accompanied him to his house.

During the walk home he scarcely spoke a word, but his taciturnity seemed only a continuance of his quiet composure at the inn. On our arrival he introduced me to his daughter Maria, and then left the room. Maria Lute was a fair and a decidedly handsome girl of about fifteen; her manner was, however, in advance of her years, and evinced that self-possession, and, in the favourable sense of the term, that womanliness, that is only seen at such an early age in girls that have been left motherless, or from other causes thrown much on their own resources.

She had evidently not been informed of the purpose of my coming, and only knew that I was to stay there for the night; she therefore excused herself for a few moments, that she might give the requisite directions to the servants as to preparing my room. When she returned, she told me that I should not see her father again that evening, the state of his health having obliged him to retire for the night; but she hoped I should be able to see him some time on the morrow.

In the meantime, she hoped I would make myself quite at home, and call for anything I wanted. She, herself, was sitting in the drawing-room, but perhaps I should like to smoke and take something; if so, there was a fire in the housekeeper's room, and she would come and sit with me, as she expected the medical attendant every minute, and he would probably stay to smoke, and take something.

As the little lady seemed to recommend this course, I readily complied. I did not smoke, or take anything, but sat down by the fire, when she immediately joined me. She conversed well and readily, and with a command of language singular in a person so young. Without being disagreeably inquisitive, or putting any question to me, she seemed desirous of learning the business that had brought me to the house. I told her that her father wished me to paint either her portrait or that of a sister of hers, if she had one.

She remained silent and thoughtful for a moment, and then seemed to comprehend it at once. She told me that a sister of hers, an only one, to whom her father was devotedly attached, died near four months previously; that her father had never yet recovered from the shock of her death. He had often expressed the most earnest wish for a portrait of her; indeed, it was his one thought, and she hoped, if something of the kind could be done, it would improve his health. Here she hesitated, stammered, and burst into tears.

After a while she continued, 'It is no use hiding from you what you must very soon be aware of. Papa is insane—he has been so ever since dear Caroline was buried. He says he is always seeing dear Caroline, and he is subject to fearful delusions. The doctor says he cannot tell how much worse he may be, and that everything dangerous, like knives or razors, are to be kept out of his reach. It was necessary you should not see him again this evening, as he was unable to converse properly, and I fear the same may be the case tomorrow; but perhaps you can stay over Sunday, and I may be able to assist you in doing what he wishes.'

I asked whether they had any materials for making a likeness—a photograph, a sketch, or anything else for me to go from. No, they had nothing. 'Could she describe her clearly?' She thought she could; and there was a print that was very much like her, but she had mislaid it. I mentioned that with such disadvantages, and in such an absence of materials, I did not anticipate a satisfactory result. I had painted portraits under such circumstances, but their success much depended upon the powers of description of the persons who were to assist me by their recollection; in some instances I had attained a certain amount of success, but in most the result was quite a failure.

The medical attendant came, but I did not see him. I learnt, however, that he ordered a strict watch to be kept on his patient till he came again the next morning. Seeing the state of things, and how much the little lady had to attend to, I retired early to bed. The next morning I heard that her father was decidedly better; he had inquired earnestly on waking whether I was really in the house, and at breakfast-time he sent down to say that he hoped nothing would prevent my making an attempt at the portrait immediately, and he expected to be able to see me in the course of the day.

Directly after breakfast I set to work, aided by such description as the sister could give me. I tried again and again, but without success, or, indeed, the least prospect of it. The features, I was told, were separately like, but the expression was not. I toiled on the greater part of the day with no better result. The different studies I made were taken up to the invalid, but the same answer was always returned—no resemblance. I had exerted myself to the utmost, and, in fact, was not a little fatigued by so doing—a circumstance that the little lady evidently noticed, as she expressed herself most grateful for the interest she could see I took in the matter, and referred the unsuccessful result entirely to her want of powers of description.

She also said it was so provoking. She had a print—a portrait of a lady—that was so like, but it had gone—she had missed it from her book for three weeks past. It was the more disappointing, as she was sure it would have been of such great assistance. I asked if she could tell me who the print was of, as if I knew, I could easily procure one in London. She answered, Lady M. A. Immediately the name was uttered the whole scene of the lady of the railway carriage presented itself to me. I had my sketch-book in my portmanteau upstairs, and, by a fortunate chance, fixed in it was the print in question, with the two pencil sketches.

I instantly brought them down, and showed them to Maria Lute. She looked at them for a moment, turned her eyes full upon me, and said slowly, and with something like fear in her manner, 'Where did you get these?' Then quicker, and without waiting for my answer, 'Let me take them instantly to papa.' She was away ten minutes, or more; when she returned, her father came with her. He did not wait for salutations, but said, in a tone and manner I had not observed in him before, 'I was right all the time; it was you that I saw with her, and these sketches are from her, and from no one else.

I value them more than all my possessions, except this dear child.' The daughter also assured me that the print I had brought to the house must be the one taken from the book about three weeks before, in proof of which she pointed out to me the gum marks at the back, which exactly corresponded with those left on the blank leaf. From the moment the father saw these sketches his mental health returned.

I was not allowed to touch either of the pencil drawings in the sketch-book, as it was feared I might injure them; but an oil picture from them was commenced immediately, the father sitting by me hour after hour, directing my touches, conversing rationally, and indeed cheerfully, while he did so. He avoided direct reference to his delusions, but from time to time led the conversation to the manner in which I had originally obtained the sketches. The doctor came in the evening, and, after extolling the particular treatment he had adopted, pronounced his patient decidedly, and he believed permanently, improved.

The next day being Sunday, we all went to church. The father, for the first time since his bereavement. During a walk which he took with me after luncheon, he again approached the subject of the sketches, and after some seeming hesitation as to whether he should confide in me or not, said, 'Your writing to me by name, from the inn at L——, was one of those inexplicable circumstances that I suppose it is impossible to clear up. I knew you, however, directly I saw you; when those about me considered that my intellect was disordered, and that I spoke incoherently, it was only because I saw things that they did not.

Since her death, I know, with a certainty that nothing will ever disturb, that at different times I have been in the actual and visible presence of my dear daughter that is gone—oftener, indeed, just after her death than latterly. Of the many times that this has occurred, I distinctly remember once seeing her in a railway carriage, speaking to a person seated opposite; who that person was I could not ascertain, as my position seemed to be immediately behind him. I next saw her at a dinner-table, with others, and amongst those others unquestionably I saw yourself.

I afterwards learnt that at that time I was considered to be in one of my longest and most violent paroxysms, as I continued to see her speaking to you, in the midst of a large assembly, for some hours. Again I saw her, standing by your side, while you were engaged in either writing or drawing. I saw her once again afterwards, but the next time I saw yourself was in the inn parlour.'

The picture was proceeded with the next day, and on the day after the face was completed, and I afterwards brought it with me to London to finish.

I have often seen Mr L. since that period; his health is perfectly re-established, and his manner and conversation are as cheerful as can be expected within a few years of so great a bereavement.

The portrait now hangs in his bedroom, with the print and the two sketches by the side, and written beneath is: 'C. L., 13th September, 1858, aged 22.'

www.ingramcontent.com/pod-product-compliance
Lightning Source LLC
Chambersburg PA
CBHW020933020726
47495CB00002B/482